SOUTHERN TIDES

BOOK THREE

Distant Shores

GARY E. PARKER

HOWARD
Fiction

Our purpose at Howard Publishing is to:
- *Increase faith* in the hearts of growing Christians
- *Inspire holiness* in the lives of believers
- *Instill hope* in the hearts of struggling people everywhere

Because He's coming again!

Distant Shores © 2006 by Gary E. Parker.
All rights reserved. Printed in the United States of America
Published by Howard Publishing Co., Inc.
3117 North Seventh Street, West Monroe, Louisiana 71291-2227

Published in association with the literary agency of Alive Communications, Inc.,
7680 Goddard Street, Suite 200, Colorado Springs, CO 80920

06 07 08 09 10 11 12 13 14 15   10 9 8 7 6 5 4 3 2 1

Edited by Ramona Cramer Tucker
Interior design by John Mark Luke Designs
Cover design by Kirk DouPonce, DogearedDesign.com
Cover images by Steve Gardner/PixelWorks Studios

Library of Congress Cataloging-in-Publication Data
Parker, Gary E.
    Distant shores / Gary E. Parker.
        p. cm.—(Southern tides ; bk. 3)
    ISBN: 1-58229-492-5
        1. Plantation owners—Fiction. 2. Freedmen—Fiction. 3. Hotelkeepers—Fiction. 4.
South Carolina—Fiction. 5. Southern States—Social conditions—1865-1945—Fiction. I.
Title.

PS3566.A6784D57 2006
813'.54—dc22

                                                                            2005055052

Scripture quotations are taken from *The Holy Bible*, Authorized King James Version.

This novel is a work of fiction. Names, characters, places, and incidents are either the product of the author's imagination or are used fictitiously. Any resemblance to actual events, locales, organizations, or persons, living or dead, is entirely coincidental and beyond the intent of either the author or publisher.

Dedication

A long time ago, when I was a history major at Furman University in South Carolina, my dad told me, "Son, you can't make a living with a history major."

Well, to some extent he was right. Yet if I hadn't majored in history, I don't think I ever could have written a story like the one you'll find here. Being a history major gave me an interest in the large canvas of the human story, and that interest in the human story keeps me ever curious. It seems to me that without that curiosity, life gets pretty dull. With it, however, life takes on rich meaning.

So I dedicate this series to all the history majors out there. Maybe you can't make a living with it, but perhaps you can make your life and the lives of those around you a little bit fuller, more colorful, more worth living.

Acknowledgments

Although this is a work of fiction, the social culture of the South Carolina lowland rice plantations just before, during, and after the Civil War certainly wasn't fictitious. The men and women—both black and white—of this time and place lived the lifestyle reflected in the pages of the Southern Tides trilogy. Books such as *South Carolina: A history* by Walter B. Edgar, *Mary's World* by Richard N. Cote, *An Antebellum Plantation Household* by Anne Sinkler Whaley LeClercq, *The History of Beaufort County, South Carolina: 1514–1861* by Lawrence S. Rowland, Alexander Moore, and George C. Rogers Jr., *Roll, Jordan, Roll: The World the Slaves Made* by Eugene D. Genovese, *Within the Plantation Household: Black and White Women of the Old South* by Elizabeth Fox-Genovese, *Them Dark Days: Slavery in the American Rice Swamps* by William Dusinberre, *A Diary from Dixie* by Mary Boykin Chesnut, *Richmond Burning* by Nelson Lankford, *The Civil War in the Carolinas* by Dan L. Morrill, *Gentleman and Soldier* by Edward Longacre, and *The Life of Johnny Reb* by Bell Irvin Wiley gave me both information and context for the telling of these stories. Any historical inaccuracies in these pages reflect on my failings, not those of these eminent researchers and writers.

In addition to the books that gave me confidence I was telling the story correctly, I also need to acknowledge the men and women at Howard Publishing for their enthusiasm for this project, especially Philis Boultinghouse. Ramona Tucker, my editor, also deserves appreciation for her diligent approach and eager attention to detail and schedule. Her sharp eye made this work better.

Finally, as always, I express gratitude to my wife, Melody. She keeps the world around me humming so I can have the time to do fun things—like sit down to read, research, and then write the stories of the people you'll find in these pages.

Note to the Reader

The years after the Civil War were tumultuous ones for the South. Life had changed for everyone—slave and plantation owner alike. Old institutions had crumbled, and the system that had kept everyone—socialite, poor white, and servant—in their places had disappeared.

In the effort to accurately reflect the time frame in which this historical fiction is set, I have used certain terms in this work that are offensive to me, personally, and that aren't reflective of our modern speech and language. Particularly is this true in reference to the men and women who had been held in slavery on the plantations depicted in the Southern Tides series. Please know when terms like *darky*, *blackey*, *coloreds*, and *Negro* are used, they are reflective of this era and not meant as any offense to today's African-American community. Other terms that referred to the slaves, among them the most offensive, are not used in spite of their common usage in the period written about in this project.

Thankfully for all of us, the evil of slavery in our country disappeared as a result of the Civil War, and many of the unfortunate racial terms and attitudes associated with it began to disappear from the American scene. There is no way to estimate—or apologize for—the physical, emotional, and spiritual damage inflicted upon generations of African-Americans through the travesty of slavery. The truths of God teach us that all people are equal, regardless of racial status. May the day hasten to come when we all fulfill God's will in this crucial arena of human relationship.

GARY E. PARKER

Part One

Returns

The day returns, but nevermore

Returns the traveler to the shore,

And the tide rises, the tide falls.

—HENRY WADSWORTH LONGFELLOW

Chapter One

The Oak Plantation, Early May, 1865
Dark clouds covered the moon over the South Carolina coastland in the wee hours of the night that Theo, a twelve-year-old black boy with an empty hole in his right eye socket, saw a vision that showed him he would die soon . . . and that his death would change everything for most everybody he knew. Instead of scaring him, though, the vision comforted Theo somehow. It reminded him of something he had believed since he first got old enough to believe anything: sometimes one body needed to suffer, even die, so others might find a straight path to their true living.

The vision hit Theo like most of his "seein's" came to him—within a few minutes after a squeezing headache started. The pain began just behind the ear on the same side as his empty eye socket—the socket his grandmammy, Nettie, had often told him gave him his peculiar ability to see what nobody else could spy out.

"You got the vision," Nettie always explained it. "Like a piercin' stick that jabs through a fog and tears a hole in it so you can see through to the other side."

Theo, who had known for as long as he could remember that he was different than other darky boys, never argued with his grandmammy.

"That missin' eye's the Lord's special gift to you, boy," Nettie said. "Make up some for all you didn't get."

"It make up for this squatty body that keeps me a hand shorter than other boys my age?" Theo asked once.

"That's right."

"And hair that's already started to gray?"

"That's for certain. The Lord made you peculiar, child, but peculiar ain't always bad."

Theo nodded as he usually did when Nettie talked like that. She meant no offense, he knew. She just faced things like they were, without any fakery in her bones. His growing had stalled out real fast before he ever turned ten, and he had never caught up with the other boys on the Rushton Plantation—a fine tobacco-growing place a day's ride from Richmond up in Virginia.

"The only thing large about you is yo' head," Nettie added. "Round as a cantaloupe and big as a bucket."

"Mama used to say my big head held a lot of smarts," Theo had reminded Nettie. He thought of the mama he had not seen since the year he turned five and the Lady Rushton sold her off to make some money when her plantation got in some trouble with the bankers.

Nettie chuckled. "You got that right. That head of yours is plumb full of wise things—you talked like a grownup almost from the day you was born."

Theo always stood taller after his grandmammy said such things. Grandmammy Nettie said it right—the Lord had plucked out his eye before he ever took birth so as to give him a different kind of seeing.

Now, as another headache started, Theo crouched behind a massive oak tree—a tree so wide it would surely take at least four boys his size to put their arms all the way around it. The oak tree's limbs swayed in the breeze that slipped in off the Atlantic Ocean, not more than three miles away. Theo put a hand on the oak, fingered its bark, and wondered at its age—at least a hundred years, he figured. Long enough to have seen a whole lot of changes come and go . . . and long enough to be tired by all those changes.

Theo took a long breath and peered around the oak. A stone's throw away sat a badly charred two-story house. Its whole left side, black with soot, sagged in on itself from some past fire. The chimney on that side lay in broken and smoky heaps.

Theo's headache arched from behind his ear and up into his skull. He shoved a finger into his ear and pushed. Sometimes that helped with the pain.

Overhead the clouds slipped away for a moment, and the moon peeked out.

Theo took his finger out of his ear and again studied the house, wondering if he had found the right place. Although he couldn't see it real plainly in the dark, the paint on the house's right side looked like it had pretty much peeled off. The wraparound porch—a big, old thing, wide enough to hold a hundred people—fell forward like it was plain worn out. Weeds grew up and around the house steps, reaching all the way to Theo's bare feet. One tiny light glowed from the right side of the house.

Theo stared at the house's front door and dared himself to go knock on it. But what if his mama wasn't there? What if he had walked barefoot over six hundred miles and searched the last eleven months in vain? What if he had journeyed these last forty miles from Charleston without stopping but found no trace of her? What if somebody in that house told him he had come to the wrong place or that they had sold off his mama a long time ago? What if . . . ? His headache got worse.

Theo tried to figure who might be burning the light in the house. Had the owners come home from the war? Or did a vagrant, maybe a darky, sit inside the deserted place? Some bad person who would just as soon shoot as spit if he found Theo sneaking around in the front yard? Maybe he ought to hide in the woods the rest of the night and come back in the morning.

Theo's mind drifted back to what he could remember of the day his mama, Ruby, and pappy, Markus, had disappeared. Since he was only five at the time, the Lady Rushton had figured him too young to fetch much at auction, so she had sold his mama and pappy off without him.

"I will care for Theo," Nettie had said as Ruby made ready to leave the Rushton house. "I will keep him till the day you come back and claim him again."

Theo hugged his mama, then took a spot in his grandmammy's lap.

"Don't reckon that day will ever come." Ruby's brown eyes were wet with tears. "Reckon I won't see my baby again in this old world."

"Don't be grievin', Mama," said Theo. "I'll set eyes on you again. I seen it."

Ruby knelt and took his tiny hands in hers. He believed what Grandmammy

Nettie told him: that the Lord gifted him with the power to see what others couldn't. How could his mama argue against that notion?

"You watch out for your grandmammy," Mama told him. "Do what she tells you."

Theo touched her cheek, as if he was the adult comforting her. "You and me be together again someday. I done seen it."

"I hope you see it right," Ruby said.

"I did. Sho as a dog likes a bone, I seen you comin' for me."

After hugging him one more time, Mama turned and left.

Now, with his headache pounding worse than any he could remember, Theo wondered if his mama had ever come for him. He had waited a long time at the Rushton place—right up until the Yankees came through one more time and burned most everything to the ground. Something told him then that he couldn't wait no more. If he wanted to find his mama, he had to go after her.

Theo's belly growled, and his hunger almost made him forget his headache. He looked down at his stomach. His ribs poked out above his belly. He had not eaten in close to four days. He sighed wearily. His journey to The Oak Plantation had about done him in. His bare feet, covered with calluses, ached, and a sore the size of a pecan oozed on his right big toe.

When Theo's eye watered with pain, he knew he had to act quickly before the ache knocked him completely out, like it sometimes did. He looked back at the house. Was his mama there? Only one way to find out.

He stood and started limping toward the front porch. Something moved to his right, and Theo dropped to the ground. Dry dirt sprayed into his face. He raised his head and eased slightly to his left. The moon peeked out, and Theo saw a skinny chicken standing dead still, its eyes huge in the moonlight. Theo's headache eased for a moment.

"What you doin' out here in the dark?" whispered Theo.

The chicken blinked.

"You come to answer my prayer?" asked Theo.

The chicken didn't answer.

Theo smiled slightly, and his teeth, the only perfect part of his oddly shaped body, gleamed. "You just stay real still," he cooed, crawling toward the chicken. When he got within an arm's reach, he paused as a touch of conscience hit him. "You a stray?" he whispered. "Or property of whoever be burnin' the light in that house?"

The chicken puffed its feathers for a second, then relaxed again.

"Seems to me the Lord done sent you," mused Theo as his mouth watered. "Providin' for my hunger. I'd be plumb wrong to let go what the Lord's set before me."

The bird didn't argue.

With a quick pounce, Theo grabbed the chicken and shoved it into the knapsack on his shoulder. The chicken uttered a squawk, but Theo quickly shut the knapsack and muffled the sound. Then he crept behind the oak again and stared around the dark yard. "You reckon we ought to wait here 'til daylight?" he asked the chicken. "See if it's friend or foe in that house? Or move on and come back another time?"

The chicken didn't answer, but Theo already knew what he needed to do. If he went to the house, he would have to leave the chicken. Otherwise, the person in the house might accuse him of stealing it. But laying down the chicken, a feast he needed to keep up his strength, even if only for a few minutes, made no sense to him. None at all.

"I come back in the mornin'," he told the night. "After I eat me a fine meal. Maybe that put my headache away."

He turned and took a step away from the oak.

Suddenly the front door of the house swung open. A man stood on the porch. He held a lantern aloft in his left hand and a pistol in his right.

"Who's there?" bellowed the man.

Theo started running, but the sore on his big toe slowed him.

A gunshot rang out.

The dirt at Theo's feet kicked up. He jerked to the side to evade the shot but stepped in a hole and fell on his face. His toe hurt like crazy.

Another shot banged over his head.

Theo heard the man moving toward him.

"I'll kill you with the next bullet!" yelled the man, his voice thick as if from too much whiskey. "Hold where you are!"

Theo raised up to run again, but it was too late. The man was rushing straight at him!

Theo pivoted toward the man and noticed an odd gait to his hurried step. He started to stand to flee again.

Another shot rang out.

Theo froze in place. He sensed that if he ran now, he would never see his mama again. Theo felt certain this man knew something about Ruby. So no matter what happened, Theo had to stay and find out what the man knew.

"I bein' real still," called Theo. "No reason to go shootin' anymore."

When the man emerged out of the dark, Theo saw why he ran funny. He had a peg leg from his knee down on the right side. He stood medium-high, and his clothes, though faded and frayed at the edges, gave evidence of having once been fine apparel—the clothing of a gentleman before hard times set in. He wore a white shirt with lace at the collar over his thin shoulders and tan riding pants. Brown hair, unkempt and a touch too long, lay on his shirt collar. His face looked rough, like he drank a lot maybe, or didn't sleep enough. Theo guessed him maybe twenty-five years old.

Theo stared into the man's eyes and shivered. The eyes, hard and red, fixed him in a mean glare. In that instant Theo knew something in this man's past had shriveled up his heart like a grape dried in the sun. The man kept the gun trained on Theo, and Theo knew the man would shoot without regret if given any cause. When Theo smelled the man's sour breath, he knew he'd guessed right. The peg-legged man had done a lot of drinking.

"What are you doing on my property?" asked the man, his words slurred.

"Lookin' for somebody."

"That my chicken in your bag?"

Guilt flooded Theo. "I don't usually do no thievin'," he explained. "But I been starved a few days."

"I ought to shoot you. Got plenty of cause."

A sharp pain cut through Theo's head. His eye watered again, then blurred. Streaks of silver light darted before his face. His knapsack slipped out of his hands and dropped to the ground. His knees shook, and he almost fell. A chill ran through his bones like a blast of snow, and he shivered. Then the vision hit. What he saw almost made him collapse.

Licking fire.

Angry, evil shouts.

Ugly masks of awful things.

Theo saw how he would die.

And he saw who would kill him.

His body warmed and he almost passed out again. But then the vision ended as fast as it had come, and strength flooded through his body.

He grabbed his knapsack and stood up straight again, his headache gone, his knees strong once more.

"I don't reckon you'll shoot me tonight," Theo stated clearly, so sure of his vision that his fear disappeared.

"That's uppity talk for a darky boy," the man growled.

"Darky people be free now," said Theo. "The war done ended. You know that, I reckon."

The man grunted. "You are still a thief on my land, free or not. The law won't blame me for shooting a trespassing robber."

"You know a woman named Ruby?" asked Theo, his tone strong and unafraid in spite of the danger.

The man lowered the pistol a notch and stared even more keenly at him. "Why do you ask that?"

"Ruby be my mama."

The man took a step closer. Theo could see he had pricked the man's curiosity.

"What's your name?" asked the man.

"Tell yours first."

The man grunted. "Trenton Tessier. I own this place."

"I be Theo. My mama, Ruby, birthed me back in 1853, five years before she got sold off with my pa, Markus. I know from my grandmammy, Nettie, that they took Ruby off to Charleston. I been there the last few months, tryin' to find where she went from there."

"How did you end up here?" Tessier demanded.

"I figured the best way to find out what happened to my mama was to find out who did the auctioneerin' of the darkies back before the war. I talked to a lot of folks around the market over in Charleston, folks around the old auction block. People told me to find a man who always wore a blousy shirt. They said if I find him, he might know somethin' about my mama."

Tessier sneered. "You think you got a lot of smarts, don't you?"

Theo shrugged. "I carry a brain or two in my head."

"You find the blousy-shirt man?"

"Yeah, run up on him outside a saloon close by the market area a few weeks after I showed up. He's a touch frail now and wasn't too talkative about what he done before the war. But after I hung around the saloon a few days, hauled him his drinks when he needed them, aided him as he came and went, he softened some. I asked him if he remembered my ma and pa, and he said no, he didn't recall much of anythin', but he did have some records."

"He showed you those records?"

"Yeah, I offered to work a week for him, so he took me to a little room where he stays while he's in Charleston. He pulled out some old books and found my ma and pa's names, sure as the world. Told me Mama ended up on a place called The Oak and my papa on the Robertson Plantation, near a town called Columbia. I asked a little more, and he gave me some directions. Since this was closer than Columbia, I come here first."

Silence settled. Theo knew by instinct that the time had come to wait. Whatever Tessier wanted to say, he would say it easier if he didn't feel pushed. In the distance a dog barked.

Tessier studied Theo for several minutes, then spoke, his words soft as if talking to himself. "We used to work over three hundred darkies here. Grew more rice than most anywhere in the state. Marshall Tessier, my father, made The Oak the envy of people everywhere. Kept eighteen hundred acres in crops, a hundred and fifty head of cattle, sixty horses, seventy hogs, did fifty thousand bushels of rice a year. Over a million pounds. But then the war started. The Yankees took over Beaufort in December of 1861, then Charleston this February."

Tessier paused and glanced at his peg leg.

"You take that injury from the war?" asked Theo, hoping to keep Tessier talking.

"If that were only so," grunted Tessier.

"Somebody shoot you?"

Tessier flinched as if he'd been struck. His jaw tensed. "In a duel. So I ended up looking after this place. Did all right until the darkies ran off."

Theo could see Tessier remembering, looking back on what had been, knowing those days would never return.

"Yankees burn yo' house?" asked Theo.

Tessier shook his head. "A bunch of darkies raided through here and set fire to the house. I shot at least two of them before they ran off. If a storm hadn't sprung up and dumped a lot of rain, the whole place would have ended up in ashes."

"The war been hard on everybody."

Tessier stopped and studied Theo, as if trying to make up his mind what to do. "You think getting your freedom makes it all better, don't you?"

Theo couldn't help but shiver. There was a coldness, an emptiness in Tessier's eyes.

"It set me loose to find my mama," said Theo simply. "That's a good start."

Tessier laughed slightly. "It's all changed. But it's not all better. You people got to care for yourselves now, pay for your food, your medical care, clothes, shelter. Not as easy as you think."

"Life be hard whether a man is free or slave," Theo replied.

Tessier suddenly shook his head and came out of his trancelike mood. The pistol pointed at Theo again. Tessier's eyes narrowed. "I don't know why I'm talking to you. Hand me the chicken."

"Tell me if you know my mama," Theo bargained. "Then I give you the bird."

Tessier's lip curled. "I could just shoot you and take the chicken when you fall."

"It's not my time tonight."

"You are mighty sure of yourself for such a little boy."

"The Lord done told me my hour ain't come yet."

Tessier raised an eyebrow. "You sure you're hearing the Lord right?"

"I expect so. You know my mama or not?"

Tessier grinned. "You almost amuse me."

"You know my mama?" Theo insisted.

The grin disappeared. "Yes." Tessier spat. "Ruby showed up here in November 1858. Captain York, our overseer back then, brought her from Charleston. A pretty thing."

Theo clenched his fists. "A white man ought not speak of my mama that way."

Tessier's face bunched into a snarl. "What do you plan to do about it?"

Theo took a breath. "You know my mama's whereabouts or not?"

"Yes. She's in the dirt. Dead." Tessier seemed to take pleasure in saying the words.

Theo's knees almost buckled, but he quickly braced up again. "How you know that?" he asked, not willing to believe it without more details.

"I saw it happen. Back in Richmond—I just returned from there a few days ago. The Yankees came through and about burned the whole city. Your mama stayed at a place called the Victoria Hotel. I stayed there, too, for a while, with my mother, the Lady Katherine. The fire caught in the hotel, and your mama tried to fight it. But she didn't have much luck. She was hauling up a bucket of water to throw on a burning wall when the wall fell on her."

"You do anythin' to help stop this fire you're tellin' about?"

"It was not my concern."

Theo studied Tessier, trying to figure whether he told the truth or not. Theo usually found it easy to read people. But something about Tessier's face clouded his view—something dark, like the surface of a pond on a moonless night. He couldn't see to the bottom of it one way or the other.

"I don't know that I believe what you be tellin' me," Theo said softly.

"Believe what you want. Just give me that chicken."

Theo kept his hands tight on the knapsack. The bird squirmed but didn't squawk. "Things must be pretty hard around here for you to fight so much over one skinny bird."

"That's not your business."

Theo wanted to protest, but he knew when he was licked. He handed the knapsack to Tessier.

"Now get on the ground," growled Tessier. "Face to the dirt."

Fear gripped Theo's empty stomach, but his vision still gave him courage. "You ain't the one doin' the directin' around here," he said in a stern tone. "You ought to know that."

"Do what I tell you!"

Theo started to drop down, but a shout from the house stopped him.

"What's going on out here?" a woman called out.

Theo squinted in the moonlight toward the house. A middle-aged woman in a dark robe descended the steps.

Tessier wheeled to face the woman. "Nothing to bother you."

The woman moved closer, and Theo got a look at her face. Her skin glowed pale. Her eyes appeared dark. She carried a touch of thickness around her chin and neck, and her eyebrows almost touched in the middle. Gray streaked her hair. *Tessier's mother*, Theo figured.

"Something woke me," said the woman. "I looked for you in the house."

"I caught a thief, Mother," explained Tessier, pointing the gun at Theo again. "Stealing a chicken." He held up the knapsack. The bird squawked and cackled. "He says he's Ruby's boy—here all the way from Virginia. I told him I saw Ruby die in the fire in Richmond."

A look passed between mother and son, but Theo couldn't tell exactly what it meant.

The woman faced him. "Are you truly Ruby's son?"

Theo nodded. "I've looked for her nearly a year."

Mrs. Tessier raised her chin. "Let him go," she ordered Tessier.

"I planned on shooting him," Tessier said casually.

"You won't put me away today," Theo replied. "I already spoke clear on that."

Mrs. Tessier faced Theo again. "Go on. Get out of here before you get hurt."

Theo held his ground for a second. "You see my mama die like he said?" he asked her.

"No. I wasn't there when it happened."

Theo glanced at Tessier once more, but the man's face revealed nothing.

Tessier scowled. "I better not see you around here ever again," he warned, giving in to his mother but still haughty.

Theo stood as tall as he could. "Oh, you be seein' me again. I know that for certain."

"You step foot on this place again, and it will be the last thing you ever do."

Theo shook his head, remembering his vision. "You got troubles comin'. Best you take note of that before it's too late to stop them."

Tessier did not reply, but he cocked the pistol.

Knowing the time had come for him to leave, Theo turned and slipped away, the big toe on his right foot aching almost as much as his most recent headache.

As Theo left, Trenton Tessier turned to his mother. "Why didn't you let me shoot him?"

"Are you that thirsty for blood?"

"Blacks think they can do what they want now that the Yankees won the war and set them free. They will try to destroy us in the years to come."

His mother shrugged and headed for the house.

Trenton followed her.

"Why did you tell him that lie about Ruby?" she asked.

"How do you know it's a lie?"

She stopped and faced him. "I know you, Trenton. Better than you realize. You're the image of your father, God rest his soul. You take what you want without thinking about consequences to others. You lie when it suits you, cheat when you can, and devil take the hindmost. Telling that boy his mother was dead pleased you for reasons only you know."

Trenton took his mother by the hands and smiled. "Some would say I'm just like you, Mother dear."

14

Mrs. Tessier shook her head as if to argue. Then a small smile crawled onto her face. "Of course they do. That's why your father and I made such a perfect couple."

"I wish he were still alive."

"Of course you do."

Trenton squeezed her hands. "You plan to stay with Hampton York?"

"Captain York is my husband now. You need to accept that."

"But he shot my leg off," Trenton whined.

"You gave him plenty of cause—even you have to agree with that."

His eyes smoldered. "You know I hate him."

"And you know I love you."

"You saying you don't love him?"

Katherine pulled her hands away. "You know I married York to save The Oak. We needed cash before the war, and he had it—twenty-seven thousand dollars."

"He stole that money behind your back," Trenton accused.

She lifted her chin. "I can't prove that. Neither can you. He said he won it gambling."

"He lied so he could get you and become master of The Oak."

"Either way, we're married now—have been for almost four years. It's about time you accept that."

Trenton placed his hands on his mother's shoulders. "What about Calvin, Mother?" he asked derisively. "Are you forgetting that York didn't protect him in the war like he promised he would? Have you forgotten that your son died while fighting the Yankees with your dear, precious husband?"

Katherine sighed. "No man can see after another during a war. Besides, we don't know for sure that Calvin is dead. No one ever found a body."

Trenton stepped back. "He's dead, Mother. You might as well accept the truth. I'm all you have left."

Katherine's eyes watered for an instant.

Trenton stared toward their house. "If it comes down to me or York, who will you choose, Mother?"

"You know better than to ask that."

"I asked you if you love him."

She touched Trenton's elbow, and he faced her once more. The moon dipped behind a cloud, and a shadow covered her face. "Love has nothing to do with it," she said. "I need him, and so do you, even if you won't admit it." She pointed at the house, then waved a hand over the rest of the plantation. "You see all this? You think you can restore it to its former glory?"

Trenton shook his head.

"Neither can I," she whispered. "But Hampton York knows how to get things done, and he will work until he drops. He'll do whatever it takes to make this place come alive again. Can you see that? Do you understand it?"

"You will stay in a loveless marriage for the sake of The Oak?" asked Trenton.

Katherine chuckled lightly. "I'll do what I've always done: whatever is best for me and mine."

Trenton grinned knowingly. "York best keep his wits about him, or the black widow will devour him."

"You think me ruthless, don't you?"

He ignored her question. Instead, taking his mother's arm, he led her back to the house. "One thing Ruby's boy said is right, I expect," he offered.

"What's that?"

"I have troubles coming my way."

"Don't we all?"

Chapter Two

Not more than twenty miles away a man named Josh Cain stood by Hampton York on a slight rise under an oak. Both early risers, the two men had started a campfire close to an hour earlier. Now they watched as, fifty yards away, a group of nine other people rose from sleeping and stoked up the fire. A creek meandered a few feet from the camp.

Cain, a man of average height but thick in the shoulders, stared out through tired blue eyes from under a floppy, sunbaked, brown hat. His hair, a wavy, sandy blond, touched the collar of his tattered brown shirt. His pants, torn in at least three places, hung loosely around his food-starved hips. The night before he'd taken a bath in the creek—his first bath in at least a week. Although he had slept soundly after that, weariness still rode his bones. He wondered if he would ever feel completely rested again.

"We're a sorry-looking lot," he told York as he nodded toward the group below.

"No wonder," York replied. "We've traveled hard for close to a month. Covered over four hundred miles. Plumb wore out the horses we brought, fixed three different wagon wheels when they broke off. Ate next to nothin', except what little we could find and shoot."

"The land's about stripped bare," agreed Josh. "Lots of people scrounging to survive, eating anything they can find."

"I don't know what's worse sometimes—a war or all the troubles that follow."

Josh lifted the cup of water he held to his lips and drank. "Wish I had some coffee."

York scratched his black beard. "Might as well wish for a white silk suit. Not likely we're gonna see either for a long time."

17

Josh finished the water and gazed down at the group. His two off-spring, Beth, almost grown at seventeen, and Butler, three years her junior, stood by the fire as it started to smoke. Two white women, Camellia and her mother, Lynette, and one white man, Camellia's brother, Jackson, moved down to the creek as he watched. Ruby, a black woman with fine features and buttery skin, stood just a few feet from the fire. She took care of Leta, her three-and-a-half-year-old child, and Nettie, her ancient and frail mother. Johnny, York's grown son, stood off to the side.

Running from the last days of the war, those in the camp were as thin as skeletons and as tired as dogs after a coon chase. Worse, all had a haunted look in their eyes. In Josh's case, at least, the pain came from carrying around a ton of bad memories from the fighting he'd just left behind.

Josh refocused on York. "We need to talk before we go any further. Clear up some matters."

York, tall and broad-shouldered, spit tobacco juice on the ground. "You're right," he agreed, squatting by the tree. "We got to figure out what to do next."

"I've decided what I'm doing," said Josh. "I'm picking up whatever is left of my belongings at The Oak, marrying Camellia as soon as I can find a preacher, then taking Beth and Butler and heading out."

York studied him suspiciously. "Where you plan on goin'?"

"Don't know yet, but it'll be somewhere pretty far off. Folks in South Carolina will not take to me too well anymore, what with me fighting for the Federals like I did."

York grunted unhappily. "You plan on leavin' me, Brother? Simple as that?"

Josh eased down and sat back against the oak. Its leaves shadowed his face against the early sun. He placed a hand on York's elbow for a second, then pulled it back.

York spat again.

"We just survived one war," Josh murmured. "Let's not start one now between us."

"We've survived two, all totaled," said York. "Don't forget Mexico."

Josh set his cup on the ground. "We were so young then. I was sixteen when it started."

"We fought side by side in that war. Too bad that didn't happen again."

"You know why I chose the path I took," said Josh, glad the two half brothers finally had a chance to talk openly of what had happened during the Civil War.

"Yeah—you and your almighty conscience," York growled.

"I didn't think it was right to wage a war to keep the blacks in bondage."

"You'd rather let the Yankees tell us how we ought to live our lives?"

Josh started to defend himself, to explain to York why he, a man born and raised within a few miles of the Atlantic Ocean in South Carolina, the most Southern of all the states, had betrayed his native land and fought for the Yankees. He wanted York to understand how he didn't believe Jesus would ever have owned a slave or approved anybody else doing so either. But, fearing that York, who was Southern to the core, would never see his point, Josh let it go.

"All that is past," Josh finally said. "We need to start over."

"But we're brothers," insisted York. "You should have told me what you planned to do instead of runnin' off to the Yankees with no word about it. I could have shot you out there somewhere and never known. We fought in the same battle more than once, so it could have happened. In fact, I heard it did a few times. Brother shot brother. Then right there at the end I come up on you, almost dead from your wounds. I picked you up where you had fallen at Burgess Mill. If our luck had been real bad, it might have been my bullet that took you down."

Josh took off his hat and stared into it as he remembered that awful day in October 1864. They hadn't known it then, but the war was nearing its end. As part of the Union General Winfield Hancock's boys, Josh and forty thousand other Federals attacked an area southwest of Petersburg. They hoped to cut off the Southside Railroad and prevent any more supplies from going into Petersburg and Richmond beyond it. During the fray, Josh took a number of wounds—a pistol shot, a crack in the head with a rifle, a saber in the side. If York had not recognized Josh as the Union soldier who had saved Johnny's life and pulled him away to safety, Josh would surely be dead right now.

"I owe you my life," Josh told York.

York's eyes lit up as he faced Josh. "Then stay with me!" he pressed. "Though it frets me to admit it, I need you. I can't do what I have to do without you beside me!"

Josh studied York, his elder by twelve years, and wondered, as he had a hundred times, how two men sired by the same father could turn out so different. To his way of thinking, the difference had to come from the fact that they had different mamas. Although Josh had never known the woman who birthed York, his own mama—a schoolteacher—had raised him with as much refinement as she knew how. She had taught him to read and how to hold a napkin at a fancy dinner. More than anything else, she had impressed on him the need for a strong faith in the Lord.

Sadly, York had never received training in any of those matters. Although Josh never thought of himself as any better than his half-brother, he did recognize that they often looked at things from opposite angles. They treated situations and people in ways that sometimes caused great troubles between them.

"I can't stay on The Oak," Josh finally said. "We both need to accept that."

York picked up a stone and flung it away. He remained silent.

Josh noted the weariness around his brother's gray eyes and the gaunt skin over his cheekbones. "We've traveled a long journey. Barely eaten in days."

"All the more reason for you to stay at The Oak a while once we get there," York argued. "Let everybody rest up some, then decide what to do next."

Josh didn't want to argue anymore but couldn't stop himself from telling the truth as he saw it. "I'm thirty-five. Time for me to get on with my life. Marry Camellia like I've wanted to since before the war. Settle down somewhere with her, Beth, and Butler."

"Beth is a growed woman now. Some man will come for her soon."

Josh nodded. His little girl truly had grown up. How he wished her dead mother could see her now. Deep brown eyes, hair the color of beach sand. Although Beth had never had much chance to go to school, she had learned to read and write from him and Camellia.

"What if I said I wouldn't give you Camellia's hand?" asked York.

Josh tried to read how serious York was. "You're not really her pa," he stated firmly. "I want your permission, but I don't have to have it."

York frowned. "I raised her like she was my own. Nobody can say different."

Josh looked toward Camellia as she bent near the creek, cupped her hands, and took a drink of water. Her rich brown hair, cut shorter than normal, fell in waves around her face. Although he couldn't see them from this distance, her eyes were as blue as the sky, and her teeth were white and straight. Her smile lit up the whole outdoors.

Camellia loved to read like he did and, most important, she loved the Lord like he tried to do. That he loved her and she loved him back had been a sweet, unexpected miracle.

A light smile crossed Josh's face as he recalled how long and winding the path had been that had finally brought him and Camellia together. After Anna, his first wife, had died of seizures and headaches, Camellia had helped him with Beth and Butler. The children loved her from the start, but Josh denied his love for her for a long time. First, because loving her seemed like a betrayal of Anna. And second, and even more complicated, at the time Camellia believed Josh was her half uncle. To protect her from sad truths, York had never told her that a man other than himself had fathered her.

"You did well by her," Josh agreed with York. "Everybody knows it."

"I did as good as I could . . . what with her mama running off like she did. Camellia was just four."

Josh glanced back at Camellia, then over to her mother, Lynette Swanson, standing beside her. Lynette had two-year-old Camellia and was pregnant with a boy she named Chester when she married York back in 1842. For a couple of years she and York had done just fine. She'd even birthed Johnny, sired by York. But then, still in love with Wallace Swanson, the man who had fathered Camellia and Chester, and unable to cope with life as the wife of an overseer, even one on a plantation as fine as

The Oak, Lynette had run off one day, leaving her three children behind.

Although York had searched for her for months, his hunt had proved futile. Finally he had returned, heartbroken, to The Oak and moved on with his life.

Josh's thoughts returned to the present. "Camellia is as fine as any woman who ever lived. Too good for me—I know that."

"She ought to at least marry a man her own age," teased York, his mood lifting for a moment. "Not an old coot like you—ten years her senior."

"You got no room to talk."

"You got that true. I'm just three years short of fifty."

A bird chirped from where it sat in the branches of the oak.

"I already said it once, but just in case you didn't get it the first time—I need you if I'm gonna restore The Oak to what it used to be," York said.

"You will do fine on your own."

"I have no help now that the darkies are free."

Josh looked down at the group by the creek and wondered if he had made the right decision. Was it best for Beth and Butler to leave The Oak? Or should he return them to a place familiar to their hearts and souls? Let them recover from the war before going anywhere else? But still he held back from considering staying.

"I don't see The Oak as a good place for any of us anymore," he explained. "Too many bad memories there."

"You worried about Trenton?" asked York. "What he will do?"

Josh shifted from foot to foot as he answered. "I want to avoid any more trouble with him."

"I'll take care of him if need be."

"He's mean as a rabid dog, and you know it. He killed old Stella, hurt Butler, tried to . . ." Josh let the rest of the sentence drop. "Trenton hates you, me, and just about everybody else."

"Everybody but Camellia. He says he still loves her."

Josh picked up a stick and threw it into the sunlight, past the tree's shadows. "Trenton doesn't know what love is. He just wants Camellia because he can't have her. If he actually had her, he'd treat her like he does everyone else—without respect, without love." It made Josh's blood boil just to think about anyone treating Camellia that way.

"He and Camellia grew up together, played together as kids," York reminded him. "When they were young, Trenton and Camellia always said they would marry someday."

"That was before Camellia grew up enough to see the kind of man he is," Josh explained.

"You think he will stay at The Oak with me giving the orders?"

"Hard to say." Josh scrubbed at a clump of grass with the toe of his boot. "But where else would he go? I expect he'd find too many Yankees in Charleston for him to feel comfortable. Columbia too."

When York stood, he stomped the dirt off his cracked black boots.

Josh eased up too.

"Trenton's got good reason to hate me," York reasoned. "I shot him."

"You left Calvin behind at Burgess Mill too. Trenton won't forget that."

York spat. "It was a hard choice. I could haul you or Calvin off that battlefield but not both. I chose to save you because you're my brother. Trenton ought to understand that. He would do the same thing."

"He understands only what he chooses to understand."

"Yep. I expect someday I'll have to finish the job I started when I shot off his leg."

"I pray neither of us will end up with his blood on our hands."

York grinned at Josh. "You're a kind and gentle man, Brother. The war didn't put you off your religion?"

Josh raised an eyebrow. "I don't know why it should."

"All that death and dyin'? Where is the Lord in such things as you and me saw these last four years?"

"I agree it's hard to understand . . . harder even to accept. But maybe the Lord loves us enough to let us loose. To see what we'll do when we're free."

York shook his head. "Seems like we always do purty rough things."

"Not always, even in a war. You saw kindnesses in the war, same as I did. Sacrifices on behalf of others. Heroism. Courage."

GARY E. PARKER

"Not enough of it to make a believer out of me," said York, his eyes on his boots.

"Nobody said life was easy," Josh continued. "The Good Book says we'll have our tribulations."

"I've seen more than my share of those."

"I expect we have more on the way."

York chuckled briefly. "Don't know that I can survive them if we do."

"Good Lord's willing, you can."

"You depend on the Lord if you want," York fired back. "As for me, I'm taking care of myself."

"That's a lonesome way to live, I expect."

A bird chirped again and, as he usually did when matters came around to anything too religious, York changed the subject. "You expect Katherine is back at The Oak?"

"If she traveled safely, she is. She left a while before us. Probably rode the train to Columbia, then headed on from there. I expect you'll be glad to see her."

York faced his brother. "You know I married her to get The Oak. I never lied to you about that."

Josh dropped his eyes. Although he loved his brother, he still found some things about Hampton York hard to swallow. Like the way he drank more than he should, gambled for dollars he didn't earn, and cared for power more than Josh figured worthy. "You plan to stay with her, don't you?"

York glanced toward the creek.

Josh knew why. Lynette, Camellia's mother and York's first and only true love, stood next to Camellia beside the water. Her hair, dark like Camellia's but with some gray streaking it at the temples, was pulled up in a tight bun. A tall and stately woman, she had eyes as blue as Camellia's and a face that made men take a second look when she stepped into a room. Her son, a young man with black hair, a black mustache, and black eyes, knelt beside her, a bucket in his hands as he dipped water into it.

"It's crazy how life goes sometime," said York. "How Lynette ended up here with us."

Josh smiled at the memory.

24

In 1858, fourteen years after Lynette had run away from The Oak, Lynette and her husband, Wallace Swanson, had sent a man named Sharpton Hillard to find Camellia and her brothers. Although it took him three years to track them down, Hillard had shown up at The Oak just before the war started. He offered Camellia and Johnny, the only surviving brother, the chance to return with him to Richmond to meet their mother. Not trusting their mother, both refused to go. But York, fearing Trenton's threats against Camellia because she had refused to marry him, forcefully packed Camellia away to Lynette in Richmond. She lived there until the Southern capital fell to the Yankees. As the city began to burn, York had gathered up the whole bunch—Lynette, Jackson, Ruby, Nettie, and Leta—and brought them out, connecting with Camellia and Josh at the south end of the bridge out of Richmond. Together they all escaped south and out of danger.

"You know I've always loved Lynette, don't you?" York asked Josh, breaking the silence.

"You tried to keep it quiet, but yes, I've known it."

"But I married Katherine to get something I wanted."

For an instant, Josh thought he saw regret on York's face.

"Then Sharpton Hillard showed up and told you Lynette lived in Richmond," Josh continued. "The war started. Lynette's husband died of tumors. You end up stationed in Richmond as the war ends and haul Lynette and everybody else out just as the Yankees invade."

"Yep, funny, ain't it?" York smirked.

"I don't hear much laughing."

"Seems like nothin' I do is right."

Josh stared back toward the creek. As he watched, Camellia walked away from the water and toward some bushes.

"You raised the woman I love and saved my life," said Josh. "I'd say those were two good things. At least I won't ever forget them, even when I'm separate from you."

York grunted again.

It was time for them to rejoin those at the camp. By the end of the day's walk, the group would reach The Oak Plantation. Within a couple more days, Josh would take his children and Camellia and leave the plantation behind, hopefully forever.

Josh moved to York. "I will miss you, Brother," he said, putting a hand on York's shoulder.

York wiped his eyes, obviously grieving but not wanting to admit it. "Best get the horses ready."

Josh nodded.

As the two brothers began to walk toward the camp, Josh's arm was firmly clasped about York's broad but slumping shoulders.

Standing by the creek, Camellia finished washing her face. She stood and waved toward Josh as he moved toward the horses tied up beyond the camp. Although weary past anything she could remember, a warm glow filled her bones. Within a few days, a week at the most, she and Josh would go to Beaufort, find a preacher, and say their holy vows to one another. Then they would take Beth and Butler and head west, maybe as far as Texas.

She glanced over at her mother, and a twinge of sadness hit her. For years she had thought her mother was dead. Then Camellia had found out the truth. She'd spent a few more years resenting Lynette Swanson for having deserted her when she was a girl. But the war had changed all that. Now she and her mother shared a deep admiration and love for each other.

Camellia tucked her hair behind her ears and slipped her bare feet into the creek. As the cool water washed over her toes, she realized how much her feet ached from the long miles she had walked. Calluses covered the bottom of her feet from where her shoe soles had worn out. She had taken them off and left them in the back of the old wagon they had brought with them.

"Look at these feet." She stuck a foot toward Lynette. "Have you ever seen anything worse?"

"Try these hands." Lynette held out ten fingers for Camellia to examine. "Scalier than a lizard's."

Camellia laughed softly, and it felt good. After all the years of war, the frantic rush out of Richmond, and the days and days of running south, she finally felt safe enough to chuckle.

"We'll reach The Oak by the end of the day," she told Lynette. "Maybe we can find some old shoes there."

"If the place is still standing," said Lynette.

Camellia gazed into the water. "Yankees could have destroyed it, I guess."

"Or the freed servants or folks like us trying to get back home."

Camellia faced Lynette. "What if it's gone?" Camellia was suddenly frightened again.

"Does it really matter?" asked Lynette. "You're not staying there, and neither am I."

"When will you go back to Richmond?"

"As soon as I can. I have to find out if my hotel, my house, survived the Yankee invasion. Ruby won't stay either . . . you know that. She'll take her mama and Leta and go somewhere as soon as she can."

"She'll try to find her boy, Theo," Camellia guessed. "Once she found Nettie and learned he came south looking for her, she has sworn she will do all in her power to track him down."

"Only York will stay at The Oak," said Lynette. "Maybe Johnny with him—at least until he takes a wife and starts his own family."

Camellia's heart sank as she recognized a truth she had not yet fathomed. With everybody else departing, the man she had known for most of her life as her pa would remain alone on the plantation with Katherine, now his wife, and her son, Trenton Tessier.

"Can I just go off and leave Pa?" she asked, more to herself than to Lynette. "Desert him like everyone else?"

Lynette's eyes grew misty. "You know you can't stay, no matter how loyal to your pa you are. Trenton Tessier won't allow it, at least not happily. He made that plain enough with his actions in Richmond."

Camellia nodded as she recalled the last few hours before the city fell. In the awful chaos of that night, Trenton had once more declared his undying love for her. But, when she again refused his advances, he kidnapped her and forced her onto a fleeing train. "If Josh had not shown up at the last minute and rescued me from Trenton, who knows what Trenton might have done?" she wondered aloud.

"That's why you cannot stay on The Oak." Lynette's voice was firm, but there was also fear in it.

Camellia thought again of her father. "Pa wants The Oak more than anything. He often spoke of having his portrait hung over the staircase at the entrance to the house. But too much has happened for him to get that done yet. Well, now he's got his chance."

"If he wants it enough to deal with Trenton, the only thing I can do is wish him well and pray God's protection on his endeavors."

Her mind settled, Camellia stepped to Lynette and hugged her.

Lynette accepted the embrace without reserve. When the hug ended, she stepped back. "What was that for?" she asked Camellia.

"I'm just glad you sent for me," said Camellia.

"Your real father was dying," Lynette explained. "He wanted to see you and Chester before that happened."

Camellia remembered her dead brother—a victim of malaria at the age of seventeen. "It's sad that Chester never got to meet him."

"At least you did."

Camellia nodded. "He loved me, didn't he?"

"More than you'll ever know."

Camellia sighed, then stepped away from Lynette and toward some bushes to privately finish her preparations for the day.

After hitching two horses to the wagon, Josh headed back to camp to get his bedroll to toss in the back. As he rounded a stand of brambles, he heard a scream. Instantly recognizing it as Camellia's, he broke into a dead run toward the bushes where he had seen her disappear.

Lynette rushed from the creek—also toward Camellia. She reached Camellia first. "Hold on for a second!" she shouted to Josh. "Let me get her decent!"

Josh halted and everyone gathered around him.

"It's a snakebite!" yelled Lynette. "On the right wrist!"

Not waiting any longer, Josh rushed through the brush just as Lynette led Camellia toward him. As the rest of the group gathered, Camellia held her right hand out. Josh spotted two tiny cuts in the flesh just above her hand.

Camellia's eyes were wide with obvious fear and pain. York moved past the group and stomped into the bushes, obviously searching for the snake that had bitten her.

"I think it was a copperhead," Camellia managed. She began to sob.

"Lay her down," Josh ordered. "Get her arms and legs flat and straight out."

"How big was the snake?" asked Lynette.

Camellia gulped back her tears. "I couldn't tell."

Josh removed the knife from his pocket as Lynette helped Camellia stretch out on the ground. "Let's ease her to the creek," he said. "We'll need to cleanse the wound after I finish."

Camellia eyed the knife.

"It's OK," said Josh, soothing her. "Stay easy. I'll just make a little cut above the fang marks—nothing too deep, but we have to get the poison out."

As gently as possible, Josh and Butler lifted her by the shoulders while Jackson took her feet. Together they moved her quickly toward the water's edge. A moment later they set her down again.

"Just close your eyes," Josh told her. "Stay as calm as you can. Any extra fuss makes the blood move faster. Spreads the venom in your body."

Obeying quickly, Camellia shut her eyes and held out her hand.

York showed back up, a bottle of whiskey, half full, at his side. "Let me pour this on it before you cut," he told Josh.

Josh nodded.

York drenched the snakebite in liquor, then poured more of the whiskey over the knife in Josh's hand.

"You ready?" Josh asked Camellia.

She nodded, her eyes still shut.

Josh touched the blade to her wrist and cut into the flesh above the wound. Blood poured out. Finished with the incision, Josh handed the knife to Lynette, lifted Camellia's hand, touched his lips to the wound, and sucked inward. The blood filled his mouth and he spat it into the creek. He repeated the act three more times.

"Wash it out," ordered York, "then we'll need to keep some pressure on it. Slow down the blood flow."

Josh dipped Camellia's hand and wrist into the slow current and sloshed the water through the cut. After he finished, he took her hand out and examined it closely. Swelling already surrounded the wrist, and the fingers of her hand resembled red sausages.

"It's already in her bloodstream," he said softly, worry crossing his face.

Lynette handed him a handkerchief she had produced from the pocket of her long skirt. Quickly Josh washed it and pressed it over the wound.

"Had to be a big snake," said York. "A small copperhead wouldn't cause so much swellin' so fast."

"Or maybe she's especially sensitive to the venom," Josh reasoned.

York thought a second. "Yep, she must be. A wasp stung her on the neck when she was nine or so. Her whole face swelled up fat as a hog. Took it close to two weeks to finally go down. She's avoided bees ever since. Spiders too."

Josh's heart pounded with fear. Some people hardly reacted to snake-bites. Others, those somehow weaker against the poison, sometimes died. "We need to get her to a doctor," he insisted.

"Beaufort's too far to go straight there," said York. "We need to split up. One of us can go for a doctor. The other should take her and everybody else to The Oak."

Josh recognized the logic. A man riding fast could get to Beaufort and back to The Oak a lot quicker than the whole group going straight to town. "I'll go to Beaufort."

"Right," York agreed. "Trenton won't be glad to see either of us. But since I'm married to his mother, he'll have to let me stay there, even if he hates it."

"Let's move," Josh said.

"I'll ride with you," Jackson offered. "Lots of dangerous people still running about."

Josh studied the young man for a moment. A tall, quiet sort, Jackson had said little on the trip south. It was almost as if he kept a secret close to his heart that he didn't want to take a chance on letting out by saying anything. Not more than twenty years old, if that, Josh figured. Jackson was dark of face and beard, his chin and eyes like . . . Josh shrugged off the notion as absurd.

"You're right," Josh said. "Roving bands of blacks, Yankee patrollers who tend to shoot first and ask questions later. I'll like the company."

"Load up!" shouted York.

Everybody moved.

Within minutes Josh and Jackson had climbed onto their weary horses. They headed immediately south toward Beaufort, where they hoped to find a doctor capable of making sure Camellia didn't die before Josh Cain got a chance to marry her.

Chapter Three

After Theo left The Oak, he spent a long time just wandering in the woods, trying to figure out what to do next. Although he suspected Trenton Tessier had lied to him about his mama, he had no way to know for sure. Either way, he didn't figure it smart to go back to the plantation anytime soon and let Tessier take another shot at him. Best to let the man calm down some before taking a chance on showing up there again.

His toe ached more and more as he walked. His body began to heat up with fever as the sun beat down on his head. The fact that he hadn't eaten for a long time continued to take its toll. By the time midday arrived, his steps had slowed to little more than a crawl, and his belly felt as empty as a hollow tree. Reaching a narrow creek, he sat down at the edge of the water and examined his toe. The swelling had spread into the whole foot. The skin on the toe had cracked, and yellow pus slid out of the wound just below the first joint.

Theo tried to remember how he had hurt the toe, but the miles and days and stubs and cuts all blended together. No single moment of pain came to his thinking. Dipping his foot in the water, he cleaned the toe as much as he could, but the ache didn't ease up any. Gingerly he bent to take a drink of water and to wash his sweaty face. A tiny fish floated by, and he grabbed for it but came up empty. Frustrated, he pounded his fists into the creek.

He tried to figure what to do next, but nothing stayed in his head for long. His thoughts were scrambled. His whole plan since leaving Virginia had centered on going to his mama. "Find her," he had repeated over and over again during his dangerous trip. "Find her and then go look for Pa."

Theo lay back on the ground. Now all his plans to find his ma and pa seemed as crazy as his try to catch a fish. The fever gripped his whole body,

32

and his hunger hurt so bad that everything began to blur before his eyes. He tried to stand, but his toe hurt too much. His body wobbled, and he plopped down by the creek again, the wet dirt seeping into his badly torn britches.

Unable to go another step, Theo lay down on his stomach and stared into the stream's crystal-clear water. A line of black ants slipped by his cheek toward some unknown destination. He stretched out a finger and picked one up. Pushing it into his mouth, he crunched down, but the ant tasted bitter. It felt so small that Theo knew not even a thousand ants would make a dent in his empty belly. He didn't eat another. Sighing, he rolled over onto his back, gazed into the sky and, for the first time ever, doubted his visions.

A long time ago, on the morning before his mama had come and told him she had to leave, a flash of pain had swirled behind his eyes just as he awakened. Images rolled through his head—a night, his mama, men with mean faces, his mama coming after him. The pictures slid real fast through his thoughts and then disappeared. But Theo had seen them just the same—like a bolt of lightning flashing in the sky and dipping back into the clouds. Here, then gone.

A few hours later, when his mama picked him up and set him in her lap to tell him she had to go because Lady Rushton had sold her, Theo did not even feel that sad. She would come back, he knew. His dream had told him so. But now seven years had passed, and he was about grown up. A war had come and gone, and he still hadn't seen anything more of that porch step or that dusty road over which his mama walked to find him in his visions.

Was it all a mistake? Were his visions false? Had Grandmammy Nettie lied to him when she told him how special he was? If so, what did that mean for his future? If he never found his mama, what would he do? How would he survive?

All of a sudden, Theo got scared. He shuddered as he looked down at his hands, his legs, his feet, and noted how small everything was. If somebody attacked him, he would have no way to protect himself and, with his bad foot, he couldn't run either.

For a few seconds Theo weighed the matter as best he could in his fevered state. Nothing comforting came to him. His teeth chattered.

Then a bird sang out from a tree to his right, and he turned to stare at it. The bird, a thick-breasted robin, perched on the edge of a limb and chirped as if dancing at a party. And then he remembered his grandmammy's words.

"*The Lord takes care of the birds,*" Nettie had said. "*The rabbits and squirrels too. If the time ever comes that you get to frettin' about anythin', remember that the Lord loves you more than any of them critters. He won't be forgettin' about you, no matter what's happenin'.*"

Although almost too weak to do it, Theo lifted a hand and waved feebly at the bird. As the sun continued to bake his face, sweat poured from his brow. His foot throbbed, and he closed his eyes against the glare and the pain. Pulling his legs to his chest, he curled up like a baby.

Rest, he thought. *The Lord gone take care of you.*

The face of his pa rolled through his head. Theo almost smiled as he saw what he needed to do as soon as his fever ended and he got some food. Go find Markus, the man who sired him. If his mama was gone, his pa was left. Find him, then find out the truth about Ruby.

With his pa's face dancing in his head, Theo passed out, his toe aching, his stomach rumbling, his fever baking through his brain.

Josh and Jackson rode all day toward Beaufort, stopping only enough to keep the bone-tired horses from falling over with weariness. They met a variety of folks on the road as they passed—numbers of thinly clothed Rebel soldiers limping home after years of hard fighting, scores of blacks free for the first time in their lives, and a few whites who had lost their farms or plantations to the fires of the Union army as it burned its way through the countryside.

Neither Josh nor Jackson said much as they rode, but they did talk a little when they stopped to water the horses. From Jackson's clear speech and good use of words, it was evident the young man had received a quality education, but Josh didn't ask him where or when. For the most part Josh learned pretty much the same things York had already told him about the young man. Jackson had served on a Confederate ship during the war, a raider called the *Alabama*.

"The *Alabama* took sixty-four Yankee ships," Jackson proudly told Josh as he drank from his canteen on one of their stops. "We made headlines all over the United States and England too. The Federals finally sunk her in June of 1864, near Cherbourg, France."

"How did you survive?" Josh asked.

"A British boat called the *Deerhound* picked me out of the water and hauled me to London."

"You came to Richmond from there?"

"My skipper on the *Alabama*, Raphael Semmes, survived the sinking too. He ended up leading the James River Squadron, protecting the water entrance to Richmond. I signed on with him. Right before Richmond fell, Semmes ordered us to scuttle all the ships, then said we were free to go. I went home to protect my mother. That's where I met Hampton York."

After their short rest, the two men mounted again and thundered on toward Beaufort. Once again silence fell between them. Josh glanced at Jackson every now and again, studied his dark face and hair, the cut of his chin, the thick shoulders and tall frame. As he had on a number of occasions, Josh noted how much the boy looked like . . . but no, that notion made no sense, so he let it drop. They rode on together, two strangers bent on one thing—finding a doctor to take to The Oak as fast as possible to help Camellia.

At dusk, a couple of miles out of Beaufort, they ran up on a sight Josh had heard about but not yet seen: a shantytown. It was filled with all kinds of dwellings—a few worn tents and lots more lean-tos, their sides and tops made of all manner of scrap wood, sticks, leaves, and mud. A couple of cave-like places were cut into the bushes and covered by limbs and sticks. The smoke from several smoldering fires in and around the dwellings drifted into the sky like a long black cloth. An odd smell hung over the area, something akin to sweat mixed with smoke and animal grease to form a combination that made a man's nostrils burn and drip. Scores of ill-clad blacks sat or stood in and around the fires, their eyes watching Josh and Jackson as they rode through. The former slaves' faces were masked with hidden emotions.

Josh and Jackson slowed as they entered the area. Thinking he recognized a couple of the men, Josh nodded to them. They, in return, stood as still as statues. Evidently, everybody in the shantytown took their cues from those men, so nobody acknowledged the presence of the two intruders.

Josh sensed seething anger, a fury that might boil over at any time, in the stares of those who watched them. He noted fear too, a lot of it, and thought he understood, at least a little. The unusual times created anger and fear for everyone—blacks and whites. Many of the whites who had survived the war had lost their homes, their land, and their belongings. The blacks, although free, had no work, no place to stay, no garden to grow food. No wonder things felt scary.

Spurring his horse slightly, Josh increased the pace as far as he could without breaking the horse into a trot. Several minutes later he and Jackson passed the last of the campfires and moved onto the empty road again. By now the sun had just about disappeared.

"We need to put some ground between us and the shantytown before it gets any darker," Josh called.

"Those folks did look mad," said Jackson.

"Fearful too, especially the children and women."

"Nobody knows what will happen next," Jackson added.

When they rounded a bend, Josh pulled up his horse and whipped it around to make sure no one followed them. Jackson did the same.

"The old ways have passed, but the new ways aren't set yet," Josh explained. "It's a confusing time for everybody, a time almost as dangerous as a war."

"You think trouble will come between blacks and whites?"

"I don't see how we can avoid it. The blacks have to survive but aren't sure how. Most of them have never fended for themselves. They don't know what it means to labor for a wage."

"Whites won't like paying them."

Josh grimaced. "Most will pay as little as possible."

"Rumor says the Yankees will insist on giving the blacks the right to vote."

Josh nodded. "That will cause great upset, I am sure. The South has lived so long with a certain way of doing things that it will be difficult to change. Even if the old way wasn't just."

Jackson turned to study Josh. Josh could see the questions in the young man's eyes, but he didn't ask them aloud.

"Change will come slow and hard," Josh continued.

"What happens if blacks elect their own people? If they put blacks in power over whites? Talk about trouble," Jackson said, shaking his head. "Those who used to own slaves in the South aren't going to stand for that."

"The blacks will want land, too, and property. As is their right if they are free citizens."

Jackson appeared startled. "Do you think they will expect whites to give it to them?"

"The Yankees might enforce it. I've heard some say that all lands abandoned during the war will go to the blacks."

"Won't the owners come back for it?"

"Maybe, maybe not." Josh settled his brown hat more deeply onto his head.

"What will happen if they do and the blacks already have it?"

"No way to tell," Josh said slowly.

"I guess the end of the war didn't settle everything, did it?"

"Not by a long shot. Throw on top of it all that the Yankee soldiers will surely occupy the South for a good many years, and you've got enough powder and fuse to blow up a whole lot of things."

Jackson nodded.

Josh spurred his horse and faced it back toward Beaufort.

Again he and Jackson stopped talking and rode for a long time in quiet. Josh kept thinking about Camellia—how he didn't know if he could survive if she didn't make it, how his love for her had seen him through the war. Then, just when they had thought they were safe and almost home, she was bit by a poisonous snake. Why had the Lord allowed this random thing? Was it another test they needed to pass? Another purifying moment? But hadn't they had enough of those, both before and during the war?

Unable to answer his own questions, Josh hunkered down in his saddle and rode forward. The rest of the day passed, and they reached the main road on the outskirts of Beaufort. About a mile out a Union picket hailed them to stop; they reined their horses in, dust kicking up at their feet.

"You boys ridin' mighty fast," said the army private, sounding slightly suspicious in the gathering darkness, his rifle on the ready. "What's the rush?"

"Looking for a doctor," Josh explained.

"Somebody shot?" asked the private.

"A woman's been snakebit," said Jackson.

The soldier nodded gravely and lowered his rifle.

"How long have you been stationed here?" asked Josh.

"Close to two years," the private replied. "Hope to go home soon."

"You know if Doc Stone is still around?"

"Never heard of him. But there's a Doc Rankin on Main Street, not far from the city bank."

"Mind if we pass?" asked Josh.

"You comin' home from the fightin'?"

Josh gave a nod.

The soldier appeared to think a second, then waved them through.

Josh and Jackson spurred their horses on past the guard.

Jackson glanced back at the soldier, then forward again. "I'll never get used to Federal soldiers in charge of our towns. How long do you think they'll stay here?"

Josh wondered if Jackson knew he had fought against the Confederates. In all the time their group had traveled together after the war's end, Josh had never discussed it openly. "Until everything is calm," he offered. "They'll make sure the blacks get fair treatment and the Rebels don't start something up again."

Soon they reached a hitching post on Main Street. Josh hopped down, tied up his horse, then gazed up and down the street. Except for the presence of Union soldiers, everything looked pretty much like he remembered it before the war. People headed this way and that as night took hold.

Although not nearly as large as Charleston, Beaufort held a charm all its own. Countless fine houses shaded by oaks and palms bordered the streets. Four good churches—Baptist, Methodist, Episcopal, and Catholic—gave people places to worship come Sunday. A library with over three thousand volumes housed great books. Before the war the Beaufort College provided education for the richest of the area's young men. From what he could see at the moment, the fighting of the last four years hadn't done the place much harm.

"The Yankees occupied Beaufort without a fight early in the war," said Jackson, who had also dismounted.

"November of 1861," Josh added. "The Yankees attacked the water-way down near Hilton Head with steamer ships. They did something no one had ever seen . . . changed the way ships attacked forts."

Jackson stared at him in surprise. "You know a lot about it."

"I helped build Fort Walker to defend this town." Josh strode toward a sign that read DOCTOR and hung off the side of a board building. "I didn't want to kill anybody, so I signed on as a construction man. Two forts were built—Walker and Beauregard, down near Port Royal Sound. But the Yankees beat us, fair and square. Like everybody else, I took off when the retreat order came."

"How did the Yankees do it?"

When they reached the building, Josh knocked, then continued. "They brought steamer ships, which meant they didn't have to worry about wind or ocean currents like the old sailboats did. They brought the ships in on an elliptical path, stayed out of range of our guns, then swung around and came in from the north. Since we figured they would set up and fire point-blank at us from east to west, like ships have always done, we didn't have our north flank fortified. They hit us there, then kept moving. Attacked us broadside as they passed to the south. They had no reason to sit still and fire at us. That would have given us the advantage since we had the fixed positions. But when they kept moving, we had to shoot at passing targets. That gave them the upper hand."

Jackson nodded as Josh knocked on the door again.

"So they fired at you and moved on south," said Jackson. "Wheeled around and went back north out of range again. Then swung around and hit you again as they sailed past."

"That's it. Fort Beauregard was over two and a half miles away on the other side of the sound. The Federals had plenty of room to go by them, then us, and never get caught in a cross fire."

Jackson appeared impressed. "Like you said, a new way of fighting."

"After they beat us, they headed right on up here, at least fifteen warships, a hundred and fifty guns, and close to ten thousand men. The whites in Beaufort took everything they could haul away and headed in-land without a fight."

Josh stepped to the office's only window and peered inside. There were several chairs and some shelves, but nobody moving.

"Where did you go?" asked Jackson.

Josh faced Jackson again and decided he might as well tell him the truth. "I made a hard choice. I went north and put on the Union blue."

Jackson's eyes flashed. "York told me, but I didn't want to believe it."

"I did what I thought right," said Josh.

"York told me that too."

"I never felt good about owning a person," Josh explained. "No matter their color."

Jackson spat like Josh had seen York do a thousand times—an act of disgust. "I didn't fight the war to keep the blacks in bondage," Jackson retorted. "My folks never owned slaves. They paid them a wage. But letting the Yankees tell us how to live our lives . . . no Southern man can abide that. Not then, not now."

A pair of Union soldiers marched past. After Josh nodded at them, he faced Jackson again. "You might have to get used to it."

"Never," Jackson declared.

Although fearful that Jackson's rebellious spirit might someday cause him trouble, Josh couldn't help but smile just a little. "You sound a lot like Captain York."

Jackson seemed to ignore Josh's observation. The young man simply took off his hat and ran his hands through his hair. "The doctor isn't here," he said, pointing at the door. "What do you want to do?"

"We wait." Josh sat down on the street by the door. "He's got to show up sometime."

Jackson shrugged. "You think there's a saloon around here anywhere?"

"You think it's wise to go searching for a saloon?"

Jackson stared at his boots a moment before sliding down and taking a spot by Josh. "Mother told me you stayed on the straight and narrow."

"Probably a bunch of Yankees there anyway," said Josh.

Jackson smiled but said nothing else.

The two of them sat side by side on the plank walk, waiting for the doctor.

Chapter Four

York led his group onto The Oak's grounds just after dark fell. Not wanting to explain anything to anybody at the manse, he bypassed the main drive leading to the big house. He headed his horse and the wagon through the back way, then straight toward his old house. Although intent on getting Camellia comfortable in bed, he couldn't help but let his gaze roam as he hurried across the outskirts of the property.

Although he couldn't quite see it, he knew the manse stood about half a mile away. He wondered if a light burned in the windows . . . if Trenton and Katherine had made it home safely. He would need to go see them as soon as Camellia turned for the better.

Although he couldn't see much in the dark, he remembered the plantation beyond the manse—the thirty bunking houses for the Negroes that sat over five hundred yards away and downwind to the left of the manse. Three different barns stood halfway between the manse and the bunking houses. Out of sight past all that, along the banks of the Conwilla River, lay the rice fields.

York tried to smell the water of the river as he used to on soft nights like this. The Conwilla River, its fresh water rising and falling with the flow of the ocean tide that pushed it in and out every morning and night, made the rice growing possible. For a few seconds he forgot about Camellia and recalled his days as overseer of the operation that produced barrels and barrels and barrels of rice.

Banks of wood and earth about eight feet wide at the base and three feet high—what they called check banks—had allowed Hampton York to flood the fields separately from each other on a regular schedule. The hard labor of the field hands built the banks with great precision and kept them up by constant care, clearing the ditches and drains with hoes and shovels.

During the winter the servants plowed the fields and dragged them with a harrow to break up the earth and keep the field flat—a necessity for growing good rice. In April they sowed the seed for a new crop, pressing the seed into balls of wet clay and then drying the balls before putting them into the ground.

After the sowing they immediately flooded the fields, keeping them wet until the seed "pipped" or germinated, a step that usually took somewhere between four to fourteen days. After that, they drained the fields, hoed them for weeds, and kept them dry until the young, needlelike rice plants formed rows across the field.

Then came the flooding again, a series of water flows that gave the rice protection from weeds and provided all the moisture it needed to grow strong. Finally, the harvest flow of water came—the flooding occurring in late summer, after the rice plants had grown to about fifteen inches. This flood supported the stalks until shortly before the harvest that started in late August and lasted usually until almost the end of October.

Everybody worked at a frantic pace at harvest time—from sunup until late at night. A couple of days before the harvest, they drained the water from the fields and sent in the field hands to cut the stalks with sickles—rice hooks, they called them. After they'd cut down the stalks, they left them in the fields to dry for a couple of days. Next, they stacked the stalks in ricks about seven feet wide, twenty feet long, and as high as a man could make them. When all the rice was cut and dried, they hauled it away to a mill on a mule-drawn cart or a rice flat—a flat-bottomed barge. After milling the rice, they stored it in barrels made of pine and banded with birch and white oak hoops. Each barrel carried about six hundred pounds of rice.

Lots of things made the work hard—stifling heat, swarming horse flies, field rats and mosquitoes, the danger of malaria and yellow fever. For York, though, the sight of a smooth field of swaying rice in the middle of a gentle flood of water made it all worthwhile. He liked the ebb and flow of it, the way it connected to the ocean, the way it tied to all things natural.

York spat into the dirt from the back of his horse as his mind returned to the present. His days of growing rice might have ended forever, he realized. Without the labor of the blacks, such work was certainly impossible.

A minute later he reached the front yard of the house where he had once lived. It was surrounded by oak trees on all sides. The thick moss on the branches draped downward, like an old woman's gray hair, almost touching the ground. Even in the dark York could see the outline of the four-room square home, with its two shuttered windows, one on each side of the door in the front. In times past, scores of chickens had darted across the well-swept yard as he walked up. Not anymore. No sounds of chickens scratching in the dirt greeted him. Instead, weeds grew up right to the edge of the steps. Everything about the property looked worn and old.

York hopped down from his horse and stepped quickly to the wagon, where Camellia lay. He touched her head and felt the heat rising from her skin. "Let's get her inside."

Lynette nodded and moved into the wagon to Camellia's head. Johnny helped on Lynette's end, while York gently took Camellia by the ankles. Together they carried her into the house. Ruby ran ahead and shoved open the door to the bedroom. To York's relief, the bed was still there. There were no covers on it like before the war, but at least the worn mattress was undisturbed. After they settled Camellia on the bed, Ruby rushed into the room with a tattered blanket that she tucked around Camellia.

When York bent to Camellia, her eyes stared at him but held no focus. He lifted her injured hand and saw that the arm from wrist to elbow had swelled to almost twice its normal size. Butler, holding a bucket of water, and Beth stepped into the room.

"The well still works," Butler said, handing York a dipper.

York took the water and held it to Camellia's mouth. A sip dripped through her lips but little more.

Lynette moved to York's side. "Take everybody out. Let me get Camellia in her nightclothes. She'll be more comfortable. I'll wash her down with this water . . . try to get her skin cool."

York stood and led the group out of the room. "You two best check your old house," he told Beth and Butler once they were on the porch. "See if it's OK to live in. If it is, haul your things off the wagon and put them in the house."

"Pa says we don't plan to stay," said Beth.

"You'll have to stay until Camellia is better."

Beth and Butler nodded and left.

Ruby, with Leta on her hip, and Nettie walked onto the porch.

"We got four cabins here," York said. "Pick one of the two that are left and put your things there."

"You reckon Mr. Tessier will agree to that?" asked Ruby. "Darkies living in houses not built for them?"

York's chin tensed. "I can assure you he will. I'm married to his mother, remember?"

Ruby lifted an eyebrow and adjusted Leta on her hip. After a minute of silence, she shrugged and led her mama down the porch steps.

Fingering his beard, York waited for them to disappear in the darkness before he took a deep breath. He started to go back to Lynette and Camellia, then realized they needed privacy for a while. So he left the porch and strode toward the wagon to unpack.

After looking around to make sure nobody saw him, he slid a rectangular box off the wagon, hauled it into the shadows, and squatted beside it. For several seconds he stared at the box, wondering, as he had every night since he left Richmond, what he might find in it. He recalled how he had come into possession of the box. It was on the night the city of Richmond fell to the Yankees . . .

At the foot of Fourteenth Street, near the north end of Mayo's Bridge, a line of train cars stood waiting to leave the city. Most of the cars were already loaded with Southerners, fleeing the conquerors soon to arrive. Two of the cars, however, waited for bags, barrels, and wooden boxes. Each of the containers was loaded either with papers from the archives of the Confederate government or with coins, dollars, or bullion from the half-dozen safes of the Confederacy's treasury.

A row of oil lanterns threw a yellowish glow onto the rail platform as sixty young men stood guard with fixed bayonets around the last two cars. Hundreds of people rushed past the guards, each of them so intent on his own survival that they paid little or no attention to the loading of the valuables. A troop of soldiers marched toward the cars, a line of wagons behind them. Each wagon was loaded with at least eighty boxes and barrels. When the soldiers reached the platform, they halted, and Captain Hampton York slid off his horse and approached the man leading the guards.

"I got everythin', Superintendent Parker," York reported. "We been workin' for hours loadin' the wagons from the bank."

Parker nodded. "Treasurer Hale will be pleased. Got to get it all out of here."

York noted that the guards were all youngsters from the naval academy. They had been assigned to protect the Confederate treasury because the navy they once served no longer existed.

All hope for victory was gone, York realized. He resigned himself to defeat. "We best get everythin' on the train," he suggested. "Another few hours and somebody might want to shoot us for it."

When Parker saluted, York turned back to his men. Over the last few hours they had loaded up more money from the Treasury Department than York had ever dreamed of seeing. He'd heard his superiors whisper that it was about a half-million dollars' worth. Everything—from gold bullion, Mexican silver dollars, double-eagle gold pieces, ingots in square, squat boxes, and bags and small kegs of assorted coins—lay in the boxes, satchels, and barrels he and his men had hauled into the wagons.

"Unload the wagons," yelled York. "Pack it tight. We're short on room."

His men moved quickly, while York pondered what to do next. From what he could see, even if the Confederate General Lee managed to escape the Union leader Grant at Richmond, he didn't have much of an army left. Within weeks, if not sooner, Grant would surely catch Lee and the war would end. What would happen then? Would the Northern Bluebellies put every Southern Rebel they caught in prison? Would they shoot them? Nobody knew.

York spat. No matter the outcome, he figured his presence no longer mattered. Now was the time to do what he could to take care of his own family. Although he risked life and limb over and over again for the cause of the South, the time for such heroics had ended.

Determined now, York walked up a wood ramp into one of the rail cars his men continued to load. Both sides of the cars were open, and the chilly night air rolled in. York spat the last of his tobacco out the side of the car. When he smelled smoke, York wrinkled his nose and peered out. Light glowed in the distance. Fire.

It's already starting, he thought. Before morning, all of Richmond will be in ashes. Maybe from the Federals. Maybe from the people of Richmond as they burn anything they think the Yankees might want.

Two soldiers—one of them his son, Johnny—entered the car. York nodded as they placed a box the size of a piece of luggage near his feet and shoved it into the corner. Johnny wiped his hands, then followed the other soldier out to get another box.

York considered his future. Should he go back to The Oak with Katherine? Was The Oak still standing? And what about Katherine? Although she had come to Richmond, he had not seen much of her since his recovery and reassignment to the military. Was she still in the city? Did she still have his money, about twenty-seven thousand dollars of U.S. cash? What had she meant when she told him so many years ago that she had taken care of things after she didn't go to London? Could he trust her?

York stared at the box Johnny and his companion just placed in the corner. He tried to imagine its contents—gold, silver, Confederate script? What if he ended up back on The Oak without money? What if Katherine had wasted his dollars—everything he had earned, gambled for, fought for?

Lynette's face entered his mind. He hoped she had taken Camellia and everybody else and fled from Richmond. But what if she hadn't? Since he had stayed away from Lynette, even more deliberately than he had Katherine, he had no way to know what she had done.

York stepped to the box and studied it for another moment. Then, without further thinking, he lifted a boot, pushed the box over to the back opening in the train car, and kicked it onto the ground. It hit the dirt with a soft thud. York froze, wondering if anyone had noticed what he had done. When no one raised an alarm, York waited until the next box arrived, then stepped past Johnny and back onto the platform.

About an hour later, just as his men were finishing the loading, York walked to the box he had kicked out, shoved it closer to the track, where the shadows from the boxcar completely covered it, then headed back to his men. After ordering the lieutenant to lead the men back to the War Building, he told Johnny to wait with him. When the men left, he commanded Johnny to ride straight to the Victoria Hotel and wait for further instructions. As Johnny rode off, York stepped to the hidden box and lifted it quickly onto his shoulder. He carried it to an alley several yards away.

Dropping the box, York checked around to see if anyone was watching. When he saw no one, he shoved the box into a corner. After kicking a pile of *dirt over it, he wiped his hands and pulled out the last good chew of tobacco he owned—the one he'd saved for the day the war ended. For him that end had just come.*

He stuck the tobacco in his cheek, left the alley, climbed onto his horse, and urged it toward the Victoria Hotel. Although he didn't know exactly what was in the bank box, he was determined to come back for it when he was ready to leave the city.

And that's exactly what he did a few hours later, as the city sank into burning chaos . . .

Now that York was back on The Oak, the time had finally come to open the box. He took out his knife, shoved the blade under the locked clasp, and pried it open. A stack of black books—battle manuals he noted instantly— lay just inside. Not interested in the notebooks, York dropped them on the ground. He tossed out the several pistols that lay under the manuals too. Beneath the pistols he found a stack of papers, all of them dusty.

His heart pounding, York pushed the papers to one side, hoping, believing he would find something valuable underneath. But he didn't. He reached the bottom of the box and cursed under his breath. For a second he searched through the box once more but again came up empty-handed. No money, no jewelry, no watches or silver chains—nothing of value.

York spat in disappointment, then stood and gazed into the sky, as if looking for a long-lost lover. Nothing seemed real; nothing seemed right. He had counted on finding something he could use for money here!

The door to the house opened.

York shoved the contents back into the box and pushed the box up against the house. Hurrying to the front porch, he saw Lynette standing there. Her hair, unpinned from its usual tight bun, brushed her shoulders as she gripped the porch rail.

"You unloading?" she asked as York stepped onto the porch.

"Yep. A few things to unpack yet."

"Camellia is resting," Lynette reported. "Her breathing is ragged, and her face is hot, but Ruby is keeping her as cool as she can with wet rags."

"Not much more we can do for now," York said. "Except hope the doctor gets here before too long."

Lynette's blue eyes studied him. "We can pray."

York spat off the porch. "Between you and Josh I'm plumb surrounded by religion."

She cocked her head. "You see that as a bad thing?"

"Not unless you expect me to get the infection."

"You try so hard to seem rough . . . but I know it's not true."

As York looked at Lynette, there on the porch, he forgot the box for a minute. Even with the privations of the war and their hard journey south, Lynette still took his breath away. He recalled the first time he had seen her.

Lynette Ruth Wheeler had grown up in a Columbia church orphanage. Her parents were victims of a fire that burned down their house when she was only eight.

In June of 1842 York met her in a saloon in Savannah, where he lived at the time, making his wages, for the most part, at a poker table. She came to the bar with a card player named Wallace Swanson, a man who'd seen her obvious beauty and taken up with her soon after she left the orphanage the year she turned sixteen.

Although Swanson had a good eye for women, his card playing didn't amount to much. When York won most of his money that night, Lynette quickly shifted her affections to him and left Swanson broke of pocket and heart when the bar closed.

It didn't take York long to fall in love with Lynette Wheeler. How could he resist? What a woman! Lynette carried her wondrous body like a goddess, and her face melted a man's heart. When she smiled—and she always smiled when she wanted something, he found out later—the whole room lit up. Nobody could resist that smile.

York didn't find out she had a two-year-old daughter until two weeks after they met.

"A woman friend takes care of her most of the time," Lynette explained. "I give her money. She keeps my baby."

"Whose is it?" he'd asked bluntly.

Lynette didn't bat an eye. "Swanson's."

"You two married?"

"No."

"Why not?"

"He never asked."

Lynette's straightforward manner had surprised but not shocked York at the time. After all, he wasn't a saint either.

"I'm with you now." She smiled and snuggled her head on his shoulder. "You won't throw me and my baby out because of my wanton ways, will you?"

York remembered the feeling—she needed him! No woman had ever moved him so. "No. I won't throw you out," he promised.

Within the month York and Lynette married.

A few weeks later he found out she had another child on the way—and it would be too soon for this baby to have been his. Anger boiled in him for a few days . . . until Lynette favored him with a kiss that made him feel like a king. Then his anger disappeared.

Later he asked her why she'd chosen him over Swanson—the father of her two children. Lynette shrugged. "I'm almost twenty. Had another baby on the way and needed somebody to take care of us. Swanson loved me but didn't do well when it came to making a living. You seemed better at it."

The words cut York as she spoke them. She had not even pretended to love him. But York had not worried about that then. She would love him someday, he figured. He would treat her so well she would eventually come to that.

But, of course, she never had. As York continued to stare at Lynette on the porch, he wanted to hurt her for her betrayal. Much later he had found out she lied to him about not being married to the gambler Wallace Swanson. And then, less than two years into her marriage with York, Lynette had fled The Oak, leaving York with three children to raise on his own—two of which were Swanson's. "You weren't so religious when we were together twenty-three years ago."

She dropped her eyes. "I made a lot of mistakes when I was young."

He bristled. "Bein' with me was a mistake?"

"I didn't say that."

"Sounds to me like you did."

"I grew up after I left you," she murmured. "Came to faith in the Lord in Richmond years later."

"Swanson get right with the Lord too?" York asked sarcastically.

She nodded.

He spat. "You both had a lot to repent of."

"That's true," she admitted. "I lied to you about not being married to Wallace."

He gave an abrupt nod. "I found that out later."

"I'm sorry."

"Then, when my luck at cards ran out and I moved you to The Oak so I could make a steady livin', you ran out on me. I woke up one day and you were gone . . . like a puff of smoke," he accused.

"All of that was wrong." Her tone was filled with regret.

"I made a thousand dollars a year at The Oak, but that wasn't enough for you."

Lynette looked back up and her eyes flashed. "I didn't leave you and the children because of the money."

"Then what? You told me at the time that bein' the wife of an overseer wasn't your idea of fine livin'. You tried to talk me out of goin' there from the first. But we had three kids by then. I couldn't count on a turn of a card anymore to take care of you and them."

Lynette shook her head. "It doesn't matter."

"But it does matter!" he exploded. "If you had a good reason for leavin' me, maybe I could understand. But you didn't. Other than the fact that you didn't love me . . . there was that, of course." His voice calmed as he reached this final conclusion. He swept off his hat and stared into it. "Who knows what might have happened if you had stayed? I might have turned out a better man."

"It's all past," she said, almost in a whisper. "I don't want to remember it anymore. I want to put it behind me."

York grunted. "Seems like you put it behind you a long time ago."

She took a step toward him and put a hand on his elbow. "I did. Most of it, anyway. But there's one thing I still need: your forgiveness for the way I hurt you."

"You already asked me once. I told you I couldn't do it," he fired back.

Lynette sighed. "I'll keep asking."

"Do what you want." He pulled away and put his hat back on.

Lynette reached for him again, and her touch warmed his forearm. With all his soul he wanted to take her in his arms and tell her he forgave her. Even after all this time, he still loved her, so how could he refuse? But York couldn't let himself do it. Couldn't say the words. Couldn't tell her he still had feelings for her. If he did, he feared she would just reject him. He couldn't take that. Not again. Not after the way she had hurt him so long ago. Besides, he was a married man now—even if he didn't love his wife.

"I want you to understand," she pleaded.

"Then tell me why you left." As York searched her eyes, his heart hurt. So much had gone wrong. They had both made so many bad choices. He wished he could fix it all, change the past. That he could alter what he had become. But in the next instant he knew he couldn't.

"I . . . can't." Tears glimmered in her eyes.

His heart turned hard. "Then don't ask my forgiveness."

"I'll pray for us. Pray the Lord can get us through this."

"Save your prayers for Camellia," he replied. "I'm long past them doin' me any good."

"None of us is ever past the power of prayer."

"So you say."

She lifted her head, and York saw the familiar flash of determination in her eyes. "The Lord may need to break you before you see it," she told him.

York raised an eyebrow. "Seems like the Lord missed His chance at that. When you left me, when Chester died, when I left Calvin back at Burgess Mill—things can't get much harder."

Lynette sighed, obviously at her wit's end.

"I need to finish unloadin'," said York.

"We all have things to finish."

"Indeed we do." With those few words, York left the porch and headed to the wagon to unload the last few belongings he had brought home from the war.

Chapter Five

Theo awoke with a jerk early the next morning.

An old black man, squatting beside him, was peering into his face. The man's head was set slightly sideways on his neck, and a patchy gray beard covered his cheeks and chin. The man wore what appeared to be a cat's paw on the end of a string necklace. His eyes—yellow where white should have been—blinked real fast over and over. He wore a rough gray hat with a single feather stuck up from a band on the front.

The man touched Theo's forehead with a stubby finger, then drew back and clucked. Theo got a glimpse of gums, tongue, and a few scattered teeth. The sun beat down from behind the man's head. The glare hurt Theo's eyes, so he closed them and rubbed his head with both hands. For an instant everything felt like a dream.

Then the man clapped his hands and shouted.

Startled, Theo opened his eyes again. Everything was real.

"Wake!" yelled the man. A blast of foul breath rolled out with the one-word command, and Theo jumped up as it hit him. The man grabbed Theo by the shoulders and pulled him to a sitting position.

Theo wobbled a little, then gathered his strength and held still, his feet folded under his body, his hands propped on the ground to hold himself up. The man reached back, picked something off the ground, and held it out. It was an ax, a dull-looking blade attached to a thick handle. Small bits of hair and something dried stuck to the blade's edge.

Theo's heart pounded. He tried to get to his feet, but his right foot didn't work. Looking down, he saw that the swelling in his toe had spread to his ankle, and it now showed blue and yellow streaks of thick infection.

His big toe was completely black, and the skin had split in a couple of places.

When the man stood and stepped back, Theo relaxed just slightly. The man pointed the ax at Theo's foot. "You gone die with that foot."

Desperately wishing for a drink of water, Theo ran a hand over his mouth. He didn't want to move, lest the man see it as a threat of some kind. The man moved to his left, and Theo followed him with his eyes.

Two wagons were nearby, with a pair of slump-backed mules hitched to the reins of each wagon. A dirty canvas covered the back of one and at least four cats—two of them black and white, one a dull yellow, the last a solid gray—sat on the wood bench in front. The cats meowed but otherwise seemed bored. A younger black man—his body thin, still, and almost formless—held the reins of the wagon with no cover. A plumpish woman with lighter skin sat on the seat beside the younger man. As she stared at Theo, she tucked her dirty gray skirt around her ankles.

When the man with the ax reached the wagon, the second man handed him a bottle. He uncorked it with his teeth, then strode back and handed the bottle to Theo. "Drink!" he ordered.

Theo took the bottle. His nose wrinkled at the sour smell, and he almost handed it back, but the man lifted the ax slightly. Theo had no choice but to obey. He touched the bottle to his lips and sipped the liquid inside.

"More!" growled the man.

Theo took a big gulp, then another. As the warm liquid seeped into his stomach, he retched. Then his stomach settled and accepted the drink.

"All of it!" yelled the man.

Theo obeyed without argument this time, pouring the last of the bottle's contents into his starved belly. When he finished, he handed the bottle back to the man and lay back on the ground. The man took the bottle back to the wagon and returned to squat again over Theo. The yellow cat suddenly appeared in the man's arms, its tongue licking at his fingers.

"I am Marquis," said the man in an accent Theo didn't recognize. "Hail from New Orleans. Sell da medicine." He pointed to the wagon.

"What you just took. Dat man"—he indicated the one sitting in the wagon—"he be Rufe, do my deeds for me. Da woman, she be Mabel. Menfolks pay me for her favors."

Theo started to speak, but his tongue, swollen from fever and a lack of water, made it difficult. "Th-e-o," he finally managed, the word sounding strange. "V-i-r-g-i-n-i-a."

"What you doin' out here all by yo' lonesome?" asked Marquis.

"Lookin' for . . . my mama."

Marquis seemed to consider that awhile before he spoke again. "You a odd-lookin' boy. Stumpy of body, round of head. Eye not with you."

"What . . . was in . . . the bottle?" Theo managed.

Marquis laughed. "A little dis, a touch of dat. Good for what ails you, dat it is."

"I need water," Theo pleaded.

"No water," said Marquis. "Not yet."

Theo closed his eyes.

"Where you lose da one eye?" asked Marquis.

Theo considered the older man again. "Born missin' it."

"Bad fortune."

Theo shook his head. "I see things," he muttered. "Better than folks with both eyes."

Marquis raised a gray eyebrow. "How you mean?"

Theo's voice sounded faraway to him, like somebody else talking. Although something told him maybe he shouldn't say so much, he couldn't hold back. "Visions," he mumbled. "I see . . . beyond . . ." His head began to swirl worse again, and he wondered what caused it—the drink or his fever.

Marquis touched Theo's forehead again. "You took with da fever. Hot as a skillet in da fire. Everybody see da visions when dey got fever."

"Not from fever," argued Theo, trying to stay conscious. "I always seen them, since soon after I could talk."

"You sayin' you got the sight? See portents and such as dat?"

Theo licked his lips and nodded.

Marquis lifted an eyebrow again. "A body with da sight can do right well in this old world. Peoples pay cash money to hear what a body with da sight got to say."

"I don't . . . do that," Theo said weakly. "Can't make a vision come . . . they just happen . . . no way to conjure them up, to demand them."

"You sayin' you never took a nickel for tellin' things?"

Theo shook his head.

"You a crazy boy," Marquis concluded.

Theo's eyelids grew heavier. When the yellow cat meowed, the sound seemed a long way off.

"What you sayin', Yellow Boy?" Marquis asked the cat. "You sayin' dat a body with da vision maybe do better than a man sellin' medicine?"

Yellow Boy simply licked a paw.

Theo tried to protest. He wanted Marquis to understand that he didn't know how to see anybody's future. Even if he could, he wouldn't make somebody pay for it. But Theo's tongue didn't cooperate. His body felt numb, like a lump of flesh basting in the sun. Although his eyes were open, he didn't know if what he saw truly existed or not. Everything seemed out of his reach . . . beyond his fingers, past his touch.

Yellow Boy cried again.

Theo dimly sensed movement. He tried to see what was happening, but his vision blurred worse than ever. Black dots swirled before his eyes. He felt Marquis move to his bad foot and lift it off the ground for inspection.

"I believes what you cryin'," Marquis told Yellow Boy as he studied Theo's foot. "Maybe dis boy here got more than he knows. Maybe peoples pay a nickel to hear what he could see for them."

Theo felt his foot touch the ground again; then a heavy weight pressed down on it. He forced himself to open his eyes. When he did, he saw Marquis sitting on his leg, a knee squarely planted on his foot to hold it in place. Theo tried to push Marquis off, but his legs barely moved. He raised a hand to knock Marquis away but couldn't close his fist. His whole body seemed frozen in place, and his eyes saw nothing but swirling images.

"Don't want no man with the vision dyin' on me," mumbled Marquis. "Or runnin' off lookin' for his mama neither."

Theo tried to figure out what Marquis meant, but none of it made any sense. He figured the effects of his fever or the drink had finally taken hold.

"Take more of this." Marquis produced another bottle from somewhere and handed it to Theo.

Unable to argue or fight, Theo took another long swallow.

Marquis grabbed the bottle from Theo and swigged from it too, then put it away.

Theo sensed something was about to happen but couldn't figure out what. A second later, when Marquis lifted the ax, the sun glinted off the dirty blade and into Theo's eyes. He squinted into the glare and wondered what Marquis planned to do with the ax. Only when the blade crunched down and bit into the bone just above his injured toe and he heard Yellow Boy screech did Theo figure it out. He screamed along with Yellow Boy.

Marquis lifted the ax again. Again there was a crunch and a scream. By the time the ax chomped into his foot for the third time, Theo could no longer tell his screams from Yellow Boy's.

Yellow Boy darted away.

And Theo collapsed into a nightmare from which he never expected to wake.

Feeling something sharp digging into his side, Josh Cain awoke with a start. He glanced up to see a man with a brown beard, slumped shoulders, and thick hands prodding him with a boot. Josh quickly stood, wiped the sleep from his eyes, and slipped on his hat. Jackson stood beside him, his young face marked with sleep lines.

"What you doin' here?" asked the man who had poked him.

"Waiting for the doctor," said Josh.

"That's me," the man announced.

Something in the doctor's voice sounded familiar. Josh studied him carefully, wondered where they had met before. The Beaufort doctor wore a dirty white shirt, faded brown pants, and scuffed boots. It took

only one more look into the doctor's face before everything flooded back
to Josh.

*Ferry Point. The day Fort Walker fell. Although wounded in the hip, Josh had
a black man named Lester in tow as he waited on a boat to take them off Hilton
Head to safety on the mainland. Blood poured from a head wound Lester had
taken in battle. A doctor moved to Josh to check his wound, but Josh pointed
him to Lester.*

*The doctor shook his head. "Let me check your hip. Then get you on a
boat."*

"I'm OK," Josh insisted. "He's not."

*The doctor glanced at Lester but didn't do anything. "I got soldiers to
check."*

"Take care of him!" Josh demanded.

*"I got more hurt soldiers than you can shake a stick at," the doctor told Josh.
"No time for darkies. You want my aid or not?"*

*Josh grabbed the doctor by the front of his shirt. "That man took that wound
defending you!" he shouted. "Now tend to him!"*

*The doctor pushed Josh away. Josh threw a punch but lost his balance and
fell before it landed. The doctor kicked Josh in the side. Josh struggled to get up
but, exhausted and in pain, couldn't manage it. The doctor held Josh down with
a boot on his back.*

Josh pushed up, ready to fight, but the doctor walked away, with an expression of disgust.

*That's when Josh decided to go north. No way would he fight for a man
like that doctor.*

Now that same doctor, Rankin by name, stood before Josh Cain, who
needed his help to save Camellia's life.

"You need to ride with us to The Oak Plantation," Josh urged, hoping the doctor didn't remember him. "A woman is there with a bad
snakebite."

"The Oak still standin'?" asked the doctor.

"We think so," said Jackson.

Rankin eyed the two of them. "You have any money?"

Josh almost hit him—not only for the question but for the incident at Ferry Point. But, for Camellia's sake, he held his temper. "Not on us. But this woman needs your services."

Rankin shrugged, moved past them to his door, and stuck a key in the lock. "I got plenty of folks without money to tend right here," he groused. "Don't need to take a day's ride to The Oak to find another one."

Josh grabbed the doctor by the shoulders, spun him around, and glared right in his face. "What kind of a doctor are you?"

The doctor's gaze held his. "Who are you?"

"Josh Cain."

Rankin pushed Josh's hands away. "I've heard of you. You and Hampton York ran The Oak before the war."

"That's right." Josh tried to relax.

"I heard you fought for the Yankees," Rankin said scornfully.

Josh glanced at Jackson, then back to Rankin. "You heard right," he said, seeing no reason to lie. "Met you once too, when Hilton Head fell. Perhaps you recall that?"

Rankin stuck his chin close to Josh's. "Don't recollect," he growled. "But men like you aren't welcome here."

Josh's eyes narrowed. "You want me to call a Yankee soldier here, to see how welcome he says I am?"

"The Yankees will leave soon enough."

"Probably not for years."

"Folks can wait. You'll see."

Jackson suddenly stepped between the two older men.

"You *will* go with us," Jackson calmly told Rankin.

Rankin faced him. "Why should I?"

Jackson pulled a gold coin out of his pocket. "Because I have this."

Rankin eyed the coin. "I thought you boys said you didn't have any money on you."

"He said it, not me," said Jackson.

Rankin again eyed the money—a five-dollar gold piece.

Jackson grabbed his hand and pressed the coin into the palm. "We need to hurry!" he said firmly.

Rankin frowned, then nodded. "Just give me a couple of minutes to gather my things."

As Rankin walked into his office, Josh turned to Jackson. "How many of those coins do you have?"

"Just the one."

"But you would give it to Rankin?"

"For Camellia, yes."

"But why?"

"She's my sister."

"But you barely know her."

Jackson stared at his boots. "Hampton York told me to bring back a doctor, and I do what he tells me."

Josh scratched his head. "I don't understand."

Jackson began to explain. "Captain York is my superior officer. And he told me to bring back a doctor."

"But the war is over . . . Lee surrendered; they caught Jefferson Davis a few days ago."

Jackson put his hat on. "It doesn't matter. York is . . . my superior."

Josh studied the young man for a few seconds. He started to voice a suspicion, then decided to let it go. It was not his business how York treated Lynette's boy. Not his business at all.

Rankin poked his head out the door. "Got everythin'," he said, holding up a black bag. "Ready to go."

Hurrying now, Josh led Jackson and Rankin to their horses. Together they galloped out of town and back toward The Oak.

When Camellia's eyes fluttered open, she saw Ruby, wet rag in hand, sitting beside her on the bed. A sliver of sunlight filtered over her face from the broken window that overlooked the barn not far from the manse. Camellia's mouth felt like somebody had filled it with dirt, then forgotten to clean it, and her right arm was swollen and aching. Ruby laid down the rag and brought Camellia a dipper of water from a pitcher on the floor. Camellia raised her head slightly to drink the water, then lay back down again.

"Josh," she whispered.

"He's gone for the doctor," Ruby explained.

Camellia took a deep breath. "We're . . . at The Oak?"

"Yes, arrived yesterday."

"Not where you want to be, I don't guess."

Ruby's dark eyes were soft. "You don't worry about that. Just lie easy until the doctor comes."

Camellia licked her lips, and Ruby touched the cloth to her head again. When Camellia raised her right arm, it shook from weakness. But she managed to inspect the swelling that reached from the tips of her fingers all the way through the elbow and into the upper arm and shoulder. "How sick am I?" she asked, lowering the arm again.

"It's a good sign you can talk," said Ruby. "The doctor will come soon. You just stay calm and quiet."

Camellia attempted a smile. "You are a . . . friend, Ruby."

"Sounds odd to hear you call me 'friend'—with you white and me black and all. But we have been through a lot."

Camellia nodded. "Seven years . . . since you showed up . . . here."

"A lot has happened," agreed Ruby. "You and Mr. Tessier parted ways. You fell in love with Mr. Josh, who disappeared during the war, then showed back up again just as it ended."

"You lost Markus . . . took Obadiah as your husband."

Ruby hung her head.

Obadiah was a good man, Camellia knew. A free man of color, he lived near Beaufort and built furniture and coffins to make his living. Ruby had married him in 1859, after her first husband was sold away from her.

Over forty years old when they married, Obadiah had gotten his freedom papers the year his pa—a white shipbuilder and land baron from Savannah—died. That happened every now and again: a white man who sired children by a slave woman would let his offspring go free once he had passed on. Obadiah's pa had left it in his will that his mixed children would receive twenty acres of land, fifty dollars in cash, and papers of freedom ten days after he died. Nineteen at the time, Obadiah had immediately left Savannah, moved to Beaufort, and started building coffins.

Laboring hard, he'd soon become one of the richest black men in the county. A caring, loving man, he had helped Camellia when her brother, Chester, had died of the fever.

"I wonder where Obadiah is?" asked Ruby.

Camellia opened her eyes again. "You figure to go . . . looking for him?"

"I got to find my boy, Theo, first," Ruby said. "You know my mama said he left Virginia to come looking for me."

"I remember."

"I plan on searching for him, then Obadiah after that."

"Maybe Obadiah will come here," Camellia offered. Suddenly she was weary again.

Ruby rubbed her eyes. "Obadiah's a fine man. Handsome and strong as an ox. He treated me well. Gave me presents even before I showed him any favor. I remember once he rode over to see me seven Sundays in a row and brought me a pretty thing every time—a red ribbon one week, a piece of mint candy another, a small hand mirror on a third. If he comes back while I'm gone, you hold him right here, OK?"

Camellia smiled and remembered Obadiah and Ruby's courting days.

Obadiah had called on Ruby for months before she yielded to his charms. They married in August 1859, after Trenton Tessier gave his permission. When his work allowed, Obadiah stayed with Ruby. And when he couldn't, he picked her up in his buggy on Saturday and drove her to his place, a four-room house with two glass windows on the front, a small spot for a garden out back, and two red rugs he'd bought from a dead man's widow in the main room. Camellia had visited Obadiah's house with her pa once when she was a child.

There she'd seen what she would never forget. Obadiah had cabinets in his kitchen that covered one wall from floor to ceiling. Finely cut figures of men and women in all manner of dress and doing all sorts of labor decorated the cabinets. The figures included white folks and black. Camellia studied the wood, then asked her pa—who stood by her in Obadiah's kitchen—who the figures were.

"It's everybody he's ever cut a box for," York explained. "Black and white cut in the same wood."

Camellia had been fascinated.

As Camellia's breath grew more ragged again, she asked Ruby, "When will you go for . . . Theo?"

"After I know you are better."

"Leta will . . . stay with your mama?"

"Yes."

A bird chirped outside the window. Camellia longed to sit up but couldn't find the strength. Yet she needed to say something important. "I will . . . look after Leta until . . . you return," she gasped. "Your mama too."

"I can't ask you to do that," Ruby said.

"You didn't ask . . . but . . . I'm telling you . . ." Camellia's words faltered as she finished the sentence.

"You're not strong enough."

"I will be . . ."

"But what about you and Mr. Josh? I know the two of you want to leave here as soon as you can. You need to get away from Mr. Tessier. Flee the bad memories of this place."

"We will do that. But . . . we'll stay . . . until you return," she promised.

"Mr. Tessier will let you do that?" Ruby's voice was skeptical.

Camellia's heart ached as she thought of Trenton. A man with so much potential, he had fallen so far. "He still has good in him," she whispered.

"After all he has done to you or tried to do?"

Camellia stared toward the window and considered all that had happened. She and Trenton Tessier had once thought they loved each other. They had hoped to marry. But then, when The Oak had fallen on hard times, he had pledged to marry a woman of financial means from Columbia. Tragically, that woman had died in a carriage accident, and Trenton had come back to Camellia. By then, however, she had come to realize she loved Josh Cain and had denied Trenton her hand. From that point, Trenton's life had taken a turn downward. His drinking became constant, his temper foul. When he discovered that his mother had agreed to marry Hampton York in exchange for his help in saving The Oak from the bankers, things got even worse. Trenton challenged York to a duel and lost his leg in the exchange. The war followed, but due to the continuing infection in his amputated limb, Trenton never received a commission. Shamed, he sank lower.

Tears wet Camellia's cheeks as she remembered Stella, the old Negro housewoman whom she had loved so much. In the absence of her own mother, Stella had served as an able substitute. But Trenton had killed Stella . . . and hurt Butler too. Truly, Trenton had become an evil man. He had even kidnapped her on the night Richmond fell. If Josh had not rescued her . . . well, she wouldn't even think of what might have happened.

A touch of strength returned to Camellia as she faced Ruby. "I know Trenton is . . . a bad man," she whispered. "But maybe if I had . . . I don't know . . . treated him better, I might have made a difference. He's suffering, that's all. Hurting."

"You are a good woman," Ruby replied. "But he is too far gone—you might as well admit it. Not even you can fix that man."

Camellia closed her eyes, the last of her strength abruptly gone. Was Ruby right? But how could a man fall so far? It hadn't happened all at once, she knew that. But had Trenton been evil all along and she simply hadn't seen it? Or had he been a good man who had turned bad as the result of a series of choices . . . one leading to another until he dropped so far he couldn't climb back up again?

"You take your rest," said Ruby, touching Camellia's forehead with the wet cloth again. "I've let you talk too much."

"I will care for Leta . . . your mama," Camellia repeated. "Don't forget that."

As Ruby rubbed Camellia's forehead with the damp rag, Camellia took a long breath and relaxed.

Soon sleep overtook her again.

Chapter Six

Although awake and busy several hours before anyone else, York waited until the sun had climbed fully into the sky before he made his way up to the manse to see if anyone was home. Standing on the front porch, he took off his hat and looked out at the place he owned, his greatest dream come true. But now it was half-burned, rotting, and empty of laborers to tend the fields and repair the barns, the sheds, the fences, the canals, the manse. What should he do? He took a deep breath, pivoted back, started to enter, then decided maybe he should knock first. He rapped lightly on the door, shoved his hat back on, and waited.

For at least a minute he didn't hear anything. Since he had seen no fire in the one remaining chimney, he wondered again if the place was empty. Had neither Trenton nor Katherine made it safely home? If not, he'd have free rein of the place and nobody to cause him problems. The thought almost made him smile, but he knew he shouldn't feel that way. Katherine was his wife after all, so he quickly cut off the grin.

As he knocked again, he thought of the box he had unloaded last night, and his mood dropped once more. He had counted on finding money in that box or at least some valuables of one sort or another—a bit of jewelry maybe, a man's watch or two. What a letdown war manuals were, action reports from various battles. Since he didn't read too much, he had no use for any of that. He might as well burn the box and be done with it.

He knocked again. Without money from the box, he had only one source of funds left—the twenty-seven thousand he had left with Katherine when he went off to war. At first they had planned for her to take the money to England, but the Yankees had blockaded the Southern ports and made that impossible. Now he wondered if she still had the money. She had written him once and said that she had taken care of things, but what did that mean? Today he would find out.

Finally he heard footsteps. A second later the door opened.

Katherine stood before him in a long brown dress with a white ruffle around her neck. He studied her features—her skin as white as flour in a skillet, brown eyes with thick brows that almost touched in the middle. A light mustache fanned out over her lip, but nobody could see it without looking real close. She was a touch thick at the waist and hips but not overly so. She certainly didn't take his breath away when he saw her, but he had also seen less attractive women. Truth be told, Katherine was slightly above ordinary—nothing more, nothing less. But he had loved beautiful women before, and that had gotten him absolutely nothing. Maybe this way was better. Katherine had attractions other than a toss of a pretty head and a figure that made your heart flutter.

"Hampton," she spoke calmly, almost as if she had expected his arrival.

York felt awkward. How does a man greet a woman he married for reasons other than love? Does he take her in his arms or not?

"I'm home," he said simply. "You goin' to ask me in or not?"

She stepped back without emotion, and he walked inside. As always, York took off his hat as he entered the house. In spite of the fact the war had taken a hard toll on the place, it still awed him. He peered around the entryway, as if expecting somebody to shoo him out. All the fancy furnishings were gone, including the large table with the oblong mirror that had stood to his left and all the smooth rugs—most of them a shade of burgundy or gold—that had once covered the hardwood floor. Even the immense full-length portrait of Mr. Marshall Tessier, Katherine's first husband, in his red jacket with a black collar and gold buttons and laced white shirt, buttoned at the neck, was gone. York reverently studied the spot where the picture had hung. It had long been his dream to put *his* picture up there, dressed fancy and everything. But now would that ever happen?

"Things have changed some," he said.

Katherine nodded.

"Not all is bad, though." York checked the roofline and the spiral staircase that led to the second floor. "Ceiling looks OK. The staircase is intact."

"Most everything in this half can be fixed, I think," Katherine agreed.

York faced her now. "You look like you survived all right."

"I left the night before Richmond fell, had me a hired man and a few U.S. dollars. It took me close to a month, but I made it back. Even got a train down from Columbia. The Yankees kept the line together most of the way."

"I tried to find you that night, but you were already gone."

"Sorry but I couldn't wait for you. I hadn't seen you in weeks. Didn't know where you were."

York rubbed his eyes. Although he didn't really love Katherine, he had not been a good husband. He felt ashamed and guilty for his failures. "I'm sorry we didn't talk more when you came to Richmond to find Calvin," he offered.

"You were wounded," she said, obviously trying to give him a way out of his apology. "And . . . well . . . with the way you and Trenton are with each other, I figured it best we keep our distance. Then you got assigned again when you recovered."

"Still . . . we were in the same city."

She waved him off, then led him through the entryway and into a huge room where a fireplace covered most of the wall. A small stack of wood lay beside it. Katherine perched on the end of the only furniture in the room—a single, sagging sofa—and took a white handkerchief from her dress pocket to wipe her mouth. York moved to the fireplace and threw a new log on it before he turned to face Katherine.

"We need to figure some things out," she said.

"I know," he agreed. "Where do we go from here?"

"Who did you bring with you?" she asked.

He began to count them off on his fingers. "Ruby, her mama, and baby girl. Plus Lynette Swanson and her son, Jackson. My boy, Johnny."

She interrupted. "What about Josh Cain and Camellia, Mr. Cain's boy and girl?"

"Them too, but Camellia got snakebitten. We've sent for a doctor."

"I hope she recovers."

"She is gravely ill right now, but we are hopeful."

"I'm surprised all of you survived the war."

"Josh would say the Lord protected us."

Katherine wiped her face again. "Then what about Calvin?" she asked, her tone taking on an edge. "Why didn't the Lord protect him?"

York took off his hat as if in reverence. "I didn't say it; Josh did."

"You said you would protect Calvin," she accused.

"I did all I could."

She faced him squarely but not in anger this time. Her eyes seemed to have softened, gentler than he could ever remember. York wondered if losing a child did that to a woman—made even the hardest, coldest of them become kinder in spirit. What about a man? He'd already lost Chester to the fever. That had made him angry and then plunged him further into hard work at The Oak. But if he lost Camellia, what would it do to him? Make him a better person or a more bitter one?

"What kind of man was Calvin?" asked Katherine, tearing up a little. "Seems I can hardly remember what he looked like, how he talked."

York's heart hurt as he remembered the young man, a brother to Trenton but so completely different than his evil sibling. Had the freckle-faced Calvin always possessed the bravery and loyalty, the honesty and good humor the war revealed in him? Had he been such a fine man of good character all along, and it simply took the war to bring it out? Or had the war created something in him he never would have discovered if he had stayed at ease on The Oak?

"Calvin fought with a steady courage," he said. "His temper stayed even, his eye sharp and his aim true. He took orders without complaint and accepted the rough life of a soldier as if he had been raised to it, as if he had never slept on silk sheets or sipped French wine."

"He sounds like a good man." Katherine's eyes grew misty.

"One of the best. He and my Johnny became constant companions. Told me once that when the war ended, he wanted to come back and bring some peace between our two families. He wanted us to put the past behind us and move on."

"How did he die?" Katherine asked, ignoring the last statement. "You never really told me."

"I didn't know how to say it."

"Just tell it plainly."

York took a breath, not wanting to tell the story but knowing he couldn't avoid it. A mama deserved to know how her son died. "You know we were at Burgess Mill," he began. "Everythin' happenin' all at once— bullets flyin', horses runnin', men shoutin' and screamin'. I saw Calvin halfway across a pasture, off his horse, with his back to a tree. Three Union soldiers were rushin' at him, bayonets out. I spurred my horse, plowed through the Yankees. Then I heard a yell behind me and, even in battle, recognized Johnny's voice. I turned and saw Johnny on his knees about thirty yards away, blood pourin' down his face. A Yankee stood over him, a pistol in hand. I glanced back at Calvin. A couple of Yankees were down, but a couple more were at him, their bayonets thrustin'."

He stopped as he remembered the terrible scene.

"You went to Johnny, didn't you?" asked Katherine.

York didn't want to finish but, again, knew he couldn't escape it. "I wheeled my horse around and galloped toward Johnny, my pistol firin'. A Yankee shot my horse from under me, and I hit the ground, saber in hand, and ran as fast as I could toward Johnny."

"You were already shot in the heel?"

He nodded and continued. "A Yankee grabbed a rifle off the ground and aimed, but I threw myself at him, stabbin' with my saber. I jabbed him purty good, and he died on the spot. Then I looked back toward Calvin. Saw him by a tree, three Yankees at his feet. I wanted . . . wanted to go to him."

"But you still had to care for Johnny."

"Blood poured from his head, but I couldn't tell how deep the wound was. I yanked a dirty cloth out, stuffed it in the wound. Johnny opened his eyes. For a second all fell quiet. Darkness started to fall."

"*Pa*," Johnny moaned.

"*You're OK*," I told him. "*I'll get you to a doc.*"

"*How's Calvin?*"

"*I'll check on him after I get you safe.*"

"*I'm steady. Find Calvin,*" Johnny insisted.

Katherine took a deep breath. "He truly cared for Calvin, didn't he?"

"Like they was brothers. Johnny told me to come back after I'd provided for Calvin. So that's what I did. I went to Calvin as fast as I could. When I got to him, I pulled a bayonet out of his chest. He opened his eyes. I picked up a handful of mud and spread it over his wound to stop the bleedin'."

"He was still . . . alive?" There was a catch in her voice.

"Yep. I tried to lift him, to take him to a surgeon. He pushed my hand away, but I grabbed him anyway and lifted him up. As we headed back to Johnny, I told him, *'Don't give up. I'll get you home.'*"

York paused again, wishing the next part had never happened. His eyes watered, but he brushed away the tears. "I almost got back to Johnny. But then Johnny stood up and began to come toward us. I yelled at him to stay down, but he didn't seem to hear. Then I saw four Yankees runnin' at us—three from the left and one from the right. I lay Calvin down and ran at the three. I hit one with a pistol shot. Then I tripped and fell in a hole.

"When I looked up, I saw a Yankee facedown, not more than twenty feet from Johnny. The other two Federals were squared off in front of the dead soldier, their bayonets thrustin' at each other! I tried to move but couldn't get up. At first I couldn't figure out what was happenin'. What were the Yankees doing? But then, all of a sudden, I understood. One of the Yankees stood with his back to Johnny, defendin' him from the other Federal!"

"That was Josh Cain, wasn't it?"

"Yep. Though I didn't know it at the time, Josh was defendin' Johnny from the other Yankee. He saved Johnny's life but almost lost his own. Josh took a bullet wound and a bayonet stab that day."

"So now you've got three wounded men to tend," Katherine reasoned.

"Yep. Once I saw it was Josh, I figured out what was goin' on."

"You had to choose who to rescue."

"I had no horse and couldn't carry all three—hard enough to haul two out of there. Johnny wanted me to take Calvin and Josh first, but I wouldn't do it."

"A rough predicament."

69

"We were on an open patch of ground between two stands of trees about four hundred yards apart. Other than a shack in the middle of the pasture, I saw no other shelter. I looked around for Yankees, wondered when they would come back. I figured I didn't have long, so I moved back to Calvin to check on him."

"Was he still alive?"

York nodded. "Just barely. I grabbed him, hauled him to the shack, laid him inside, and went back to Johnny and Josh. Took them off the field. That's the end of it."

"You think it's possible Calvin lived? That maybe he ended up in a Yankee prison? That he's still there, recovering from his injuries?"

"Maybe."

"I could write the Yankee authorities, ask of his whereabouts."

"True but—"

She held up a hand. "I know; he's probably dead."

Silence fell for several seconds.

York thought of the letter he had in his coat. He pulled it out and handed it to her. "It's from Calvin. He asked me to give it to you if anythin' happened to him."

Katherine took the note and held it with shaking hands.

"He gave me a letter before every big fight," York explained. "He was superstitious that way."

Katherine unfolded the note and read it. Her eyes filled. She wiped the tears away with her handkerchief.

York wanted to ask what Calvin had said but didn't. Katherine put the note in her lap, dabbed her eyes again, and looked up. "I won't believe he's dead until I see his body."

York wanted to comfort her but didn't know how. To his relief she took a deep breath, put the note away in a pocket, and faced him squarely, determination in her demeanor.

"I expect you came to talk about the money," she said, obviously done with talking about Calvin.

"I came to see my wife."

"But the money you left with me is part of that."

He rubbed his hands together. "Yep, sure, if we're goin' to put this place back together, we'll need cash to get it done."

"I still have the money," she said. "Least most of it."

York's heart settled a little. "Glad to hear it. Cash will be hard to come by for a while for most everybody."

Katherine glanced down. "I'm going to keep its whereabouts to myself for now, if you don't mind."

York gripped his hat. "What?"

She stared at him without fear. "I will determine when and how we spend the money. To do that, I have to keep its location to myself."

York bit his tongue to stay calm. "I brought you that money—are you forgettin' that?"

"No, but I still don't know that you didn't steal it from me in the first place. As overseer of this place, you could have done that easily enough."

York paused, recognizing at least a little truth in what she said. For several years he *had* skimmed off the top of the profits on The Oak. Using the stolen money as his cash stake, he had chosen the right horses at the February races in Charleston back in February of 1861 and came away a big winner. If he divided it all up honestly, he owed Katherine about one-third of the cash he had given her to keep. "That money is mine," he said, not willing to admit the truth. "I will not let you steal it from me."

She smiled grimly and stood. "If I give you the money, you might not even stay here."

"I've always wanted this place, you know that. Why would I leave now?"

Katherine moved to the fireplace, stared into it for a moment, then faced him again. "Lynette Swanson. I know you loved her once, and now she's here. What's to keep you from taking the money and running off with her?"

York strode to Katherine and grabbed her elbow. "She cares nothin' for me, never did. You're talkin' crazy. I'm your husband. I want this place, and I don't plan to go anywhere with anybody but you."

"But I don't hear you saying you don't love her." It was a statement, but there was a question in Katherine's brown eyes.

York pulled her close. "Just give me my money," he said firmly. "And I'll show you who and what I love." He took her chin in his hands and moved his lips close to hers. For the right to place his picture over the staircase of a restored Oak, he would do what needed doing. He started to kiss her, but footsteps sounded behind them before he could.

"What a touching scene!"

York wheeled at the voice and saw Trenton in the doorway, a shotgun in his hands. York stepped back and held up his hands. "Trenton?" he asked, his eyes not believing what he saw.

"We don't want you here," said Trenton.

York would not have recognized him if not for the peg leg. Trenton's face looked swollen, flushed with liquor. He seemed to have aged at least twenty years since York had last seen him.

"This is not your affair," Katherine told her son. "Leave us alone."

"I've been listening for a while," Trenton replied, a crazed gleam in his eyes. "I heard you talking about the money. Glad to hear you managed to keep some of it."

York took a step forward, but Trenton held up the gun.

York paused. "Keep your grubby hands off my money," he growled.

Trenton chuckled. "You're not one to talk about grubby hands. The notion of your kind living in this house sickens me."

York almost laughed too, but the shotgun kept his mirth at bay. "It's over, Trenton, but you don't even see it. The war changed everythin'— your way of life, mine too. But men like me will survive in this new world. Men who know how to use their hands and their brains. Men who have made it on their own in the past because nobody ever give them nothin'. Boys like you, born on silk sheets, brought up in boardin' schools, what can you do? Read a book? Shoot straight so long as a man ain't on the other side of the bullet? Speak some French? You know what that will get you these days? Nothin'. Just be glad you're still alive and I'm goin' to let you keep stayin' here." York paused, out of breath from a longer speech than he could ever remember giving.

Trenton eyed his mother. "You with him on this, Mother dear?"

Katherine glanced from one man to the other, then finally settled on

Trenton. "I want you both to leave the other alone. Let some time pass. Get The Oak back up and going. Then we'll see what happens."

York actually admired her for her practicality. For now she would stay in the middle, a wise course for one in her predicament.

"I have no cause to bother Master Trenton," York said, feigning neutrality. "So long as he leaves me and mine alone, I'll do the same to him."

Trenton lowered his weapon. "I want you out of my life," he told York. "But I can see Mother's point. We need you alive to rebuild The Oak." He swiveled to face his mother. "For now, then, I will do as you wish and refrain from shooting your dear Captain York."

Ignoring Trenton, York turned to Katherine. "We are not done with the issue of my money."

"I will provide what we need as the situation arises," she said.

Knowing he couldn't do anything else for the time being, York put on his hat. "I will stay in my old house so that Trenton and I don't bump into each other too often."

Katherine lifted her chin. "I believe that is a wise decision, until things settle some."

With one last look at Trenton, York walked out.

As York left the room, Katherine took Calvin's letter from her pocket and held it up. "It's from your brother," she told Trenton.

Trenton stepped closer but didn't take the letter. "What does it say?"

Katherine smiled. "It says he loves me, and that if anything happened to him, he wanted me to know that."

"Anything else?"

Katherine shoved the letter in her pocket. "He praises Hampton York, says he admires him. Calvin says that if he doesn't make it home, I should know Hampton cared for him as well as anybody could expect, and we shouldn't blame him."

"You believe that?"

Katherine shrugged. "Hampton is many things—some of which I greatly dislike. But he is a man of his word. He said he would try to protect Calvin, and I believe he did."

"But Calvin is still dead." Trenton's words were flat.

"Probably so."

"That's all the letter said?"

"Just one more thing. Calvin said if he lived through the war, he wanted to come home and try to bring peace between you and York."

Trenton stepped to his mother, grabbed the letter from her pocket, and read it quickly. When finished, he handed it back and eased away from Katherine. "But Calvin didn't make it back."

Katherine gently ran her fingers over the letter. "No, he didn't."

"Then we can forget the notion of peace between me and York, is that right?"

"I expect York will kill you one day," said Katherine.

"Unless I kill him first."

Chapter Seven

Josh and Jackson rode back onto The Oak with Dr. Rankin just before sunset, their horses lathered with sweat and dirt and their backs aching from the hard, steady ride. His black medical bag in hand, Rankin left them in the front room and went immediately to Camellia. Within a couple of minutes everyone had gathered in the room with Josh and Jackson, each of them anxiously awaiting the doctor's report.

Josh stood by the small room's fireplace, watching Beth in a rocker and Butler on the floor. Josh couldn't believe how much they had grown up. For a second he felt fearful. Who knew what life would bring in the next few years? What changes would come to their lives?

York stepped to the center of the room, his hat in his hand, and everyone fell silent. "This is about the first quiet moment we've had since we left Richmond," he started. "Figure we ought to talk through a few matters."

Everybody nodded.

York continued, "First thing is, we all got to take care of Camellia. If you believe in prayin', do it extra hard."

Josh almost chuckled. When it came to somebody York loved, he would even ask for prayer.

York spoke again. "We don't know exactly what will happen next, with her or anybody else. But I plan to stay here, make sure Camellia gets well, then rebuild The Oak. I ask the rest of you to join me if you want."

Ruby held up her hand. "I expect I'll be leaving, least for a while. Got to find my boy, Theo."

"That's no surprise," said York. "But when you find him, come on back. I'll pay you a fair wage to labor here." York nodded at Josh. "I know Josh wants to take his leave, too, as soon as he can, and I don't reckon I can blame him. But until Camellia is better, he's stuck here."

"Miss Camellia says once she is well, she will look after Leta and Mama until I return," Ruby added.

Josh's eyes widened at the news.

York rubbed his beard in thought but stayed quiet.

"I will go back to Richmond," Lynette announced. "Not immediately, but . . . once we know how Camellia is."

"I'll go with her," said Jackson.

"What about you, Son?" York asked Johnny.

"I'm with you, Pa," he replied. "We'll build this place back better than ever."

"OK," said York. "For now, we're all stayin' but Ruby. We got just enough houses. We'll work on fixin' them up first, then the barns and other buildin's."

"What about the rice fields?" asked Jackson.

York almost smiled. "It will take a whole lot more help than we got to do anythin' with those. We won't even touch them this year. We'll put in a garden. Grow what we can to get us through winter, then worry about the rice fields when spring comes next year."

"What about the manse?" asked Lynette.

"Is Trenton Tessier in the manse?" added Josh.

York frowned. "Yep. And Katherine too."

"When are you moving in there?" asked Jackson.

"Not for a while," York said quickly.

Josh saw the surprise in the eyes of the rest of the group.

"I got my reasons," York defended, "so keep your tongues to yourself. As to the manse, part of it is all right to live in as it is. We'll decide later what to do about the rest. Agreed?"

No one spoke, so York continued, "Things ain't gonna be easy. Lots of rough labor ahead of us—whether we stay here, go to Richmond, or anywhere else. Nobody knows what the future holds. But if we stick together and help each other, we can do most anythin' we set our heads to do."

Josh marveled at York's ability to look at the best side of things. No matter how hard life got, York managed to stay hopeful.

The door to the bedroom opened, and Dr. Rankin stepped out. "She's resting. I gave her medicine to keep her at ease. That's the best thing for right now—to keep her as still as we can so the poison doesn't move any further in her body."

"She'll be OK though, right?" asked Johnny, his young face anxious.

Rankin shrugged. "My best guess? Yes, she's a strong woman, so I think she will be fine. But long-term, she will have some things still to worry about."

"What kind of things?" asked York.

"Snakebites can weaken the heart," explained Rankin. "Nobody knows for sure why. But the venom goes through the blood, we do know that. Figure that it makes the heart sick somehow and, in some folks, it never gets a lot better. She might get weak at odd times, not have much breath. She could shake some, like a fit or somethin', a seizure of the arms, legs. Travelin' might come hard to her, or labor on anythin' too strenuous."

"You saying that *will* happen or that it *might* happen?" asked Josh, suddenly fearful for Camellia's future.

Rankin stared hard at Josh. Josh wondered if the man liked giving bad news. "I'm sayin' it *might* happen," said Rankin. "Might happen for a while, then go away forever. Or it might happen from now until the day she dies. Or it might not happen at all."

Josh took a deep breath. So long as he had hope that Camellia could end up normal, he could live with that.

"Anythin' in particular we can do to help her?" York asked the doctor.

Rankin pulled a brown bottle from his bag and handed it to York. "Give her this three times a day for about a month . . . a couple of spoonfuls at a time. It should help her stay calm. The rest is up to her."

York took the bottle and handed it to Lynette. "Anybody got any questions, anythin' else to say?"

Nobody did. "Bed down here for the night," York told Rankin. "You can head back to Beaufort in the mornin'."

After everyone had gone to their own houses—Leta, Ruby and Nettie in one, Lynette and Jackson in another, with Josh, Beth, and Butler in a third, Josh left York and Johnny by the fireplace of the fourth house and went to Camellia's room. She lay quietly on the bed, her hair fanned out around her pillow. The room now looked spotless. Somebody had dusted the floor, the window sill, and the small table by the bed. Josh pulled a chair close to her bed, sat down quietly, and smiled in relief when she opened her eyes.

"How are you feeling?" he asked her.

"Like I'm in the middle of a fog. But a lot better than yesterday."

He shook his head. "You make it through a war, then almost die from snakebite. Pretty loony, don't you think?"

She smiled and he touched her chin.

"You look tired," she said, her blue eyes searching his.

"I about killed my horse. A long way to Beaufort in one day."

"You need to rest."

His fingers brushed her lips. "Doctor says you're going to get better. That medicine he gave you helping any?"

"I don't hurt since I took it."

"Good."

Josh peered out past the window, wondering how to bring up what he wanted to say. If he didn't take care, he might sound angry and upset her, and he didn't want that.

Camellia took his hand and kissed his fingers. "You look fretful."

"I am worried about you."

"It's something . . . else."

He pulled away his hand. "You told Ruby you would stay here until she got back."

"Yes."

"But you know I want to leave this place."

"So do I. But I couldn't let her go with nobody to care for her mama and little girl."

"So you took it on yourself to watch after them."

"Of course . . . you would do the same thing . . . in my place. You know how much I love Ruby." Her eyes pleaded with his for understanding.

Josh took a full breath and told himself to stay easy but found it hard. In spite of his desire to avoid argument with Camellia, her promise to

Ruby had put him in a hard spot. "I just feel like The Oak is bad for us. Always has been. The sooner we get away from here the better. We can get married, start our life together."

"I agree. But since I'm going to need time to regain strength anyway—"

"But what if it takes a long time? What if Ruby is gone a year or more? I can't stay here that long, and neither can you. Trenton is here. His mother too. They will cause us trouble; they always do."

Camellia took his hand once more. "Trenton knows I don't . . . love him. He'll come to accept that. And when he does, his mother will be . . . fine."

"You're so trusting," Josh said. "Too much so sometimes."

Camellia closed her eyes and didn't say anything for several seconds. Josh thought maybe she had fallen asleep.

Then she spoke softly, wearily. "We will take it a day at a time. Like we should. Ruby knows we want to leave, so she won't stay away a day longer than she needs."

"But what if something happens to her? That's possible in this day and time, you know."

"Then we'll just take Leta and Nettie with us when we go."

Guilt washed over Josh in waves for bringing up a hard subject while Camellia remained ill. "OK," he said finally, a hand touching her cheek. "But I want to leave before winter sets in. We need to marry, then get somewhere and settle in before the weather turns cold."

"Ruby will . . . return before then."

"I trust she will."

Camellia smiled but said nothing else.

As he sat by her bedside, Josh resigned himself to staying a little while longer on The Oak. Hopefully Trenton would stay out of his way and away from Camellia. If not, well, like Camellia said, he would deal with that when it came.

Chapter Eight

Ruby spent the rest of the month of May in and around Charleston, searching for Theo. Since her mama had told him to go there when he left Virginia, she figured it made good sense to see if he might have made it there and stayed. She found Charleston a sad scene. The proud city had been reduced to near ruin. Weeds and bushes grew wildly in the yards of the once primly trimmed houses. Much of the city lay in ashes, the result of terrible fires. Many of the best houses stood empty, their contents looted, their outer frames beaten down and forlorn. Even more amazing to Ruby, black folks brazenly roamed the streets, some of them quite rude to the whites they happened to pass. Some of the black men carried weapons and acted like they owned the place. With Yankee soldiers present on almost every corner to protect their newfound freedoms, the blacks seemed bent on taking every advantage of it.

Although uncomfortable with the haughty spirit of some of the blacks she saw, Ruby couldn't help but feel good about the fact that she could move without restraint and go where she wanted to go. She had dreamed of such a thing all her life. Although she didn't know exactly how she would make her living now, at least she would get to decide that for herself. Even better, her new freedom gave her the chance to do the one thing she had sworn to do someday—find Theo.

Ruby slept each night near the battery area, her few belongings under her head in the burlap bag she had stuffed with food and a few clothes before she left The Oak. The beat-up horse Josh had insisted she bring stood nearby, the reins tied to an oak. Hundreds of other blacks slept around her, so she felt pretty safe except for times when some man set his eyes on her horse like he wanted to take it.

During the day Ruby spent her time with black folks—sometimes in one of the makeshift camps the Negroes had set up in and about the city, at others going from house to house in the places she saw where blacks had set up their neighborhoods. She asked them all if they had seen a smallish boy with a big head and only one eye, but so far she had come up with nothing. Many of the blacks told her they would surely have remembered a boy like the one she described, but no, such a boy had not come into their sight.

Now, as the first week of June came to its end, she lay down to take her rest for the night. Her stomach growled with hunger, and her body ached from all the walking she had done. Although she had managed to survive on meager rations since her arrival in the city, she had run out of food and had no provisions for more. She would have to take a job soon if she didn't want to starve, and doing that would slow down her search for Theo.

Unable to sleep, she rolled onto her back and stared up into the stars. A sense of loneliness hit her. She wondered about Obadiah. Where was he? What if he had heard she was back at The Oak and had come for her?

For the first time since leaving the plantation, she wondered if she should give up her quest to find her boy and go back, try to find Obadiah, and settle down with him. They could make new babies and live a good life together.

Tears welled in her eyes. She wanted to go home, but how could she give up on Theo? Did she think she could forget him? Wipe him from her memory? She had looked everywhere but with no luck. Where else could she go? Who else could she ask?

She searched the stars for an answer. Suddenly one came to her, and she realized she had gone at this all wrong! Theo was a smart boy. He would have thought of this too—maybe even before she did! Knowing she had ended up on the auction block in Charleston, Theo would have gone to the selling area. He would have sought out the people who sold the servants. He would have asked any he could find if they remembered her, if they had any records of the sale that sent her away. If he found such a person, Theo would have asked where her owners took her after she was sold.

Ruby closed her eyes . . .

The next morning, when she awoke, Ruby knew exactly what she had to do. The notion scared her and made her empty stomach want to retch with dry heaves. But she made herself stay steady on the idea. She needed to look for the blousy-shirted man, needed to find the auctioneer who had barked out the bids taken on her when she first came to Charleston so many years ago. Ruby gritted her teeth as she remembered the awful day.

Close to fifty people had stood around a raised wood platform not far from the center of town. Most of the people in the crowd were men—rough men, fancy men, men in hats with tobacco in their cheeks, men in frock coats and ruffled shirts, all kinds of men from the best to the worst that South Carolina and its neighboring states had to offer. The smell of sea air and poorly washed bodies drifted in and out as a light breeze rose and fell. A variety of dogs mingled in and out with the men.

A line of nine coloreds stood on the platform—seven men and two women. The men wore chains on their ankles; the women were unshackled. A bald, stocky white man in a blousy shirt stood slightly in front of the darkies, his voice booming constantly as he tried to jack up the prices on the men and women he wanted to sell.

Ruby stood at the end of the line, the last of the coffle for auction that day. She kept her head up and her eyes straight, almost as if she dared any man to make too low a bid on her.

The man in the blousy shirt moved to the first darky and started the bidding, explaining all his fine qualities. Ruby tried hard to keep from listening. Her lips pouted; she wished she had a last name other than one stuck on her by a white man. People with their own last names didn't get sold off when the fever burned through their plantation in late summer and killed off their master and two of his children. But since she didn't have a true last name, the banker man had come to the Rushton Plantation only a month after the fever and poured out the harsh news that some Negroes had to go to sale.

Ruby spent the night in a building one street over from the ocean, just two streets from where she stood. She listened to see if she could hear the waves wash-

ing in but didn't hear anything. She wished the water would reach all the way to where she stood. That it would come in one large wave and wash her away forever. It didn't matter if it drowned her; in fact, that would please her greatly.

Her mouth set with anger, Ruby glanced at the others on the platform. Some were as black as cooking skillets. Others were almost yellow brown. The tallest man stood as high as a horse's ears, the shortest no higher than three washtubs stacked on each other. The blousy-shirted man pointed at the crowd, his tongue moving like a lizard in and out over his lips.

Ruby glanced at Markus, the tallest of the black men. The two of them had taken each other to marry six years ago. Part of her dared to hope she and Markus would end up at the same place, but the other half knew better. The chances of it didn't add up to much. People with no last name got split up all the time—no matter that they had spent lots of nights on a pallet together, and in spite of the fact they had made Theo out of their union.

The auctioneer sold off one black after another as men stepped in and out of the crowd, buying and leaving, shouting and spitting streams of tobacco and snuff juice into the cobblestones under their feet. Ruby wished she could die. When the auctioneer reached Markus, Ruby stared at her man. Markus had shoulders like an ox and wide, clear eyes. He knew how to keep horses and fix wagons. Markus tried to look her way, but the auctioneer grabbed his chin and squeezed it until he turned back to the crowd. Ruby saw Markus's muscles tighten. She knew if he got the chance, he would pick up the auctioneer, bear hug him, and crack his back like snapping a twig.

The bidding started at nine hundred dollars. Within a few minutes a man with a curly mustache ended it all at the price of eleven hundred.

Ruby listened hard to see if anybody mentioned the man's name or where he lived, but nobody did. She ached to follow Markus as they took him away but knew she couldn't. A man in the back would take the dollars from the buyer and write up the papers that sent her man to his new master. She wondered how far away from Markus she would end up. If they lived close enough, maybe he could get a pass every now and again and come see her on Sundays when they rested from their labors.

Only one more Negro stood between her and the blousy-shirted man. She wiped her face, then brushed down her hair, straighter than most of her people and not nearly as coarse. The auctioneer finished quickly with the next to last

Negro man, moved him off the platform, and turned to her. She kept her eyes on her bare feet.

"Now look at this one," said the man, pointing to the spot where he wanted Ruby to stand. "She's straight from the house of Mr. and Mrs. Thomas Rushton outside of Richmond, Virginia. She's named Ruby, and she was raised for the house: for cookin', cleanin', sewin', and tendin' children."

Ruby moved to the spot where he pointed. She felt the crowd studying her, felt the men's eyes moving up and down her body. Her skin seemed alive, like ants crawling on her arms and legs. She hated the way the men looked at her. It didn't seem right somehow. Why should a man get to study a woman this way? Look her over as if she were a prize cow he might want to purchase?

At least five men had come by her stall that morning, walking one at a time into the small space where she'd slept last night. The men made her stand up, made her open her mouth so they could see her teeth, made her pull up her skirt so they could see her feet and legs.

Ruby had glared at each man and wished she had a pistol to shoot him.

"She's twenty," said the auctioneer. "Took care of the Rushtons' babies since they first drew breath."

"Why did they get shed of her?" yelled a man from the middle of the crowd. "Mr. Rushton set his eyes for her and his missus take offense?"

The crowd laughed, and Ruby wanted to shrink up and disappear. Although Master Rushton had always acted the gentleman, a few other white men had tried to make advances on her since she first got her womanhood nearly seven summers ago. Donetta, the Rushtons' daughter, had warned her about such things. She had told Ruby that her light skin and curvy figure might prove a strong enticement to menfolk of all colors.

"Best marry up fast," Donetta had advised, when Ruby was near her fourteenth birthday. "That won't guarantee a white man won't come for you, but it'll give you some protection. Least on our place it will."

Ruby's marriage to Markus followed soon after, and so far she'd escaped any white man's advancements. But now, with Donetta out of her life forever, who knew what might happen?

The crowd's laughter died away. "She's a clean woman," said the blousy-shirted man, making sure to get the selling points stated early. "No diseases, no scars of any kind. I got the papers to prove it. She got sold when her master died. The family needed money."

The men nodded with understanding.

"Who'll start the biddin'?" asked the auctioneer. "Openin' price is eleven hundred."

"I'll go twelve," said a man Ruby recognized from her stall earlier in the day. "Make it thirteen," said a second man, this one to her right.

The final bid, the one made by Hampton York of The Oak, came in at eighteen hundred, as high a price as most any slave ever took. The auctioneer pointed to his left, and Ruby moved off the platform and down the steps.

From there she ended up on The Oak.

Ruby shook her head. It was hard to believe seven years had passed since that day she was sold to The Oak.

Now she had come to Charleston once more, but this time as a free woman. Strangely, she was free to go back to the very man who had sold her and ask him for help. Sighing deeply, Ruby stared up at the night sky. Her heart pounded. She had to find the blousy-shirted man. For as soon as she did, he would tell her he had seen her boy. Somehow she knew that to be true.

Just over 120 miles away, Theo sat on a box on the back edge of Marquis's covered wagon. It was parked with its mate under a grove of tall pine trees that just about shut out the sky. Theo's feet dangled over the side of the wagon. Thirty raggedy black people crowded around him, their faces upturned as they stared at him on the high box. At least six cats circled in and among the people, their purring and meowing a steady sound as they rubbed up against the folks' legs. A smoky fire burned behind the crowd, casting a heavy cloud over the scene, and a candle burned in the wagon behind Theo, making everything a little spooky. He looked around for Mabel but didn't see her. She was probably on a blanket in the woods where she sometimes took a customer.

Theo wore clothes he would never have picked for himself—a pair of red pants that ballooned out on his legs from his waist down, a white shirt that almost looked clean, and a belt with a big buckle with a metal star on it. A yellow cape, made of some kind of cloth that felt almost hairy, hung off his shoulders. His hair, thick, high, uncombed, and completely gray now, sprigged out in all directions. His right foot, wrapped in a soiled brown rag made stiff with dried blood, ached like a bad tooth. Chopped off about midway between the toes and the heel, the foot bled any time he bumped it on anything and hurt almost constantly.

Only one thing gave Theo any relief from the pain—a bottle of the elixir Marquis kept ready-made for sale to the sorry mix of folks he managed to talk into buying his foul-smelling drink. If not for that elixir, Theo didn't know if he could have made it through the worst days, the days when his foot hurt so bad it made him wail and cry like a tiny baby. True, the elixir kept his head all swimmy and his vision out of focus, but the more he drank of it, the more he seemed to want it, no matter what it did to his thinking. He knew he ought not to crave the drink like he did, but what else could he do? Without the drink and the fog it put on his mind as it dulled the hurt in his foot, Theo probably could not have survived.

Marquis and Rufe stood on the ground below Theo. Marquis held a walking cane, wore a tall black hat, and spoke fast in his thick Cajun accent. "Now look here, my peoples. Dis boy got da sight. See dat empty eye?" He pointed the cane at Theo's face. "He see through dat socket. I don't know whether da Lord done give him dis sight or da devil, but he got it, dat's for sure. You want to know what da future gone hold for you? Dis boy da one can tell you. One nickel, dat's all it take. One cheap nickel to know what da days to come hold for you. You want to know if you gone find work, where you gone lay yo' head come nightfall, whether dat man you want gone come knockin' at yo' door? Dis here boy can tell you."

Marquis kept talking, but Theo shut his ears to the speech. Over the last few weeks, he had heard it more than once . . . in fact, every time Marquis could find a new group of folks to offer his elixir and his fortuneteller.

Theo licked his lips and took a drink from a bottle of the elixir. Although he hated the taste of the stuff, he knew he needed it now.

Needed it to ease the pain in his foot and to make his mind dull enough to forget his search for his mama and to keep on doing what Marquis forced him to do—make up futures for the poor and ignorant folks who gathered around, paid their money, and listened to his lying tales . . .

At first Theo had resisted the plans Marquis had for him. Within a day after emerging from the week-long coma caused by pain in his chopped-off foot and Marquis's elixir, Theo gathered enough strength to get up and try to run away, but to no avail. A body made weak from no food and a foot missing all its toes made fleeing impossible. Rufe caught him before he ever got out of the campsite.

"You ain't runnin' from me," said Marquis when Rufe hauled Theo back, laid him at Marquis's feet, and pushed him down. "I done saved yo' life by cuttin' off da gangrene in yo' foot. What kind of Christian boy goes runnin' off before he pay back his debt to da man who kept him alive? Here, eat dis." Marquis shoved a piece of moldy bread at him, but Theo refused it.

"Suit yo'self," said Marquis. "You eat when you get hungry enough."

For almost two more days, Theo held out. Finally he couldn't do it anymore. His body demanded food and water, and though he hated the notion of giving in to Marquis, he knew he had no choice but to eat or die. When Marquis gave him a dipper of water, a piece of moldy bread, and another bottle of his drink, Theo took it and finished it all. As he did, he knew something had changed between him and Marquis—something that made him less than what he had been. Although resigned to that change for the time being, Theo refused to let himself think it would last forever. Somehow, someday, he would once more become strong enough to run away, just as soon as his body could stand the strain of the flight. For the time being, though, he had to live, had to do what Marquis told him to do.

For another week or so, they drifted northwest. "We goin' up toward Columbia," said Marquis when Theo asked about their direction. "Lots of darky folks livin' in dat city, yes dey is."

Theo knew The Oak lay behind them, and Charleston too. He figured his mama, if still alive, lived in the opposite direction of where he was headed. "You figure we ever goin' back south?" he asked, trying not to sound too eager.

"Could be," said Marquis. "Never know where the road gone take you, no you don't."

At the end of that week, Marquis had put him in front of people for the first time. "Just take der hand when dey hold it up to you," Marquis explained, holding Theo's palm to show him how he wanted it done. "Turn it over so da palm shows up. Lay dis buckeye in da palm." He handed Theo a brown-and-black buckeye. "Let the buckeye rest in der palm for a jiffy, then pull it out and hold it up to yo' empty eye, like you peerin' right into everythin' dat's yet to come."

"But I won't see anythin' in that buckeye," argued Theo.

Marquis stomped a boot onto Theo's bad foot, and Theo's eye watered from the pain. Marquis eased off. "It don't truly matter to me what you see or don't. What matters to me is dat you say somethin' dat makes the peoples happy dey done laid down a nickel to hear yo' words. Make it up if you don't see nothin'. Dey won't ever know the difference."

That night, as the sun went down and the candle burned in the wagon and the cats slid in and out around the ankles of the crowd, Theo pretended to tell his first fortune.

A squatty woman with a wart on her chin the size of a pecan and a baby daughter clinging to her knees paid Marquis her nickel—the Lord only knew where she had gotten it—and stepped to the back of the wagon. She held her hand out, as if reaching up to a god. Sitting above her, Theo took her hand in his and glanced down into her face. His heart ached over his sin, but he didn't know how to get away from committing it.

Marquis had told him what to do, and now he had to do it or suffer hard things as a consequence. He turned the woman's palm up toward the sky. For a long time he didn't say a word.

Then the woman spoke up. "You seein' a bad thing? That why you not usin' your tongue?"

Theo glanced at Marquis, who, for maybe the first time, paused from the selling of his elixir. Marquis glanced at Rufe, who stood nearby, and Rufe climbed up by Theo on the wagon. "You tell this woman what she want to hear," Rufe whispered in Theo's ear, "or you lose the toes on yo' second foot."

Theo swallowed hard. He hated himself for what he had to do next. "You takin' care of your baby girl," he said softly.

The woman nodded.

Rufe grunted. Theo knew Rufe wanted him to talk faster, to finish with this woman and give somebody else a chance to spend a nickel.

"You not sure what gone happen next," said Theo, a little louder this time.

Again, a nod from the woman.

"Anybody knows that," whispered Rufe, his teeth clenched. "Say somethin' like you got a seein'."

"You need a man to help you," offered Theo.

"Oh, yes," said the woman.

Theo spoke a little faster now. "You know the man you want."

"Yes, yes."

"You go on after that man and he be yours," said Theo, gaining a little confidence. "He need you as bad as you need him. He need you to fix his clothes, cook his food, give him love at night."

"I know that's for true," said the woman.

"He wantin' you to show him what you feel in your heart."

"I can do that."

"Then go forth to it."

Theo dropped her hand and took a deep drink from the bottle he kept close by all the time. The woman stepped back, lifted her baby into her arms, smiled at Theo, and walked off toward a tall, bald man near the back of the crowd.

Rufe whispered quickly to Theo, "You done real fine, real fine for sure."

A man without a shirt walked up, and Theo gave his attention to him.

This night again Theo sat in the back of the wagon and prepared to lie to the people below him. His heart tensed in his chest, but he told himself what he had vowed over and over again since the day he found out what Marquis wanted from him. The only future he knew for certain said that one day he would run off from Marquis and Rufe and find his mama. Until then, he would do what he had to do and say what he had to say to stay alive.

Chapter Nine

As Hampton York yanked a usable plank from the side of a half-burned barn, rain began to fall for the first time since he'd returned to The Oak. Tired, he dropped the plank to the ground, wiped his brow, then took off his hat and stared up into the gently falling rain. It felt cool and good.

After a few minutes York put his hat back on, glanced toward the manse, and wondered what Katherine was doing. Probably working on the house, he figured—scrubbing spider webs out of a corner, rubbing the wood floors with a rag, or cooking a rabbit in the fireplace. He smiled briefly. Although Katherine had depended on the servants and done little in the way of labor before the war, she had surprised him with her set jaw and willingness to pitch in since coming back home. Hard times made people do things not usually suited to them, and Katherine's response to her hardships showed that truth better than almost anybody he knew. But even her hard work had not caused him to forgive her for not returning his money. Nothing would do that, short of her laying his dollars straight into his hand. Until she did that, he would have nothing to do with her except as a fellow laborer on The Oak. No connection as husband and wife, no aid to her decisions about the plantation, no comfort to her rough times or lonely nights.

York spat, then hefted the wood plank to haul it to his house where he planned to use it to repair a spot on the porch. Josh suddenly appeared from behind the barn with a rectangular box on his shoulder.

"Mornin'," said York.

"You all right?"

"Passable."

"How's Camellia today?"

"A little better. Seems a bit stronger every day."

"I'll stop by later. Tell her if you see her before I do."

York smiled at Josh. "You bad in love with her, that's the truth."

"I can't argue."

York pointed to the box on Josh's shoulder. "What you got there?"

"I found it by your house," Josh explained. "Took a look inside; saw some journals. You bring this from the fighting?"

"Found it in Richmond," said York, not wanting to admit he had stolen the box.

"You read the journals?" asked Josh.

"Not really."

Josh stared at him a second as the rain began to fall a bit harder. "You might want to take a look at them."

"Why?"

"I know you don't take much to reading," Josh continued, "but these are logs, journals describing the activities of General Jeb Stuart's cavalry unit."

"You know, I served under Stuart," said York, surprised. "With General Wade Hampton, the commander of my brigade."

"That's why I thought you might want to read through the logs." Josh handed the box over to York.

Not sure what else to do, York propped the plank on the barn and took the box. The rain fell faster.

"You might want to get them out of the rain," Josh suggested.

York nodded and Josh walked away. York glanced down at the box and saw the lid was still half open where he had hurriedly left it when Lynette came out on the porch weeks back. He started to set the box down, to leave the journals in the rain, but then decided to put the box in the one barn left standing. Who knew? Although he had no real interest in reading the logs, somebody else might want to do so at some point in the future. Seemed wrong to just leave them out in the weather.

Hoisting the box to one shoulder and the plank to the other, York made his way to the barn. After setting the plank down, he looked for a dry spot for the box. Outside the rain fell in sheets, a hard, soaking wet. A lantern cast a soft glow as he set the box by the barn door and squatted to rest a second. He took a deep breath and stared at the box. If only it contained what he had dreamed it might.

He took off his hat and wiped his face. Dreams never seemed to come true, he decided, at least not his. Nothing he ever wanted had panned out: not his love for Lynette, not his hopes for him and Katherine, not his wishes to keep Calvin and Johnny safe in the war, not this box by his knees.

Resigned to his fate, York pulled a plug of tobacco from his pocket and bit off a chew. As he tucked the plug back into his pocket, his eyes fell on the box again. He peered at the journals inside. A little rain had dripped onto the bindings of the books, so he took one out to wipe off the moisture. Curious now, he opened it and studied the writing. An unnamed aide to General Jeb Stuart had obviously kept daily notes detailing the exploits of the great general and his men.

York smiled as he remembered General Stuart, who favored polished jackboots, golden spurs, crimson-lined capes, and ostrich-plumed hats. Although the general sometimes took enormous risks with his men and their horses and seemed a little too fond of the ladies for a married man, York served gladly under Stuart. After all, his men rode horses, raided the Yankees with near impunity, and always seemed able to procure as good a provision as any other Southern soldier . . . and often better.

York stood and glanced outside. Rain now poured from the sky. Unable to go back to work, he decided to read a little more. He eased the lantern off its peg, set it on the back of a wagon, and took a spot beside it, a journal in hand. Although not reading in detail, York scanned the pages in order, finished the first book, then picked up a second. After a couple of minutes, he saw the notes were in chronological sequence, so he dropped the journals describing action near the end of things and moved to the ones telling of the beginning of the war. Of the glorious times when Stuart and his men seemed to win every battle, long before the Yankees cut off their supplies and wore them out with superior numbers and better boots and weapons. Before Jeb Stuart died six miles above Richmond at a place called Yellow Tavern in May of 1864.

York's eyes landed on a journal with notes from 1862. He read with greater zeal as the events unfolded before him—events he knew and recognized well. The rain fell harder, but York barely noticed. The journal described the fighting in October of that year, specifically the raid into Maryland and Pennsylvania that Stuart had led from the tenth to the thirteenth of the month. York and eighteen hundred other topnotch horsemen had taken part in that great adventure.

Starting just south of the Potomac River near Hedgesville, Virginia, the troop had flowed north over the river, through northern Maryland, and into southern Pennsylvania. At a spot near the town of Mercersburg, the riders came across a boot factory and gladly supplied themselves with new Yankee footwear.

Newly shod, the Confederate riders continued their raid toward the town of Chambersburg and their most-prized goal of the expedition—the destruction of a bridge over which General George C. McClellan's army received many of the supplies that fed and clothed its men.

York remembered the dashing ride. They arrived in Chambersburg a couple of hours after dark under intermittent rain. To their surprise they found no resistance. The town fathers surrendered without condition under a flag of truce. Through that night and into the next morning, the soldiers secured the town. The next day the soldiers found a Federal warehouse full of new blue uniforms and put on the warm garments under their tattered gray uniforms to go along with their recently acquired boots.

As the journal noted the success of the foray into Chambersburg, York chewed his plug and relived the glorious night. What days those were, what victories! If only the Yankees had not had such superior factories and so many more men. York paused and closed his eyes. If only the South had won!

He shook his head and studied the journal again. Suddenly he sat up straighter as his eyes landed on surprising words. He read slowly to make sure he didn't miss anything:

General Stuart's men spent that night and the following morning trying to fulfill the secondary objective of the expedition—the task of relieving the local bank of as much gold and greenbacks as possible. After finding a reasonable amount of both, a contingent of handpicked men hauled the financial contraband to a wagon, secured it under guard, left Chambersburg, and headed immediately toward the southwest, back toward Virginia, while General Stuart and his cavalry continued on toward Cashtown.

York reread the sentence and tried to remember everything he could about the events at Chambersburg. When the town fathers gave up without a fight, the soldiers had laid only a light hand on the place, taking all the livestock, the chickens, and the valuables of the citizens. Only a few people had resisted and required whipping.

Yep, he recalled the town—and everything the men confiscated—but not any gold or cash. He closed his eyes and pictured the town's bank in his head. He had seen a wagon pulled up in front of it through the night but paid it little mind at the time. Armies always took what money they found, but usually, given the warning most towns had before the army rode in, they found cash and gold scarce.

York turned back to the log.

Unfortunately for our cause, a troop of Yankee horsemen attacked the wagon and its defenders a few miles south of Chambersburg. Our guard found it necessary to find a hiding place for the valuables before the Yankees overwhelmed them. Only one Southern boy survived the ordeal, and although he gave me a brief sketch of the escapade, he died from wounds suffered in the battle before being able to fully describe the place or return to the spot of the fight or the burial place of the valuables.

York held his breath and finished the page.

General Stuart and his men returned to the Virginia side of the river on October 13 with hardly any loss of men and the glad capture of dozens of Yankee soldiers, thirty hostages, and over twelve hundred horses.

York flipped to the next page and then the next but found nothing else about the missing treasure. Dropping the book into his lap, he scratched at his beard. Had anyone gone back for the buried money? There was no way to tell. For all he knew, the writer of the journals, whoever he was, might be the only man with any knowledge of the events he described. If, as he said, nobody from the Rebel side of the fray survived, then who else could know? A few Yankees maybe? But the journal said the Rebels hid the money before the Yankees arrived. Maybe nobody knew about it but the author of the journals and York. But who was the author? York searched the front and back pages of the log, then flipped through the others in the box. No name was listed. Had the journal writer ever gone to find the valuables? Who knew?

York stood, walked to the barn door, and looked out at The Oak. Rain continued to fall. More than anything else he wanted to stay right there and rebuild the plantation. But what about this story he had just read? Were gold and U.S. dollars hidden somewhere just north of the Potomac River across from Virginia? If so, how much? What did the writer mean by "reasonable amount"?

He thought about Lynette, soon to make her return to Virginia now that Camellia had gained some strength back and seemed out of danger. Should he accompany Lynette and Jackson back to Richmond? Escort them safely home, then go to the area north of Mercersburg and see what he could find? How many places could somebody hide a stack of money and gold while running from Yankee horsemen? How much money might be there, if any?

York stared into the rainy sky and remembered Katherine. What would she do if he suddenly left with Lynette, a woman Katherine guessed he still loved? Would she figure he had left her for good? But how could he tell her he wanted to go search for treasure?

York pondered the question of why this information had come to him. Josh might say the Lord had sent it to him. Did the Lord want him to go back to Virginia? Had God indeed directed Josh to find the journals and bring them to York's attention? Of course, York had never believed in anything like Providence. But this seemed so much more than a co-incidence. Could he believe this had just dropped out of the blue with nothing divine about it? That's what he had always thought before . . . but should he change his views now? Was Someone "up there" trying to get his attention?

Unable to answer, York spat into the rain and watched the tobacco juice mix with the muddy earth. Although he didn't know if God had anything to do with this or not, he did know he wouldn't let the chance pass him by. If some good old Yankee gold and dollars lay hidden some-where between Chambersburg and Mercersburg, York saw no reason in the world, except for what Katherine might think, for him not to go find it. Katherine's opinions just didn't mean that much to him, at least not at the present time.

Set on his thought, York turned back to the journals. Best read them all, he figured. Who knew what else they might reveal?

Chapter Ten

Except for a four-day trip to and from Beaufort to buy flour, sugar, coffee, a new set of clothes, boots, and a barrelful of whiskey, Trenton spent all of June sitting on the front porch of the manse, watching Hampton York, Josh Cain, and the rest of their brood busy themselves about The Oak. Thanks to his mother's carefully preserving hidden funds that he used to pay for their supplies, Trenton didn't suffer from too much want. The pants leg on his stump was pinned snugly again. He neatly combed his hair every day and kept his shirt clean, his boots polished. Yes, the world had changed, but maybe he could still do all right in it. With the money his mother held, he still felt confident in the future.

Trenton tried to figure how much money his mother actually possessed—five thousand, ten thousand? Who knew? One thing he had to admit about his mother: she watched out for herself, no two ways about it. Maybe that's where he had inherited the art. And it was an art; he felt convinced . . . a gift only a few received.

Every now and again he thought of Calvin and wished he had not died in the war or that their two sisters, Martha and Miranda, weren't suffering in occupied Charleston. But since he couldn't do anything to help them or Calvin, Trenton usually took another drink of whiskey, pushed his bad thoughts away, and went back to observing the goings-on around him.

It pleased him to see York and Cain and all the rest labor so hard. The men started on their houses first, using scrap materials from an old barn to repair the four dwellings where everybody lived. The women, meanwhile, began to lay out a garden. Although the season had already passed for them to grow some things, that didn't stop them from putting in some others—squash, okra, beans, potatoes. Not being much of a gardener,

Trenton had no idea what else they planted. Within a couple of weeks, the women had cleared out the weeds, hoed out a big patch of rows, and set out some seed Lynette Swanson had bought at the Crossville General Store, which had sprung up at a crossroads about eight miles down the dirt road that led to Beaufort. To Trenton's surprise his mother had given Lynette the money to buy the seed.

"We all have to eat, you included," Katherine had told him when he complained about her generosity. "And since you don't seem eager to lift your hand to much, somebody needs to get some crops going."

Although still angry at her generosity, Trenton admitted her logic made sense and let it go.

Another surprise showed up about halfway through the month. Obadiah, once married to the troublesome Ruby, appeared one morning, looking for his former wife. It pleased Trenton when he saw Obadiah's shoulders slump as Josh Cain told him Ruby had gone looking for Theo. A day later Obadiah left, headed back to his house outside Beaufort. *Good riddance*, figured Trenton. No need for a black man around the place unless that man planned to work real cheap, and he knew Obadiah didn't do that.

After Obadiah's departure Trenton went back to watching people work. York and the rest of his crew finished the repairs on their houses pretty fast, then moved on to the big barn that once stabled the horses. A cow appeared from somewhere and went into the barn. Two days later a couple of chickens showed up. Soon The Oak, all except for the manse, began to take on a renewed look. No, the plantation was nothing like its former glory, but the main buildings did receive a fresh coat of paint and were patched up where they had been most damaged.

Although he tried to seem disinterested, Trenton's anger and resentment boiled within at the successful endeavors of those around him. Preferring them to fail, he growled even quicker at his mother when she dared to speak to him and drank more and more whiskey. His face stayed red and puffy, and his new clothes became drenched with sour liquor and lazy sweat.

Inside the manse his mother labored just as hard as York or anybody else. With the help of a couple of darkies who had drifted in and asked for paying work, she had started fixing the manse up too. Under Katherine's direction the Negroes rebuilt the roof over the house's main room, then fixed the chimney in the cooking area. Next they put glass back in the windows and repaired the spiral staircase. When finished with that, they started on the chimney in Katherine's bedroom.

Every now and again Katherine stepped out on the porch, her face pouring perspiration, and urged Trenton to get up and do something to help.

He always refused. "Why bother?" he would ask. "The place belongs to you and York, not me."

Usually Katherine just shrugged and went back inside. But one late afternoon, at the end of the first week of July, she lingered a bit longer after she had once again chastised him for his laziness.

"The Oak will be yours when York and I pass on," she said, taking a seat on the porch railing. "Fixing the place up ought to be something you want to do."

"You think Martha or Miranda might show up here again someday?" he asked, hoping they wouldn't.

"Not likely. They'll make it on their own or not at all."

"They write you a letter?" he questioned, knowing full well they had and wanting to know its contents.

"Yes. Said they were leaving Charleston for Savannah; Luther and Gerald both have family there."

Trenton sighed with relief. His sisters were out of the picture. Then he thought of another bad possibility. "The Yankees will probably give The Oak to the darkies."

"Don't talk nonsense."

Trenton grunted. "You know as well as I that a lot of white folks lost their lands to blacks the Yankees freed during the war."

Katherine stayed quiet as Trenton took another drink. His anger grew as he considered the audacity of the Federals. On January 11, 1865, the rampaging General Sherman had issued his famous Special Field Order 15—a command stating blacks could claim all abandoned coastal lands up to thirty miles inland from the ocean all the way from Jacksonville, Florida, to Charleston, no matter who owned them before the war. From that they would carve out a forty-acre plot for each family. The Oak lay right in the heart of that vast expanse.

"If I hadn't stayed on The Oak for most of the war, who knows what might have happened here?" Trenton continued. "A horde of darkies might be sitting on this porch right now, staking claim to our land."

"It grieves me you didn't get to go fight like you wanted," said Katherine. "But perhaps your staying here did keep the land in our hands."

Trenton sat up a little straighter. For the moment it seemed he had been heroic—that he had willingly stayed home to protect his property. "I heard some gossip in Beaufort that said the blacks would eventually get all that land anyway, whether white folks still live there or not."

"I will not let that happen," Katherine announced.

"How will you prevent it?"

Determination gleamed in her eyes. "You know I have my ways."

Trenton leaned back in the rocker. "How much money do you have, Mother?"

A light breeze played with Katherine's hair. "That is not for you to know."

"What if I started looking for the money? It's got to be around here somewhere."

"Go ahead. You won't find it," she challenged.

As he swigged more of the liquor, he gave up hope of prying information out of his mother. Instead, he focused his attention beyond the manse. Lynette Swanson labored in the garden about fifty yards away, just up from the barn in a sunny spot. Beth Cain worked beside her, a hoe in hand. A long skirt and beige blouse covered her slender body. Camellia, not yet completely recovered from the snakebite but apparently gaining strength, sat in a chair under a nearby tree, a lapful of sewing in her hands, the baby, Leta, at her knees, and the old woman, Nettie, in a chair close by.

Trenton watched Camellia for several minutes. Such a lovely woman. Yet, to his surprise, he felt no love, no longing for her anymore. Nothing but a little anger and a touch of resentment. Truth was, he had finally figured out she didn't deserve him, wasn't worthy of his affection. What had he ever seen in her—a poor, ignorant daughter of a plantation overseer—anyway? He deserved someone else, someone more appreciative of his status, someone who would recognize his wisdom, his education, his refined character.

"You need to think about finding a wife," said Katherine, almost as if reading his thoughts.

Trenton stopped rocking. "You trying to get rid of me, Mother?"

"No, but you're a grown man of twenty-five. You expect to stay alone all your days?"

He took another sip of whiskey. "I've thought some about that," he admitted.

Katherine shifted to where she could face him head-on. "I know you loved Camellia, but that is past. You know it as well as I do. There are lots of women without men these days. You'll have no trouble finding a proper bride."

Trenton pointed his bottle at his leg. "No good woman wants a cripple."

"Men are in short supply, crippled or not," she said bluntly. "You can make a match if you want."

Trenton wiped his face. "You think you're one to be giving me matrimonial advice?"

"I'm your mother. I can give you all the advice I want."

Trenton gazed back toward the garden. "I see Mr. York has not moved into your bedroom," he countered, hoping to move the talk away from his lack of a woman.

Katherine shrugged. "York is a stubborn man."

"He wants the money before he comes to you, doesn't he?"

"Something like that."

"That can't be good for a woman's ego."

"My confidence is not dependent on whether Mr. York comes to my bedroom or not; I can assure you of that."

Trenton spoke slowly, savoring the uncomfortable position his mother found herself in. "I see you give him money from time to time."

"He needs it to do his work on The Oak."

"You suppose he keeps any dollars for his own purposes?"

She shrugged. "I would if I were him."

"Does that not bother you?"

"It would bother me more if I had married a man who would not look out for himself."

Trenton laughed, stood, and fixed his eyes even more intently on the garden. His eyebrows arched as he noted how much Beth Cain had changed in the last few months . . . how she had rounded out in most attractive and womanly ways. Even from this distance he could see her beauty, the arch of her chin, the high cheekbones, the softness of her eyes, her lovely blond hair. Such an innocent young woman, so pure, so . . .

A pleasant and slightly wicked thought entered his head in the midst of the fog of the whiskey he had consumed.

Lynette picked up her garden tools and headed out of the garden. Camellia, Leta, and Nettie followed her. Beth moved to a bucket of water under the tree, pulled out a dipper, and took a long drink. Without saying anything else to Katherine, Trenton made his way down the steps.

"Where are you going?" asked Katherine.

Trenton glanced back at her. "I thought I'd see what I could do in the garden."

"Leave Camellia alone."

"I have no more feelings for Camellia York; I assure you of that."

Katherine shaded her brow with a hand and gazed at the garden for a moment. "Don't even think of it," she warned Trenton.

"I don't know what you mean," he lied.

"Beth Cain is what I mean," she retorted. "She is too young for you."

"She's seventeen. Lots of women are married with babies at her age."

"Stay away from her."

"I'm just going to say hello," said Trenton. "Not planning to offer her a proposal of marriage."

"You stay careful with her."

"Maybe she would like a beau," he suggested.

"True, but it shouldn't be you. Camellia won't stand for it. Mr. Cain either."

Trenton smiled. "Mr. Cain is a Christian gentleman. Surely he will look kindly on a repentant man."

Katherine placed her hands on her hips. "And where are the signs of your repentance?"

Trenton laughed, lifted his whiskey bottle, and took a drink. "Repentance is easy. I can do it every day."

"Just don't trifle with Beth Cain," insisted Katherine. "She is an innocent child, and you could hurt her badly."

"Like I said, Mother dear, I'm just going to say hello."

Beth Cain finished her water and wiped her mouth with the apron that hung around her waist. Although tired from digging in the garden, she knew she would bounce back soon. At her age even the worst weariness lifted fast. Picking up her hoe, she saw Trenton Tessier headed her way. Scanning the yard to see who he was approaching, she was puzzled. No one else was there.

She started to walk away.

"Hold on," Tessier called to her.

Although confused and fearful, she didn't want to be rude, so she stopped and waited for him to approach. Tessier stepped to the rail fence around the garden and propped an arm over the edge. "You have a nice garden going here."

Beth didn't know what to say. Although she had known Trenton Tessier all her life, she couldn't remember any real conversation with him, especially anything nice.

"I want to apologize to you," he said, startling her even more. "For what happened . . . what I did to you and your brother back in Richmond."

Beth wished somebody would come and rescue her. In the last hours before Richmond fell to the Yankees, Trenton Tessier had kidnapped her and Butler and used them as bait in the effort to make Camellia go with him as he fled the city. She remembered that awful night and a city in chaos as people tried to run from the approaching Yankees.

Fires burned everywhere in the streets of Richmond on April 2, 1865.

Trenton Tessier and some other man burst into the room where Beth and Butler Cain stayed at a hotel owned by Mrs. Lynette Swanson. They held a pistol on the children, tied them up, stuffed gags in their mouths, covered them with blankets, and hauled them out the back of the hotel to a waiting buckboard wagon. There they made them lie down while they hid them under a blanket. A short while later the children heard Camellia's angry voice, but all they could do was groan in response.

The wagon bounced through the streets of the panicked city until it reached the city jail. At that point, Tessier ordered the other man to untie them, take off their blindfolds and gags, and lead them into the jail. Butler jumped at the man, but he laughed and slugged the boy in the stomach.

Tessier hopped out of the wagon. "Stay here while I take these brats inside," he ordered the other man. Then, to Camellia, *"Don't try to run. Not if you care about these two."*

Without waiting on her response, he waved his pistol and led Beth and Butler into the jail. Using his authority as a deputy of the provost marshal, he accused them of sympathizing with the Union and left them with the jail keepers. If their father and Captain York hadn't found them later that night and taken them out of the jail, terrible things would surely have happened.

Beth shuddered against the memory. She finally found her voice. "What happened in Richmond is past. I would prefer that it stay that way."

"My feelings exactly," said Tessier. "That's why I am seeking to make amends for my awful behavior. The Lord has shown me the error of my sin."

Beth's brow furrowed. "I've never known you to speak much of the Lord."

He nodded sadly. "For that I am also sorry. But you believe a man can mend his ways, don't you?"

Beth studied his eyes for deceit. Although she was still young and blessed with the most innocent of faces, war had a way of growing up a body real fast. She had survived the worst of a truly bad war, and she no longer saw herself as a little girl. Laboring in the Victoria Hotel in Richmond— which had become a Confederate hospital during the fighting—she had met and talked with a lot of men, many with less-than-honorable intentions. Given that experience, she could usually smell a story a mile away. And, since she expected nothing but meanness from Trenton Tessier, she expected the one he was giving her to stink to high heaven. Yet right now she couldn't quite tell whether he was telling a story or not.

"I believe the Lord can give a man the power to mend his ways," she said cautiously.

"So will you forgive me for my offenses against you and your brother?"

Beth thought of Stella, the old servant woman who had raised Camellia as if bringing up her own child. Trenton Tessier had killed Stella the day Camellia returned from Richmond and tried to take Stella away from The Oak. A vicious fight had broken out: Camellia and Stella against Tessier. Tessier had kicked Stella in the ribs as she and Camellia struggled with him, and the ribs had punctured her insides. Camellia had held Stella's head in her arms as the old woman breathed her last. How could Beth forgive such terrible deeds?

"How can I tell if your repentance is real?" Beth asked.

"By the way I will now live. Isn't that what the Good Book says? We know the redeemed by their fruit?"

Beth raised an eyebrow, surprised Tessier knew so much Scripture. "The Good Book also says that some folks go about like wolves in sheep's clothin'."

He chuckled lightly. "Well spoken, Beth Cain. Like a woman with a clear head."

Beth glanced around, again wishing somebody would come back so she could escape this encounter. "I should go. I have lots of work to do."

He leaned closer over the fence. "A beautiful young woman like you should not have to work so hard. The sun will burn your fair skin, and a hoe will callus your soft hands."

In spite of her misgivings, Beth blushed at the compliment. It was the first she could remember receiving from a grown man. She tilted her head. Had Trenton Tessier truly changed? True, he had treated her rough in the past, but didn't the Lord love all people, forgive them, make them into new creations? Tessier still had his charms and, except for the infirmity of his bad leg, he cut a handsome figure. *With so few men around . . .*

Beth shuddered and pushed the thought away. What would Camellia think of her entertaining such a notion, even if only for a second!

"Why do you not work?" she blurted, not sure what else to say.

"Isn't that a rude question?"

Ashamed at her blunt manner, Beth dropped her eyes. "I'm . . . sorry. I know a man of your background isn't accustomed to labor."

"I wish I could do more, but my injury . . ."

She glanced at his leg.

"I tried to take a commission in the war," he reminded her. "But they would not accept me. So I stayed behind, took care of The Oak, kept it out of Yankee hands. That was no easy thing, I assure you."

Beth tried to make amends for her rudeness. "I'm sure your mother is most pleased with what you managed."

He gazed back at the manse. "I'm afraid my mother doesn't often appreciate the contributions I make."

Beth felt a surprising touch of sympathy. After all, life had not been easy for Trenton Tessier. His father, dead now for seven years, had demanded much from him and, from all she had heard, seldom had much to say in the way of praise. And his mother? Well, Beth knew how selfish Katherine could be, how stern and unfeeling. Maybe Tessier had turned out mean because of the way others had treated him.

Just then Beth heard footsteps rounding the side of the barn. She picked up her hoe.

Her pa strode her way. "What's going on?" he asked, eying Tessier.

"Just saying hello to Beth," said Tessier.

Josh glanced from him to Beth. "You OK?"

"Yes," she murmured, relieved her father had come.

Josh advanced on Tessier. "Leave my girl alone," he growled.

Tessier eased back a step and held up his hands as if to surrender. "I apologized to her for my past behavior. That's all it was."

"Keep it that way," said Josh, taking Beth by the arm.

As she walked away with her pa, she couldn't help but glance over her shoulder at Tessier. He smiled at her and gave a little wave. In spite of all he had done to her, she couldn't help but feel a slight thrill at his attentions. Although she knew not to trust him, she had to admit she liked the way he had spoken to her, the way he had treated her as a grownup. For the first time in her life, a man had talked to her like a woman instead of a little girl.

Chapter Eleven

Ruby had made little progress through June and into July in her search for the auctioneer who had sold her. For weeks and weeks she had gone almost door to door through the burned-out city of Charleston, asking of his whereabouts. In a lot of places the people just stared at her blankly and sent her on her way. Others cursed her and she fled. A few people did remember the blousy-shirted auctioneer. One man in a worn-down saloon named Sam's, near the old slave market, even gave her the auctioneer's name.

"Benton Jones," said the helpful man. "He often took his refreshment in this place."

"You got any idea where to find Mr. Jones?" Ruby asked.

The man shook his head. Sadly, nobody else seemed to know either. One lady Ruby met at a general store near Sam's said she had heard Jones had caught the malaria and died. A lot of people in Charleston and the neighboring area had died from it in the past few months.

Unwilling to give up until she talked to somebody who knew for sure, Ruby kept searching. After talking to a woman from James Island who said she thought she had seen Jones there, Ruby headed across the water on a ferry and spent over a week talking to people in that area. Did anybody know a man named Benton Jones? Did anybody know if he still lived? Nobody did, so she traveled back to Charleston.

Ruby slept outside most nights. The hot summer air was relieved only by the breezes blowing off the Atlantic Ocean. When it rained, she sought shelter in a corner of some vacated building—and she had a lot of those to choose from. The war had treated Charleston poorly. The city and the area around it lay mostly in ruins. Many of the wealthy whites who had once ruled the place had lost everything. Most had not returned to their former homes. Weeds grew where lush gardens once flourished. Charred remains stood where majestic mansions once towered. A grieved hush hung in the air where the music of balls and banquets once poured forth. For the most part Ruby ignored the destruction. The city got what it deserved, she figured: a comeuppance for the way its people had treated blacks for so long.

In spite of the tattered city and all the displaced people, Ruby felt pretty safe as she searched for Jones. True, every now and again some man—black or white—took a look at her that lingered a little too long. Once she had to pick up a rock and throw it at a darky who lunged at her as she walked past a pier in Secessionville. But other than that, nothing scared her too much. She kept a knife tied to her ankle with a strip of brown cloth. She figured if a rock wouldn't keep dangerous menfolk off her, the knife surely would.

To pay for enough food to keep her alive, Ruby took a job from time to time to make a dollar or two to buy provisions. From washing sheets for a woman here to hauling out rugs and window drapes there, she did whatever she could find to do. Like a lot of other freed blacks, she had always dreamed of earning her own living but had a lot to learn about how to go about it. Every time she ran out of money and got hungry enough, she just stopped her search for Jones, started knocking on doors of the houses left standing, and asked for work. Sometimes she found some; other times she didn't. When she did, she labored for as many hours as the boss needed her, took her money, and moved on.

She wondered about Obadiah every now and again as she survived those days. She even thought some of Markus. Had either of them lived through the war? If so, where were they? What if they both still lived? What would she do if they both suddenly appeared? Whom would she choose? With no way to answer her own questions, Ruby let them drop and focused on the thing she had come to Charleston to do—find her boy.

By the time the month of July had entered, Ruby had searched just about everywhere she knew to look. For the first time she began to feel lowly. Since she'd lost considerable weight, her ragged skirt and blouse hung on her as if draping a scarecrow. Calluses as thick as silver coins covered her feet. With baths available only rarely, she looked a sight—her hair dirty, her fingernails chipped and broken, her face dried out from the sun beating down as she switched off riding the old horse or walking from place to place.

At the end of the second week of the month, Ruby decided Jones had either died or moved away. She needed to leave Charleston and search somewhere else. But where had Jones gone? Where should she go to find him? Columbia? Georgetown? Farther inland?

Every now and again the notion of giving up the search for Theo entered her head, but she never let it stay long. Somehow she knew her boy was still out there, waiting for her, and all she had to do was keep looking. *Patience*, she told herself more than once. *Perseverance. Press on.*

Needing money to leave the city, Ruby worked with a woman who needed her for childcare, then gathered her belongings and headed to the general store near the marketplace to buy a few provisions. The route took her by the old slave auction block, and she paused on the busy street to take one last look at the area. Her fingers closed into fists by her side as she stared at the building where so many blacks had suffered such awful humiliation. Shadows covered the area as the sun began to go down.

"Never again," Ruby reminded herself aloud. The Yankees had seen to that. No matter what happened in her future, no matter if she never found Theo or Obadiah, "Master" would never again cross her lips. Tears of thanksgiving formed in her eyes, and she slowly wiped them away before heading toward the general store. Half a block down she passed Sam's and stopped at the window to take a final look inside the faded building. Somebody bumped into her shoulder, and she turned quickly as a hand grazed her bosom.

A skinny white man in a brown jacket and gray pants stood beside her. He wore an odd grin. "You standin' in a public spot," said the man, his words bathed in the smell of whiskey.

"Excuse me?" said Ruby.

The man raised an eyebrow and nodded to the left. "You standin' in the walkway to a saloon."

"Sorry. I'll move on." She started to walk away, but the skinny man grabbed her by the elbow.

"Not so fast."

She tried to jerk away, but the man held her firm. "Leave me be!" she commanded.

A second man stepped out of Sam's. "What you doin, Raeford?" he asked the man holding her.

"Found this one peerin' in the window," Raeford slurred. "She's a fine-lookin' thing."

"She must be lookin' for a fella to buy her a drink," said the second man.

Raeford licked his lips. "You want to take a drink with us?"

Ruby pulled against Raeford's hands, but he didn't budge. He was stronger than he looked. "I'll call the Federals," she warned.

Raeford squeezed her wrists like a vise, while the other man pulled out a knife. "You'll be bleedin' on the street, and we'll be gone before anybody can get here," he hissed. "So just stay steady and have a drink with us. That's all we askin'."

Ruby glanced up and down the street but saw no Yankee uniforms. "OK," she agreed, knowing she had no choice. Raeford drew her close and steered her into the saloon. Several men stood at a bar; a few others sat at a couple of tables. Two of the men wore the last remnants of Confederate uniforms. The pants were almost in rags and the hats badly soiled. Lamps flickered here and there but not enough to really light the place. Raeford and his friend pushed Ruby toward a table near the back.

"Bring us a bottle!" Raeford yelled at the bartender. When the bartender eyed Ruby, she knew he probably didn't like it that Raeford and his buddy had brought a black into his establishment. But the bartender said nothing. One of the men in the Rebel clothes looked up, his eyes haggard and empty. A scraggly beard covered his face and a sore the length of a little finger rose out of the skin on the left side of his face. Ruby tried to make eye contact with him, to let him know by her expression that she needed some aid, but he glanced away.

Cowards! she fumed to herself. *Every man in the place!*

Raeford and his pal tugged Ruby toward the next to last table in the saloon. Frantically she looked at the lone man sitting there. *Help me!* her eyes pleaded. *I'm not a slave anymore!*

The man leaned back in his chair and studied Ruby as she passed. Ruby's eyes widened. She took a second look just to make sure. The dingy shirt, almost exactly like the one she remembered from so many years back, hung off the man's round shoulders. Although older and more sagging in his face and eyes, the man's face dispelled any questions about his identity. It was Benton Jones, the auctioneer, in the flesh!

"Wait!" shouted Ruby, digging in her heels. The bearded soldier glanced their way, then turned back to his drink. Raeford struggled to keep her moving, but Ruby grabbed a corner of the auctioneer's table and held on. "One second!" she begged.

"What?" asked Raeford.

"Him!" She pointed at Jones.

"You know him?"

She nodded quickly. "One question," she told Raeford. "I ask him one question, then go with you."

Raeford looked at his pal, then shrugged. He let her turn to Jones, who stared dully at her, a beer in his hand.

"You were the auctioneer," she said as calmly as she could muster.

Jones nodded slightly but seemed too tired to care.

"You sold me," she stated.

Jones raised up a little, a touch of fear in his eyes. "I did my job," he said wearily. "No more or less."

Ruby saw instantly she had scared him. A lot of blacks had probably threatened Jones since the war ended. "I don't care about that. I just need to ask you one thing."

Jones took a sip of his beer as Ruby continued. "I had a son. He came to Charleston looking for me. I expect he searched you out, hoping to ask you who bought me, where I went from here."

Jones chuckled. "Lots of people have searched me out in the past few months. Not many of them with my good health in mind. That's why I don't stay in one spot too long. I don't need folks knowin' where to find me."

"My son isn't like most other boys," Ruby said. "He's short, missing an eye. And he's got gray even though he's still a boy."

Jones furrowed his brow. "That be a strange boy."

Ruby nodded and Jones pondered a few moments longer. Suddenly a light glowed in his lifeless face. "I might recollect a darky like that. Come through here back in . . . I don't know, April maybe, early May?"

Ruby gasped. "What did you tell him?"

Jones sipped his beer again. "Hard to recall."

Ruby pulled out the two dollars she had earned the last week and handed it to Jones. "It's all I've got. Just tell me what you told my boy."

Jones took the money and shoved it into a pocket. "My memory just loosened a little. Seems your boy named Theo, am I right?"

"Yes!" Hope again sparked to life in Ruby.

Jones nodded. "He did right by me."

Ruby's face wrinkled in confusion.

Jones continued, a light smile on his tired lips. "He hung around over a week. Did errands for me. I took him to my place, showed him the books where I recorded all the sales." He paused to sip his beer.

"And?" demanded Ruby.

"I told him Hampton York bought you; took you to The Oak."

Ruby almost collapsed. "You telling me the truth?"

Jones lifted his beer as if saluting her. "That boy of yours got a strange look. No way to tell him no for too long."

A mix of joy and fear ran through Ruby. Theo was alive! But if he had talked to Jones in late April, early May, why hadn't he made it to The Oak by the time she had returned? Or had he, and Trenton Tessier hadn't said anything?

Raeford yanked Ruby's arm, forcing her back to the matter at hand. "You got what you wanted," he said roughly. "Now come on."

Ruby gritted her teeth. She decided right then and there she wouldn't go another step with Raeford and his awful friend. "Leave me be!" she shouted, jerking as hard as she could against his grasp.

The knife appeared again, and Raeford spun her away from Jones and toward the back of the saloon. When Ruby kicked Raeford in the knee, he cursed and grabbed her by the hair. She kicked again and hit a chair at Jones's table. The auctioneer stood, swaying, but didn't do anything to help. Raeford and his friend held her by both arms now and, although she fought with all her strength, they dragged her across the floor, her feet sliding behind.

The knife was now at her throat and Ruby screamed. Glancing over her shoulder, she hoped, prayed, that somebody would come to her aid. But the men in the bar merely stared at the commotion. The soldier with the beard caught her eye but didn't move to do anything.

When Raeford touched the knife blade to her skin, she realized she needed to stop resisting or Raeford would surely kill her on the spot. *No,* she decided. No matter what terrible thing happened to her now, she couldn't let herself die. Theo was alive! She had to endure whatever momentary suffering came her way so she could see him again.

Determined to live, she relaxed into Raeford's grasp as he and his buddy dragged her toward the back door of the saloon. Her eyes closed as she accepted her fate.

Then something scraped behind her. She opened her eyes for one last look at the bar. To her surprise the bearded soldier was headed their way. His eyes were intense—but whether with fear or energy, she couldn't tell.

"Hold it there!" shouted the soldier.

Raeford and his pal glanced back but kept moving.

The soldier pulled out a pistol and pointed it at them. "I got a gun!"

Raeford stopped and pivoted, a gun appearing in his hand too. Everybody in the saloon put down their drinks and held still. The bartender dropped his towel on the bar.

"You wantin' to go with us?" Raeford asked the soldier. "Two dollars and you can have her when we're done."

Ruby studied the man's face and saw more youth in him than she first recognized. His clothes, rags that they were, hung loosely on his visible bones. Cracks covered his lips, and the sore on his face seemed redder than a few moments ago.

"I want nothing of the sort," said the soldier, his tone far more refined than Ruby had expected.

"Then leave us be," said Raeford. "This is none of your affair."

The soldier took a deep breath, and pain crossed his face. "You will not do harm to that woman," he said bravely.

Ruby noticed something vaguely familiar in the soldier's voice but didn't know from where. She studied his eyes again but didn't believe what she thought she saw there.

"I will do what I want with her," Raeford insisted.

"No, you won't," the soldier said calmly.

"I warn you a last time," Raeford hissed. "You got no claim in this."

The soldier cocked his pistol. "I got every claim. I used to own her."

Everyone in Sam's froze.

The soldier looked right at her. "It's me, Ruby."

It took her a second to find her voice, but when it came, she almost wanted to shout. "Calvin?"

The soldier nodded, and a tear crawled out of his eye.

For the first time Raeford seemed a little unsure of himself. He eyed his buddy and then Calvin.

Ruby couldn't believe her eyes or her ears. "We figured you dead," she whispered.

"Just about was," Calvin replied. He turned then so all in the bar could hear him. "My name is Calvin Tessier," he barked. "Son of the late Marshall Tessier of The Oak Plantation. I fought with Jeb Stuart. Took wounds at Burgess Mill. The Yankees captured me and took me to a prison in Maryland. They let me out just over a month ago. I've been traveling home ever since."

Everyone nodded and Ruby knew they recognized the name. Before the war the Tessiers had been a leading family in the low country, and Charleston society knew them well.

Then Raeford stiffened beside her. She sensed him regaining his spine.

"All that is fine and dandy," Raeford spouted. "But names like Tessier don't matter anymore."

Calvin's eyes landed on him again. From behind Calvin, the second man wearing gray pulled out a pistol and moved up beside Calvin.

"Does it matter that you now have two pistols pointed your way?" asked Calvin.

"You gone shoot a man over a darky?" asked Raeford. "Take a chance on gettin' shot yourself?"

Calvin held steady but said nothing.

Raeford looked at his buddy, cursed, and lowered his gun. "Take her!" he spat. "Ain't no darky woman worth takin' a bullet over."

Ruby quickly moved to Calvin as he waved his weapon at Raeford and his crony. "Move on out of here," Calvin told Raeford. "And don't come back tonight."

Still cursing, Raeford led his friend out of Sam's and into the street. Everyone in the saloon except Calvin and Ruby turned back to their drinking, murmuring over the excitement of the conflict.

Trying to bring her breathing back to normal, Ruby faced Calvin. "I can't believe it's you!"

He touched her hand and sighed heavily. "I never thought I'd make it back. But seeing you gives me living proof I did."

"You figured Mr. Trenton and your mother were in Charleston?" she asked.

He pulled out a chair at the table and pointed her to it. Then he took the one opposite her. "I didn't know what happened to them. Whether they lived or died; whether they were here or The Oak. But this was closest on my trip back, so I checked here first. Got here early today and went by our old home. It's burned out now."

"Sorry to hear that."

"War." He shrugged.

"Mr. Trenton and your mother are alive," she offered. "At The Oak. They went back after Richmond fell."

"I'm surprised you ended up back down here."

"Nowhere much else to go—at least not yet. Mr. York, Mr. Cain, all the rest are at The Oak too."

"Why are you in this place?" He waved a hand over the bar.

"It's a long story, but mostly because I'm searching for my son, Theo."

Calvin's eyes grew sad. "I remember you speaking of him."

"He's alive; I found that out."

"Good."

Ruby paused and studied Calvin. The war had changed him, she could tell that already. Although still brave, he no longer wore the arrogance Tessier men usually carried around like a birthright. She wondered how Calvin and Trenton would get along now.

"I expect you'll go back to The Oak," she offered.

"As soon as I wake up tomorrow."

"Mind if I go with you?"

He smiled and touched her hand again. "I'll be happy for the company."

Ruby smiled, too, and why not? Somewhere out there Theo still searched for her. And now that Calvin had showed up in such an unexpected place and time and saved her from heaven only knew what, she felt certain, one way or the other, it was her destiny to eventually find her boy.

Chapter Twelve

Calvin's return caused quite a stir on The Oak. He spent most of his first days back recovering from his injuries. From what Camellia could tell, even from a bit of a distance, Katherine gave Calvin almost constant attention, feeding him as much as he could eat, making him sit on the porch and rest, fawning over him like what he was—a dead son now come to life again. Although Camellia didn't see much of Trenton for the first couple of weeks after Calvin's return, she knew him well enough to realize he probably felt rather odd—glad to see his brother alive and home again but maybe also resentful that his mother treated Calvin with a lot more love than she ever seemed to give Trenton.

Every now and again Calvin walked off the manse's front porch and strolled down to the garden where Camellia and Beth spent a lot of their daylight hours. Other than offering them polite greetings, he didn't say much, just sat on a tree stump by the fence around the vegetables and took his rest. Gradually he gained his strength and by the middle of August had offered a couple of times to help them, an offer Camellia always gently refused.

"No need for a man in the garden," she told him more than once as Beth looked quietly on. "Especially one as sick as you've been."

"But you've been sick too," he countered.

"I'm better now."

Calvin smiled each time and left them.

But one day Camellia saw him at the side of the manse, a bucket in hand, spreading a fresh coat of paint on the wall.

"He seems almost well again," Beth whispered.

"Getting closer, that's sure," said Camellia.

Beth's gaze lingered on Calvin for a few seconds.

"You think he's a handsome man?" asked Camellia, deciding to tease the shy, young woman a little.

Beth blushed. "I reckon he's handsome enough."

"Enough for what?"

Beth grinned. "Enough so as he wouldn't scare a girl if she run up on him at night."

They both laughed and went back to their hoeing.

The rest of the day passed. Although she couldn't understand how it happened, Camellia began to feel joyful again. Even though she fretted that she and Josh hadn't married and left The Oak yet, she stayed content by knowing their day would come, and soon too. About the only thing that kept her from complete peace was her concern for Ruby.

The next day as she and Ruby worked in the garden, Camellia decided the time had come to discuss Ruby's future. She reminded her, "Obadiah came for you. Maybe you should go to him."

"Theo is still out there," Ruby replied.

"But you're all alone. Maybe Obadiah would go with you to find him."

"I'm real pleased Obadiah is well, but I can't ask him to drop his labor and go with me on my crazy hunt. He needs to make a living. When I come back with Theo, he'll have to care for all of us."

"Why don't you just stay here?" Camellia asked, worried for her safety. "Theo will show up here sooner or later."

"I can't wait on that," said Ruby. "Winter is coming. The auctioneer said he sent him this way. He's got to be out there, close somewhere. I just know it."

"You ask Trenton if Theo came to The Oak before we returned?"

"He swore not."

"But I fear for you," Camellia warned her. "Things are mighty dangerous right now. Yankee soldiers running around without a lot of supervision. Bands of blacks stealing and fighting. Poor white boys still crazy from the war."

118

Ruby nodded. "Wonder when it will all settle down again."

"Not for a long time I expect."

"You'll still look after Leta and Mama?"

Camellia thought of Josh and their postponed wedding plans. But since she didn't know how to deny Ruby, she nodded.

"You're a mighty good friend," said Ruby, her brown eyes moist.

Seeing she couldn't change Ruby's mind, Camellia sighed and let it go. "Least you've fattened up some since we got home," she said, noting Ruby's figure.

"These weeks of rest have done me a lot of good."

"I pray your boy is OK," said Camellia.

"I feel in my bones he is."

"Which way you headed when you leave here?"

"Toward Columbia, then maybe down to Savannah. If I don't find him by then . . . well, I will just have to see which way to turn from there."

The two women hugged.

The next morning Ruby left, head held high and eyes focused straight ahead. She carried a burlap bag filled with as much food as Camellia could find and stuff into it.

Camellia visited with Josh on his porch at the end of the day Ruby left, while Beth cleaned up in the kitchen. Josh took her hand and held it as they sat in matching rocking chairs and stared out into the yard. The air lay flat and hot against the ground. Bugs flitted in and out around the lantern that hung on the post by the steps.

"We have made a lot of progress on this place," Camellia said. "Got a good crop of vegetables going—maybe enough to tide us through winter."

"Houses are fixed pretty well too," Josh added.

"When will Lynette and Pa leave?" she asked, aware of York's plans to escort Lynette and Jackson back to Richmond but not sure of the timetable.

"He wanted to make sure we had finished repairing the main barn before he took off," Josh explained.

"Is that done?"

"Not quite. York will probably go by the first of September."

"Did it surprise you that he decided to escort them back?"

"A little. But he loves Lynette, you know that. He won't take a chance something might happen to her."

"It shocked Lynette though."

"Yeah, she protested some. Told York she could take care of herself."

"She's a strong woman. You think they might ever . . ." Camellia couldn't voice the rest of her thought.

"York is a married man; don't forget that."

"But he's not living with his wife."

Josh shrugged. "People do odd things because of pride."

"Katherine still won't tell him where she hid his money?"

"Guess not."

"Has he searched for it?"

"Not that I've seen, but knowing your pa, it would not surprise me."

"He won't be her husband until he's got that money?"

"Guess not."

Camellia paused. A bird chirped. "Did Katherine make a fuss when she found out he'd be leaving with Lynette and Jackson?"

"York doesn't tell me everything, but I would expect so."

She sighed. "I will miss Lynette and Jackson. I've been with Lynette four years now."

"You still don't call her Mother?"

She shrugged. "Though she birthed me, she is more friend than mother. I guess growing up with her not around . . . it doesn't feel right to call her anything but by her name."

As Josh ran his fingers over the back of Camellia's hand, she wondered when he would bring up the matter of their wedding. When Ruby had come back from Charleston, they had both thought that meant their nuptials could happen and they could start their lives together. Sadly, though, it was not yet to be. Ruby still had not found Theo.

"I suppose your promise to Ruby is still in place," he said.

"I don't see a way out of it."

Josh withdrew his hands from hers. It was a gentle gesture, but still she felt his disappointment seeping into the late-day air.

"I'm sorry," she offered, "but what can I do?"

He faced her, his eyes grave. "I'm not faulting you, but . . . well, the notion of marrying you got me through the war. Now, even though we're with each other every day, I still can't make you my wife. First, the snakebite. Then this promise to Ruby. It doesn't seem fair somehow."

She sighed. "The Lord never said much about life being fair, so far as I can tell."

Josh sat back and started rocking again. An awkward silence fell. A bird chirped and a squirrel ran across the yard.

Camellia broke the quiet. "I suppose we could go ahead and marry and live here on The Oak until Ruby comes back."

Josh searched her face. "I have thought of that, but—"

"I know," Camellia interrupted him. "It seems wrong for some reason. Like if we marry here, we'll never leave."

"My thoughts exactly," said Josh. "I want a proper wedding for you—in a church like you deserve. Then a chance to start a whole new life away from the bad memories that haunt this ground."

Camellia leaned toward him and rested her head on his shoulder. "So I guess we're stuck until Ruby comes back."

"Looks like it."

"Promise me you're not mad."

He paused, as if carefully choosing his words. "I'm not. Well, not too much anyway. Worried is more like it."

She lifted her head from his shoulder. "About what?"

He gestured toward the house. "Have you seen Trenton around Beth much?"

"Some . . . but not too often."

"But you're not with her all the time, are you?"

"No, why do you ask?"

Josh balled his fists on the arms of the rocker. "I saw him talking to her down by the river a few days ago. She goes there some in the afternoons. Likes to rest there, bathe her feet."

Camellia nodded. She sometimes did the same thing. "You afraid Trenton is up to no good?"

"You ever know him to be up to anything else?"

"Maybe—a long time ago."

"A real long time ago."

Camellia sighed and remembered her younger days with Trenton Tessier. How had he fallen so far? No, not all at once, but through a steady series of bad choices that seemed to make him more and more evil. Is that how people turned bad? she wondered. Not in one fell swoop but as gradual as the drip, drip, drip of water that wore down a rock in a creek bed?

"Have you talked to Beth about Trenton?" she asked.

"A little but she stays quiet when I bring it up . . . like it's something I shouldn't touch."

"Young folks sometimes squirm against the strong hand of a parent," said Camellia. "Want to think for themselves, make their own choices."

"I have tried not to sound too harsh when I talk to her about him."

"That's wise, I reckon."

"I think she's afraid I want her to stay away from all men."

Camellia smiled. "Is she right about that?"

Josh chuckled. "Not really. But I do want her to find a good match, and I fear that will be hard to do around here. The only men she ever sees are Trenton and Calvin. That's another good reason for us to move: to give her a chance to make some new acquaintances."

"You want me to bring up the subject of Trenton with her?"

Josh shook his head. "Let it be. She might feel we're ganging up on her. She's a smart girl. She'll figure him out soon enough."

"He can be charming," said Camellia, not sure about Josh's decision to leave the matter alone.

"I know." Josh stood and moved to the porch rail, reseated himself and faced Camellia again. She knew from the look in his eyes he had something important to say. "I want to offer another option than just staying until Ruby comes back."

"What?"

"Why don't we leave in the spring—whether Ruby is back or not?"

Camellia started to protest.

Josh held a finger to his lips to keep her quiet and added, "We will take Leta and Nettie with us if Ruby isn't here."

"But where will we go?"

Josh shrugged. "Not sure yet, but perhaps Hilton Head. You know I have friends there. Or further west. Who knows? Wherever I can find work."

"You think it's wise to head out with no labor guaranteed?"

Josh took off his hat and stared into it. "I feel we have to do it. We'll keep in touch with York. When Ruby comes back, he can tell her where to find us."

Camellia understood his fears without him even stating them. "You want Beth away from Trenton, don't you?"

Josh put his hat back on. He walked back to her, squatted down, took her hand, turned it over, and kissed her palm. "Yes. But it's for our sakes too. We've waited long enough to start our life. And I feel . . . I don't know . . . that if we don't get away from here by the spring, something bad is going to happen. Something maybe we can't reverse."

"You have been so patient with me."

He kissed her hand again, then gently let go. "I expect you to make up for that when we are finally married." A smile twinkled at the corners of his eyes and mouth.

She grinned. "I will do my best to see that I do."

She stood and he did likewise. As they hugged and then, arm in arm, looked out at The Oak, she knew for sure, no matter what happened, they would leave this place when the winter had passed.

Part Two

Regrets

Make the most of your regrets;

never smother your sorrow,

but tend and cherish it. . . .

To regret deeply is to live afresh.

—HENRY DAVID THOREAU

Chapter Thirteen

At dusk, near the end of September, Hampton York rode his worn-out horse across the Potomac River and into Richmond. Lynette and Jackson followed in a mule-drawn wagon. Their trip had taken just under a month. Except for a couple of times, when somebody approached them begging for food, they made the journey without much contact with others. Due to the hard march they made every day, they hadn't talked a lot with each other either. Just said the minimum of what they had to say and when they had to say it.

Slouched in the saddle, York inspected the former capital of the South. His heart sank. It lay in ruins—much of its former glory almost completely blackened by the fire that had raged the night the city fell to the Yankees. Whole streets lay in rubble, many of the buildings nothing more than charred shells of their former state. Others were missing their roofs and all their windows were shattered, but the fronts of the buildings were still standing. Former stately mansions now lay in ashes.

A strange smell, like burned wet wood, hung in the air. Yankee soldiers stood on almost every street corner, many of them sullen in expression. It was obvious they were ready to stop guarding this hollowed-out city and go on home. Blacks milled about as plentifully as the soldiers, many of them idly standing on the corners. A few of the Negroes stepped toward York, Lynette, and Jackson as they rode into town, as if ready to take their horses right out from under them. York glared at the blacks as they approached. When he touched the side of his hip, as if wearing a pistol under his shirt, the blacks left them alone.

As they reached the main entrance to the city, a Yankee sergeant stopped them and asked what their business was. York quickly told him.

When the soldier asked if they had sworn the oath of allegiance, York almost choked on the word *yes*. But he asked Lynette to pull from the box under the wagon seat the papers that showed all three of them had gone into Beaufort with the rest of his folks in mid-July and stood before a Yankee official.

It was then that York had been forced to speak the hardest words he ever had to say: *"I, Hampton York, do solemnly swear, in the presence of Almighty God, that I will henceforth faithfully support, protect, and defend the Constitution and Government of the United States against all enemies, whether domestic or foreign, and that I will bear true faith, allegiance, and loyalty to the same."* Those words had given him official forgiveness for fighting the war he had thought it his right to wage and had allowed him, along with Katherine, to stake permanent claim again to their property on The Oak.

The Yankee examined their papers before handing them back to Lynette. "You boys got any firearms on you?" asked the sergeant.

"Just a hunting rifle and one pistol," replied York, again grinding his teeth at the humiliation of having to declare his weapons to a sorry Yankee. "In the back of the wagon."

The Yankee studied him. York decided he needed to stay calm even if the Yankee made him dismount so he could search his body. To his relief, the sergeant merely moved to the back of the wagon, lifted the canvas cover, peered at the contents under it, and dropped it again.

"You look clear," said the soldier.

York tipped his hat, and the Yankee let them pass.

Chewing hard on his tobacco plug, York rode through the streets with Lynette and Jackson toward the Victoria Hotel, the place Lynette and her deceased husband had run before the war. They reached it in half an hour and stood, stunned. Little or nothing remained of the formerly stately building.

York remembered the place as a three-story stone building with a black wrought-iron fence around it. Large iron lions had guarded the two columns that framed the doors. Now only the tall maple trees bordering the cobblestone walk that led to the double front doors remained intact, and even their trunks showed black near the base where the fire had burned them.

Tears rained down Lynette's face when York caught her eye. He put an arm around her back, Jackson joined them, and the three of them stood in a tight circle for a long time. Lynette's sobbing was the only sound.

Finally, York couldn't stand it any longer. "We can rebuild it."

She shook her head. "We have no money," she sobbed. "No insurance of any kind."

York ground his teeth again. The Federals weren't accepting insurance granted during the war by Southern companies. "We'll find a way," he insisted, not willing to let Lynette feel so hopeless.

"But how?" she asked.

York thought of the journal in the box under the wagon seat and of the treasure he hoped to find. A touch of guilt ran through him because he had used Lynette and Jackson as his excuse to come back to Virginia. "You are a woman of faith," he offered. "Shouldn't you trust the Lord?"

Lynette's brow furrowed in puzzlement.

"We've still got the house," suggested Jackson. "Perhaps it's OK."

"That's right," agreed York. "Maybe the fires didn't spread that far."

When Lynette's eyes brightened, York hoped with all his might that her home had escaped. "Let's go to the house," he said. "We'll come back here later and see if there is anything we can salvage."

Lynette wiped her eyes and nodded.

They left the hotel and headed to her house. A few minutes later they turned a tree-lined corner and spotted it about halfway down Clairemont Street—a two-story brick house with a fountain out front.

Lynette hopped from the wagon, even before it stopped, and ran toward her home. York spurred his horse to catch her. Seconds later they stopped and took a deep breath. The house, although blackened in spots near the lower corners and missing all its windows and the front door, looked reasonably intact.

"The fountain is still there." Lynette pointed toward the center of the yard, to the brick fountain that held a carved bird in a birdbath.

"No water in it," said Jackson.

"We can put water in it," Lynette replied.

She hurried toward the front door, and York and Jackson followed. Once inside the house, York paused to inspect the place. High ceilings stared down at an empty entryway. All the furnishings were gone—the rugs, the chandeliers, the furniture, the pictures from the walls—every stick of everything that had once graced the house. Cobwebs cluttered the corners, and bits of clothing lay here and there. Glass was scattered on the hardwood floor and, though he tried to avoid it, York still stepped in some.

This time Lynette kept her composure. She didn't cry. "It's OK," she said as she sized up the situation. "We can fix it back up."

"That will take a lot of money," Jackson stated.

York noted the somber expression on the young man's face. And something else—a flicker of pain?

Lynette glanced at her son. "York's right," she told him. "We will trust the Lord, find a way."

York walked ahead of them to examine the rest of the lower floor. A man's scuffed boot sat in the corner in the parlor, a battered hat beside it. Chewing-tobacco stains covered one of the walls, where it looked like somebody had spit without regard to where it landed.

When Lynette and Jackson stepped up behind him, York pointed at the items. "Somebody else has been here. Don't know how long ago."

"You figure they might come back?" asked Jackson, obviously seeing the danger.

York paused, torn between scaring Lynette and warning her. "Not sure," he finally said. "But I do think you two ought to stay careful. Make sure you keep your pistol handy."

Jackson nodded. "At least the Yankees didn't make us give up all our weapons."

York grunted, then left them to search through the upstairs of the house. When he found no other signs of trespassing, he headed back downstairs.

Lynette was sitting on a broken chair in the parlor.

"Where did you find that?" he asked, pointing at the chair.

"In the room over the carriage house. There are a couple of items there we can use—an old bed, a few utensils. Guess nobody thought to rob it. Jackson is bringing everything over."

"I'll go help him."

Lynette held up a hand. "I . . . I want to thank you. You didn't have to come with us."

York shrugged. "I want you safe."

"Still . . ."

York's guilt returned. He almost told her about the gold he hoped to find. How he planned to bring it all back and give it to her if that would make her happy. She could rebuild her hotel again and start all over.

She interrupted his thoughts before he could speak. "You are a good man, York. Though I know you will not admit it."

He hung his head. "You don't know me, or you would not say that."

She stood. "What will you do now?"

"Go back to The Oak," he said, lying only a little since he did plan to do that once he found the gold. "Plenty there to keep me busy for a long time."

"You still want your picture over the staircase, don't you?"

He frowned. "Who told you that?"

"Camellia mentioned it."

"That child ought to keep her mouth shut," he said, half joking.

"You still think you can restore The Oak?"

He rubbed his beard. "Not like it used to be, I don't expect. But it can still be the best place around."

"What about Katherine?"

York stared past Lynette, toward one of the broken windows. "She's doin' well now that Calvin is back."

Lynette exhaled in frustration. "I mean you and her. You're married, for heaven's sake! When are you going to act like it?"

"She took my money," he defended.

"I know that story, but it's crazy. From what I can see, she's spending wisely, taking care of things pretty much as you would if you were making the decisions."

"True, but it's my money."

Lynette smiled. "You have to be in control, don't you?"

York walked to the window, spat out, then turned back to Lynette. "That ain't it," he argued.

"No?" She obviously didn't believe him.

131

He stepped close to her, his heart pounding. "Well, it's part of it. But there's something else, and you know it. I've—" He didn't know if he could admit once more what he wanted to say, if he dared speak it out. Yet he knew he had to do it now, or he may never have the chance again. "I've not moved in with Katherine because I still love you," he declared. "Whether I'm married or not, that's the truth. I'd leave her tomorrow if I thought you might love me, even a little, or that you would someday in the future."

Lynette didn't pull away, so York took her hands and held them to his chest. "I've always loved you," he continued. "That's not a secret."

Lynette stood still for a second, as if stunned, then pulled away and fell back into her chair. "You're Katherine's husband," she stammered. "So it doesn't matter what either of us feels."

"But it does!" he exploded. "I will leave her this instant. Let her have the money. Divorce her—a barrister in Charleston can tell me how. Katherine will probably welcome it!"

Lynette shook her head. "You don't know women too well, do you?"

York raised an eyebrow. "I don't know what you mean."

"Katherine would never give you a divorce," Lynette said.

"You're the one who doesn't know what she's talkin' about."

"I see the way she watches you when you're around. It might not be the kind of love most of us expect between a man and a woman, but she loves you as much as a woman like her can."

York waved her off.

But Lynette continued. "She argued hard when you told her you were coming here with us, didn't she?"

"How do you know that?"

"It's a guess, but I'm right, am I not?"

He shrugged his acceptance of her words and she kept going. "Katherine knows what she's got in you—a handsome, powerful, smart man."

"But I don't love her, I love you."

"I would never marry a man who left his wife, no matter how much I loved him."

"But you left me! What's the difference?"

Now Lynette hung her head. "It was a long time ago, and I had my reasons."

"I know—you loved Wallace."

Her head jerked up. She stared at York for a long time, then bowed again, as if praying. "That's not the only reason."

"What?"

"There's something else . . . something I never told you."

He fell to one knee before her and lifted her chin so he could look into her eyes. "What?"

"I can't tell you," she murmured.

"Why not? What's keeping you from it? I'll be gone in a day. Maybe you'll never see me again. Now is the time for honesty if there ever was a time."

Her shoulders slumped. "I guess you're right. I need to tell the truth."

"Yes."

"Marshall Tessier," she said softly. "He . . . well, he tried to take advantage of me."

York almost fell over, but he knew instantly she had told him the truth. Tessier treated women—black or white—like property, and his immorality knew no bounds.

Pain and anger rose from deep within.

Lynette continued. "Tessier approached me over and over. I kept dodging him, running from him. But I knew I couldn't escape him forever and that if you found out what he was trying to do, you would kill him or he would kill you. Either way, your life would end. If you killed him, they would hang you, no matter how you explained it."

York's mind reeled. "So . . . you didn't leave me . . . run off from the children because you didn't love me or them!"

She smiled sadly. "I was a confused woman. I loved both you and Wallace—hard to say which one I loved more. Wallace took care of me when I was young, starving; then I met you. I didn't love you at first; I admit that—but you were strong, handsome, adoring. How could I not eventually come to love you?"

York got up abruptly and walked toward the window. As he stared outside, thoughts tumbled in confusion. How could this have happened?

Why hadn't he seen it, known it? What would have happened with him and Lynette if he had discovered Tessier's advances? Would he and Tessier have dueled to the death?

He turned back to Lynette. "You should have told me. We could have left The Oak. Started over somewhere else."

Her hands clenched into fists. "Maybe. It's hard to say."

He strode back toward her and squatted down. "Look," he pleaded, "I don't want to hurt Katherine. But we don't love each other. She knows it and so do I. All the secrets between you and me are out now. We can be together. I'll find a way. Katherine will understand."

"No," Lynette said firmly.

York wanted to yell, to force her to listen to him. How could she refuse him now, after she had admitted she loved him?

She touched his chin, then dropped her hand. "I've got one secret left."

"What?"

She took a deep breath, then opened her mouth to speak.

Just then Jackson burst into the room.

Lynette closed her mouth.

York knew the moment had passed . . . for now. Although he desperately wanted to press her, to make her tell him so they could get everything out and plainly spoken, York knew he had to wait. When the right time came, Lynette would reveal her secret. Until then he had to keep steady, be patient. Give her what she needed from him.

Thankfully, with some gold to find, he had something to keep his mind occupied until that moment came.

Chapter Fourteen

Ruby wandered from town to town for weeks in her quest to find Theo. Jacksonboro, Willtown, Branchville, Fort Motte, Orangeburg—she passed through all the towns, one at a time, and visited in the sections where her people had settled. She asked everybody she met if any of them had seen a boy with a big head but no right eye. A lot of people looked at her kind of funny. A number of the men said no, but for a favor or two, they might be willing to help her search. And a few folks, mostly the older women, even seemed to take some pity on her. But nobody said anything that even remotely pointed her on a path to find her son.

As she had done while in Charleston, Ruby stopped at a white family's house and labored awhile every time she ran out of food or needed a place to rest for a couple of days. Sometimes people paid her with a little cash, while others just fed her what they put on the table and said that's all they had. Ruby always took whatever the people gave her and offered no complaint. Times were hard, and everybody knew it.

Knowing that men usually liked what they saw when they looked at her, Ruby kept her head covered and her eyes down most of the time. She stayed away from menfolk whenever she could so as not to attract too much attention. No reason to make the kind of trouble that had happened in Charleston spring up again if she could help it. With the law as lax as it was, a woman on her own needed to do all she could to protect herself.

By the time September reached its end, Ruby had searched out almost every town of any size between The Oak and Columbia. Without really thinking about it, on the last day of that week, she found herself on the main road that led from Charleston to Columbia. As she had done through all her travels, she kept her ears open for horses, wagons, and walkers on the road. Every time somebody approached, she ran into the woods and hid until she could determine whether she thought them safe or not. White folks weren't safe, so she always let them pass unless she needed a job. Black men weren't safe except when they traveled with women and sometimes not even then. When she saw a black woman alone or in a group of other black women, Ruby always jumped out and walked with them awhile, asking about Theo as they traveled.

She was alone as the day neared its close. Her feet ached and her stomach rumbled. She reached a crossroads and stopped for a drink from the canteen she carried on a string over her shoulder. A touch of nostalgia rolled through her as she realized she had walked this road once before, back in February of 1861, when she had fled The Oak in the effort to find her husband, Markus.

For the first time in a long while, she wondered what had happened to him. Should she take a little detour from her search for Theo? See if Markus had made it through the war? If he still lived somewhere around the Robertson Plantation? She recalled the last time she had seen him.

Robertson's place stood southeast of Columbia, not far from a small river called the Richland. She had traveled by night, found the old chimney that stood at the curve in the road that Camellia told her to look for. Passing the chimney, she reached the outskirts of the plantation near the morning of the fourth day after she ran. She knew so because she saw a sign with the plantation name painted in black hanging on a white fence as she walked down the road. The sign turned her to the left, and she followed the road until the sun came up. Then, heart pounding, she crept off the road, lay up for the morning under a thicket of heavy brush, and studied what to do next.

About midday she slipped out of the thicket and headed through the woods in the direction the sign had pointed. She found a creek about an hour after she started and crept up the creek bed until she rounded a corner and saw the plantation several hundred yards away. Tall pines and heavy brush surrounded the cleared cotton fields.

After finding a spot that gave her a good view of the fields and barns that lay about a hundred yards away, Ruby squatted and watched. Fifteen darky houses sat about three hundred yards behind the plantation manse. She spotted Markus about an hour later, his broad body strolling toward the barn. He looked as fine as ever, strong and healthy. He ducked into the barn, then came out later with his arms full of tools he carried into a shed nearby.

Ruby stayed patient as the day moved past. Then, as dusk fell, she saw Markus again, this time by the well. His thick shoulders were straining as he pulled water up in buckets and poured it into a trough. A few minutes later the field hands came from all over the plantation and started washing in the trough.

Suppertime had come. Ruby kept waiting—past supper and into the darkness. Then, leaving her belongings, she eased from the forest and crawled across the field, keeping her eyes on the water trough. A few minutes later she reached the back of a small shed and squatted by the chimney. Markus stood less than thirty yards away, his back to her. When she heard his low voice, she wanted to jump out of the shadows and run to him. But she knew she didn't dare. A little while later the field hands scattered to their quarters.

Ruby kept her eyes on Markus as he took his food into a house about forty feet away. Satisfied now, Ruby eased back to the ground and waited for every- body to fall asleep. The birds stopped chirping; the frogs ceased croaking. Dew settled on the ground and bushes, and a chill fell on Ruby's head. When the moon climbed high, crossed the middle of the sky, and started to drop, Ruby stirred. The time had come.

She rose silently and slipped across the ground to the front stoop of the house Markus had entered. She smiled, feeling blessed. Although she didn't put such store in God, she sure felt that something—or was it someone?—watched her tonight.

She opened the front door without a sound. In the glow of a small lantern sitting on the mantel over the fireplace, she counted six men on pallets in the front room. But as she peered at the faces, she didn't see Markus.

Then she spotted the blanket hanging over a doorway, tiptoed to it, and pulled it back. Markus lay on a pallet on his side, facing her direction. She gasped and almost dropped the lantern. A woman lay beside him, her head sticking out of the blanket that covered them both.

Tears threatened Ruby's eyes. Markus had taken up with a woman! What could she do now? Keep on running? Leave here and go north all alone? But wait! Just because Markus had a woman didn't mean he didn't still love her; that he wouldn't still leave with her. After all, she had taken Obadiah in marriage but left him. How could she leave now, without talking to Markus, offering him the choice?

Ruby put the lantern carefully on the floor and touched Markus. When he woke, Ruby pressed a hand over his mouth to keep him quiet and pointed to the door. His warm brown eyes recognized her and became gentle. He and she eased out of the house and into the woods. By a tree she pulled him down beside her. He embraced her. Stars twinkled. Ruby felt like heaven had come down. She kissed Markus and he responded.

"We been apart a long time," she said softly when the kiss ended.

Markus held her close, rubbing her shoulders and back. "You scared the fool out of me. Thought you was a dream. But I reckon not."

"I'm real enough." She kissed him again, then leaned back into his arms once more. They stayed that way for several minutes, the quiet of the night making it seem like old times back before they were sold. Ruby relaxed, believing Markus would run with her. That they would make it to freedom, and life would turn out wonderful.

But when she told Markus she planned to go north, he turned his eyes toward the ground. She took his chin, pulled it up so she could see his eyes.

"I don't reckon I can go with you," he said. "I done run twice to find you. One more time and they will kill me for sure." He lifted his shirt, and she saw in the moonlight the scars cut deeply into his flesh.

She ran her hands over them. They felt like knotty ropes, all raised on his back. She sighed with understanding. A darky who ran three times almost always got whipped until he died.

Tears welled in her eyes. "What about that woman?" she asked, tilting her head toward the shanty.

Markus shrugged. "I ain't gone lie. She nursed me after the second whippin', kept me alive. I took up with her after that. Figured I wouldn't ever get back to you."

"You love her?"

Markus took Ruby back into his arms. "Not like I love you. But what am I gone do? Robertson wanted me with a woman. I got to do what he says."

"What about Theo?"

"I don't know. I think of him every day. But I got no way to go to him."

Both of them cried, then talked a while longer. Suddenly she knew what she

*had to do—go back to The Oak. Without Markus she couldn't go north—least
not yet. Not without some time to scheme.*

*After she kissed him one last time, she stood and walked off without looking
back. From what she knew, she would never see Markus, her husband, again . . .*

Now, over four years later, she was again only a few miles from where
she had last seen the first man she had ever truly loved. She desperately
wanted to find out if he was still alive. Not for the purpose of leaving
Obadiah and going back to Markus, but . . . well . . . Theo's vision said she
and her man would come to him. And for that to happen Markus had to
come back into her life.

It took Ruby just over an hour to make it to the outskirts of the plantation. By the time she did, the sun had almost completely disappeared.
As she rounded the last corner of the path, she saw instantly, even in the
gathering dusk, that almost everything she remembered had changed.
The plantation house lay in a heap of ashes. Only the chimney remained
standing.

Ruby hurried forward. Her gaze searched the area where the slaves'
houses had stood. Only two of the houses had survived, and the roof over
one of them was burned out. A sliver of smoke curled out the chimney of
one house that still looked livable. Ruby ducked behind a tree, wondering
whether to risk going up to the house. Who knew what waited inside?

The night fell quickly, and the moon poked its head out. After an
hour Ruby eased beyond her tree, crept closer to the house, and crouched
behind a stack of old wood. A few minutes later a heavy, elderly woman
carrying a wood bucket slipped out the door, down the steps to a well about
a hundred yards away, filled her bucket, then returned to the house. Just
before she stepped back onto the porch, Ruby moved out of the shadows.

"Hey," Ruby called.

"Who there?" asked the darky woman, looking Ruby's direction.

Ruby raised both hands. "I mean no harm."

The woman set down her bucket and cupped a hand behind both ears.
"What you say? I don't hear so good."

"My name is Ruby. I am no danger to you," Ruby yelled.

The woman nodded vigorously. "You by yo' lonesome?"

"Yes."

The woman walked closer. "What you want?"

Ruby also took a step forward and spoke loudly. "A long time ago I knew a man who labored here. I came looking for him."

"I been here awhile," said the woman.

"His name was Markus," yelled Ruby. "A broad-shouldered man."

The woman picked up her water bucket. "Come on in, child," she offered.

"You knew Markus?"

The woman paused. "My head gets addled. Ain't sure what I recall and what I don't. You hongry?"

Ruby licked her lips. "I could eat a bite or two."

"It's meager fare, but what's mine is yours."

Ruby followed the woman inside. To her surprise a young man, no more than eighteen or so, was sitting on a wood chair just inside the door. The side of his head was wrapped with a dirty cloth. The house smelled like grease and burned wood and contained just one long, narrow room. A blanket sectioned the room off into two different areas.

"My name is Melva," hollered the woman as she put the bucket in the corner. "This be Walter. He's my son. Took a knock on the head a day or so ago. Waitin' on the knot to go down and the cut to heal."

"I'm Ruby." She eyed Walter, wondering how he got his injuries.

"He's a good boy," said Melva. "Won't hurt you none. Have a sit."

Although not sure she believed what Melva said about Walter, Ruby pushed back her bonnet and sat in one of the two chairs in the room, while Melva dipped out two cups of water and handed her one.

"She say she's lookin' for a man named Markus," Melva told Walter, her tone still loud.

Walter shrugged, his expression sullen.

"We lived here since Walter just a little boy," said Melva. She looked back to her son. "You recall a man named Markus?"

"Maybe."

Melva kicked him in the shin, and he squirmed away from her. "You recall him or not?"

Walter nodded. Melva walked to a shelf and lifted down a skillet. She took three pieces of bread from it and handed one to Ruby, one to Walter, and kept the last one.

"Markus served here till about halfway through the war," Walter replied.

"Where is he now?" asked Ruby, her appetite quelled for a moment.

"He dead," Walter announced.

Ruby's heart dropped. "Dead?"

"Yeah. Took a bullet from a Johnny Reb not too far from here, about a year ago."

Ruby fought to keep the tears from welling up. "You saw this happen?"

"Not directly, but I knowed a man who did. He told me later that Markus took a shot in the chest. They buried him and about ten more up the road toward Camden."

"You his woman?" asked Melva.

The tears broke loose. "A long time ago I was," sobbed Ruby. "Before we got sold off from each other and he came here."

"He had another woman here," Walter said bluntly.

"I know," Ruby fired back.

"Too bad for you he's gone," said Melva.

Ruby wiped her eyes. "What happened to Markus's woman?"

"She took smallpox," Walter explained. "Died a couple years before Markus ever left."

Ruby tried to take it all in. So much had changed. She took a bite of her cornbread and wondered about Theo's vision. He had said she and her man would come back for him. But now at least part of that vision had been proven wrong. What about the other part? Did this mean she would never find Theo either?

"Where you livin' now?" Melva asked loudly.

"I come from The Oak, about seventy, eighty miles from here."

"It come through the fightin'?"

"Damaged some, but not too bad."

"You workin' there?"

"Yeah."

"You come a long way to find a man you ain't seen in such a long time," said Walter.

Ruby took a sip of water. "I'm looking for someone else too."

"Who that be?" asked Melva.

"My son," said Ruby.

"Markus had a boy here with him?" Melva asked.

"Not here," Ruby explained. "But, yes, Markus and I had a son—Theo. He stayed in Virginia when Markus and I got sold, then left there near the war's end. Came south searching for me. A man told him I'd gone to The Oak and Markus here to Robertson's."

Melva placed hands on her heavy hips. "Your boy not find you at The Oak?"

"I don't know if he ever came there."

"But you figure he might have come here lookin' for his pa?" asked Walter.

"Yes."

Melva ate her cornbread for several moments.

"What your boy look like?" asked Walter.

Ruby described Theo for them.

"Ain't seen nobody like that," said Melva.

Walter threw another log in the small fireplace in the center of the room. "Cold for this time of year," he said.

Ruby finished her bread and wondered if she should ask to spend the night. Although Walter and Melva had treated her nicely, she didn't want to push her luck or take advantage of their hospitality.

"I might have seen your boy," said Walter, his tone softer than previously.

Ruby jumped from her seat. "Where?"

"I ain't sure," said Walter, still quiet, almost as if he didn't want his mama to hear. "But I saw a fella, couldn't tell how old. Sittin' in the back of a wagon with a man lots of folks speak about—Marquis by name. He sells elixir, about anythin' else he can put his hand to steal and get a nickel for. The fella I saw didn't have no eye, just like you say with your boy. He's all fixed up, like a soothsayer, tellin' fortunes. Cost you a nickel to get yours spoke."

"When?" repeated Ruby. "How far from here?"

Walter stepped closer to Ruby and almost whispered again. "I reckon I might just hold what else I know."

"What you tellin' her?" yelled Melva.

Walter held up his hand at his mama. "Let's you and me go out on the porch," he said to Ruby.

Ruby glanced at Melva, then back to Walter. When she saw a gleam in his eye, the hair on the back of her neck stood up. Her earlier fears of him returned.

"I ain't gone hurt you," he said softly. "Just want to talk private-like."

Not knowing what else to do, Ruby nodded. Walter turned to Melva. "We goin' out for a spell," he yelled to her.

Melva opened her mouth to speak, then evidently thought better of it.

Ruby followed Walter out to the porch. He waved a hand over the fields. "Gets lonesome out here."

Ruby had no patience for small talk. "I want to know when and where you saw this boy with no eye," she challenged.

Walter looked her over, head to toe, the gleam back in his eyes. "I can tell the way you talk you are a smart woman, educated even. You know what I hanker for."

"You seem a little young for such grown-up notions."

Walter smiled. "War makes a boy grow up fast."

Ruby's heart pounded. Why did men insist on doing such mean things? "If I do what you want, how will I know you'll tell me the truth?"

"Don't reckon you will until you go and see."

"So I'm supposed to just . . . you know . . . let you have your way with me and then take your word for what you say?"

"It beats all, don't it?" chuckled Walter.

Ruby bit her lip, her heart aching. In spite of all the bad men she had met and all the tough spots she had faced, she had always managed to escape the unwanted advances men kept throwing at her. But how could she say no to this if she wanted to find her boy?

"What if I deny you?" she asked Walter.

"Like my mama said, I'm a good boy. I won't force nothin' on you that you ain't willin' to do of your own free accord."

"You think your way makes it my free accord?"

"I just sellin' somethin'," he said. "I give what I know, and you give what you got. That be the way of the world, I reckon."

Ruby hesitated and stared into the sky. Stars twinkled down at her. *How odd,* she thought. *Something so pretty as stars looking down at something as ugly as what Walter suggests.* For the first time in her memory, she said a prayer. *What should I do, Lord?* she silently breathed into the heavens. *How do I make a choice like this?*

Almost instantly her answer came—whether from the Lord or not, she didn't know. Turning to Walter, she raised a hand and caressed his cheek.

His eyes gleamed brighter as he moved to put a hand on her back.

Just before he touched her, she lifted her hand from his cheek and drew it back into a fist. Then she smacked him in the head right on his knot!

He bellowed and grabbed for her, but she dodged him. Scrambling off the porch, she ran into the night. A hundred yards away she turned to see if he trailed her, but he didn't. She slowed her pace and caught her breath. Whether she'd find Theo or not, she didn't know. But she would not sell short her virtue in the effort. Somehow she knew that down that path lay nothing but destruction.

Chapter Fifteen

The next day dawned bright and chilly on The Oak. Trenton Tessier woke early. Having sworn off liquor for the last couple of months, his eyes were clearer than in months and he felt better than he had in a long time. He shaved and dressed in a hurry before making his way downstairs.

His mother and Calvin were sitting at a small table eating biscuits with a touch of grape jam.

"What are you doing up so early?" asked Calvin.

Trenton ignored the question. Instead, he sized up his brother as he had done almost every morning since Calvin had returned from the war. He noted again how mature Calvin had become. Although thinner than ever, he seemed to weigh a lot in terms of wisdom. In many ways it felt like Calvin had become the *older* brother and Trenton the younger . . . at least their mother appeared to have reached that conclusion. She talked with Calvin far more than she did with him. Of course, it might have helped if Trenton had taken a little interest in business matters at The Oak and if he helped out some with the labor. However, except for his almost daily walks to wherever Beth Cain might be on the property and his weekly rides over to Crossville General Store to visit with some men for a little gambling and manly conversation about the state of affairs in their area, he hardly seemed to move. Calvin, of course, labored like a darky, and Katherine loved him for it.

"Want some coffee?" his mother asked Trenton.

Trenton moved to the pot, poured some, and drank it quickly. "The air is cool this morning," he offered.

"Winter is coming," said Katherine.

Trenton almost shivered at the thought of the winter approaching.

With no servants to do his bidding, only simple food to eat, and a scarcity of amusements, he didn't know if he could manage another winter. Which made it all the more vital that he accomplish the mission he had set out for himself today.

He finished his coffee and headed to the back door.

"Where are you headed?" asked Calvin.

Trenton turned back. "What's it to you?"

"We have a lot to do, that's all. I could use your help."

"You and Mother seem to have things under control."

Calvin didn't respond. He simply took a bite from his biscuit.

Trenton left the house and headed across the back field toward the Conwilla River. *How can two brothers turn out so different?* he wondered as he walked. *Calvin so high and mighty, thinking that because he fought in the war, he holds the upper hand. But look what I've done in the past few weeks—completely quit drinking, I talk politely to almost everybody . . . and I've even traveled over to Beaufort to go to church one Sunday. But do I get any credit for any of that? No, none at all. Nobody has even bothered to say anything about any of it.*

Resentful at not receiving any attention for his efforts at character change, Trenton stopped by a shed near the edge of the field. He ducked inside the shed and rummaged for a burlap bag he'd hidden in a toolbox. Pulling a bottle and a simple, heart-shaped gold locket out of the bag, he held the locket in his palm for a moment and studied it. He had filched every dollar he could from his mother over the past two months to pay for the jewelry. It felt cool to his touch and glistened with a burnished glow.

Pleased with his purchase, he slipped the locket into his pocket, clutched the bottle in one hand, and headed to the river. Several minutes later he reached the riverbank and stopped. The water eased by on its way to the Atlantic, a few miles away. A bird chirped and a frog jumped. The sun warmed his head in spite of the cool air. The tranquility of the place soothed Trenton some, steadied his nerves. The lack of liquor made him a little shaky; he wanted a drink more than anything. Whiskey made words come easier for him, and he needed help if he planned to carry out what he had come to the river to do. He looked at his clothes; they were clean and neatly pressed. He had seen to that last night. His eyes searched the riverbank and landed on the sight he had come to enjoy more than anything else.

Beth Cain. She came to the river almost every morning after she fed her father and brother and cleaned up the dishes.

As always, Trenton stayed completely out of sight, never allowing her to know he watched her every move, except for her most private bodily attentions. He loved to see her bend and drink from the river. Loved to see her sit on the bank with her feet dangling in the gentle current. Loved to see her shed her clothes and slip into the water for her bath. With colder weather coming, he knew he would not find her here for several months, so he needed to act now.

Trenton smiled without guilt. A man should admire the kind of beauty the Good Lord had granted to Beth Cain. No sin in that.

When Beth moved to the river, Trenton leaned behind a giant oak and set his bottle on the ground. Long strands of gray moss hid his face as he watched her. She lifted her skirt slightly, kicked off her black boots, and dipped her toes in the stream. The sun's rays glistened on her blond hair. Her chest filled out her plain brown blouse nicely.

Trenton's eyes brightened at her beauty. He knew he could have her. Why not? He had spent hours cultivating her over the last few months— gently approaching her, usually at the end of the day as she finished her labors. Although skittish at first, she had gradually become a little more at ease around him and their talks had moved from brief formalities to what felt to him like genuine conversations between two friends.

At first Trenton had held no grand design to any of his interactions with Beth, except perhaps to jab a little at the high-and-mighty Josh Cain and Hampton York. To make them worry maybe he could worm his way into Beth's heart. Now that seemed pointless, almost childish. He no longer cared what they thought about his conversations with her. After a while the visits with Beth became the only thing he looked forward to, the one bright spot in an otherwise bleak life. She carried herself with such innocence, such openness, such purity. How could he not feel drawn to her? How could he not . . . fall in love with her?

Carefully, so as not to startle her, he picked up his bottle, stepped from behind the tree and called out her name. She glanced up, obviously surprised, and backed up out of the water.

He walked quickly to her before she could dart away. "What are you doing here?" he asked, pretending he didn't know she came here almost every day.

She dropped her eyes in obvious embarrassment. "I-I come here," she stammered, "t-to take some minutes of quiet . . . after we eat."

"It is a lovely place," said Trenton, waving a hand over the bank.

Beth bent to put on her shoes, and he offered her his hand for balance as she stood back up. The touch of her fingers sent a tingle up his arm, and his breath moved faster.

She dropped his hand and smoothed her skirt. "I best get back."

"What's your rush?"

She tucked a strand of hair behind an ear and glanced around nervously.

"It's fine," he replied, "I'm your friend."

"I know, but . . . well . . . a man and a . . . woman ought not be alone like this. You know my pa would not approve."

Trenton chuckled. "So you do admit you are a woman now?"

She blushed and smiled a little. "I turn eighteen come late December."

"That's right, and a woman of your advanced years does not need her pa's approval to spend a moment talking to a beau, does she?"

Beth smiled a bit more. "I guess not, but still . . . Pa doesn't think well of you, Trenton, you know that. If he knew we talked as often as we do, he'd tan my hide, grown woman or no."

"Have I been anything but a gentleman with you?"

"No."

"Have I been anything but a friend?"

"No."

"OK." He grinned and held up his bottle. "I have something for you."

"What is it?"

"Wine."

She tilted her head at him, and he handed her the bottle. "I don't understand," she said, examining the bottle.

"I bet you've never had a drink of wine, have you?"

"My pa doesn't take of the spirits—me neither. And who drinks this early in the day anyway?" She handed back the wine.

He laughed. "I already loosened the cork. Wanted to offer you a drink to celebrate."

"To celebrate what?"

"You'll see."

"But I don't imbibe," she insisted. "I already told you that, more than once."

"But aren't you curious about the taste? Or the way it makes you feel?" He held the bottle to his nose and sniffed it. "Ah . . ."

She dropped her eyes. "Maybe I *am* a little curious."

He took half a step closer. "It's a fine wine. There's not much wine this good around these parts these days. I bought this especially for you."

When she glanced back at the bottle, he could see her interest. She held so much potential. Dress her up in good clothes and shoes, teach her some proper grammar, and she could make any man proud. "I could teach you so much," he said, his voice quieter, his breath a little faster.

She backed away from him. "I need to go."

Realizing he had gone too far, Trenton shoved the cork back in the wine bottle and smiled warmly. "I have one more thing, and it's not something on your taboo list. You can't refuse this."

She stopped, obviously fearful, but also intrigued by his mysterious actions.

He placed the wine bottle on the ground, then reached into his shirt pocket. Covering the locket with his fist so she couldn't see it, he took it out slowly. "Close your eyes."

She looked at his closed fist, and her brow furrowed. "What are you doin'?"

"Just close your eyes."

She hesitated, then obeyed.

Trenton unclenched his fist and touched her on the arm. He studied her as she opened her eyes. When her eyes widened with excitement, he thought he had her.

"For you," he offered. "I bought it in Beaufort." Heart pounding, he extended his hand toward her.

To his surprise she held up a hand, palm out. "I don't understand. Why are you—"

Trenton pushed the locket toward her. "I want you to have it," he insisted.

"But I can't take it," she argued. "It's not right."

"Why not?"

"Well . . . a man gives this kind of thing to . . . to somebody he . . ." She couldn't finish the sentence.

"Somebody he loves," concluded Trenton. "That's right. That's what I'm doing." He tried to keep his voice calm.

Beth looked stricken. "I'm so sorry, but . . . there's been a mistake."

"What kind of mistake? You love me too—you know it. We've spent hours talking. I've been nice to you."

"I'm glad to be your friend, but . . ."

"But what?"

Beth turned to walk away, but he grabbed her arm and held her.

"Let me go!" she ordered.

He ignored her command. "Listen! I know I have little virtue in the eyes of your pa. But you believe men can change, don't you? Isn't that part of your Christian teaching—that the Lord can cause a leopard to change its spots?"

Beth stopped struggling as he talked, so he dropped his grip on her arm and kept going. "I have not taken a drink in weeks," he said, proud of his accomplishment. "I went to church too, all for you. I can change; I know it. Somebody just needs to give me a chance, to believe in me."

"I do believe you can change," Beth murmured. "But it won't matter. I am your friend but not . . . well, I care for you, but not the way you want. I never dreamed you meant your attentions this way."

"You are lying," said Trenton, unable and unwilling to believe what he had just heard. "You knew exactly what I wanted."

"But I didn't," she insisted.

"No one is that naive," he challenged, a little angry now. "Why else would I confer my time upon such as you?"

Her eyes narrowed. "Such as me?"

Realizing with horror what he'd said, Trenton tried to back up from it. "I just mean . . . we come from different classes, that's all."

"Classes mean nothin' now, don't you know that?"

"That is all temporary," he said. "One day we will all know our places again."

Beth shook her head and turned again to go.

"Stay with me," he pleaded. "Take the locket—not to promise me anything but to tell me you believe I can amend my ways. You can help me; I'll do it for you. I can become a better man."

Beth rubbed her eyes, her confusion obvious. "Don't do anythin' for me. Do it for yourself."

"But I need a woman like you," Trenton pleaded again. "Somebody innocent and pure. Someone who can take my vices and patiently love me in spite of them. Somebody who can call out the best in me . . . make me better than I am."

"Only the Lord can do that for a person," she claimed.

Trenton grunted. "The Lord is not as warm in the winter as a lovely woman."

When Beth took a step away again, he knew he had offended her once more. But this time her offense made his anger rise a notch higher. Why did she want to play such games? She liked him—he knew it, and so did she.

He jumped at her and grabbed her again. "You can't leave yet!" he shouted.

"I have to go."

His fingers cut into her flesh. "You will go when I say."

"You're hurtin' me." Tears glimmered in the corners of her eyes, but he ignored them.

"I've been so sweet to you, so gentle, and this is the reward I get!"

"I thought you were my friend," she sobbed.

"I want more than a friend."

"I'm sorry, but it can't be me."

He jerked her closer, wrapped his arms around her back, and pressed his body against hers. She fought him, but he pinned her arms against her body.

"You're just like Camellia," he seethed, his anger now full and loose. "Nothing but a tease! But I won't have it, won't put up with it. I won't let your hatred keep me down!"

"I don't hate you," she said, her breath ragged.

He pressed his lips close to her neck. "I'll teach you to love me!" he snarled. "I need you!"

She screamed into the morning air as his lips touched her skin.

Her smell drove him wild. He kissed her neck, and one hand moved up her back toward her hair. She wrenched away, but he held her by the neck of her dress so she couldn't move. He pushed his body harder against hers.

She screamed again and tried to pull herself away from him.

When the fabric of her dress tore, he shifted his grip to her neck.

Smack! Something hit him hard in the back of the head. Pain throbbed behind his ears. For an instant he kept his grip on Beth.

Then another blow struck. He felt something wet and warm on the back of his neck. Blood was rushing from a wound in his skull! He let Beth loose, pivoted, and saw Calvin standing there, a dead tree limb in his hand. Beth ran away, her dress torn.

"Leave me alone!" shouted Trenton.

"You're a disgrace!" Calvin shouted back.

"This isn't your business!"

"Everything that happens on The Oak is my business!"

Trenton reached for the pistol in his waistband, pulled it, and pointed it at his brother. "I said leave me alone."

"You would actually shoot your brother?"

"I will protect what is mine." Trenton's breath came in gasps. The wound on his head continued to bleed.

"You saying Beth belongs to you?" Calvin demanded.

"If everybody would stop telling her of my evil ways . . ."

"From what I saw, she wanted nothing to do with you."

Trenton weighed his next move. Should he shoot Calvin? Or walk away? But if he shot Calvin, he might end up in jail, maybe at the end of a noose. Who knew what would happen with the Yankees in charge?

Trenton's hand trembled. He detested Calvin—resented his calm demeanor, the way their mother doted on him, the stature he seemed to have gained from what happened in the war. But could he shoot his brother in cold blood? Had he sunk so low?

Trenton lowered his pistol and sighed heavily. "I wish it had not come to this."

Calvin fixed his eyes on Trenton. "You are not an easy brother to understand."

Trenton tucked his pistol away, stepped back, and pressed a hand against his head wound. "I'm not sure it matters anymore whether you understand me or not."

Calvin handed him a handkerchief. "You've done bad things, Trenton. You have to admit that."

"I'm sure we all have."

"True, but some bad things are worse than others."

"You really believe that?" Trenton pressed the handkerchief to his wound.

"I do, yes," said Calvin. "What you were attempting to do with Beth . . . what kind of man does that sort of thing?"

Trenton picked up the wine bottle, popped the cork out, and took a long drink. "I love her."

Calvin lifted an eyebrow. "So you force your favors on her? That's how you demonstrate your love?"

"I tried to give her this." He showed Calvin the locket.

"She does not want it."

"So I gather." Trenton removed the handkerchief and studied it. He noted that the flow of blood had slowed some.

Calvin stepped closer to examine the wound. "Not too deep. I suppose you will live."

"Is that a disappointment to you, Brother?"

Calvin didn't reply. He merely stared at Trenton, then shook his head and retreated toward the house.

For a long while Trenton stayed by the river and tried to figure what to do next. Keep striving to make Beth love him? Leave The Oak and never come back? Shoot Calvin?

He drank several more times from his wine bottle before the answer came to him. When it did, it made all the sense in the world. Since everybody thought so poorly of him, maybe he should go ahead and prove them right. He had tried to live virtuously recently, but what had that gotten him? Beth had led him on, made him believe she cared for him, then dropped him the first chance she got. If Christian conduct brought nothing of value to a man, why even bother to try?

Trenton finished his wine and thought of the men who gathered almost every night at the Crossville General Store. Those men didn't bother too much with the notion of living virtuously. They drank, gambled, chased women when and if they wanted. They even took the law into their own hands when needed. Like when the darkies got too uppity or a white man seemed too friendly to the Yankees.

Men like those would understand him, Trenton decided. Maybe he needed to spend more time with them. If folks like Beth Cain didn't appreciate his capabilities, perhaps men like that would.

Chapter Sixteen

Hampton York slowly made his way across the two hundred miles that separated Richmond from the area south of Chambersburg, Pennsylvania. He saw the signs of the war's destruction everywhere he rode—burned-out houses and barns, whole sections of forest chopped down for firewood or blown to bits by cannon fire, people with vacant looks in their eyes, stray animals of all kinds. With the first winter since the war's end coming on, he knew most people lived in fear. Fear of the cold days and nights. Fear that they would go hungry. Fear that somebody would come and steal from them the meager harvest they had managed to gather and store from their summer crops.

The lonely ride gave York a lot of time to think. His mind skipped from the treasure he hoped to find to Lynette and Jackson, to Katherine and The Oak, and back around again. What would he do if he did find a substantial sum of money? Would he go back to Katherine and demand that she grant him a willing divorce? Although few people did such a thing, he knew a man with money could make almost anything happen. But what about Lynette if he did that? Would she marry him if he divorced Katherine? Probably not. She held fast to her ways these days—no two ways about that. And what about The Oak? A divorce from Katherine guaranteed the end to his dream to own that place.

Unable to decide what he most wanted to do, York thought about Lynette and worried about her more than anything else. With no money at hand, she would find it almost impossible to rebuild her house, much less her hotel. How would she pay her taxes, much less find enough money to do anything else? He had already heard of a lot of people losing their property for the simple reason they had no dollars to pay the government the taxes they owed.

Frustrated at the notion such a thing could happen to Lynette, York spurred his horse forward. Money would solve a lot of problems, so the best thing he could do was try to find some as fast as he could.

Wanting to avoid Yankee soldiers and bands of roving hooligans, York stayed off the main roads as much as possible and approached the farms he often encountered only when he needed to buy some food. Using what little money he had managed to squirrel aside from what Katherine gave him for repair provisions, he paid for a meal here and there—a sack of biscuits, a jar of jam, a slice of cured meat—when he didn't find any game to shoot. Eager to get their hands on cash dollars, most people sold him whatever they could spare.

Every now and again, as he rested by his fire at the end of the day, York reread the notes he had jotted from the war journal and hoped to find some new clue to the location of the treasure. But nothing fresh came from his readings. His only hope lay in searching the area a few miles south of Chambersburg and seeing what it revealed.

About halfway through October, York bypassed the town of Mercersburg, about seventeen miles south of Chambersburg. His plan was to simply ride the main road south to north into Chambersburg to see if any spot stood out as a likely place for somebody to hide a wagon. The way he figured it, if a band of Yankee cavalry had attacked Confederates guarding a wagon full of valuables, the Confederate horsemen would have stopped to fight the Yankees while the men in the wagon fled the road and drove as far as they could into the countryside. Once the terrain became too rough or too thick with trees for the wagon to pass, the guards would surely have gotten out, unloaded the valuables, and buried them somewhere.

Since the journal hadn't mentioned the exact distance south of Chambersburg where the attack occurred, York decided to start his search in earnest about ten miles out. From there he planned to go straight to Chambersburg, inspecting each side road wide enough to let a wagon pass.

Figuring the distance as best he could, he reached the spot where he wanted to start his search. It was about midday of the day he bypassed Mercersburg. To his regret the next ten miles didn't reveal much, except that he had a lot of searching to do. Slowly making his way up the main road, it took him two days to reach the outskirts of Chambersburg. As he had expected, numbers of side roads, ruts, and overgrown trails led off the main thoroughfare. A Confederate wagon driver could have chosen any one of them as an escape from a Yankee patrol.

Marking each of the small trails on paper he took from his saddlebags, York figured he had to give them all some attention in the days to come. If any treasure waited for him, it almost surely lay somewhere down one of the dirt paths running off the main road.

As he neared Chambersburg in the late afternoon of his second day of searching, he wondered whether he should enter the town or not. With people still mighty suspicious, he knew it was a risk, even if only a small one, that somebody would take offense at his presence and cause trouble. Yet, given his focus the last few days, he had stayed too busy to stop anywhere and buy provisions, so his bags were pretty empty of food. And, after sleeping outside for days on end, the notion of a night inside from the fall chill sure sounded enticing.

Bundling up inside his thin black coat, York decided to chance it and rode into Chambersburg just as the sun began to fall. The trees outside the small town already wore their fall colors of gold, red, and orange leaves. The beauty stood in sharp contrast to what he saw as he dismounted on the main street in front of one of the few buildings that looked open.

Rubble and ash covered the ground on almost all sides. Most of the buildings lay in total ruin. Several stray dogs roamed the street. A few people walked by York but didn't speak. A little spooked but also hungry and tired, he tied up his horse, tugged a plug of tobacco from his pocket, and stared at the devastated town.

Although he hadn't remembered it until he rode into town, York recalled that sometime in July, 1864, the Rebel General John McCausland had ordered his men to put the torch to Chambersburg in retaliation for the Yankees' destruction of the Virginia Military Institute. As the only Northern town burned by the Rebels, Chambersburg now faced the task of rebuilding almost everything.

People here probably don't like Johnny Rebs too much, he figured, *so I best buy food and get out of here as fast as I can.*

York stuck his tobacco in his jaw and noted the sign above the building before him: GENERAL GOODS AND SUNDRIES.

His eyes sharp and nerves on edge, York strode, straight and tall, into the building. A man wearing a round, brown hat stood behind a counter talking to a second man, this one much thinner and bald. The thin man wore a long, black coat like a preacher or an undertaker, a white shirt with a soiled collar, and black boots with pointy toes. He looked maybe sixty years old or close to it.

"Evenin'." York nodded.

The men eyed him in an unfriendly manner.

York glanced around. Several bolts of cloth lay on a shelf to his left. An ax, a few hoes, and several shovels leaned in the corner to his right. On a wide bar straight ahead was a barrel of whiskey and a basket of red apples.

"I need some hardtack," York requested. "A little coffee, and maybe a few of these apples."

"You doin' some travelin'?" asked the man in the brown hat as he reached for the apples.

"Yep." York wanted to keep the information exchange as limited as possible. No reason to tell them his origins or his sympathies in the war.

"Where you from?" asked the thin man.

The clerk held up four apples and York nodded. Then he answered the thin man. "Richmond."

"What you doin' all the way over here?" asked the thin man.

York didn't know how to answer without raising more questions, so he said nothing. The Chambersburg men exchanged glances, then the thin and bald one eased his way out of the building.

York slowly chewed his tobacco but knew he needed to move quickly. Something was up. "You got that hardtack?"

The clerk stepped to his right, squatted, and pulled a burlap bag from behind the counter. "You got cash?"

"Nothin' else."

The clerk unwrapped a piece of hardtack, held it up for York's inspection, wrapped it back up when York nodded his OK, and handed it to York. He turned for the coffee next, put some in a bag, and gave that to York too.

As York took money from his pocket and started to hand it to the man, he heard footsteps behind him. When he twisted around, York saw two Yankee soldiers—one a lieutenant, the other a private. They thumped into the room, their hats sitting at jaunty angles. The thin, bald man in the long coat followed them.

"He's the one," said the bald man.

The Yankees studied York for several seconds. "You from Richmond?" asked the lieutenant.

York kept his voice steady. "Yep. I rode in a little while ago. Just want a few provisions, then I'll be on my way."

"You a Johnny Reb?"

"Not anymore."

"But you admit you were at one time?"

Although now regretting his decision to come into Chambersburg, York managed to keep calm. "Yep. I'm Captain Hampton York, and I fought like most all of us did. But that's over now, and I'm a peaceful man."

"What you doin' in these parts?"

"I lost a friend near here," York said, telling a truth. "Wanted to go back to where I buried him, pay my respects."

"You fought around here?"

"Yep, early in the war when Jeb Stuart rode through. We didn't burn the place though. That happened long after I left."

"Johnny Rebs burned my town," hissed the bald man. "And you admit you were a Johnny Reb. I suppose that makes you as guilty as any of them that actually set the fires."

York fixed his stare on the skinny man. He wanted to tell him to shut up. Instead, he faced the lieutenant again. "Look, I ain't lookin' for no trouble. Just want to do my business and be on my way."

The soldiers eyed each other, then York again. "You got your oath of allegiance document?" asked the lieutenant.

York stayed steady. "On my horse outside. In my saddlebags."

The lieutenant grinned.

"I think I'll check those bags," said the bald man.

"Good idea, Jukes," said the lieutenant.

Jukes scurried out.

York fixed his gaze on the lieutenant, a man not more than thirty or so. His blond hair was long, but it looked clean. The Yankee's eyes were clear; he didn't look away when York stared at him. The man didn't seem like a bad sort, if York was any judge of character.

"You been here long?" York asked the lieutenant.

"About a year."

"You here when the town got burned?"

The lieutenant shook his head.

York relaxed a little. At least the lieutenant wasn't a native.

Jukes bounced back into the room, York's saddlebags in hand.

"You find the paper, Able?" asked the lieutenant.

"Nope," said Jukes with a big grin.

York's heart raced. He knew he had put his paper there. No former Confederate soldier would dare travel without proper documents. Everybody knew the Yankees would throw a man without papers in jail faster than you could flip a winning hand in a card game.

The lieutenant raised an eyebrow as he faced York. "You sure your paper was there?"

York glanced at Jukes and noted the satisfaction on his face. "It was there. Unless somebody took it."

The lieutenant also looked at Jukes. "You swear he's got no papers in his bag?"

"Search for yourself." Jukes handed the bag to the lieutenant.

It was obvious Jukes had taken his document, but why? York wondered. He thought of the pistol in his waistband in the small of his back but hoped he wouldn't have to use it. "Search him," he told the lieutenant, pointing to Jukes. "He took my papers. I'm sure of it."

The lieutenant took off his hat and scratched his head. "Can't do it. He's the mayor here."

York chewed his lip and wondered whether it was time to fight.

Instead, he tried once more. "Look, just give me my bag and I'll leave. You'll never see me again. That's all I ask. I aim to cause nobody any heartache."

The lieutenant put his hat back on. "I tell you what. You come with me overnight, and I'll send a telegram to Richmond, see if they got a record of your oath there. If so, I'll let you go in the mornin'."

"I swore my oath in Beaufort, South Carolina," said York.

"I thought you said you came from Richmond." The lieutenant sounded a little confused and maybe a touch irritated.

"I did, but I hail originally from South Carolina."

Jukes smirked. "He lied to you."

"South Carolina boys are the worst of the whole Rebel lot," said the clerk behind the counter. "Started the whole war."

York shook his head. "I didn't lie. I did come here from Richmond. I got a friend there, and she owns a hotel. I got her safe in her house, then come on this way."

The lieutenant sighed. Obviously he was stuck in the middle of something he didn't particularly want to handle. "I need you to come with me," he told York, "until I can clear this up."

York weighed the situation. He decided he couldn't just let the Yankee take him. For all he knew, Jukes and some of his friends might show up in the middle of the night, overpower the Yankee guards, and haul him into the woods and shoot him. "Just let me go," he pleaded one last time.

"No can do," said the lieutenant.

York jumped before anybody could stop him, his head a battering ram into the stomach of the Yankee lieutenant. As his head slammed into the Yankee's ribs, York grabbed for his pistol. He smacked the man with it as he tried to fight him off. The lieutenant fell, his head bleeding.

Spinning, York rushed the second soldier and knocked him down before the private could react. Jukes dove behind the store counter, his hands over his head. York kicked at him but missed. As York ran for the door, the Yankee lieutenant reached for his ankle and grabbed hold, his fingers burying into York's flesh. York kneed him in the face and rushed to the door once more. The second soldier pulled a pistol and fired a shot.

Pain sizzled in the back of York's right thigh, but he didn't fall.

Almost to the door, York ducked to avoid a second shot as it rang out. This time it missed.

York pushed open the door, but a hand grabbed his neck from the back and spun him around. The blocky store clerk held a double-barreled shotgun while the lieutenant clamped both hands around York's throat. York fought the soldier's fingers.

Then the clerk drove the butt of the shotgun into York's face. Blood spurted from his nose. His vision blurred.

And he lost all consciousness.

Chapter Seventeen

For almost a month after leaving the Robertson Plantation, Ruby searched for Theo. To the best of her calculations, she figured Walter had probably seen him at a darky shantytown, a likely place for the Marquis fellow to visit as he tried to sell his elixir and get people to pay Theo to tell their fortune. If so, she needed to find the nearest such town and ask some questions.

With no money to buy food, she did the best she could with what she found as she traveled—a piece of bread an old woman gave her, a handful of pecans she gathered, four apples she earned by doing a white woman's wash for half a day. Gradually, Ruby's weight had wasted away to almost nothing, and her cheekbones nearly poked through the skin. Blisters covered her heels where she had walked without rest when the horse had grown too tired, and her lips were chapped from the sun and wind that blew in her face every day. For the most part, though, she didn't care or notice the hardships—she had her mind on one thing—finding Theo.

After badgering practically every darky she met in hopes of getting information, Ruby finally found a makeshift Negro village about thirty miles away from the plantation. She walked into it as inconspicuously as possible, her bonnet tied tight, her shawl gathered about her neck. At least three hundred blacks lived there, she estimated—all of them in lean-tos patched together from bits of wood taken from heaven only knew where. Smoke billowed up from scattered fires, stray dogs prowled here and there, and children in all manner of dress peeked out from their shacks as she slipped into the place. The whole sight made her sad—her people with no real shelter, no way to grow crops, and no medical care as winter approached. What kind of world did she live in where people got their freedom but no aid to survive? Where they could go where they wanted but found no house when they got there? Where they could labor for a wage but could find nobody with enough cash to pay them much of anything?

Disturbed but unable to solve any of the problems her questions raised, Ruby brushed off her sorrow. She had to find Theo; nothing could interfere with that.

To her pleasure she found a chubby black woman with six children who told her that a man named Marquis had indeed passed that way a couple of weeks earlier. And yes, he had a soothsayer with him, but nobody could say exactly how old. The soothsayer looked out from only one eye, and his head seemed right large for such a small body.

"They got a woman too," said the chubby lady as she smacked a kid's bottom with an open hand. "She sells her wares in the back of one of the wagons, if you knows what I mean."

"He got anybody else?" Ruby asked the chubby lady.

"A skinny man with a mouthful of bad teeth. Somebody say his name be Rufe."

Ruby thanked her and moved on to talk to several other ladies. A couple of them had actually seen the soothsayer. One said, "Yes, he looked right young in spite of his gray hair."

Ruby's heart soared. "Any idea where Marquis was headed next?" she asked each of them.

"Not for certain," each one replied. "But they's a big town of black folks over near Orangeburg. Wouldn't be no surprise if Marquis headed there. It be further south, so warmer for the winter."

Spurred by the excitement of finally hearing word of her boy, Ruby left the camp and hustled toward Orangeburg, barely stopping to eat or sleep as she traveled. If Marquis had taken Theo to a spot outside of Orangeburg, she wanted to reach them before Marquis wore out his welcome there and took off for somewhere else.

Almost panicky to find Theo, she threw caution to the wind. She stopped almost every black person she met—man or woman—and asked them if they had seen or heard of a man named Marquis or of a fortune-teller with no right eye. To her dismay nobody had. Yet she kept asking, often telling the people that the fortuneteller was her son, and she hadn't seen him in seven years. Many of them shook their heads and spoke their sympathy for her, but none seemed to know anything.

Finally she reached the edge of Orangeburg. Her body was so weary, she could barely move. A light rain fell on her head as the day headed into evening. Too tired to go on, Ruby paused at a turn in the road and looked around for a place to bed down for the night. An old man, wearing faded overalls with only one strap around his shoulder and no shoes, led a mule around the bend in the road. The man's face was as long as his mule's.

Ruby waved the man to a halt and asked if he had heard of or seen a man named Marquis.

The old man wiped his mule-face with a blue cloth and pointed behind him. "Other side of town. A few miles south of here."

Ruby's heart leaped. "He got a boy with him? A fortuneteller missing an eye?"

The rain fell faster.

The man nodded. "I paid a nickel. He tell me to watch out for bad sickness this winter. Say it can cause ill fortune for me and mine."

Ruby couldn't contain her excitement. "I'm the boy's mama!" she declared. "Did he seem healthy?"

"Reasonable so, I reckon. He look old for his age though. And he seem all swimmy headed too, like he been drinkin' or somethin'."

Ruby wondered why Theo would be drinking, then decided it didn't matter. Her boy was alive! She could go find him.

"You figure to go after your boy, don't you?" the man asked.

"Soon as I can."

"That might be a danger to you."

"I don't care."

The man looked up, and the rain slicked down his long face. "Weather too bad for you to go on tonight. They's an old shed not far from here. You ought to bed down there. Go for your boy in the mornin'."

Ruby checked the black sky and realized the old man was right. Although she wanted to go on, it made no sense. Marquis wouldn't travel on a night like this; neither should she.

"Can you show me that shed?" she asked the man.

Leading his mule, the old man started walking. In less than ten minutes, he pointed to a spot off the road.

Seeing a shed's dim outline in the open field, she asked, "Is it safe?"

"Whoever owned this place ain't showed up since the war ended. They's a little straw in the shed. Reckon you be just fine until mornin'."

"You stayed here before, am I right?"

"I travel this road from time to time."

Ruby smiled warmly toward the old gentleman. "Thank you."

"Hope you find that boy of yours," said the man.

"You going on?"

"My place be about two miles down the road. I reckon I can make it. You take care now."

As the man moved on into the wet night, Ruby hurried to the shed, slipped inside, and shut the door. After feeling around a minute in the dark, she found the straw, stretched out on it, and curled up to try to sleep. At first she had no luck—too many things running through her head. But then, although more anxious than ever, her body gave up and, in the dark of the rainy night, she finally dozed off.

Just over four miles from where Ruby lay on the bed of old straw, Marquis sat in the back of his wagon with a thick blanket pulled around his shoulders. Rufe sat beside him, his skin blacker than coal, his teeth a collection of gaps and gums between the few remaining teeth. A lantern hung from the center of the wagon. Marquis smoked a brown cigar. Rain continued to fall. Several cats purred at Marquis's feet. Yellow Boy lay in his lap.

"They be a woman askin' about you," said Rufe, his eyes eager.

"What she askin'?" asked Marquis.

Rufe hesitated until Marquis reached into his pocket for a nickel and handed it to him. A small price to pay for the kind of information that Rufe, a man hired specifically to help protect Marquis from drunks and angry customers, often provided.

"She askin' 'bout our fortune-boy. I hear she sayin' she be his mama."

"Where you hear this?"

166

"Here, there, peoples tell me things . . . you know . . . I got my ways to gather what I needs to hear."

Although almost always on the run because of his tendencies toward thievery, Marquis rubbed his chin. This threat surprised him a little. He leaned sideways and stared out at the smaller wagon next to his—the wagon where Theo lay sleeping.

"Fortune-boy tell me often dat he got a mama," said Marquis. "Say more dan once he wants to find her. Dat why I keep him drunk up on da laudanum. A boy on da opium not one much for runnin' nowhere."

"Maybe this be her."

Marquis pondered what to do. Load up and leave before morning? But he had not been here but a couple of days—not long enough to make hardly any money at all. And he hadn't thieved anything from anybody since he arrived, so he had nobody coming after him. Fact was, he had figured maybe he would spend the winter in this spot. It was a good place—warm enough and friendly too. Better than Charleston, where he knew the law wanted to ask him a few things, and safer than Columbia, where roving bands of blacks and whites made a man fear for his life every time he lay down to take some sleep.

"Where dis woman be?" he finally asked.

Rufe licked his lips, and Marquis gave him another nickel.

"She right out of town . . . not sure exactly where but can't be but a few places she able to find shelter on a night like this."

"You figure we can find her?"

"Theo be right valuable to you, ain't he?"

Marquis puffed his cigar. "He do good, dat's true. Offers somethin' for the womenfolk dat don't take to my elixir. Peoples pay to hear da future deez days, yes dey will."

Rufe grinned. "Reckon it a good thing he only got half of one foot. A body can't move fast like that."

"Dat be true."

"I reckon we don't want his mama comin' to take him away from us, do we?"

Marquis stroked Yellow Boy. "Reckon not."

"What you figure we ought to do?"

Marquis stubbed his cigar out on his boot heel, tossed it out the back of the wagon, and dropped Yellow Boy to the floor. "I figure we best go find our fortuneteller's mama."

"You leave him here by hisself?"

Marquis moved to the back of the wagon and stared out into the rain. "Tell Mabel to keep an eye on him."

Rufe smiled. "Theo ain't goin' nowhere in this rain. Nowhere at all."

Ruby slept with her hands and arms tucked between her knees as the rain fell and the night deepened. Every now and then she shivered and rolled over in the thin straw but didn't awaken. Dark images flickered through her dreams, but she couldn't make out what they were.

In the latest hours of the dark, something splashed in the rain outside the shed. Ruby stirred. When a thump sounded, she sat straight up in the dark. Her nerves instantly on alert, Ruby wondered if the shed contained anything she could use as a weapon—a hoe, a pitchfork, anything she could stab with or use as a club. She scooted up against the wall, then stood, turned, and began to quietly move her hands across the wall, hoping to find the door so she could escape through it and into the night. She thought she heard a creak, then knew for certain she saw a sliver of light slip through a crack in the side of the shed. The light cast just enough of a glow for her to see a thick stick leaning against the wall near her knees. She grabbed the stick as the door shut and the light disappeared.

Breathing hard, she rubbed her hands up and down the stick's smooth sides. It felt like an ax handle but without the ax—thick and smooth and long. She grasped it near the end, as if holding a club, and waited.

The front door of the shed burst open, and a man, lantern in hand, rushed through. The light lit up his face: it was blacker than any face she had ever seen. As the man's eyes landed on her, he screamed at the top of his lungs and jumped her way. Without knowing it, she screamed, too, and lifted her stick over her head.

The man dropped the lantern and grabbed for her waist, but she spun to her left and swung the stick at his head. He dodged and ducked, and she missed him.

Then he reached for her legs. She pounded the ax handle downward and caught him on the back. He groaned and fell backward.

She turned to run, but he kicked out a leg and tripped her. She fell hard, her stick dropping from her grasp. The lantern was straight ahead, on its side, so she grabbed it and swung it around just as her attacker climbed to his knees and stumbled toward her. The lantern caught him across his forearms and shattered, the oil streaming across his arms and face and catching on fire. He shrieked and tried to brush off the oil as she grabbed her ax handle, stood, and ran to and through the door.

Once outside she paused just long enough to see the rain had stopped and the moon had peeked brightly out of the clouds. Ax handle in hand, she sprinted toward a grove of trees a stone's throw to her right. Mud clung to her shoes, and she slipped a couple of times as she hurried away. A minute later she reached the trees and fell to her knees to catch her breath.

Facing the shed, she saw it had started to burn, the flames casting eerie shadows into the black night. She wondered if her attacker had escaped the fire. Even more she wondered who he was. Marquis? She thought not. Although she had glimpsed the man only briefly, it was enough to see that he wore ill-fitting clothes and looked poorly fed. A man like Marquis— and she had known some like him in her day—surely took better care of himself than that.

Her fears still high, Ruby stood with stick in hand and turned to move deeper into the woods.

Then something moved to her left. Heart pounding, she pivoted to face it.

A man stood there, visible in the moonlight. Instantly she knew who he was. A patchy beard covered his cheeks and chin. His eyes glowed yellow, even in the dark. A single feather stuck up from the front of the band of his hat.

"Marquis," she said.

"Dat be me," he replied. "You name of Ruby?"

"Yes."

"I hear tell you lookin' for me."

"That is true."

"Yo' boy Theo speak fine of you."

"I have come to take him home."

"He home with me now. I feed him, keep clothes on his back, pay him a good wage."

"Why don't we ask him who he wants to live with?"

When Marquis chuckled lightly, a shiver ran down Ruby's back. She knew he would never let her take Theo without a fight.

"You a fine-appearin' woman," he said, his tone soft. "I can see that even in the dark. Maybe we make us a deal where all of us come out happy."

Ruby squinted. "What do you mean?"

Marquis grinned and waved a hand at her, head to toe. "You make a fine dollar with a shape as good as that. I protect you, have my own taste every now and again, make others pay for the privilege."

Ruby's stomach rolled as she realized what he meant. "You disgust me."

"You reject my offer?"

"Yes."

He shrugged. "You best go on then; let matters lay as they are."

"I can't do that."

"Too bad for you."

Ruby gripped her stick tighter. Theo waited on the other side of this fight. All she had to do was survive it and go get him.

Marquis stepped a pace closer. Ruby drew back the ax handle. Marquis reached into his waistband and held up a knife with a long, curved blade. Ruby's breathing quickened.

"Come on now," cooed Marquis.

Ruby stayed still. Marquis moved at her quicker than she expected and the knife cut through the air. She jerked back and whipped her stick at him but missed. The knife dodged her neck, but barely.

When Marquis giggled, as if enjoying the sport, Ruby wanted to kill him—for trying to kill her and for holding Theo for so long.

He came at her, and she swung the ax handle again. This time it caught Marquis in the wrist, knocking the knife from his hand. Seeing her advantage, Ruby lifted the stick once more, but Marquis rolled to the ground and went after his knife before she could whack him. A second later he bounced back up, the knife ready once more.

"I tire of this," said Marquis, his breath short.

"Then give me Theo and let me go."

"I think not. I have another notion."

She lifted her weapon, ready for his attack. But, to her surprise, he didn't rush her at all. Instead, he turned the knife blade toward his face, grabbed the blade in his fingers, flicked his wrist, and threw it at her. Although stunned at the swiftness of the act, she threw herself to the right, hoping to dodge the blade.

The steel caught her in the left side of her rib cage and she fell to the ground faceup, the knife handle sticking from her side. She touched the knife, felt the warmth of her blood on it. Breathing hurt like fire burning in her chest.

Marquis moved to her and peered down into her face. "You a worthy woman. Too bad for you to cross my path."

Ruby opened her mouth to speak but managed only a whisper. "Theo . . ."

"Your boy be fine," said Marquis. "He valuable to me. I care for him good."

Ruby raised a hand. She wanted to grab Marquis by the throat and strangle him for what he had done to her boy, what he had done to her to keep her from going to him. "Theo . . ."

Marquis laughed gleefully. "I'll tell him I saw you," he offered. "Saw you in a saloon sellin' your body to whatever man brought a quarter to pay you for the favor."

Ruby tried to raise herself but couldn't manage it. When Marquis reached for his knife still sticking from her side, she didn't have enough strength to push his hand away. Marquis grasped the knife handle and twisted it before pulling it from her body. The pain made her wail. Marquis wiped the knife on the leg of his pants, then slipped it back into his belt.

Ruby moaned and pressed her hands over her wound. Blood poured onto the forest floor. Her fingers felt sticky and warm.

Just then something moved behind Marquis and he turned.

A man emerged from the woods.

"Rufe," Marquis called.

Rufe walked quickly to Ruby and leaned over. Ruby saw that burns had swelled up on one side of his face. He kicked Ruby in the ribs where the knife had been, then stepped away.

Marquis spoke to Rufe. "She be dead before the day breaks."

"No heartbreak to me."

"We move on with a hurry," said Marquis. "Lest somebody find her body and recall she been lookin' for me."

Ruby closed her eyes, the pain unbearable. From somewhere off in the distance, she felt somebody kick her one more time.

As footsteps moved away, she became numb. She heard nothing, felt nothing, saw nothing.

All went black.

Chapter Eighteen

The month of October moved slowly off the calendar for Katherine on The Oak. With the colder weather she was outside less and found she missed the hard labor she had taken on with such reluctance in the spring. *Odd,* she thought more than once as she busied herself about her house, *how a person's worst fears can become something they actually appreciate once they experience it.* All those years spent in the parlor doing nothing while the servants took care of all the chores, inside and out . . . and now she yearned for the chance to go to the fields and lay her hand to some task. In fact, she found her mood getting darker each day because she couldn't.

York's absence only added to her melancholy. Although the two of them had kept their distance, even when he was there, she still thought of him as her husband and figured eventually they would end up in a normal marriage arrangement. When he had told her of his plans to escort Lynette and Jackson back to Richmond, she had argued quite vehemently against the idea.

But to no avail. "When you start actin' like a wife, I will start bein' a husband," he had told her.

"But I am your wife!" she protested.

"A woman don't make the decisions for a household. That's a man's business, and you know it."

She shook her head and he walked out.

Now, as October drew to a close, she sat in the parlor in the manse with a pair of pants that needed mending in her lap. As the fire burned low, she wondered if she would ever see York again. Even though bad weather might have slowed him some, enough time had passed for him to have reached Richmond, gotten Lynette and Jackson in place, and come back home. So what had happened to him? Did he ever plan to return? Or had Lynette talked him into staying? Were they even now happily spending their days together—and their nights?

Another notion occurred to Katherine. Could something bad have happened to York? Had he finished his mission to Richmond and headed back, only to run into some kind of trouble?

She glanced over at Calvin sitting beside her, a book in his hand. In spite of her misgivings about York, a sense of gratitude washed over her. No matter what other unfortunate event rolled her way, she still had her boy home and alive from the war. Although she didn't put much stock in matters of Providence, she saw this as a true miracle—perhaps not one caused by the Lord, if a Lord even existed, but a miracle nonetheless. That notion calmed her a lot—something or someone had protected her younger son through the war.

"What are you reading?" she asked Calvin.

He held up a thick black book. "Bible."

Katherine's eyebrows arched. She had not seen him doing this previously. "I didn't know you had become religious."

"The war changes a man," he explained. "I . . . find . . . comfort in the words. They settle my spirit."

"Where did you come by it?"

"Beth gave it to me."

"Beth?"

He dropped his eyes. "We . . . talk from time to time."

"What about your brother?" she asked.

Calvin stared back at her. "I don't know what you mean."

"Trenton has shown interest in Beth Cain, you know that. Is it wise for you to spend time with her against his wishes?"

"I can assure you Beth has no interest in Trenton."

"You sound quite confident of that."

"I am."

"What makes you so sure?"

Calvin placed the Bible in his lap and shook his head. "I prefer not to talk about it."

Katherine stood and tossed another log onto the fire, then faced

Calvin again. Something had happened between Trenton and Calvin; she felt certain of it. Trenton stayed gone almost every night now and, from what she could see, he and Calvin barely spoke to each other anymore. At first she had passed it off as the result of a jealousy between them, mostly from Trenton's side of things. But in the last month or so, matters had gotten even worse.

"Have you and your brother had words?" she asked.

"We are different men, Trenton and me."

"Brothers always fight some; it's natural for that to happen."

"It's worse than that, I fear," Calvin said sadly. "He . . . I don't know . . . I think he hates me, wishes I hadn't come home."

Katherine stiffened as she recognized the truth in Calvin's words. "Do you know where he goes each night?"

Calvin stood and walked to the window. "I think he's with the raiders."

"What?"

He faced Katherine once more. "You've heard the news. The violence seems to worsen each week."

"I hear the Negroes have attacked some homes close to us," Katherine admitted. "People everywhere are fearful of them."

"And they are afraid of the raiders. You know that's why Obadiah returned here a couple of weeks ago."

Katherine folded her arms. "The raiders burned down his house."

"He's afraid of living by himself now." Calvin shook his head. "A man of his strength and courage. So who is terrorizing whom?"

"Will he be safe here?"

"So long as he labors hard and keeps his head down. Doesn't get the raiders' attention."

"He is working with Mr. Cain's family?"

"Yes." Calvin sighed. "The Negroes thought the Yankees would give them everything they wanted. Sherman promised each of them forty acres of land and a goat. But most have received little or nothing. Now they've found they have to labor like everyone else. But most whites pay them as little as they can, and the blacks are starving, without shelter, clothing."

She frowned. "So they steal what they want."

"What they need to stay alive," Calvin emphasized.

Katherine paced to him and put a hand on his back. "The darkies outnumber us greatly."

"By the thousands."

"Should we be afraid?"

He put an arm around her. "We should pay a decent wage to those who work for us. And be careful."

"So Trenton rides with the raiders?" she asked.

"Yes. In fact, I hear he is the leader of them."

She frowned. "Do you think he's doing it to keep us safe?"

"I'm certain he sees it that way. Grown men with their faces covered with hideous masks and skulls on their saddle horns, prowling the countryside at night. They dispense vigilante justice—burning homes, scaring women and children—to any black they decide has gotten above himself. That's keeping us safe?"

Katherine faced him but ignored the question. "I hear some of the raiders pretend to be the ghosts of Confederate dead."

Calvin ruefully shook his head. "Some wear sheets. They ride up to a Negro's house and demand water. When the darky brings the water bucket, the raider gulps it down and demands more."

Katherine's brow furrowed, and Calvin explained the trick. "The raider carries a large canteen under his robe; a tube runs from it to his mouth. When he drinks—or pretends to drink—the water runs down from the bucket into his canteen. After he drains two or three buckets from the darky, the raider declares that he's not had water since his death on the battlefield at Atlanta. Then he gallops into the night, leaving the impression that ghosts of Confederate dead are riding the countryside."

"He plays to the superstition of the blacks."

"Yes, any tactic to scare, intimidate, control."

Katherine sat back down, her motherly instincts torn between her two sons. "You said yourself the blacks outnumber us," she argued. "And you know the Yankees let them do what they want. How else will we protect ourselves? Our property?"

Calvin shook his head. "I don't know the answer to that, but what Trenton does will lead to bigger troubles. It can't be the way to handle things."

"Do you have a better solution?" she asked, chin held high.

Calvin moved back to his chair. "Treat people fairly. That may be the only defense we have."

"You learn that from the Bible?" She pointed to the book he held again in his lap.

"Maybe," he said. "From Beth too."

Katherine's suspicions rose once more. "Something happened between you and Trenton. Don't deny it. Did you and your brother come to conflict over Beth Cain?"

Calvin brushed back his hair. "I caught him."

"Caught him what?"

Calvin told her how he had caught Trenton trying to force his way on Beth, how he had stopped it before it got any worse.

Katherine held her breath as she listened and knew that nothing more terrible could have possibly occurred. Two brothers fighting over the same girl always caused great anguish, and she had no doubt Calvin and Trenton would prove to be no exception.

"You need to talk to him," Calvin said when he finished his story. "Tell him to leave Beth alone, me as well."

"You no longer defer to your brother?"

"I am long since past that, Mother."

"Do you have designs on Beth Cain for yourself?"

Calvin focused on the fireplace. "I have not come to a conclusion about that."

Katherine wasn't sure whether to believe him. From what she could see in his eyes, he had reached a lot of conclusions he didn't perhaps want to talk about yet, but which were nonetheless quite true. Yet, how could she blame him? Calvin needed a wife, and Beth Cain would prove a good one. The old days of searching for a mate from within one's own social circle no longer held; nobody had a social circle anymore. She thought of her two daughters in Charleston—both of them scratching for a living as best they could, all the old customs and finery long since gone.

Katherine focused on Calvin again. If it came down to a choice between her two sons, what would she do? She recognized Trenton's meanness, but he was still her elder son. How could she desert him when he needed her so badly? But she knew in her heart that virtue lived within Calvin—an honesty his older brother had long since lost, if he ever had it at all.

Which of the two sons would survive in the world where they now lived? Which of the two did she want to survive?

"Read it to me," she said, pointing to the Bible.

Calvin appeared surprised. "Are you sure?"

"You think I am not a woman of the Word?"

He hesitated. "Not to this point."

"You say it comforts you?"

"Yes."

"Then perhaps it will comfort me also," she said in a determined tone.

"OK."

So Calvin started to read, and Katherine listened. Although the words meant little to her, the sound of Calvin's voice slowed the thumping of her heart and somehow, for the moment at least, brought to her a slight sense of peace.

Sitting in his house with Beth, Butler, and Camellia, Josh Cain drank down the last of his coffee and searched the faces of everybody at the kitchen table. Although tired from riding from Beaufort that afternoon, he needed to get some things straight. He set down his coffee cup and took a paper from his pocket.

"I got this in Beaufort this morning," he said, holding up the paper. "It's a telegram from Richmond, a response to one I sent a few days ago. Lynette sent it."

"She say anything about Pa?" asked Camellia.

Josh nodded. "She said York left there near the end of September, headed back here."

"Then he should have made it home by now," said Butler.

"Exactly," said Josh. "I need to go find him. Something has kept him from returning."

"That's got to be true," said Beth. "Captain York would never desert The Oak without tellin' us he wasn't returnin'."

Josh smiled at his daughter, such a woman now.

"But what could have gone wrong?" asked Butler.

"Lots of trouble out there," said Josh.

"And Pa knows how to find it," said Camellia.

Josh folded the telegram and put it back in his pocket. "We've repaired the houses, laid aside enough food for the winter, and Camellia is strong, well again. I see no reason I shouldn't leave day after tomorrow."

"Can you take a train?" asked Camellia. "Save a lot of time."

"We have no money for that," Josh replied.

"Katherine might pay for it if you asked," said Camellia.

Josh shook his head. "I can't take her money. I'll ride hard. Take my horse and Butler's. Cut the time in half."

Everybody nodded solemnly. Josh eyed Butler. "I need you to take care of everything," he told him. "Stay close to Beth and Miss Camellia. This place still has its dangers: bands of roving blacks, thieving and fighting, white raiders attacking them when they get the chance."

"The Yankees are in charge, but they're not doing much to stop the violence," said Camellia.

Josh looked straight at Beth. "I need you to stay away from both Trenton and Calvin."

Camellia reached for Beth's hand, and Beth dropped her eyes. "Master Trenton made advances," she said softly. "I tried to be nice to him . . . but he wanted more."

"I know," said Josh. "That's why you have to be careful."

"I have not talked to him any lately," Beth continued. "Don't want to either."

"I'd prefer you stay away from Calvin too, at least until I return," Josh suggested.

Beth looked upset and he knew why. Calvin had showed up pretty often at their house lately, often sitting on the porch with Beth as the sun went down. Although careful to keep his eyes on them, Josh hadn't seen any reason to interfere with their meetings. He figured Beth was old enough to make some of those choices now. Besides, from what he could tell, Calvin had changed during the war, become a soft-spoken man, older than his years. With Josh himself away, though, he didn't want her near either one of the Tessier brothers.

"Why Calvin?" asked Beth.

"It might upset Trenton," explained Camellia.

"Without me here I don't want the two of them in a spat over you," continued Josh. "Any trouble between them will only lead to trouble for you. Do you understand?"

Beth sighed as he placed his hands over hers and Camellia's and gently squeezed. "You and Calvin will have time to figure out your feelings for each other when I return," he soothed. "A couple of months . . . that's all I'm asking."

When Beth smiled, he knew she now understood. He motioned toward Butler. "Help me get ready. I've got a lot to do."

Over four hundred miles away, Hampton York rolled over in his bunk and touched his fingers gingerly to his nose. Although weeks had passed since he had taken the rifle-butt hit, his nose still bled some and his head ached at the strangest times. Thankfully, the wound in his right thigh had healed nicely. A local doctor had pulled out the bullet, washed it out real clean, and wrapped it up. No infection had set in, and now it felt fine.

York glanced down at his body—at least ten pounds thinner than when he had been thrown in the jail. For close to a week, the swelling in his nose and mouth had prevented him from eating anything. Gradually, as the swelling went down, he began to take soft food—a biscuit, some gravy, a scrambled egg. Only in the last week or so had he gotten to where he could eat whatever the guards at the jail brought him.

York sat up and touched his bare feet to the cold jail floor. A soldier he knew as Ludwig sat on a chair at a small wood desk a few feet away.

"You figure to feed me tonight or not?" York asked the guard.

Ludwig waved a finger at York. "You eat when I eat."

York pushed back his hair, much longer now since nobody had cut it since his arrest. He knew his beard looked bad too, scraggly and almost all gray. "You boys sure you sent that letter I gave you?" he asked, as he did every day, when he scribbled another note to be sent to Lynette.

"You bet," said Ludwig. "Just never got back no reply."

York walked to the cell bars and clutched them in his hands. Two other men lay on cots in cells on either side of his. "Somethin' must have happened to my letter," he told Ludwig.

"Yeah, you done told me that a million times."

"What about checkin' with the Yankees down in Beaufort? They will tell you I swore the oath down there."

"I think Lieutenant Rider wrote them a letter," said Ludwig. "But the mail moves slow. No tellin' when we hear back from them. Spring probably, when the weather turns better."

York started to curse but held back. One thing he had learned since his arrest—resistance and ranting did him no good. The first and last time he had tried it, grabbing for Jukes one day when the man got too close to York's cell, he'd ended up locked in a three-by-four-foot outhouse behind the jail for a whole week with no fresh air and almost no food or water. By the time they let him out, his brain felt crazy, right at the end of its endurance, and his whole body ached from the cold weather and cramped quarters. His nose bled almost every day during that confinement. A few times he had wondered if he would bleed to death, right then and there. If Lieutenant Rider hadn't sent for the doctor a couple of those times, that surely might have happened. Since then York had tried to keep his temper down and his charm up.

The door to the jail opened, and Lieutenant Rider walked in with Mayor Jukes right behind him. York's jaw tightened as he saw Jukes. Although the mayor seemed to stay away from the jail for days at a time, when he did show up, he usually caused some kind of trouble. One time he had even encouraged Rider to put York in the outhouse again—for the whole winter. York wanted to strangle the man with his bare hands every time he saw him.

Rider pulled off his gloves and took a seat at a desk in the front room. Jukes warmed his hands over the wood stove.

"He givin' you any trouble?" Rider asked Ludwig, indicating York.

"Just keeps askin' about his letter."

Jukes laughed.

In spite of his vow to stay calm, York was furious. "You find that mirthful?" he shouted.

Jukes clomped to him and thrust his face close to the bars but just out of reach. The lieutenant exited the room toward a back area of the jail.

"You have no clue, do you?" Jukes, eyes blazing, asked York.

"I know you hate me 'cause the Rebs burned down your town," York countered. "But that wasn't me—you have to believe that."

Jukes leaned forward slightly, then whispered where only York could hear him. "Yes, your boys burned down my town," he hissed. "But that ain't the half of it. They killed my wife and son too. Burned them to a crisp right inside their own house."

Stunned, York stepped back a pace. He wondered how he would act if somebody killed Johnny, burned his loved ones. "I am truly sorry for what happened," he said quietly.

Jukes grunted. "Sorry don't bring them back to life."

York tucked a lock of hair behind his ear and leaned closer to Jukes again, hoping to make him understand. "Look, I did no harm to your family. I am not to blame."

Jukes shrugged. "You Rebs are all the same."

"No, we're not!"

Jukes laughed. "That letter of yours never got sent," he said with glee. "I saw to that."

York gritted his teeth and tried to stay steady. After all, the mayor had cause for treating York harshly. But as he watched Jukes, his anger boiled higher and higher. Before York could stop himself, he lunged for the mayor, his hands grasping like talons.

Jukes jumped back, his reflexes saving him from being strangled on the spot.

"You never sent my letter?" York bellowed.

Rider strode back into the room.

"Lieutenant Rider!" York shouted. "Jukes said my letter never got sent! What does he mean?"

"I don't know what he's talkin' about," said Jukes.

"He's lyin'!" screamed York. "He just said my letter never got sent! What else didn't get sent? Have you contacted Beaufort?"

Jukes laughed while Rider walked over to York.

"He said the letter didn't get sent," pleaded York. "Make him tell you the truth."

Rider folded his arms. "I have done all I can do for you for now, Captain York. These things take time. Stay steady. If you're tellin' the truth, it will all work out just fine."

York glowered at Rider as he stepped away but reserved his intense anger for the mayor, who now stepped close to him again.

"You want out of here real bad, don't you?" whispered Jukes.

York just stared at him.

"You tell me where that gold is buried, and I'll give you back the document you need."

York made a grab for Jukes again.

The mayor leaped back. "You think I'm a fool?" he asked, still quietly. "I know that gold was stolen. I was the mayor when it happened. Then you show up, all innocent-like. I figure you were part of the gang of hooligans who come through here that night."

"I don't know what you're talkin' about."

"I found your scribbles from your saddlebags, so don't waste your breath lyin' anymore. You rode into Chambersburg only because you needed provisions. You've already marked the dirt roads. How many of them have you searched?"

York dropped his head. Jukes had figured him out so easily.

Rider got up and left the jail.

Jukes spoke again. "If you want out of here, you got just one thing to do—tell me the trails where you already looked so I can leave those alone. No use me takin' months to find somethin' if I can do it in a week."

York rubbed his beard. Why had the mayor decided to make this offer? Then he realized, "You've tried to find it, haven't you? That's why you're here, then gone for days. You've been searchin', but you've had no luck, and now you need my help!"

Jukes grinned and York continued. "You figure others might show up here too, don't you? That if I know about this treasure, somebody else will. You expect they'll show up in the spring. That gives you the next few months before they arrive, and you want me to narrow the field for you so you can find it before anybody else comes."

"You a smart man," said Jukes. "Tell you what: you tell me where you already looked, and I'll check the rest. When I find it, I go halves with you."

York grunted. "I don't trust you far as I can toss you."

The mayor hooked his thumbs in his belt loops. "Suit yourself. But with you or without you, I plan on findin' that gold."

York stared at the man. "Listen to me good," he growled. "When I get free of here—and I will, sooner or later—you will pay for what you've done to me."

Jukes snickered and backed away. "A man in your situation ought not to make threats."

"We'll see."

"Indeed we will."

York hung his head. Unless somebody figured out what had happened to him, he might be here for a long, long time. Or at least long enough for Jukes to find out if any treasure lay out there for either of them to find.

Chapter Nineteen

Ruby stirred and rolled over. Her eyes blinked—once, twice, three times—then opened for good. She sucked in her breath and tried to sit up, but her head wobbled and she fell over like a loose wagon wheel. She wiped her mouth with a shaky hand and rubbed her eyes. Her stomach felt hollow, like somebody had dug out her insides with a big shovel, and she craved water. She tried to sit up again, but when her body refused, she lay back down and stared around the single-room shanty where she lay on a pallet. Plain, unpainted board walls, a dirt floor, a hole dug in the ground for a fire, a slight opening in the ceiling for the smoke to drift out. The fire burned low, not making a lot of dent in the chilled air. A pair of men's pants hung on a nail on the wall; a rifle rested in the corner. She glanced down at her body, covered by a coarse blanket, and saw her thin frame dressed in a brown flannel shirt of some kind, a garment she had never seen.

Ruby tried to figure matters out but with no success. She didn't recognize anything. She closed her eyes and tried to recall what had happened. Parts of it resurfaced. She had searched for Theo . . . found out Markus was dead . . . got word of a man named Marquis and gone looking for him. That's where everything turned fuzzy.

Opening her eyes, she looked around for water and saw a bucket in the corner of the tiny shed. Again she tried to sit up; this time she managed it. As she started to crawl toward the bucket, she heard a voice. Jumping back onto her pallet, she pulled the blanket over her head.

Footsteps sounded and the door to the shed opened. A blast of cold air rushed in but stopped as the door shut. Ruby held her breath. A man's voice sang a song she didn't recognize. The voice rang out deep and

185

slightly familiar. She heard the man move across the shed, pour something in the bucket, then shift to the fire. Slowly she drew the blanket down and peeked out. An old man with a long face was studying her. She clamped her eyes shut.

But evidently the man had already seen her looking at him. "Glory be!"

He jumped to her side and peered down at her. His face looked like a mule's.

"You finally be wakin'!" he shouted.

"Who are you?" Ruby's voice sounded weak, scratchy.

"Buster my name." The man scrambled back to the bucket, dipping out some water in a tin cup and moving back to her.

"Where am I?"

"Drink this," Buster said, handing her the cup.

Ruby took the water and drank. It dripped down her chin, and she choked a little. She tried again and got more down. After handing the cup back to Buster, she tried to piece together who he was and how she had gotten to this place.

Buster's eyes squinted as he scratched the gray stubble of his beard. "You truly don't recollect, do you?"

Ruby slowly shook her head.

"We met on the road out of Orangeburg," he explained. "It was rainin'. I sent you to a shed, then come on here. This be my home."

A memory rose vaguely in Ruby's head.

"I come back to the shed where I put you at first light," Buster continued. "Felt sorta bad that I left you on your lonesome the night before. Found the shed burned down. Felt real bad then, for sure. I started lookin' for you. Come up on some footprints leadin' to the woods. And there you lay, most near dead, with a cut in yo' side big enough to shove a pine cone through."

"You brought me here?" Ruby asked.

Buster shrugged. "I didn't figure it the right thing to leave you in the woods. I lay you over my mule—he outside—and hauled you straight here."

Suddenly the rest of that terrible night in the shed returned to her.

Marquis and Rufe—they had Theo. She had finally found her boy, but they had come to kill her and steal him away again.

"Marquis stuck me," she said.

Buster nodded. "The man who's got your boy."

"Yes. Marquis heard I was asking about him, so he and his man came searching for me." Ruby reached for the water cup and drank again.

"It ain't right that Marquis fella tried to kill a woman."

"He didn't seem the kind of man who worried much about whether something is right or not."

Buster took a big breath. Ruby handed him the water cup. With some liquid now in her body, a bit of strength returned. "How long I been here?" she asked, her eyes on Buster.

"A couple of weeks. You barely livin' those first few days after I brung you here. I cleaned yo' knife wound, poured some water down yo' mouth, tried to keep you warm. You been through fever, shakes, most everythin' you can think of. I got a little food in you the last few days. You startin' gradual to breathin' right again."

Her heart sank. "I'm sure Marquis has left these parts by now."

"I heard that was so."

Her determination to get well renewed. "Where you figure him to go from here?"

Buster studied the matter a second. "Probably more south," he offered. "They's warmer weather there . . . maybe some customers he ain't seen in a while."

Ruby smiled at the old man. In spite of all the meanness in the world, every now and again a man like Buster happened along and gave her reason for hope again. "I thank you for your kindnesses."

Buster dropped his eyes. "I doin' what any Christian man ought to do."

"You saved my life."

Buster patted her hand. "I needed the company."

She smiled again as he took a piece of bread out of a burlap bag and brought it over to her. She broke off a bite and ate it. More water followed that.

Then she paused. "I will leave as soon as I can," she said, setting down the water cup.

Buster shrugged. "You way too weak to worry about such as that right now. It's cold and travelin' ain't easy. I say you ought to stay right here through the winter, heal yourself some. Go after your boy when the spring comes . . . after you be strong again."

Ruby thought of The Oak, of Obadiah in his house waiting on her, and wondered if she could make her way back home. She tried to sit up again, but her eyes blurred. As she lay back down, she knew there was no way she could travel anytime soon. "Maybe you're right," she said weakly. "I need to stay here awhile longer."

Buster smiled. "You bet I am right. Right as rain."

Ruby closed her eyes again, her body weary once more. "In the spring," she said. "I will go for Theo again in the spring."

Josh arrived in Richmond halfway through the month of November. A hard chill lay on the city as he entered—white frost on the trees and grass. The breath of his horses was visible as they pushed forward. Although both he and the horses were nearly exhausted, Josh quickly made his way to the Victoria Hotel, where he found it burned to the ground. Grieved, he dismounted for a moment, picked up a handful of soot, and let it sift earthward through his fingers. War carried such a high price.

His spirits low, Josh mounted again, shoving his hat lower against the cold, and headed to where he remembered Lynette Swanson's house to be. To his great relief, he saw it still standing as he approached from the road. After tying up the horses, he approached the door and knocked. Nobody answered. He walked around the front yard but saw no signs of life. Back at the door he tested the lock and found the door open. He stepped inside. No one was there. A further search revealed empty rooms on both floors.

Puzzled, he walked to the back of the house, stood in the kitchen, and tried to figure what had happened. Although empty, the house was clean. Floors were swept; the corners were empty of cobwebs. Obviously, somebody took care of the place. But who? With the hotel burned down, where did Lynette and Jackson live?

Then, outside the kitchen window, Josh spotted the carriage house at the back of the property. A curl of smoke slid from its chimney. A stack of wood rested on the ground beside the narrow stairs that snaked up the side to the rooms on the top. Curious, Josh rushed outside and up the stairs of the carriage house. He hesitated, then knocked.

Seconds later Lynette Swanson opened the door. "Josh! Come in!" She stepped back, and he followed her into a space just wide enough for the two single beds and wood chairs. He hugged Lynette, then swept off his hat and sat down in the seat she pointed him to, his hat on a knee.

"Let me get you some coffee," she offered.

"That would be good. It's so cold today."

She picked up a pot from the hearth, poured a cup of coffee, and handed it to him. As he drank the warm liquid, his body relaxed a little.

"What on earth are you doing here?" she asked, sitting down beside him.

Josh took a good look at Lynette then. He noticed the worn black shawl around her shoulders, the navy dress that, though clean, had tatters near the hem. Her cheeks were thin and wan, and her hair seemed a lot grayer than when he last saw her. "I could ask you the same," he said, waving a hand over the small space.

"Times are hard," she explained. "At first Jackson and I figured we'd live in the big house, but then . . . well . . . dollars are hard to find, and it's easier to heat this space than any room in the house. Jackson and I figured we ought to just stay here through the winter."

"I saw the hotel." He sighed. "Sorry the Yankees burned it."

She brushed back a stray hair that had fallen over her eyes. "At least the house made it."

"Yes, reason for gratitude for sure."

Josh saw the worry in her shoulders and became concerned. "Is Jackson OK?"

"Yes, though the Yankees seem to harass him every chance they get. He works at the docks, does repair on ships, makes a few dollars here and there."

"That's how you get by?"

"For now. I plan to rent some rooms in the house once we save enough to buy some furniture for it."

"The furniture get stolen?" Josh asked.

"Before we ever got home."

"How are you paying the taxes?"

She stood and placed another log on the fireplace. "Why are you here, Josh?"

Her tone was weary, Josh thought. Like she didn't want to think about hard things anymore. He set his cup on the floor. "York never came home."

"What?"

"York never returned to The Oak. I came looking for him. Hoped to find him here with you."

Lynette frowned, as if in thought, and folded her arms. "He left here near the end of September, headed back to The Oak."

"He never made it."

Neither of them spoke for several minutes. The fire crackled.

"Where do you think he went?" Josh finally asked.

Lynette sat back down. "I have no clue."

"He didn't say anything to you about going anywhere else?"

"Not that I can remember." She touched Josh's arm. "You think something happened to him?"

Josh sighed heavily. "I don't know."

Just then the door swung open and Jackson stepped inside. With a welcoming grin Josh rose to shake his hand as Lynette poured Jackson a cup of coffee.

Josh noted that Jackson appeared as starved as his mother. Just how bad were things for them?

"Josh came looking for York," Lynette explained to Jackson. "He never returned to The Oak."

Jackson lifted an eyebrow and left his coffee untouched.

"You ever hear York talk about going anywhere else before he headed back south?" Josh asked Jackson.

He shook his head.

"I don't understand then," said Josh. "Unless something . . ."

"No!" Lynette interrupted him. "York handles himself too well. He's fine—I can't believe anything else."

Although not sure he agreed with her, Josh decided he best keep his fears to himself. "You're probably right." He attempted a chuckle. "You know York—always up to something."

"Maybe he went somewhere else," Jackson reasoned. "Charleston, Columbia, somewhere in between . . ."

But what would make York do something like that? Josh wondered. He came up with nothing. Although York liked to drink and gamble, he had no money for such things these days, and even if he did, no card game or whiskey bottle would cause him to desert The Oak Plantation for this long.

"You must be hungry," Lynette said. "Let me see what we can find to eat."

"I hate to bother you for that."

Lynette retrieved a sack from the back of the room and placed it on a tiny table. "We got meager fare, but we share it gladly."

Jackson headed to the door. "I'll get more wood for the fire."

Josh stepped to the table beside Lynette. "What can I do to help?"

Lynette stopped—a cake of bread in her hands. "You can find York," she said, eyes watering.

"I will," Josh promised.

"You have to." She began to sob. "He . . . he . . ."

"What?"

"I never told him!" Lynette cried.

"Never told him what?"

Lynette didn't reply; she simply cut the bread.

"What?" Josh repeated.

"He needs to hear it from me."

"OK," Josh said, confused but not wanting to press.

Lynette stared at Josh. "Promise you won't tell him. Unless . . ."

"Unless I don't think he'll live long enough for you to tell him?"

"Yes."

"I promise."

Lynette sank down into a chair by the table, and Josh took her hands in his.

"York is Jackson's father," Lynette confessed.

For an instant Josh's mouth fell open. Then he felt foolish that he had not already guessed it. Jackson so resembled York that even the blindest person could see it. "Does Jackson know?"

"No, I never saw a need to tell him."

Josh nodded and Lynette continued. "I regret I kept this to myself. I should have told both of them a long time ago, but . . . the moment never seemed right. It's the last secret I have, and it's eating me up inside. You have to find him so I can come clean with this. The thought of him dying without ever knowing of the fine young man he sired . . . grieves me to my soul."

"We all make mistakes," Josh said gently.

"This is more than a mistake. It is a *sin*."

"We all do that too," he soothed.

"All but you."

Josh leaned back so he could see her eyes. "I will find York," he promised. "You can trust me on that."

"I do," she said, smiling through her tears. "Or I would never have told you what I just did."

Chapter Twenty

The rest of the winter passed slowly, the cold, gray days hanging on as if glued to the sky. Inside the manse of The Oak, Katherine York did what she had to do to keep things going—she cooked, cleaned, and mended. Although Trenton spent more time at home as the days grew shorter and colder, he stayed sullen and spoke to her only when necessary. She feared for him more than ever. From what she had heard, most of it in whispers in and around Crossville General Store, Trenton had indeed become the leader of the raiders: a man known for his anger, his willingness to inflict the greatest pain on the blacks he saw as dangerous, as uppity, as unwilling to stay in their proper place. More than once, news of a lynching—a gruesome tale of a Negro strung up for some misguided action toward a white—swept through the rumors.

Every now and again Katherine tried to talk to Trenton about his deeds, to caution him against going too far. But he just pushed her off and refused to converse. After a while she gave up and plowed back into her labors, pushing away her awful imaginings and motherly fears.

Sometimes, when the day ended, as she sat by the fire, she dreamed of the old days. The grand parties she once attended in Charleston. The lavish meals. The exquisite dresses, hats, and shoes. The wonderful music that played as she and her wealthy, sophisticated friends danced and danced, their silly heads never imagining those carefree days would someday end. How foolish they had all been. How blind to the ways of the real world! Now she lived in the real world—a world of backbreaking labor and long drudgery, a world without refinement, without luxury, without beauty.

Often she considered the money she had kept hidden for so long and wished she could simply go get it all, buy what she wanted, and reclaim some of the lifestyle she had lost. Yet she knew she couldn't do that. The Yankees would immediately show up on her doorstep and demand that she tell them where she got her dollars. No doubt they would then claim her money as ill-gotten gains and take it from her, just like they had stolen all the furnishings from her house when she had traveled to Richmond to find Calvin.

No, for now she needed to keep the amount of her wealth well-disguised, spend it only in dribs and drabs . . . just enough to keep body and soul together. Nothing more and nothing less. Maybe years from now, when the Yankees returned to their homes in the North—and she knew in her heart someday they would—she could bring out her treasure and let the whole world know that she, Katherine Tessier York, had come through the war with more success than anybody she knew. She smiled a little when she thought of where she had hidden the dollars—so obvious to anyone who really thought about it. So close, but oh, so far.

Every time she thought of the money, her mind inevitably shifted to York. What a difficult man—yet also an attractive one. She longed for him in the worst of her moments, when loneliness hit her like a runaway wagon. In spite of his bullheadedness, his overweening pride, his unwillingness to give in to her control—or perhaps because of it—she realized she had come to count on him more than any other man, even her dead first husband, Marshall. One thing about York: you could trust him to do what he said he would do.

Which made it all the more disturbing that he had not yet returned.

Although she didn't truly believe it, she feared at times that somebody had killed him—that his temper had gotten out of hand and someone, probably a Yankee with a better aim than his, had laid him in the ground. The notion that York would never come back actually scared her. Did this mean she really loved him? That she had finally found a man she could respect enough to give him her heart? What a strange idea. Yet Katherine couldn't deny it. Her loneliness grew worse.

She knew, of course, that Josh Cain had gone to Richmond to search for York. But when Mr. Cain didn't come back by Christmas, she began to feel panicky. What if York never returned? She would end up a widow a second time—this time without ever having truly become York's wife.

Once in a while she felt as though she wanted to cry over that, but she fought it off—at least most of the time.

About the only thing that kept her going was Calvin's presence—his steady head and calming voice. If not for the company he offered, she didn't know how she could have managed. Sometimes, when she found him reading the Bible, which he did for a while on most nights as they sat by the fire, she asked him to read a few passages to her. He always complied. To her surprise, when she gradually started paying attention to the actual words rather than just his voice, the messages in them began to calm her a little. They made her feel more peaceful in spite of all her fears and misgivings. Although she didn't hold to any true belief in the God the Bible spoke about, she did at least confess to Calvin that the Scriptures offered her solace in her hardest days.

On several occasions she asked him to explain something he had read, and although he admitted he didn't know a lot about it all himself, he did his best to comply with her request. A few times he came back to her the next day and told her that he had asked Camellia the question she had raised, and she had explained the matter this way.

"You can't tell her I'm asking," she warned him the first time that happened.

"No, Mother," he agreed. "We will keep this to ourselves."

So they did.

January rolled through, the days bleak and short. Right at the end of the month, Calvin told Katherine about a recent conversation he'd had with Beth. Although she seemed reluctant to talk to him, he had finally gotten her to say that Camellia and Butler had gone to Crossville General Store, and the clerk had given them a letter Josh had sent. The letter said Josh had made it to Richmond; that he was asking around the city to see if anybody knew what had happened to York. As a former Yankee soldier, Josh hoped he could get some answers a Reb could never expect to hear. So far, though, he had learned nothing.

"Josh Cain is staying in Richmond until the spring," Calvin told Katherine. "He says he will explore the area around the city, then branch out from there, asking folks about Captain York."

"You think Mr. Cain will find him?" asked Katherine, trying to keep her tone calm and unafraid.

"Captain York is a strong man, Mother," Calvin soothed. "I know him. He is OK; I am confident of that."

Katherine hugged her younger son and kept hoping.

February entered. Cold gripped the land. Occasionally, a black or two, begging for food, showed up on the manse's back steps. For reasons she couldn't explain, Katherine usually gave them a little of what she had—a bite of a biscuit, a swab of jam on it, an egg or two.

One day Trenton caught her giving a Negro a biscuit and scolded her for it. But she didn't back down. Although she found it difficult to accept the blacks as equals, neither did she like the notion of letting them starve if she could do something to stop it.

"You're growing soft, Mother," accused Trenton, disdain dripping in his voice. "Listening to Calvin read you that religious drivel every night."

"That religious drivel, as you call it, is important to your brother," she defended.

Trenton sneered. "What about you?"

"You know better than that."

"Do I? You're changing, Mother dear, whether you know it or not. I fear you're going soft."

Katherine shrugged and kept her silence. Let him think what he wanted.

About midway through the month of February, a cold rain started to fall and continued for a week. Sleet mixed in with the rain some, a rare thing on The Oak. When Katherine went to the pantry near the end of the day to start some supper, she found only two jars of jam, half a sack of potatoes, and one piece of cured ham in a burlap bag. She took a deep breath, hoping spring would soon come. She longed to get back outside, start her garden again, and do something about the increasing panic she felt over York's absence.

She heard a knock on the back door, wiped her eyes, and hurried to the door. As she opened it, a blast of frigid air blew back her hair. Three black men, wearing only light coats, stood there, hats in their hands. Rain and ice pelted their faces. One wore a pair of boots with a hole in the left front. She saw his toes.

"We freezin'," said the tallest of the three, a towering man with huge hands and a light-skinned, pear-shaped birthmark on his left cheek. "Starvin' too."

Without really thinking about it, Katherine stepped back and waved the men inside. "I don't have much."

"We grateful for whatever you might can spare," said the tall man, obviously the spokesman for the three. "We got kids waitin' in the woods a ways from here."

Katherine inspected the big man. She figured him close to forty and noted he was clean in spite of his obvious poverty. He looked her in the eye when he spoke and seemed mannerly.

"Where are you from?" she asked.

"I grew up outside of Columbia, a house man for the Leigh Plantation."

"I knew the place."

"It gone now. Burned to nothin' but ashes."

"The Leighs?"

"Not sure where they all went."

Katherine sighed. The Leighs were probably dead or poverty-stricken. These men needed food, yet she had so little for her own family.

"I got children," the man reminded her gently.

Katherine hesitated, Trenton's words ringing in her head. Was she going soft? Did her desire to do something for a few starving blacks mean she had become weak? But how? Giving something, in spite of her own needs, to help keep somebody else alive felt strong to her, courageous.

"Stay right here," she said, suddenly deciding Trenton was wrong. Sacrificing for somebody else showed power, not weakness.

The man nodded, and Katherine headed to the pantry. Grabbing half the potatoes and one jar of the jam, she hurried back to the kitchen. As she did, Trenton entered the house, smelling of liquor as usual. Since the unfortunate episode between him and Calvin over Beth, he had imbibed more and more whiskey.

"What's this?" he bellowed, glaring at the blacks.

Katherine ignored him and handed the food to the Negroes. "Take it," she said, hoping to get them out before Trenton got too riled.

"You got a blanket to spare?" asked the man with the birthmark. "My boy, he be three, got a fever. A blanket might aid him some."

Katherine hesitated, wanting to fetch a blanket for the sick boy but not wanting to leave the darkies alone in the room with Trenton. To her relief, Calvin walked through the kitchen door.

"They need a blanket," she explained to Calvin.

"I'll get one," he offered.

"We don't have one to spare," said Trenton.

Calvin ignored him and left the room.

Trenton's face flushed, and he stepped toward the blacks. "You boys can wait outside," he said angrily.

The Negroes hesitated and looked at Katherine.

"It's cold out," she told Trenton. "Leave them be until we get the blanket."

Trenton glared at her, his eyes red, angry. "I'll have no darkies standing in my kitchen!" he seethed. "They wait outside!"

The tall black man stretched up a little, his back straight, and moved a touch toward Trenton. His height loomed over Trenton, making him look small and weak. "We be clean men. Good enough for yo' kitchen for sure."

Trenton's lips pulled back into a snarl.

At that instant Katherine shivered, recognizing something that truly frightened her. She should have seen it a long time ago but hadn't, perhaps because she had refused to believe it. But on Trenton's face was the proof: her son had become a beast, more savage than anything anybody had ever accused the blacks of being.

An odd thought came to her, and she weighed it for a second. Had Trenton gradually become so evil that she could now see it? Or had she, indeed, changed over the last few months—taken on a touch of virtue, a trait that allowed her, for the first time, to see her older son as he truly was? Had the Bible reading Calvin shared with her made a mark on her soul? Given her the capability to recognize meanness when she saw it?

"I said leave!" Trenton shouted at the blacks.

The blacks didn't budge.

Trenton yanked a pistol from his waistband and pointed it at the tall man.

Calvin strode back into the room. "Here's the blanket," he said, handing it to Katherine. Then he stopped in his tracks. His eyes widened as they landed on Trenton's pistol.

"No one is giving a blanket to a Negro," ordered Trenton, grabbing it from Katherine's hands. "We got plenty of need for it right here."

Katherine bit her lip and turned to the blacks. "Take the food and go!" she instructed them.

The men pivoted to leave, but Trenton threw the blanket on the floor and rushed them. "I want the food too!" he snarled.

The three men turned back to him. The tallest one dropped the potatoes and quickly produced a knife in his hand. Trenton shot at him and the bullet caught the black man in the shoulder. He rushed at Trenton and grabbed his gun hand by the wrist. The two other blacks jumped at Trenton too, both of them going for his legs.

Calvin moved then, plowing into the blacks.

Katherine jumped on the back of the tall man fighting Trenton. "Stop!" she screamed.

Nobody listened.

The man with the birthmark twisted Trenton's wrist, and his pistol fell to the floor. Katherine squeezed the black around the throat. Trenton bit at the man's face, and he jabbed at Trenton with his knife. Calvin pulled the other two blacks off Trenton's legs and fought to hold them down.

When Katherine saw the knife blade cut Trenton's shoulder, she screamed again. Trenton broke loose of the black man and dropped to the floor, his hands grasping for his gun. The black man lunged back and tossed Katherine away. She crumpled to the floor.

One of the other blacks yanked away from Calvin, pulled out a pistol, and tossed it to the tall Negro. He cocked the weapon and aimed it at Trenton. Trenton jerked to his feet as Katherine screamed for a third time. Trenton jumped at the black man, but Katherine moved even faster, throwing her body between Trenton and the man with the gun.

The gun fired, and the kitchen was filled with the boom.

Katherine staggered and slumped, then collapsed to the floor. She grabbed at the searing pain in her chest. Warm liquid oozed from the wound. Holding up her fingers, she saw they were red.

Suddenly everything grew quiet.

Calvin loomed over her. "Get a towel!" he screamed to Trenton.

The black man's marked face appeared beside Calvin. A cut bled on his birthmark. "I sorry," he pleaded. "Didn't mean to cause nobody no harm."

Katherine nodded and the man moved away. A second later she heard the back door shut. She reached up, and Calvin took her hand. He held it to his cheek.

"You will be fine," Calvin soothed her.

Trenton appeared with a towel and pressed it against Katherine's wound. But it soon turned red. "We need a doctor!" he shouted.

Calvin touched his brother's shoulder. Katherine saw the look that passed between them and knew—no doctor could reach her in time. She was at the end of her life.

She grabbed Trenton by his uninjured wrist and made him face her. "Enough!" she said, her tone as forceful as she could make it. "Enough meanness!"

Trenton's eyes glazed, and she could not read them. "You hold on, Mother. We will take care of you."

She shook her head. "You are brothers," she whispered between clenched teeth. "Tell me you will remember that."

Trenton and Calvin glanced at each other once more.

"I will remember," said Calvin.

Trenton nodded, but his eyes were cold.

"Do not blame the Negro," Katherine ordered. "He did not mean this to happen."

Trenton opened his mouth to protest, but Katherine shook her head.

She looked back at Calvin. "The Bible . . . get it."

Calvin left immediately.

Katherine took Trenton's hand in hers. "You've had it rough. I know that."

When he didn't reply, she wondered what thoughts ran through his head. "I am sorry I didn't do better by you."

"You did fine," Trenton claimed. "Always looked out for me."

"I did not know how to do better." She choked and a trickle of blood filled up her mouth and ran out the side of her lips. "Nobody ever taught me."

Calvin returned and squatted by her.

"Read to me," she pleaded. "Something nice."

He flipped open the Bible and began to read. "God is our refuge and strength, a very present help in trouble. Therefore will not we fear, though the earth be removed, and though the mountains be carried into the midst of the sea; though the waters thereof roar and be troubled, though the mountains shake with the swelling thereof . . ."

Calvin's words grew softer, and she closed her eyes. The Scripture soothed her mind, gentled her spirit. She thought of York and, for the first time she could remember, breathed a short prayer, asking God to care for him.

Opening her eyes, she saw Trenton and Calvin and prayed for the second time in her life. This time she sought God's provision for her sons.

As Calvin continued to read, Trenton bent closer to her, his lips right up to her ear. "The money," he whispered. "Where is the money?"

Katherine's breath slowed, and her vision blurred. She felt her heart ebbing, her blood flow dropping. She closed her eyes.

"Where is the money?" Trenton whispered once more.

She licked her lips. "It is . . . ," she tried to say, but nothing came out.

Trenton spoke again, this time louder.

But she could no longer respond.

The last sounds Katherine Tessier York heard were the comforting words from the Bible.

Part Three

Resolutions

If you falter, and give up,

you will lose the power

of keeping any resolution,

and will regret it all your life.

—ABRAHAM LINCOLN

Chapter Twenty-One

Spring entered gently that year of 1866, with the air slowly becoming warmer off the James River as the dogwoods began to reveal their white and pink flowers. The sky eased into more and more blue with each passing day. Josh's hours away from Lynette and Jackson increased with the better weather, and his field of search expanded into an ever-widening circle around Richmond.

As March moved past, Josh stopped wherever he could find a saloon, a card game, a general store, or a roadside inn. He always asked the same question: Had anybody seen a tall man with a thick, black beard flecked with gray? A man sharp at cards and ready with a good story? A man known for his bravery in the war as a captain under General Wade Hampton?

To Josh's distress nobody seemed to know anything, and his spirits continued to plummet. He wondered if the time had come to give up and go back to The Oak. He missed Camellia terribly and Butler and Beth too. Often he worried about them and prayed that the Lord had kept them safe from harm. He realized, perhaps more than most, that a lot of danger existed in the world. And if harm befell any of his loved ones in his absence, he would never forgive himself.

He hoped Ruby had come back with Theo, but either way he planned to marry Camellia and leave The Oak as soon as he returned. The time had long since passed for the two of them to start their life as husband and wife.

When April came and still no word on York had turned up, Josh decided the time to leave had arrived. He rode back into Richmond near the end of the third day of that month—a year since the city had fallen to the Yankees—and made his way to Lynette's house. He found her in the tiny room above the carriage house, sitting at her kitchen table, Jackson beside her. She held a paper in one hand and what looked like a tattered letter in the other.

Seeing her stunned expression, he pulled up a chair beside her. "What is it?"

"Two things. Neither of them good." She handed him the paper and the letter without further explanation.

He read both papers silently. "Katherine is dead," he said, laying the letter from Camellia on his lap.

"All the more reason to find York," urged Lynette.

Josh weighed the effect Katherine's death might have on things at The Oak. Would Trenton become more violent without her strong hand over him? Or would his mother's death bring enough grief to cause him to take a hard look at himself?

He glanced at Jackson, then focused on Lynette again. "What will you do about this?" he asked, holding up the paper she had given him.

"I couldn't pay my taxes," she explained. "So the Yankees have confiscated my hotel property . . . what's left of it anyway. I owe now on the house."

"Two hundred and thirty dollars," Josh said, quoting the document he had just read.

She sighed. "Might as well be two hundred thousand for all I have. The Yankees will take everything. They're doing it to a lot of folks. They'll get the house—and this place too. We'll have nowhere to live."

Josh bit his lip. "You've got a month," he said, indicating the paper.

"We'll find a way to fix this," Jackson promised.

Josh marveled at the young man's calm spirit. *Another resemblance to York,* Josh thought. "Maybe I can talk to some people."

"You think you can?"

"I know a few of the Yankees stationed here—found out I fought with a couple of them. I don't know if a banker will care much about that, but the soldiers can control a banker if they choose to do it."

Lynette's face lit up. Josh was glad he could at least offer her some hope. One thing bothered him though. "I'll have to stop looking for York for a while."

Lynette nodded. "I've been figuring that would happen soon anyway. And with that"—she pointed to the letter—"I'm sure you'll want to go home as quickly as you can."

Josh took her hands. "I am sorry I haven't found York. But I don't know where else to look. I've gone out close to twenty miles around the city, and nobody remembers seeing him."

Lynette's shoulders sagged again. "I can't help but think he's still alive . . . though I have no logical reason to believe that."

Josh frowned. He hated to give up but didn't know what else to do. "I don't know if York's alive or not," he admitted. "But one thing I do know is this: he loved you more than he ever loved anybody."

"I know." Her eyes glistened.

Jackson cleared his throat. "Excuse me, but we need more wood for the fire."

Lynette smiled briefly at him as he ducked out of the room. Josh heard the young man's footsteps as he headed down the stairs to the woodpile.

"Will you tell Jackson now?" Josh asked Lynette.

"Perhaps it's time. He deserves to know."

They sat quietly for a few moments.

Josh wanted to ask Lynette about York and how the news of Katherine's death might affect the two of them. Might it give them a chance to be together again? But how could he bring up such a delicate subject? Although Josh knew York loved Lynette, he didn't know how she felt about him. Besides, what if York, too, was dead? How strange if that were true.

When Jackson came back with several pieces of wood cradled in one arm and a box in the other, Josh breathed deeply. Jackson stacked the wood by the fireplace, then handed the box to Josh. "This is the only thing Captain York left. It was under the seat of the wagon we brought from South Carolina. Figured you'd want to have it."

"Thanks," Josh replied.

"Wonder what's in it?" asked Lynette.

"A bunch of war journals," explained Josh, remembering the day he found the box and gave it to York. "I found them on The Oak last fall. They're logs telling about the fighting, written by an aide-de-camp to Jeb Stuart."

"Wonder why he kept them?" asked Jackson.

Josh opened the lid, saw the journals resting inside, and pulled the top one out.

"Captain York fought with Stuart," Jackson noted.

Josh opened the journal. "York didn't read much, but guess these meant something to him."

"You figure the logs talk about him?" asked Jackson.

Grief hit Josh all of a sudden as it dawned on him that York almost certainly had to be dead. His eyes filled, and for several seconds he sat straight and still, not wanting to believe it but knowing it must be true. Although he and York saw the world a lot differently most of the time, he had still loved his half brother. Now . . .

Josh wiped his eyes and looked back at the journal in his hand. For a few seconds it blurred in his vision. But then, wanting to feel closer to York, he flipped it open and read a few pages. He leafed to a page marked by a down-turned edge and started reading. His eyes widened as he finished that page and turned to the next. He hurriedly completed that page, then one more. When finished, he stood and faced Lynette and Jackson. "Have either of you read this?" he asked excitedly.

They shook their heads.

"What is it?" asked Lynette.

Josh handed the book to Lynette and stalked to the fireplace. As he stared into the flames, Lynette read the marked pages, then gave the journal to Jackson.

"You have to go to Chambersburg!" Lynette exclaimed. "That's where he went!"

Josh turned to face her. "Doing something about your taxes will have to wait."

"I agree."

"And I can't go back to The Oak just yet either."

"I'll go with you," Jackson offered.

Josh shook his head. "Stay here. Keep working. You're going to need every dollar you can earn."

"Not if Captain York finds a Yankee treasure," said Jackson.

Lynette put her hands on her hips. "We can't profit from stolen money," she insisted in an indignant tone.

All sense of grief left Josh. Even though he still wondered why York hadn't come home yet—with or without any Yankee gold—at least he now knew where York had gone. "Leave it to York." He chuckled. "If there's even a hint of treasure buried somewhere, he's definitely the man who would go searching for it."

Chapter Twenty-Two

Ruby showed up at The Oak a week after Josh left Lynette to go to Chambersburg. The air, washed of anything cold or musty, was scented with blossoming flowers and budding trees. A light breeze from the ocean touched her hair, and the sun warmed her back. Buster walked beside her, his stride slow and purposeful.

Wanting to avoid Trenton Tessier, she eased her way around the edge of the property and approached the houses from the river side. Rounding a corner, she spotted Camellia and Beth in the yard back of Beth's house, hanging wash, and headed toward them. As she got closer, she spotted Obadiah in a garden to her left. His head was down, and he held a hoe. Her heart rose, then sank as she saw him. When had he come back and why? Had something happened to him . . . or his house?

Moving even faster now, she glanced toward the house, where she had left Nettie and Leta. Tears welled in her eyes as she saw her mama in a rocker by the back of the house and Leta playing beside her. Camellia looked up from her labors, stared at the two figures for a second, then dropped the basket in her hands. Camellia ran toward Ruby, with Beth right behind.

"Obadiah!" yelled Camellia, pointing toward Ruby. "Ruby is home!"

Obadiah raised his head, dropped his hoe, and rushed her way. Within seconds everybody else had heard and came pouring toward her—Butler and Johnny from the barn and her mama holding Leta.

Ruby ran to them, her arms open. Leta dropped Nettie's hand, and Ruby gathered her little girl into her arms and squeezed her hard. Everybody talked at once. Tears streamed down all the female cheeks, while the men stood dumbfounded, their hands at their sides as they watched.

Still holding Leta, Ruby hugged everybody—men and women—one at a time. She paused as she came to Obadiah.

"I been missin' you," he said, his wide face serious but happy all at the same time.

Ruby set Leta on the ground and stepped into his stout arms. As they encircled her, she finally felt safe again. After a long, tight embrace, he let her go.

She stepped back and took a breath. "When did you return?" she asked Obadiah.

"Middle of October. Raiders burned out my place."

"You not hurt?"

"I look hurt?"

She relaxed as she inspected him and saw no harm on his strong body. Then she turned to Buster, who stood outside the circle, his eyes down. "This is Buster," she said, smiling.

Johnny and Butler shook his hand.

"I know you have lots to tell," said Camellia. "But you're surely tired and hungry. Let's go to the house, get some water for both of you, a bite to eat, let you get off your feet. Then you can tell us everything."

The group moved to Camellia's front porch. Camellia and Beth quickly brought water and bread to Ruby and Buster, who sat in the two big rockers. Everyone else perched on the rail or settled onto the porch floor. Leta snuggled in Ruby's lap, and Obadiah perched on the rail next to her. Ruby grasped his hand.

"Tell us where you've been," Camellia urged. "We've been worried sick."

Ruby took a long drink of water and squeezed Obadiah's hand. "It's been a real journey," she started. "Almost didn't make it, but Buster saved my life."

Buster looked at his bare feet while Ruby went ahead with the tale of all that had happened to her since she had left The Oak. The faces around her shifted with the ups and downs of her story, showing fear, sadness, hope, and fear again as the adventure unfolded.

"I've been recovering at Buster's place all these months," Ruby concluded. "Soon as I got able to travel again, I decided to make my way here. Buster insisted he come along."

At first nobody seemed to know what to say. Then Beth broke the quiet. "You found Theo," she said, almost in reverence.

Ruby sighed. "Yes, but I lost him again."

"What you did once, you can repeat," Johnny encouraged. "A man like this Marquis you spoke of won't go far. He'll stay near what he knows."

"I'm not sure of that," Ruby said sadly. "Marquis came from Louisiana. Maybe he'll go back there."

Silence fell for a second, but Ruby didn't let it last long. "What's the news here?" she asked, wanting to change the subject.

"All manner of things," said Camellia.

"Katherine Tessier is dead," Johnny stated.

Ruby frowned.

"A Negro man accidentally shot her," explained Camellia. "He and two others came begging for food." She told Ruby the rest of the story.

"So Captain York owns the place now?" asked Ruby when Camellia had finished.

Camellia shrugged. "We don't know where Pa is. He left here back in September to escort Lynette and Jackson back to Richmond. But he never returned. Josh went at the end of October to search for him, but he's not back yet either."

"Mr. Cain doing OK?" Ruby asked.

"Yes, he writes us . . . mail is sketchy, but we've heard enough to know he is well, at least for now."

Ruby tried to figure what it all meant. "Who's running The Oak if Captain York and Mr. Cain are gone?"

"We are," said Johnny. "With Calvin."

"What about Mr. Trenton?"

"He's gone loco," Johnny continued. "Stays drunk most of the day. Most nights he's out with the raiders. He's tryin' to find the man who killed Katherine."

"You said it was an accident."

"Not in Trenton's mind. 'Course he wants to kill every Negro he can. If he finds this man, a lynchin' will surely follow."

"Won't the law stop him?"

Camellia sighed. "The law is spotty. Sometimes it does right— sometimes not."

"The man with the most guns seems to make his own law these days," Johnny added.

Ruby bit into her bread and tried to take in all she was hearing. What a difference a few months could make.

"What do you plan to do now?" asked Beth.

Ruby glanced at Obadiah. She wanted to talk to him alone about such matters but didn't know how to avoid Beth's question. "I need to rest some more first. Let my body get stronger."

"You goin' after Theo again after that?" asked Johnny.

Ruby caught Obadiah's eye and knew she might as well say it. He would find out soon enough. "I have no choice. I know Theo is alive. I couldn't live with myself if I didn't go find him."

"That be dangerous," said Obadiah, his tone stern. "Marquis will want to kill you for sure this time. Maybe it be time for you to settle yourself down, stay here where people can take care of you. Let the law go after Theo."

Ruby's heart broke. She knew the message behind Obadiah's words. He wanted her to stay safe on The Oak with him and give up her wild pursuit of her boy. Ruby couldn't blame him for his words. She had already made him wait far longer for her to come home than he deserved. But how could she stay here while somebody else went after her son? Nobody else would die for him, and it might take that in order to free him from Marquis.

"Theo is my son," she told Obadiah. "You would do exactly what I'm doing if he was your boy."

When Obadiah dropped his gaze, she knew she had hurt his feelings. But what else could she do? Deny her intentions, then tell him the truth later? No, she would rather have it out and said plain as day so nobody would feel confused. If Obadiah didn't want to wait on her until her return, so be it. She would go anyway. She had no choice.

"I go with her," said Buster, speaking for the first time. "I's old but not afraid to stand up to Marquis."

Comforted, Ruby smiled at the old man.

Obadiah moved from the porch rail to squat beside her. Although everybody still watched them, Ruby suddenly knew this was between her and her husband. The others on the porch faded into the background.

Obadiah took her hand and gently rubbed it, palm up. After a few seconds he raised it to his lips and kissed the top. "I loves you too much to let you go and leave me again," he said soberly.

Ruby opened her mouth to interrupt him, but he kept going. "I waited all winter for you to come home. Worried myself sick you was dead. I swore in those cold days that if I ever laid eyes on you again, I wasn't ever gone let you leave my sight. Not another single time."

Ruby's temper flared, but when she spoke, she kept her words calm. "You can't make me stay," she argued.

Obadiah shook his head. "Not sayin' I even gone try," he explained. "I know how hard of head you be, like arguin' with a tree stump. I'm just tellin' you I's goin' with you this time, that's all."

"What?"

"I got nothin' without you and Leta," said Obadiah. "So if it means I got to go with you to find your boy to be with you, then I reckon I's doin' just that."

Ruby beamed. Her heart filled with joy. She handed Leta to Camellia and leaned over to Obadiah. "I've been gone a long time, and you have been patient to wait. I promise that soon as we find Theo, we will come back home with him and never leave again."

"That's good by me," said Obadiah.

As Ruby snuggled into his arms, everybody dropped their eyes. When the ocean breeze fingered Ruby's face, something in the touch of it told her that she would, indeed, soon find Theo. Whether she would ever return with him, though, the wind did not reveal.

∼

Over four hundred miles away from The Oak, Josh rode into Chambersburg under a light rain just as the day ended, ten days after he left Richmond. He made his way down the gloomy main street until he reached a building with a light burning. A beat-up sign on the outside read, GENERAL GOODS AND SUNDRIES.

Josh dismounted, tied the horse's reins around a post, and stepped into the general store. Two men greeted him as he entered—a stout man in a dingy apron behind the counter and another, much thinner man with a bald head. The two sat across from each other, a checkerboard between them. The second man wore a long, black coat with a white shirt and brown pants.

"Evening," said Josh.

Both men nodded.

"What you need?" asked the man in the apron.

"A loaf of bread, a piece of any kind of meat you have."

"You got cash?"

"Not much but enough," Josh stated.

The man stepped to a shelf behind his counter. Josh faced the other man.

"Where you from?" asked the bald-headed man.

"Richmond."

"He's from Richmond," the thin man said to the blocky one as he returned with a loaf of bread.

"Don't get many folks here from Richmond," said the storekeeper as he wrapped the bread in brown paper. "What's your business here?"

Something about the two men made Josh a little nervous. For a second he weighed how much to say, then decided he might as well tell the truth, at least about York. "I'm searching for somebody," he admitted. "A tall man, thick, black beard, maybe came through here back in the fall, October or so. Chews tobacco. Got a little swagger in him."

The two men exchanged glances. "Who are you?" asked the clerk.

"My name is Josh Cain. What's yours?"

"Jukes," said the thin man. "Able Jukes. I'm mayor here. This is Tolliver. He runs this place." The storekeeper nodded.

215

"Pleased to meet you both," said Josh.

"Why you lookin' for this other fella?" asked Tolliver.

"He's my brother. I know he headed this way but don't know exactly what happened to him after that."

"Maybe he ran afoul of some rough men," said Jukes. "Lots of them on the loose these days."

"I know that's so."

"What was he doin' in these parts?" asked Tolliver.

Josh took off his hat, scratched his head, and set his hat back on. Although he didn't want to tell a lie, he didn't want these two to know the truth either. "Reckon you need to ask him that."

Jukes stepped a pace closer. "You sound like a Southern boy. I expect you fought with the Rebs."

Josh didn't like the tone of the question but tried not to show it. "I fought with General Hancock."

"That surprises me."

"It surprised a lot of people, but that's the way it was."

Jukes eased off half a pace.

"You seen the man I'm looking for or not?" Josh asked.

"Yeah," said Jukes. "We seen him."

Josh arched an eyebrow, his surprise evident. "How long ago?"

"A day or two. He's at the town jail."

Josh held his excitement in check. "What's he doing there?"

"He had no oath of allegiance document. We been waitin' to hear from somebody. Want to clear up the whole situation but can't seem to get any response from Richmond or Beaufort. He says that's where he swore his oath."

"He's telling the truth about that."

"You saw him do it?"

Josh hesitated but again didn't want to lie. "I wasn't in the room at the time, but I know he did."

"You saw his document?"

Again Josh knew he had to tell the truth. "Nope, not with my own eyes. But he did it. I know that as sure as you just put my bread in a paper wrapper."

Jukes scratched his chin. "Me and Tolliver here want to believe you, but . . . well, you can see the position we're in. Your brother, York, who admits he fought for the Rebs, showed up here with a pretty flimsy story about why he came to these parts. We asked to see his oath document, but he ain't got it with him."

"He say what happened to it?"

Jukes smiled slyly. "He swears I stole it from his saddlebags. Ain't that a likely story?"

Josh scowled. He knew instantly Jukes had done exactly what he had just teased about, but what could Josh do about it? He wanted to pull out his pistol and march the two men straight to the jail and make them release York. He took a breath to steady himself. *That won't work*, he told himself. *I've just got to figure something else out.* "You have Mr. York under a Yankee guard?" he asked.

"Yep."

"Mind if I see him?"

Jukes rubbed his bald head. "Don't see why not."

"Good."

Leaving Tolliver in the store, Josh and Jukes headed to the jail, about two minutes away. Once inside, Jukes led him past two bored-looking guards to the four cells in the back. York lay on a bunk in the second cell, his feet propped on the bare wall, his head turned away from Josh.

"Get up, York!" yelled Jukes. "You got company."

York rolled over, his eyes dull. Josh couldn't believe how awful his brother looked—thin as a rail, his beard ragged, his hair long and un-washed, his nose a bit crooked, like somebody had shoved it over to one side with a blunt instrument. A bit of dried blood crusted under the right nostril. "York?"

York stared at him as if seeing a ghost, then stood on unsteady legs and staggered his way.

"It's me, York," Josh called.

As York neared the bars, he reached toward Josh. Josh touched his hand through the steel rods. "It's really you?" York murmured, his voice barely more than a whisper. "I ain't just imaginin' it?"

"No," said Josh, overjoyed at finding him alive. "I'm real and I'm here to get you out and take you home."

York glanced at Jukes, then stumbled back to his bunk and collapsed wearily onto it. "He tell you why they got me here?"

Josh turned to the mayor. "Mind if I visit him alone?"

Jukes hesitated, then nodded. "Makes no difference to me. He can't go nowhere 'til we see his papers." With that he pivoted and left.

Josh faced York again. He sat on the bunk, his shoulders slumped.

"Jukes stole my papers," said York, his breath short. "I know it for a fact."

"Why would he do that?"

"You know this town got burned out."

"Yes."

"Jukes lost a wife and a son in the fire. He ain't fond of any Reb, me included. He told me to my face he took the paper. Also that my letters to Beaufort never got sent."

"You think he plans to keep you here forever?"

When York dropped his eyes, Josh figured he knew why. "You think Jukes knows about the treasure, don't you?"

York stared at Josh, obviously surprised but also a little more energized. "How did you find out?"

"Lynette and I thought you were dead, so I went through the box that held your things. I found the journal. It pointed me in this direction."

"I figured to do a lot with that money," York said.

"You don't even know that a treasure exists!" declared Josh, frustrated at York for the reckless greed that had put him in this fix.

York took a deep breath. Josh noted the weak light in his eyes. His time in jail had taken a lot out of this once haughty man. York wiped at his nose and fresh blood appeared on his upper lip.

"What's wrong with you?" Josh asked.

"A little nosebleed—nothin' to worry over."

Josh frowned. His eyes narrowed. "They beat you up in here?"

York waved him off. "I'm certain Jukes found my scribbles in my saddlebags," he said, ignoring Josh's question. "I figure he's spent the last few months lookin' for a wagon up and down every dirt road between here and Mercersburg."

"And he wants you out of the way until he's found it."

"Least until he knows if any treasure is out there."

Josh rubbed his eyes, feeling suddenly wearier than he could remember. He was weary from searching for York, weary from concern over not finding him. He felt angry too, upset he had not seen the kids and Camellia for so long. "You get into more trouble than anybody I know," he accused York.

York held up his hands, palms toward the sky. "I admit that's true. But I do what I think is right."

"You do what you think will get you ahead," Josh countered.

"That too."

Josh glanced back toward the front of the jail. "So what next?"

York stood and shuffled to the cell bars. He gripped them with trembling fingers. "I been in here six months," he whispered. "Poor food, bad treatment. You see how I look." He paused while Josh inspected him head to toe. "I can't go on too much longer like this. You got to get my papers from Jukes, show them to the lieutenant who runs this place."

"But how? He's not likely to just hand them over."

"You know how."

Josh glanced over his shoulder to make sure nobody stood within earshot. "You expect me to steal the paper from him?" he whispered.

"He stole it from me!" York's eyes lit up with some of his old fire. "He's probably out every day lookin' for the gold. You should be able to get in and out of his house with no trouble at all."

"What if he's destroyed the paper?"

"He ain't done that."

"How do you know?"

"He said he'd give it back to me if I told him what roads I already checked."

"Why didn't you do that?"

"'Cause I figure he's lyin'. I tell him what he wants to know, and what's his motive for even keepin' me alive, much less givin' me my papers? He'll kill me and destroy any trace of me if I tell him anythin'."

Josh saw York's logic but still didn't want to do any thieving. Yet, what else could he do? Since the papers belonged to York, it wasn't really theft if he simply took them back. So long as he didn't take anything else or harm Jukes's property, it didn't seem like any kind of sin.

York's nose bled again, and he wiped it with a finger. "You got to get me out. I'm about come to the end of my rope."

Josh sighed. York seemed fragile, almost humble. His injuries and being in jail had taken a lot of starch out of him.

"OK," Josh finally said.

"You'll go after my papers?"

"Yes."

"I knew I could count on you, Brother," York said wearily.

"When I get these papers, we're leaving here, right? Gold or no gold."

"You're in charge," said York.

"OK."

Silence fell for a moment.

Then York spoke. "What news do you bring from The Oak?"

Josh took off his hat and stared into it for a moment before he decided to go on and tell it out straight. "Katherine is dead."

York's face fell. "I am truly sorry to hear that," he said, shaking his head sadly. "I didn't do right by that woman."

Josh didn't argue, so York continued. "How did it happen?"

Josh told him as much as he knew from the letter.

"She was a strong woman," York said. "Deserved better than me, I expect."

"Maybe so."

"This will go hard on Calvin, I think."

"I'm certain you're right."

"She tell Trenton where she hid my money?"

Josh wanted to strangle York for thinking of such a thing right now. "I have no idea, and I don't care," he said brusquely. "All I want to do is get you out of here so we can go home."

"What about Lynette?" York asked softly. "Is she well?"

What is York thinking right now? Josh wondered. But he had to stay focused on the matters at hand. "She is healthy but needs help. Her hotel is lost, and now the government wants her house as well—taxes, you know."

York buried his face in his hands. "I have made so many mistakes. With Lynette, with Katherine. When I get out of here, I hope to make some amends if I can."

Surprised by what he was hearing, Josh studied his brother. "I hope you get that chance."

When York glanced up, Josh saw what he had never seen in his brother's eyes: a combination of fear, hope, and contrition.

York focused his eyes on the floor. "Lynette told me once the Lord might need to break me."

"Sometimes it takes that to get a man's attention," said Josh.

York looked back up. "Get me my papers," he said firmly.

"Then we'll leave?"

"Yes."

Josh nodded, hoping York was telling the truth. Somehow, though, he feared no matter what had happened back home, York would not leave a potential treasure behind when the time came without some kind of fight . . . and maybe a hard one at that.

Chapter Twenty-Three

As usual, Trenton woke up long after the sun rose, his head pounding with pain from too much liquor and too little sleep. He slipped into some wrinkled pants and a soiled shirt, splashed his face with water from a washbowl, and staggered downstairs to see what he could find to eat. Since his mother's death, food had not been a priority for him, but every now and again he did have to eat something.

He found a couple of biscuits wrapped in paper in the pantry, ate them standing up, and threw the paper to the floor. A full coffeepot sat on a table in the back room, and Trenton felt a touch of gratitude that Calvin made some most every day. He found a cup, banged it, on the table to clear it of anything left over from the day before, poured coffee into it, and made his way to the front porch of the manse. A thin wind blew over his face as he stepped to the rail and looked out.

The huge oak from which the plantation had received its name wore a fresh coat of green leaves. Trenton examined the oak for a moment, marveling at its strength in spite of its age. How long did a tree like that stand? he wondered. Far longer than a human being. But would it last forever? No, nothing did, no matter how valuable.

Trenton took a sip of coffee. The sun warmed his face. A bird sang from somewhere near the top of the oak. A bee buzzed near some azaleas blooming by the porch steps.

Trenton sighed. In times past such a day would have pleased him greatly. He would have mounted his horse—already saddled by the darkies of course—and ridden around The Oak. He would have taken in the grandeur of the rice crop already in the field, the sweat of the servants' strong bodies as they labored, the sheer size of what he and his family owned.

Today, though, no rice crop grew. No darkies worked the plantation, not even the few who had come to labor for his mother while she was alive. No grandeur existed any longer. The huge oak seemed tired, worn out in spite of the leaves now bursting forth on it. Did matters of the world affect it at all? Did it sense the harsh conditions that had torn down so much of everything around it? Did the tree know that one day it, too, would fall and die, like everything else in his world had seemed to do?

Trenton drank from his cold coffee again and anger rose in his throat. Anger at the war that had ended all his hopes. Anger at the blacks who had murdered his mother. Anger at his mother for dying without telling him where to find the money. He recalled the last few weeks since Katherine's death—days of sheer torment for him.

He and Calvin had buried Katherine near the river. Only a few people had showed up for the ceremony and no preacher among them. Calvin marked Katherine's grave with a white wood cross and spoke a few words over her dirt-covered grave. After standing there a few minutes in quiet, he had walked away. Trenton stayed far longer, hours after everyone else had left. His eyes were puffy with tears—a constant state, it seemed, since her passing.

At times he felt his tears came from genuine sorrow that his mother had passed and with such little ceremony too. She should have been buried in Beaufort, at the Episcopal church his father had largely funded. Hundreds of people should have come to pay her homage. A true minister should have said high-toned words over her corpse. At other times, though, he wondered if his tears sprung from the simple fact that her passing had left him a pauper—penniless in a world where a white Confederate man without money stood no chance against the powerful forces set up against him.

On many days when his loneliness got the worst, he went back to her grave and sat down on it and patted the soil. "Where, Mother?" he whispered through the liquor that almost always fogged his brain. "Where did you hide the money?"

But no answer had come from the dirt.

Today, his coffee cup in hand, Trenton massaged his head against the ache rising from his skull and wondered what to do next. Although he had searched all over the manse, he had found only a couple of hundred dollars in his mother's belongings. He knew that wouldn't last long. What would he do when it ran out?

Furious, he cursed her for dying, for her failure to tell him where to find the money, for her dependence on Calvin instead of him, for her marriage to York, for so many things. She had ruined his life. She and Calvin and the war and—

Trenton heard voices. He peered out past the oak tree and saw Beth and Camellia walk into their garden, their heads covered with bonnets to protect their faces from the sun, their bodies clothed in simple dresses. Calvin appeared beside them, a couple of hoes in his hands. He wore a floppy, black hat.

Trenton finished his coffee and set the cup on the porch. As he watched the three people he hated the most begin to work, his anger boiled even higher. Didn't they know they had no money? That any day now the tax men from Beaufort might show up with a couple of Yankee soldiers and demand they leave The Oak because they couldn't pay their taxes? That he had not found the Negroes who killed Katherine? Were they unaware that the blacks and the Yankees ran the world now? That life held no hope, no cause for pleasure?

Sweat poured down Trenton's face as his fury boiled. He rushed back to his room, slid on his boots and hat, grabbed his pistol, and hurried out of the house and down to the garden. Although he didn't know exactly what he planned to do once he got there, he knew he could no longer sit idly by and let things stand as they were. He stepped to the edge of the wire fence that kept the deer out of the vegetable patch.

Calvin looked up. "Morning."

Beth and Camellia stopped to nod their greetings, then went back to their hoeing.

Trenton fumed for a couple of seconds before he spoke without thinking. "I want you two gone from here," he announced, pointing to Beth and Camellia. "Take Johnny, Butler, that old darky woman, everybody else too. I want the whole lot of you cleared off this place before nightfall."

Camellia and Beth froze. They eyed Calvin, who stepped between them and Trenton.

"Who will grow your food if they leave?" Calvin asked Trenton.

Trenton blinked. Such a notion had not crossed his mind. "Doesn't matter," he said, quickly recovering. "I will buy what I need in Beaufort."

"With what? The last of Mother's money is gone."

Trenton swallowed hard but didn't let the truth stop him. "I don't care if I never eat again. It's time they left and fended for themselves."

"You don't have the authority to throw us off," Camellia retorted. "My pa owns this place since your mother's death."

Trenton balled his fists. He wanted to hit something. But instead he said, "I expect your father is dead, and so do you. That means The Oak comes back to me."

"And me," Calvin interjected.

"But I'm the elder son," argued Trenton.

Calvin carefully laid down his hoe. "Excuse us, ladies," he said as he eased over to Trenton and took him by the elbow. "I need to talk privately with my brother."

Camellia and Beth turned away, pretending to go back to their labors. But Trenton could see out of the corner of his eye they were listening. He allowed Calvin to steer him away from the women.

"Leave us alone," Calvin said softly but firmly once they stopped. "Go on about your business, whatever that is these days, and stay out of the way."

"You are choosing them over me?" asked Trenton, equally as firm.

Calvin slowly shook his head. "You force me to make choices I would just as soon not make."

Trenton grunted and glanced back at Beth. "You want her, don't you?"

Calvin stared hard at him. "She is not under discussion here."

"But it's true, isn't it? You have a hankering for her. I've watched you two since . . . since the day by the river. You spend time with her whenever you can."

Calvin shrugged. "Beth and I have become friends. Anything beyond that will have to wait until her pa returns from Richmond."

Trenton jerked away from Calvin. "You stole her from me!"

"She never belonged to you for me to steal!"

"Yes, she did," Trenton countered. "She liked me—at least until *you* interfered."

225

Calvin paused, obviously trying to keep peace between them. "Look, I don't want to fight with you. You're my brother. Just leave them alone; that's all I'm asking. Josh Cain will surely return soon. When he does, we will leave and you will have the place all to yourself. I will give my share to you."

"You're going with them?" Trenton asked, stunned.

"If Beth will have me, yes, I am."

Trenton blinked. Although he had suspected this, it still hit him like a rock dropped off a cliff. "You would truly leave me? The Oak?"

Calvin gazed over the plantation. "I never dreamed I'd say this, but yes, I will leave The Oak."

"But how can you do that?"

"The Oak is not important to me anymore. The war . . . it changed me, shaped me in ways I never thought possible. Nearly dying will do that to a man, I guess. Make him check his priorities, what he believes important. The Oak is gone. It will never be what it was. Like the world we lived in . . . it's all gone. We have to deal with that, accept it. Change with the times or die."

"Never!" said Trenton. "If we change, we lose!"

"We've already lost!" insisted Calvin. "That's what you can't seem to get in your head. We lost and that's it. Maybe it's a good thing."

Trenton laughed sarcastically. "You sound like a Yankee—or a darky."

Calvin eyed him sadly. "You think that's the worst insult you could offer, don't you?"

"It's not one I'd want thrown at me."

Calvin took out a handkerchief and wiped his face. "I'm through with the past. I want to make a better future—for me, for Beth."

"What about Mother? Revenge for her death?"

"Mother is dead. I grieve that. It hurts deeply. But I can't do anything about it now."

Trenton was indignant. "You don't care if I find her killer or not, do you?"

"No, I don't. Mother said not to blame him. I would advise you to let it go at that. To not make it the most important thing in life, like you seem to have done. What will you do if you catch the man anyway?"

"I will dispense justice."

Calvin's jaw tightened. "That's the work for the law."

"It's the work of any man who loves his mother and wants to see her death avenged."

Calvin shook his head. "Sometimes I don't feel like I know you at all."

The words cut. Trenton wanted to hurt his brother as much as he could. He grabbed Calvin by the elbow and spun him to where they faced each other, eye to eye. "You caused Mother's death, you know," he charged.

Calvin's eyes widened. "How can you say that?"

"All that Bible spouting you did." He squeezed Calvin's arm tighter. "She listened to that. It changed her. She never would have tried to help those Negroes if you hadn't filled her head with all that religious nonsense."

"My reading soothed her, gave her peace."

"It led to her death, and I'll never forgive you for it." Trenton's fingers dug into Calvin's flesh. He wanted to tear away his brother's arm—to rip it off just as York's bullet had torn his leg away.

Calvin jerked his arm away from Trenton and backed up. "Believe what you want!" he snapped.

Trenton stepped close again. "I know what I know."

Calvin's eyes were accusing. "You don't know anything about anything that's important."

Trenton took a swing at his brother, but Calvin grabbed his fist and held it fast. When Trenton yanked his hand back, Calvin let go.

Trenton lost his balance and fell to the ground. His face reddened with anger, and he ground his teeth. Calvin bent to help him up, but Trenton pushed him away and scrambled up, his wooden leg unsteady but holding. Without another word, Trenton moved past him and back to Camellia and Beth.

Calvin followed him.

"I told you I wanted you gone!" Trenton shouted to the two women. "That has not changed, in spite of my brother's little talk with me!"

"They're not going until they want to go!" Calvin declared, standing by Beth. "I told you that."

Trenton jerked out his pistol and waved it at Calvin. "You can go too; it matters not to me. But I mean what I say!"

"You best put that weapon up!" ordered Calvin.

"You are no longer a brother to me!" seethed Trenton. "I am ashamed you carry the Tessier name. Are we clear on that?"

"Clear as glass."

Trenton held his pistol on his brother for another few seconds. He wanted to shoot Calvin on the spot. Then he thought of his mother's dying words and knew he couldn't do it—at least not this way, not at this time, and in cold blood. Forcing down his hatred, he lowered his gun and backed away. *Real soon now*, he thought as he left, *real soon Calvin and I will settle our differences . . . regardless of Mother's final desire that we cease the hostilities.* Circumstances made it such that Trenton saw no way for them to avoid it any longer.

Back in Chambersburg, Josh carefully trailed Jukes for the next three days, wanting to make sure of the man's schedule before he took the chance of breaking into his house. Finally, he decided he knew enough. Jukes left every morning a couple of hours after sunlight, his thin frame on a big black gelding. As Josh had suspected, Jukes spent the days riding up and down the dirt trails that ran off the main road between Chambersburg and Mercersburg, searching for the gold he believed York's scribbles described. On the days Josh followed him, Jukes rode almost eleven miles south before he broke off the main road. Josh wondered if the mayor had started his search from the north to the south or the other way around. If he had started in Chambersburg, that meant he had only six more miles before he ran out of trails to inspect.

If not for the fact that York sat sick and despondent in a dirty jail cell, Josh might have laughed. What if somebody had already gotten the cash and gold? That would mean both Jukes and York had gone to a whole lot of trouble for absolutely no reason.

On the fourth morning after his arrival in Chambersburg, Josh watched as Jukes rode out. Confident he could expect Jukes to stay away all day, Josh simply waited until the mayor disappeared. Then Josh left his horse, sneaked past a shed and a well, and approached Jukes's house from the back. The house, a square box of a place with a stoop on the back and a simple porch on the front, stood on a little ridge about a hundred feet from the woods. On the back stoop Josh paused and looked around. Nothing moved in the spring morning, so he turned back to the door and pushed it. It didn't open. Not wanting to damage anything, Josh spotted a window to his left. To his relief the window opened. He quickly crawled inside and dropped to the floor.

As expected, he landed in the kitchen area. A square table sat in the middle of the room, with a couple of clean plates on it and four chairs surrounding it. Several wood shelves hung on the walls. A big bucket of water sat in the corner to his right, and a small fireplace burned low to his left.

Waiting for a second but hearing nothing, Josh left the kitchen and moved down a short hallway until he spotted a closed door. He figured it to be Jukes's bedroom. He eased to the door and pushed it back.

A man waited on a chair directly in front of him, a shotgun pointed Josh's way.

Josh froze in place.

"You are an adventuresome man," said Tolliver, the clerk from the general store.

"I'm surprised to see you," Josh replied, his pulse racing.

"Jukes ain't a fool."

"He knows I've tailed him?"

"People in these parts keep their eyes on a stranger, and Jukes *is* the mayor, you know. Folks tell him things."

"He left you to guard his house while he is away."

"It appears so."

Josh cleared his throat and decided to plow ahead. "I am looking for my brother's papers. Your friend Jukes took them from him."

"Those are serious charges. You got any proof?"

Josh tried to size up the store clerk, figure how far to push him. "I expect you know Jukes well enough to know I don't need proof."

The store clerk grinned. "But what's the motive for Jukes to steal your friend's papers?"

"York is a Reb. Jukes lost a wife and son to the war. He's not likely to do any Reb any favors."

Tolliver studied Josh, then shook his head. "That ain't all of it. It don't explain why Jukes goes out most every day when the weather allows. Or why he sent me here to keep an eye out for you."

Josh arched an eyebrow. "You got a good head on your shoulders."

"I ain't a dummy."

Josh decided to tell Tolliver the truth. "Your man Jukes is out looking for gold."

The clerk lowered the gun slightly as Josh continued the story. Tolliver sat up straighter as Josh talked.

"So that's it," said Josh when he finished the tale. "Jukes wants York in jail until he's searched all the side roads between here and Mercersburg."

Tolliver swore quietly. "You tellin' me the truth? Your man York come here lookin' for treasure?"

"As sure as I'm wishing you'd put down that shotgun."

Tolliver smiled slightly but didn't lower the weapon. Josh tried to think of something to put the store clerk on his side. After a second he came up with an idea, and although he hated the notion of having to do what it would call for, he decided he had no choice but to offer the bait and see if the clerk bit. "I tell you what," he said. "You lower that shotgun, let me collect the paper I came to find, get my friend out of jail, and we will go find that treasure together. You get half of whatever we discover."

Tolliver chewed on his lower lip. "Maybe Jukes will do the same if I ask him for it," he suggested.

Josh shrugged. "How long have you known Mr. Jukes?"

"Ten years, close to it."

"You know him as the kind of man who will share a treasure with anybody?"

"Maybe I won't give him a choice."

"You willing to go against him alone?"

Tolliver weighed the question, then asked, "Why should I trust you over Jukes?"

"I told you the truth, didn't I? Jukes didn't."

When Tolliver hesitated, Josh knew he had him. "Half of anything we find," Josh repeated. "Then Mr. York and I will disappear."

"If I take half of a treasure, I expect I will, too, if I know what is good for me."

"So you will let me finish what I came here to do?"

Tolliver put the weapon in his lap. "Search to your heart's content."

Josh exhaled with relief. He left the clerk and searched the house. Within a few minutes he found what he wanted—a small chest in the parlor with a drawer in the top. Inside the drawer was a stack of papers. Josh thumbed through them. Right near the bottom he uncovered York's oath of allegiance document and pulled it out. Paper in hand, he hurried to the kitchen, where he found Tolliver at the table, a cup of coffee in hand.

"You goin' to the jail?" Tolliver asked.

"Yes. I'll meet you at your store after I get York out."

"It ain't really my store, you know. Jukes owns it."

Josh nodded. "See you there."

"You know Jukes will come after us, don't you?"

"I would expect nothing less."

In Richmond, Lynette sat by a table in the carriage house, her head in her hands. Her hair, pinned up, turned grayer with each passing day and her eyes wearier. A pot of tea stood on the table, her one and only luxury these days. Two tin cups kept the pot company. Lynette heard a knock at the door and glanced up but didn't move. A second knock sounded, and she pushed up, shuffled to the door, and opened it.

A man in a brown coat and black pants stood there, a bowler hat on his head, a leather book under his right arm.

"Can I help you?" Lynette asked.

The man took off his hat and bowed slightly. "I am Joe Ross, from the Richmond State Bank."

Lynette started to close the door, but he shoved a foot over the threshold and held it open. "I must talk with you," he insisted.

Lynette sighed, then let him in and led him to one of the two seats by the table. Ross sat down and placed the book in his lap.

"I expect I know why you're here," said Lynette.

Ross nodded and opened the book. "You owe over four hundred."

"It's only been a couple of weeks since I got the papers."

"The bank wanted me to come remind you to vacate these premises by the end of the month."

"How am I supposed to make money?" argued Lynette. "I want to rent rooms in the main house, but I can't afford to buy furniture to make the place livable!"

"Times are hard," Ross stated. "Are you not able to find employment?"

Lynette bit her lip. "I've been busy trying to fix up the house. The war left it a mess. My son's got a job, and we've been saving what we can, but once we take out money for the necessities, there's not a lot left."

Ross shut the book. "I'm afraid the bank has no choice. We've been patient. You have to agree with that."

"Is there no way to wait a little longer?" she begged.

Ross put on his hat. Footsteps sounded on the stairs outside.

"Must be my son," Lynette said, her question still hanging in the air.

Ross stood. Lynette's eyes pleaded with him.

"Let me see what I can do," he offered.

"Thank you," she said, although she wasn't sure a little extra time would matter.

When Jackson stepped through the door, Ross exited.

"Who was that?" Jackson asked.

"The banker, wanting his money."

"What are we going to do? No way can we come up with the money we owe."

Lynette swallowed hard. It didn't really matter if Ross found a way to postpone matters for a few days, even weeks. Barring a miracle, she and Jackson would have to move. But where would they go? She thought of The Oak. Could they return there? No, she dismissed the idea as quickly as it had come. Although she cared deeply for Camellia and everyone else in South Carolina, she couldn't just show up and expect them to provide for her. Besides, she and York had too much history. He claimed to still love her, but she had turned him away because of Katherine. If he was still alive, how could she go begging to him now that Katherine had died? No self-respecting woman could do that. Besides, York would want something more from her, and although her affection for him had deepened again during the war, she didn't know whether she felt that way for him or not.

"I don't know where we're going," she told Jackson, with tears in her eyes.

He crossed the room and hugged her. "Don't worry," he encouraged. "I'll take care of you."

She smiled at his tenderness. How grateful she was for such a good son! "We'll have to find a room to rent."

Jackson leaned back and wiped her tears away with a gentle touch. "We'll need to leave word for Mr. Cain. Let him know where we are."

"Wonder where he is," she said, stepping away. "If he found York."

"I wonder if he found any gold."

Lynette chuckled. "That could solve our problem."

"You figure Captain York would give us a loan?"

"I think I could coax him into it—if he's still alive."

"He better get here fast then."

Lynette sat down at the table and poured herself a cup of tea. As she sipped it, an idea formed. But should she really consider it?

Jackson joined her at the table.

Her thoughts raced in all directions, but the idea persisted. "Maybe *I* should go find Captain York," she finally said.

Jackson arched an eyebrow. "I don't know what you mean."

"He headed to Chambersburg, we know that. If he has found any money—"

"You would truly ask him for aid?"

"I know I shouldn't . . . but . . . yes, I think I would. As a last resort."

Jackson studied the idea. "If he's found anything, wouldn't he already be headed back here?"

"Then we'll meet him on the way. There's only one main road between here and Chambersburg."

"But what if he hasn't found anything?"

Lynette sipped her tea again. "Then it won't matter. At least I won't be here when they come to take the place. There's some solace in that."

"How fast can you get there and back?"

"If I find York and he's got money, we can take a train back. If not, again, it won't matter."

Jackson grabbed a cup, and Lynette poured him some tea. "I'm going with you."

"Shouldn't you stay here and keep working?"

"I'm not sending you out there on your own."

Lynette started to argue, then realized, what did it matter? If she didn't find York—or even if she did but he didn't have any money—she would lose her house no matter how much Jackson earned in the next few days.

She smiled at her son. "We'll need to take what little money we've saved. Might as well spend it for this as anything else. We leave in the morning," she announced.

Jackson nodded and drank his tea.

As they sat in companionable silence, Lynette knew the moment had come. She took Jackson's teacup from his hands and placed it softly on the table. He looked at her curiously. "I need to tell you something."

"What?"

She spoke it straight out. "Hampton York is your father."

Jackson stayed quiet for a long time. Then he simply nodded and picked up his teacup to sip from it again.

"Aren't you going to say anything?" she asked.

"What's to say? I figured that out the moment I met him."

With York's document in hand, Josh hurried to the jail, where Lieutenant Rider met him as he entered. When Josh handed the Yankee lieutenant the oath of allegiance document, Rider examined it carefully.

"Where did you get this?" Rider asked.

"Jukes," Josh said truthfully.

"He just volunteered this to you?"

"Not exactly, but it is authentic. You can tell."

The lieutenant tensed. "You didn't hurt Jukes, did you?"

"No."

Rider eyed Josh curiously. "Does Jukes know you got this?"

"Best ask him that."

"Is he going to be unhappy if I let Mr. York go?"

"Best ask him that too."

Rider glanced at the document once more, then shrugged. "You got the correct document, so what else can I do?"

The private entered the jail and walked toward them. "Go get Mr. York's horse ready," the lieutenant ordered. Although the young man looked surprised, he nodded and left the room. Rider led Josh back to where York lay.

"Get up," Rider snapped at York. "You're free to go."

York rolled off his bunk and stood unsteadily to his feet. His beard looked even worse than a few days ago, his eyes duller. Again dried blood showed under his nose, and Josh's worry struck hard again. A day or two more in jail and York might not have made it.

"You ain't kiddin' me, are you?" whispered York.

"I'm not that cruel," said Rider.

York looked past Rider, and his eyes lit up with a bit more strength. Josh stepped past the lieutenant. "I came to get you. Sorry it took so long."

York stuck a hand through the prison bars. When Josh grasped it, it felt hot and trembled some.

"Gather your belongings," Rider demanded.

York dropped Josh's hand and turned back to his cell. Within a minute he had everything in hand.

"The rest of your stuff is in the front," Rider explained, unlocking the cell door. "Pistol, saddlebags, and such."

York wobbled a little as he stepped out of the cell. Josh hurried to him and gripped his elbow. "You all right?"

"Just leg weak," said York, pushing away his hand. "I been in this cell too many months."

The two of them walked to the front of the jail, where they picked up York's things.

"Jukes is going to raise the roof," said Rider. "So I want you two gone from these parts."

Josh nodded. "My desire as well."

"I mean *immediately*," Rider warned. "Don't let me see your faces around here again, you got that straight?"

Josh and York agreed, then strode into the street where York's horse was hitched. York threw a leg up to mount but couldn't manage it at first. Josh moved to help, but York waved him off and climbed slowly into his saddle. Josh mounted his horse too.

In two minutes they had reached the General Goods and Sundries store. There, waiting for them, was the store clerk, Tolliver.

"You ready?" Josh asked Tolliver.

"Where we goin'?" asked York, glancing from the man to Josh and back again.

Josh smiled. "We're going to look for buried treasure."

York's mouth dropped open. "What?"

Tolliver mounted.

"He had a shotgun on me at Jukes's house," Josh explained quickly. "I told him that if he didn't shoot me, and he allowed me to find your oath of allegiance so I could get you out of jail, we would help him find the treasure. I promised him half of whatever we found." He paused and grinned. "I hope you don't mind."

"Half is a high price to pay to save a man of your low status," York joked at Josh, obviously feeling a little better surrounded by fresh air and sunshine.

"Seeing as how I just got you out of jail, I would expect a little more gratitude," Josh retorted.

York started to laugh but coughed instead. Hearing the deep congestion in York's chest, Josh worried more. The jail stay had taken a lot out of his brother, no matter how much York tried to pretend otherwise.

"Let's go," Tolliver urged. "Time's a-wastin'."

Josh clicked at his horse, and the three of them rode out of Chambersburg at a gallop.

Josh hoped he would never lay eyes on the little town again.

Chapter Twenty-Four

It took Lynette and Jackson ten days of hard, fast travel to ride the 195 miles between Richmond and Chambersburg—he on a horse, she in a small buggy. They arrived in the little town right before dark and, although weary and dirty from their journey, headed straight to the first building where they saw lights burning. A hand-painted sign identified the building as General Goods and Sundries. Pulling the buggy to the sign, Lynette hopped out as Jackson tied up his horse. She brushed as much dirt as she could off her face, then the two of them entered the store together. A couple of men played checkers at a table to their left. Another two men stood by the counter—one a tall, bald fellow wearing an apron, the other a black man with a square face and a flat nose.

Jackson strode to the man in the apron while Lynette followed. "Jackson Swanson," he said, extending his hand.

"Able Jukes," replied the man in the apron, taking Jackson's hand and shaking it.

"We're looking for a bite to eat," Jackson explained. "And a room to sleep in for the night. Anybody in town take in boarders?"

"I got some food." Jukes moved behind the counter and took a loaf of bread and two cans off the shelves above his head. "And there's a house a mile or so out that rents rooms. It's got a broke wagon out front; you'll recognize it." Jukes placed the goods on the counter and glanced over at Lynette. "Where you two from?"

"Richmond," said Jackson.

When Jukes's eyes brightened, Lynette began to feel nervous for some reason. She moved closer to Jackson's side. "You had any other folks from Richmond through here lately?"

Jukes wrapped up the bread. "Now that you mention it . . . yeah. A couple of fellas, in fact."

"How long ago?"

"A while." He handed the bread to Jackson, who put a couple of coins on the countertop.

"You know who they were?" asked Lynette.

Jukes dropped his eyes for an instant. "They didn't give out a lot of information."

"You know where they went?" asked Jackson.

Jukes glanced at the black man with the flat nose, then back to Lynette and Jackson. "Why you askin'?"

Lynette's suspicions rose. Something about Jukes bothered her, but not sure why, she decided to answer his question honestly. "We're kin to one of them. Friends to the other."

Jukes tilted his head slightly, and the black man eased away from the counter as if about to pounce. Lynette couldn't tell if the tilt of the head was a sign or not, but she felt more uneasy with each passing second.

"You got any idea why your kin and friend be comin' through these parts?" asked Jukes.

When Lynette hesitated, Jackson answered for her. "Best to ask them that question."

The black man now stood by the door, almost as if to keep them from leaving. Lynette touched Jackson's elbow. "I guess we'll head on to the boardinghouse. Be real dark soon."

Jukes tilted his head once more, and the two men playing checkers pushed back their chairs and stood. Lynette whirled around to leave, but the black man placed his body directly in front of the door. Lynette looked back at Jukes. He smiled, but there was no friendliness in it.

"I said we'll leave now," she said sternly.

Jukes held up a hand. "You'll go when I tell you to go."

Jackson reached for his waist, but one of the men behind him pulled his pistol first.

"Hold it!" shouted Jukes. "Nobody needs to get frisky here!"

Jackson's hand froze.

"Just let us leave," said Lynette. "No cause for trouble."

Jukes walked out from the counter. "I know where your men are," he said, his voice soft and easy.

Lynette's brow furrowed.

"My man, Tommy here"—Jukes indicated the square-faced man— "just found them today. Been lookin' for a while too, so they been layin' low, it seems. He says if we ride hard, we can reach them by early morning."

"Why are you looking for them?" Jackson asked.

Jukes laughed. "I expect at least three of us know the answer to that now, don't we?"

Lynette nodded, certain she knew what he meant. Jukes knew about York's search for the gold, wanted it, and had paid the black man, Tommy, to track York in hopes he would lead him to it. What she didn't know was what Jukes would do if and when York actually found any treasure. Since Jukes so obviously wanted the money, he might let everyone go if he put his hands on it. Or he might kill everybody who knew anything about it. Either way, she had no choice but to follow his lead, at least for now.

"What do you want from us?" she asked.

"You ride with me to find your men."

"Why do you need us there?" asked Jackson.

Jukes chuckled. "You can figure that out, can't you?"

Lynette nodded. "Hostages. And we know what you want from Captain York."

Jukes smirked. "I knew you were smart."

"What if we refuse?" asked Jackson, threat in his voice.

"You won't."

Lynette glanced at Jackson, then back to Jukes. "We'll go with you," she told Jukes. "Willingly."

Confusion registered on Jackson's face.

"It's the fastest way to York and Josh," Lynette told him.

"Your mama's right," said Jukes. "Best you listen to her."

Jackson nodded his understanding.

"Can you ride a horse?" Jukes asked Lynette.

"Yes."

"Then we're movin' soon as we can saddle up." He pointed to Tommy. "Get a couple more boys, and prepare the horses."

The black man rushed out.

Lynette took a deep breath. Maybe, just maybe, she'd find York and Josh by the time the sun rose. After that, though, she had no idea what to expect.

Josh, York, and Tolliver had been slowly searching the back roads around Chambersburg since York had gotten out of jail. Their hunt had taken them up and down every small road they came across. Today they were almost fourteen miles out. They pulled up their horses in a clearing at the end of a dirt road and hopped down. A weather-beaten wagon with a missing wheel on the right front sat in front of them. Even in the gathering dark, Josh could see weeds growing up through the bottom. York stepped up beside him, and together they strode to the wagon to look it over. Tolliver trailed them.

"Been here long enough it looks like," said York, examining the buckboard.

Josh nodded and bent closer to the wagon's side. "Bullet holes here, maybe." He rubbed his fingers over several splintered gashes in the wood. "It's been in a fight, that's for sure."

York stepped to the back of the wagon and inspected it. "Nothin' in it though," he said, obviously disappointed.

Josh paused and looked at his brother. "You expecting somebody would just leave a bunch of cash and gold in the back of a wagon?"

York waved in disgust, and Josh finished checking the wagon. Then they stepped to the edge of the clearing where it sat. A lone chimney, its bricks charred black but still standing, loomed up from the ground about twenty feet away between two tall maple trees. Weeds and undergrowth had climbed up and around the bottom of the chimney, almost covering its base. The ashy remains of a house lay in and among the weeds, and a tiny shed stood about thirty feet away. Tolliver checked the back and sides of the shed before he disappeared through the gaping door at the front.

Josh squatted beside the chimney and peered up the dark passage until he could see through to the little bit of light left in the day. "Nothing here," he called. Standing, he looked around but couldn't see much anymore in the gathering dark.

York stepped up beside him. "Somebody fought here, that's for sure."

"But who and when?"

York grunted.

Tolliver walked out of the shed, a pitchfork in his hand. "Nothing in the shed but this."

"Check out behind it," ordered York.

Josh studied his brother, noting how frail and thin his body looked. Even though York paused often to catch his breath and blood trickled from his nose almost constantly, York had offered no complaint since his release from the jail. In spite of that, Josh figured York couldn't go on much longer without rest and good food. Josh felt weary himself.

"I figure it's time we gave up this hunt," Josh started. "We've been at it since the eighteenth—have searched every road between here and Chambersburg. Only a couple of miles left to search. We've dodged Jukes and his men every step of the way, hoping he won't find us, because if he does, something bad is likely to happen. I don't want that, and I don't think you do either."

York shook his head. "I got to keep tryin'."

Josh's frustration rose. "We've done all we can," he insisted. "I've been gone from home for months—you too. Who knows what's happening back there? They need us to get a crop in, to take care of things. I miss Camellia, Beth, and Butler."

York spat. "I know you are worried. Me too. And I know you and Camellia . . . you've waited too long to marry, and I'm partly to blame. But I want this money. Need it for . . ." He stared at the ground.

"I know!" Josh exclaimed, too upset to hold in his feelings any longer. "You want this money to rebuild The Oak. Since Katherine never gave you the money you won gambling, you figure that's gone forever now. You'll never know where she hid it, so you have to find this! It's your last chance to get a leg up on the world. Well, listen to me, Brother. Money can't buy you what you really need. I've tried to tell you that all your life, but I'm saying it now, as clearly as I can. I don't want to sound too righteous because I'm not. I know my faults better than anybody. But you've wanted wealth and status all your life, and what has it brought you? Huh? One heartache after the next, that's all. You have to admit it. Look at you—you're barely alive, yet you keep pushing to find something that doesn't even belong to you!" He paused for a breath.

"You finished chewin' on me, Brother?" York asked, surprisingly calm.

Josh scowled, not sure he was. "Maybe."

York wiped at his nose. Blood seeped from the right nostril again. "I got my reasons for wantin' this money. But they ain't what you're thinkin'."

"You always got your reasons," Josh said, wanting to choke him.

York shook his head. "You give me no credit for any honor, do you?"

Josh leaned against the chimney, trying to figure out what York meant. "Let's just say you tend to look out for yourself before all others."

York appeared grieved. "I'm sorry you don't think better of me."

Josh suddenly felt bad about what he had said. He started to apologize, but Tolliver appeared out of the dark.

"Nothin' behind the shed that I can see," he said.

"Let's camp here for the night," York suggested.

Tolliver nodded and moved away to his horse.

Josh tried to make amends. "Your heart's good, York, I believe that. But you have to admit this hunt for treasure has gotten you a bit crazy. All these years you've wanted The Oak. Now it's yours, but you're not even there. You're here, chasing a dream. I don't understand that. It's got to stop, and you know it. Jukes will come across us sooner or later, and he's likely to be real angry when he does. If anything bad happens, he's the law in these parts. It won't go well with us."

York pulled a chew of tobacco from his pocket and bit off a piece. Josh wondered how York had managed to get tobacco while in the jail. York gazed up at the sky. "I had a lot of time to think in that jail. I come to see I've been wrong about a few things."

"Like what?" Josh asked, taken aback at York's unusual tone.

York chewed on his tobacco for a second. "Well, for one thing, Lynette didn't run off from me back in forty-four because she didn't love me."

"How do you know that?"

"She told me."

York filled him in on what Lynette had revealed before he left Richmond. "I hated her for a long while for what she did. But now I know that wasn't right; she couldn't help it."

"But you didn't know that at the time."

"Still, I should have given her the benefit of the doubt. I should have trusted her."

"You were heartbroken," Josh said, defending his brother.

"True, but it's just like me to think hard of someone, even when I shouldn't."

Josh put a hand on York's shoulder. "I'm glad you know the truth now."

"Me too."

Josh glanced at Tolliver as he built a fire. "What's all this got to do with this treasure hunt?"

York spat. "I can't tell you right now. But I ask you to trust me—that's all."

Josh sighed. "You do what you need to do, but I will leave in the morning."

York patted him on the back. "You go on. I can't ask you to stay any longer."

"You healthy enough to keep looking?"

"I got no choice."

Josh started to ask "Why not?" but knew York wouldn't say. Whatever he had up his sleeve, he wouldn't reveal it until the moment he chose to reveal it.

"Just don't let your greed get you killed," Josh cautioned.

"I'll do my best to see that it don't."

Josh woke right after dawn the next morning and quickly ate a piece of biscuit, drank a cup of thin coffee, and began to pack for his trip home. He would stop by Richmond first and tell Lynette that he had found York and that he was safe, at least for the time being. Then he would point his horse south and ride as hard as he dared. If all went well, he and Camellia could finally leave The Oak and be married, maybe as early as the end of June. Filled with excitement, he paid little attention to York and Tolliver as they searched the area around the burned-down house. *Let them look*, he figured. They would surely come up empty-handed—just like they had done at the end of every dirt road between here and Chambersburg.

After rolling up his bedroll, Josh loaded it on his saddle and glanced one final time around the camp. Then he strode to the edge of the clearing and peered past the house, hoping to see York and tell him he was leaving.

"York!" he called.

"Over here."

Josh started walking toward York's voice. About fifty feet past the old chimney, he spotted something out of place on the ground. It shone slightly as it rested in a clump of scrubby bush, tall weeds, brambles, and vines. Drawn toward the object, Josh took a couple more steps. Then he saw the dim outline of rusty metal. He wondered for a moment if he had found a cannon or a shell from one, but as he reached the object, he saw that it was longer and had a piece of old, weathered rope tied to it.

Josh squatted, pushed back a handful of vines, dead limbs, and leaves, and saw the remains of a decaying rope attached to a small pulley system. He picked up the metal piece and rope, examined them, then realized what he was holding—the rope and pulley of a water well.

Dropping the materials, he stood and inspected the area. About ten feet to his left, he saw what he was looking for—an outcropping of stone almost completely covered by heavy undergrowth. Rushing to the stone, he knelt, pushed thick vines away, and saw exactly what he expected—a well with a stone wall about four feet high built around it.

Standing by the well, he grabbed a handful of the brambles and tugged them away. They reluctantly let go of the rocks. He clutched another handful and pulled them off too. A couple more handfuls and he could see a section of the top of the well. A round piece of wood covered the opening at the top. The well appeared to be about four feet in diameter. Josh cleared away more vines and dead leaves. The well looked like a barrel of stones covered by a wood top.

Josh glanced around for York and Tolliver but didn't see either of them. He studied the well for a moment. Whoever had built it had done a good job. The wood top kept the leaves out when the well wasn't in use. He wondered how long it had been since anybody had drawn water from it. From the looks of the heavy growth, it had been a long time. Had the house burned down before the war—or during it?

Josh scraped off more leaves, revealing a notch in the wooden top. He shoved his fingers under the notch and lifted. The top creaked, then slipped off a little. Brushing off more debris, he yanked hard. The top broke from the stone opening and came completely off. A piece of tattered rope snaked down from the well's side and into the darkness at the bottom. Josh stared into the well. Although he didn't know why, the hair on the back of his neck stood up. If somebody wanted to hide treasure, a place like this made perfect sense.

He could easily see it happening—a group of Confederates with stolen treasure in the back of a wagon running from the Federals. They rushed their wagon off the main road and down this path. They reached a dead end. The wagon stopped. The soldiers set up a line of fire facing the road from which the Yankees would attack. Others lifted the containers holding the money out of the wagon and quickly searched for a place to hide them.

They wouldn't put the containers in the chimney; that was too obvious. But they had no time to dig a hole, bury the treasure, and cover it.

Where, then, could they put it? Not in a well in use. Again, that was too obvious.

But what about a well already covered with brush and brambles? One where the house it belonged to had been burned out for a while, perhaps early in the war?

The soldiers could have ripped the pulley system down and tossed it away, lifted the wood top of the well, tied the treasure box to a rope, and eased it down into the darkness. Then they covered the well again and rushed away, letting the natural growth of the vines and brambles do what no human could have done—hide their deed.

Josh took a breath and grabbed the rope that snaked down into the well. Suddenly York appeared beside him.

"What you got there, Brother?" asked York.

"Not sure," said Josh.

York stared into the well. "Draw it up."

Josh pointed to the frayed rope. "You figure it will hold?"

"Only one way to tell."

Josh held the rope with both hands and gently tugged it upward. "It's got weight on it."

"Could be a bucket of water," reasoned York.

Josh lifted the rope further. York peered down as Josh kept pulling. The rope got thinner and more frayed as he hauled it up.

They heard a noise behind them and Josh paused.

Tolliver hurried their way from the woods. "Somebody's comin'!"

"Pull!" ordered York.

Josh yanked harder. York ran to his horse and grabbed his rifle off the saddle.

Josh could almost see the end of the rope.

His pistol in hand, Tolliver joined Josh and York.

Josh heard the sound of horses pounding down the road.

"Hurry!" urged York.

Josh hauled the rope up another few feet and then saw the end of it. He yanked the contents dangling on the end of the rope out of the well.

"Spread out!" York commanded Tolliver.

Josh glanced at York, who pointed his rifle at the rectangular metal box now sitting on the ground. "Get it out of here!" York commanded.

Josh untied the box, lifted it, and ran toward the woods. A few steps past the tree line, he spotted a hollowed-out oak, flat on the ground, and shoved the box into the rotted space. Wiping his hands, he rushed back toward the chimney, his pistol ready.

Hiding behind the chimney, he spotted York at the edge of the shed.

Seconds later, seven horses appeared from the last bend in the road. Jukes was at the front of the pack, his rifle in his hands.

Not sure Tolliver or York wouldn't shoot first and ask questions later, Josh fired a warning shot into the air.

Jukes jerked his horse up about seventy-five yards away, and he and the other riders thundered to a stop. Jukes yelled something at one of his men, and he and two other riders peeled off to the right, disappearing in the trees before Josh could get a look at them.

When York stuck his head out, Josh prayed nobody would get shot. He had seen enough bloodshed for at least two lifetimes.

"Leave us!" York shouted to Jukes. "This ain't your affair."

"We got you outnumbered!" called Jukes.

"But we got cover and you don't."

Jukes glanced around the clearing, obviously trying to locate Josh and Tolliver. "You find anythin'?" he called to York.

"Not your business what I found."

Jukes pointed his rifle, and one of his men headed toward the chimney where Josh hid. Josh fired another warning shot, and the man veered off to the left. Tolliver popped off a round from that direction, and this time the man stopped completely, his horse rearing slightly as he wheeled to a halt.

Jukes rode twenty-five yards closer. His eyes scanned the area and landed on the well. Josh groaned softly.

Jukes kicked his horse and trotted it toward the well. York let him go.

At the well, Jukes hopped down and stared into the water. "What did you find here?" he yelled.

"Leave us!" ordered York.

Jukes faced York again. "I want what you found."

York fired his rifle and a spray of dust kicked up at the feet of Jukes's horse. "I ain't wantin' to shoot you, but I will if need be," York challenged.

"You figure to kill all of us?"

"I expect if I kill you, the rest of your boys will go on home."

Determined to stop things before they went any further, Josh stepped from behind the chimney. "We don't exactly know what we found," he told Jukes. "But there's a box over there in the woods, in a hollow log. I'll show you where it is if you will put down your guns."

Jukes turned to him, then back to York. "Your brother ain't too loyal."

York glared at Josh. "You don't know what you're doin'!"

"I'm preventing bloodshed," called Josh, moving toward Jukes. "We don't know if there's anything in that box, but I won't see men killed for it, not even if it's a million dollars."

"You're a fool!" fumed York. "You don't bargain with a man like this!"

Jukes faced Josh. "You got a deal."

"You promise no shooting?"

"That box is what I want."

Josh lowered his pistol and waved to Tolliver, who appeared from behind his tree, his weapon at his side.

York shook his head. "You ain't gettin' my weapon," he told Jukes. "You go get the box if you want, but I ain't lettin' you put me back in prison."

"I won't do that," said Jukes. "You have my word."

York spat. Josh noticed blood once again dripped from his brother's nose.

Jukes glanced to the woods to his right. "Bring them out!" he shouted.

His man rode forward from the trees, his rifle aimed at the two riders with him.

"I had hoped to avoid this," Jukes said to York.

As the three riders drew closer, Josh's heart dropped. He recognized Lynette and Jackson. What were they doing here? The riders stopped by Jukes.

Jukes aimed his rifle at Lynette. "Drop your rifle or I shoot her," he told York.

"You wouldn't kill a woman in cold blood," York growled.

Jukes tilted his head, then shrugged. "All right," he said, now aiming the gun at Jackson. "But I would shoot a Johnny Reb, and you know it."

York eyed Lynette, then Jackson. Josh knew York wanted to fight but couldn't risk it. York spat again, then placed his gun on the ground. Tolliver did the same.

Jukes looked at Josh. "Where's that hollow log?"

Josh pointed in the direction. "Over there, a few feet in the woods."

Jukes ordered one of his men to go get the box. The man spurred his horse and disappeared into the woods.

Everybody waited. A bird chirped. A breeze blew. Josh held his place. Two or three minutes later Jukes's man rode back out, the treasure box on the front of his saddle. When he reached Jukes, he dismounted and set the box on the ground.

"Open it!" ordered Jukes.

The man cocked his pistol and shot away the lock on the box. Jukes hopped off his horse, squatted by the box, and lifted the top. A smaller wood box lay inside. Jukes lifted it out, pried up a latch, and opened it. A second later he lifted a handful of dollar bills up where everybody could see them.

"We found it!" he shouted, starting to laugh.

"You got gold there?" asked York.

Jukes searched the rest of the box. "No gold," he chortled. "But cash dollars."

"How much?" asked York.

"Must be ten thousand, eleven maybe—good old USA cash."

Josh glanced at York, but his brother refused to look at him.

Jukes picked up the box, wrapped it in a blanket, hooked it to his saddle, and faced York and Josh again. "Thanks for the help," he chuckled, his eyes cold.

"This ain't the end of this!" snapped York.

Jukes mounted his horse, then steered it to Lynette. "Come with me," he commanded her.

She refused, but he grabbed her horse's reins and jerked her away from Jackson and the other men.

Josh tried to figure what Jukes planned to do, then it hit him. What a mistake he had made!

"Kill the men!" Jukes shouted to his crew, confirming Josh's suspicions.

The men hesitated, evidently stunned that Mayor Jukes wanted to do such a cold-hearted thing. Josh measured the distance between himself and the chimney but saw instantly it was too far to run. He wanted to apologize to York for his foolishness, wanted to tell him he should have listened to him, wanted to admit York knew far more about men like Jukes than Josh could ever imagine. Jukes would kill everybody but Lynette, then swear to the authorities it had all happened in self-defense.

How could Lynette argue against him? Nobody would believe her against the mayor of the town. Even if they did, the folks in Chambersburg hated Rebels and wouldn't care that a few had gotten shot.

"I said shoot them!" Jukes yelled.

One of his men finally lifted a rifle, but before he could fire, York fell and rolled. A pistol suddenly appeared in York's hand from behind his back. The moment he stopped tumbling, he aimed and shot at Jukes faster than a snake could strike a rat. Jukes buckled forward.

Another shot rang out, and York stumbled and fell.

Lynette's horse reared up, and she fell off the back.

Jukes tumbled off his mount as more shots sounded.

Josh grabbed his gun off the ground, dove for a tree to his right, and started firing.

One of Jukes's men sagged in the saddle but didn't fall off. Shots rang all around him.

Josh looked wildly for Jackson and Lynette. He spotted Lynette on the ground and Jackson and his horse dashing for the woods. When Josh fired at a man to his left, the man tilted and grabbed his shoulder. More shots were fired.

Jukes, wounded but not dead, shouted and cursed as he grabbed a rifle off the ground and shot at Jackson. Josh took dead aim at Jukes and pulled the trigger. The bullet caught the mayor right where Josh aimed—in his right shoulder, the rifle side. Jukes dropped the rifle and fell quietly to the ground.

One of Jukes's men, seeing his leader down, spurred his horse and galloped from the clearing, no longer a threat.

"Let's get outta here!" shouted another one.

Another shot was fired, then all of Jukes's men pivoted their horses and sped away, leaving Jukes behind on the ground.

Josh rushed to York and knelt over him while Tolliver squatted by Jukes. Blood poured from York's right upper chest. Josh shoved a hand over the wound and pressed down to slow the bleeding.

"I'm not bad hit," said York, his teeth chattering.

Jackson thundered up on his horse and dropped down to the ground by his mother.

"She OK?" yelled Josh.

Jackson lifted her up. "She took a knock on the head," he said, carrying her to Josh and kneeling beside him and York. "But breathing fine, I think."

Relieved, Josh once more gave his attention to York. "Hold still," he told his brother, pulling a handkerchief from his shirt pocket and pressing it into the wound.

"How's Jukes?" asked York.

Josh called to Tolliver, maybe a hundred feet away.

"He's hit in the throat and shoulder," Tolliver replied. "Bleedin' bad but might live if we can get him to a doctor."

"Take him then!" ordered Josh. "To Mercersburg. It's closer!"

Tolliver hesitated.

"What are you waiting on?" asked Josh.

"He's wonderin' about the money," York growled.

"The money goes back to the authorities," said Josh.

"That's not our agreement!" argued Tolliver.

Josh ground his teeth but didn't see any choice but to keep the bargain he had made. He glanced around for Jukes's horse that had carried the cashbox but didn't see it. "Take Jukes to a doctor!" he commanded Tolliver again. "I'll find his horse and send you half the money. I promise I will."

"Jukes will kill me if he lives and I'm still around," Tolliver reasoned.

"Then come to Richmond once you get him safe. To her house." He nodded to Lynette. "Her name is Lynette Swanson, and she lives on Clairemont Street. I'll leave your money there with her."

Tolliver paused again.

"You take Jukes to a doctor or he'll die, and you'll have a murder charge hanging over you. Is that what you want?" Josh demanded.

"I ain't the one that shot him," Tolliver retorted.

"As far as I'm concerned, you are . . . and that's what I will tell the jury when the time comes," Josh threatened.

"You ain't much of a liar, that I can see."

Josh's patience wore out. He stood and strode over to Tolliver. "I have no more time for this!" he barked. "I will do what I have to do to keep Jukes alive. Now move or face the consequences!"

Although grumbling under his breath, Tolliver finally hauled Jukes up and threw him on his shoulder.

"Take my horse," said Josh. "I'll find his. Now go!"

Tolliver hauled Jukes to Josh's horse, draped him over it, and mounted his own horse. Then he headed out, holding the reins of Josh's horse.

Josh hurried back to York and squatted by him. The bleeding in his wound had slowed. "You'll get us all killed one of these days," Josh accused.

"Don't fret about me," said York, teeth clenched. "Just find Jukes's horse and let's get movin'."

Josh exhaled in frustration. Lynette was still unconscious; Jackson still knelt beside her. York was bleeding. "All this for money," he complained.

"I told you. I got to have those dollars," York insisted.

"It's stealing," Josh argued. "That money belongs with the law."

"Ten thousand dollars is . . . a small payment on what the Yankees . . . did to the South."

"You're not doing this for the good of the South," countered Josh.

York closed his eyes, and Josh let it drop. Whatever his brother's motives, York had saved his life today, and not for the first time. How could he hold a grudge against him? Josh would just have to figure out what to do about the money once he got York and Lynette safe and well again.

"Hang on," he said to York. "We'll get you out of here."

York nodded as Josh motioned to Jackson. Together they lifted their wounded and put them on horses.

"Go to Mercersburg," commanded Josh. "I'll find Jukes's horse and be right behind you."

Jackson obeyed without question and, leading two horses, left the clearing. In less than five minutes, Josh found the mayor's horse and followed Jackson.

Chapter Twenty-Five

After leaving Buster on The Oak, it had taken Ruby and Obadiah almost two weeks to find somebody who had seen Marquis and his two wagons after they left Orangeburg. But once they did, it didn't take them long to find out which direction he had gone. By the time the month of April ended, they had tracked Marquis by talking to a lot of people who had seen him come through. Some of them had bought his elixir; others had gotten their fortunes told by an odd-looking young man who wore a fancy gold turban and seemed real sad around the eyes. A few of the men even whispered to Obadiah that they had found a woman with Marquis and that she had been real obliging—for a certain fee, of course.

Following the gossip of Marquis's customers, Ruby and Obadiah learned he had guided his wagons almost to Charleston after he left Orangeburg. Then Marquis had taken a southeastern route, staying close to the ocean most of the time.

"He be goin' toward Beaufort," said Obadiah on the first evening in May. "Next town of any size between him and Savannah."

Obadiah was right. At the end of the week, they found Marquis about five miles out of Beaufort. His wagons were sitting by a little creek, with a cluster of Negro shacks and shanties barely a stone's throw away. A few hours after the sun went down, Ruby and Obadiah crouched behind a tree to watch Marquis and his troupe some distance away. Between the two wagons was a fire with a pot hanging over it. A plumpish woman handed Marquis a bottle of whiskey from her wagon. Marquis fed the cats that seemed intertwined with his legs.

Folks from the Negro village drifted over every now and again. Several with a bottle of elixir, and a few others, all men, followed Rufe as he escorted the woman to the back of the second wagon. There the men handed Rufe some money, then stepped up and disappeared for five or so minutes before climbing back out and leaving.

Ruby craned her neck, hoping to see Theo, but had no luck. "He must be in the other wagon," she whispered to Obadiah. "I wish I could see him."

"Soon enough," said Obadiah. "I expect Marquis be bringin' him later in the night—once the folks have taken a bit more of the drink."

Marquis threw more wood on the fire, and it flamed up high in the center of the campground. More and more blacks joined around it. Somebody pulled out a harmonica and started to play. A few of the blacks began to clap, and a man and a woman shuffled about, as if dancing. Ruby and Obadiah watched the scene a bit more before making their way back into the woods so they could talk freely.

"I think we should go to the sheriff in Beaufort," said Obadiah, squatting by a big pine. "Now that we know where Marquis is, the law can go get Theo for us. If we leave now, we can maybe have the law back here by mornin'. "

"You believe the sheriff will stop what he's doing and come aid us?" asked Ruby.

"What better plan you got?"

Ruby weighed her choices and didn't like any of them. She and Obadiah could go after Theo, but since Marquis had already shown a willingness to do harm to anybody who crossed him, that way carried a lot of peril. What if Marquis hurt Obadiah? Killed him? Or her, too, for that matter? Maybe going to the law made the most sense. But what if the law refused to help? And what if Marquis moved while they went for the sheriff?

Ruby leaned against the tree and tried to figure what to do. When Obadiah stood, she stepped to him and laid her head against his burly chest.

"We gone make it through this," soothed Obadiah. "Then we gone go home, collect your mama and Leta, and everythin' gone be fine."

"We will go to the law," Ruby decided.

"You bein' wise," said Obadiah.

"But I will see Theo first."

Obadiah tilted her chin back and stared with puzzlement into her eyes.

"I cannot draw this close to my boy after all these years and not let him know I have come for him," she insisted.

"That's a silly notion," said Obadiah. "Too dangerous. Best you let me go to him."

"But Theo doesn't know you."

"And Marquis does know you."

"But he thinks I'm dead, so he certainly won't be expecting to see me."

Obadiah dropped his hands to his sides, his fists clenched. "You takin' too big a chance," he argued again. "I can't let you do this."

Ruby lifted her chin in determination. "You have no choice in it."

Obadiah harrumphed, clearly bothered by her stubbornness. "OK," he finally said. "But I be right beside you."

She shook her head. "I don't like having to argue with you again, but you can't. You have to occupy Rufe for a while. He knows my face too."

"How you figure me to do that?"

She smiled. "Rufe takes the menfolk to the wagon to see Marquis's woman. You go for a visit with him."

Obadiah scratched his head. "What I gone do once I get there?"

"You figure that out, I guess. But we got to keep Rufe busy while I go to Theo as he tells his fortunes. I will ask him to give me a vision. He will see my face, hopefully recognize me."

"You not afraid he'll give you away if he does?"

"He is wise beyond his years. He will know to keep quiet."

"You takin' a big risk."

"Yes, but I have to do it."

"We will cover your head up good," he said, giving in. "Keep you in the shadows until it is time."

"You got a nickel?" she asked.

Obadiah handed her a coin.

"You bring a pistol?"

Obadiah touched a lump under his full shirt and nodded. "I hope it don't come to gunplay. I not be skilled in such a thing."

"Give it to me."

Obadiah stiffened. "That be the dumbest thing you said since I knowed you."

Ruby reached for the gun. "If Marquis recognizes me, I will need to act fast."

"You a crazy woman." He handed her the weapon.

"I just want to see my boy." Ruby tucked the pistol into the back waistband of her skirt, then tucked her shawl tighter around her shoulders. "Let's wait a spell longer. Then I will go in."

Obadiah followed her back to the trees just outside the camp. "You best go in from out of the shantytown," he advised. "Like the other women."

"It won't take but a few minutes once I leave," Ruby promised. "I just want Theo to know it's me—that I'm here and going to get him free."

Obadiah hugged her. "Best not take long," he teased. "Or I could end up in a heap of trouble with Marquis's woman in the back of that wagon."

Ruby kissed him on the cheek, and they sat down to wait. In another hour or so, she would finally see her boy once more.

As he had most nights since his mother's death, Trenton again found himself at a card table at the store in the fork down the road from The Oak. A bottle of whiskey was near his shoulder as he busied his hands with a deck of cards. Five men sat at the table with him, and an odd assortment of twenty to thirty others drifted in and out as the night settled in. Some of them played cards, but almost all drank and smoked. A haze hung over the rectangular room, and the pale glow of the lanterns hanging on the wood walls cast shadows across the room. A man with one hand banged out some songs on a beat-up piano. Women with bright rouge and red lipstick drifted in and out among the men, hoping for a little business.

Trenton won close to eight dollars as the night dragged on. He pocketed five of the dollars against the possibility of losing a hand or two later. One thing he had learned since his mother's death: he now had to depend on his own wiles for his upkeep. Without the money she had dispensed on a fairly regular basis, he had no dollars for food, whiskey, or anything else if he lost all his winnings, so he usually kept a few dollars stored away just in case.

The crowd of men became smaller, and the noise level went down some as the hour grew later. A second card game started at a table to Trenton's right. He nodded at a couple of the men he recognized, then went back to his game.

About three hours before midnight, Trenton slapped down a pair of queens, won the hand, and pulled another two dollars toward his money pile. Pleased with his good fortune, he ordered another bottle of liquor, opened it when it came, and took a long drink.

Just then the door to the store opened, and a short, black man with no fingers on his left hand entered. He stopped in the doorway and waited. The men in the store looked Trenton's way, but he waved them back to their endeavors. Putting the whiskey bottle down, he motioned the black man toward him. The man, his eyes averted from any white man's gaze, picked his way toward Trenton, then bent and whispered in his ear when he arrived.

Trenton's eyes widened as he heard the information he had paid the black man to gather for him. "You sure, Stub?"

Stub nodded. Trenton thought a moment, then handed Stub half a dollar. Trenton held up a hand. The game at his table stopped, and Trenton stood and banged on the wall beside it. All talking ceased. Trenton gazed over the room. The men at the card tables held their cards still.

"We got business, boys!" Trenton declared.

"What kind of business?" asked a man to his left.

Trenton faced Stub. "You need to go home now," he told the Negro.

Stub bowed slightly. Backing up from Trenton, he left the store.

Trenton watched the black man go before he faced the crowd again. "Stub tells me he's found the darky who killed my mother," he stated.

The room filled with murmurs. "You know where the man is?" one man asked.

Trenton threw up a hand, and the noise settled again. "Stub just told me. Said he passed through a shantytown a few miles out of Beaufort on

257

his way from his mama's house today. Said he saw a man like the one we've hunted since my mother's murder—a towering man with a white mark on his left cheek the shape of a pear."

"You should go to the law in Beaufort with this," said the man to Trenton's left.

Trenton glared at the man. "We know what the law will do. It will protect the Negro, like it's done since the war ended. A white man can't get justice done these days unless he takes it in his own hands."

A number of men cursed their agreement. Trenton again held up a hand to settle the noise. "You know what we need to do," he said, his tone calm. "Go home and make ready. We'll meet back here tomorrow night, to take care of what justice demands."

Nodding their pleasure, the men pushed away from their drinks and cards and piled out the door of the store. When they had all gone, Trenton picked up his poker winnings, stuffed them in his pockets, and made his way to his horse. Although he hadn't really killed any darkies yet—in spite of what the rumors said—he felt that tomorrow night he had to do what any proud white Southern man would do. He had to bring justice upon the darky who had killed his mother.

Her bonnet snug around her face, Ruby waited quietly beside a square shack and watched Theo as he sat in a tall chair in the back of one of Marquis's covered wagons. Her heart pumped wildly as she studied her boy—he looked so different, yet so much the same. Big head, one eye missing, his hair now all gray.

Wearing a yellow cape, red pants that ballooned out on his legs, a white shirt, and a belt with a big buckle, Theo sat high in his chair, perched above the folks who gathered around him. Marquis stood by his side, obviously preparing himself to take up money as the people handed it over to hear their fortune told.

Ruby wanted to cry. Only a few minutes before, she had watched as Marquis brought Theo out. He had climbed out of one wagon and moved to the other. His gait looked unsteady as he walked, and even from where she stood, Ruby could see something had happened to his right foot. Tears formed in her eyes, but she wiped them away. No time for crying right now. She glanced toward the second wagon and wondered about Obadiah. Was he with a woman?

Not wanting to think about that, Ruby slipped away from the little house and walked toward Theo as a harmonica played in the background. The flickering fire cast shadows on her face. She glanced around but made sure not to catch anyone's eye as she reached the back of the group standing in front of Theo.

Marquis baited the crowd with his sales pitch. "Deez be perilous times," he called out. "Times when a body dat knows da future got a leg up on all da others. Dis young man here, Theodocus be his name, he got da vision. He see what nobody but him can see. You wonderin' if you gone find work in da summer? He can tell it one way or da other. You hopin' to find you a stout woman to keep you clean and fed? Dis boy can give you da nod on whether now be da time to go lookin'."

The crowd murmured in approval at the speech. It was so smooth Ruby figured Marquis had repeated it often. He made it sound like you just had to hand over your nickel—or take a chance on never knowing what your future held.

"Look right here," shouted Marquis as he moved to Theo, climbed up on a two-step box that sat by his chair and reached for his face. "You figure dis be empty." He placed his fingers on Theo's empty eye socket and tugged back the flesh until the people could see right into the gaping black hole.

The crowd gasped. One of the women shrieked.

"Dis be da hole da boy looks into. It be where he sees da visions!" shouted Marquis. "What we figure to make him blind, da good Lord uses to give him da sight!"

"I'll take a try!" shouted a fat man, whose dark face shone in the light of the fire. "I gots a sick wife and wants to know if she gone get better or not."

Marquis smiled and hopped down. The man handed him a coin, then moved to Theo and stared up at him. Two or three others, nickels in hand, lined up to hear their fortune. Taking a deep breath, Ruby pulled out her nickel and took a spot in the line. When she got to Marquis, she handed him the coin but kept her head down. His breath smelled as foul as she remembered, and she knew the odor came from a lot of whiskey. She hoped the liquor would keep his brain scrambled enough that he wouldn't remember her. He cocked his head toward her curiously, and a tiny smile played on his lips. However, he didn't seem to recognize her from the night he had stabbed her.

"You hopin' to find you a man?" Marquis asked.

Ruby kept her eyes averted. "I be hopin' for work," she said, trying to sound like a common field laborer. "Maybe your oracle can point me where to find it."

Marquis raised an eyebrow and started to speak again, but the man in front of Ruby stepped forward. Quickly she followed him. She could feel Marquis's gaze on her until another woman came up behind her and offered him a nickel. Then he gave the new woman his attention. The line shifted again a few minutes later, and Ruby got another pace closer to Theo. Her heart pounded so hard she wondered if anyone else could hear it. Sweat poured off her brow, and she found it hard to breathe. Would Theo even recognize her? If not, how would she let him know she had come for him?

The man before her took off his hat and walked to Theo. Theo took his hand and stared at it for several seconds before mumbling something in a low tone Ruby heard but didn't give any heed. When Theo finished with the man before her, he dropped his hand. The man offered what looked like a little bow, then slid away.

Her eyes down, Ruby stood as if her feet were glued to the ground. She wanted to move more than anything in the world, but somehow she couldn't find the courage to do it. After all these years her quest had ended, but she couldn't look up and see the son she loved more than life itself.

"Step forward, please." The voice came from Theo, but it was far deeper than what she had imagined. He sounded so grown up that she wondered for a second if he was the same boy. Head still down, she lifted a foot and managed to take one step, then another.

"Let me see your hand," Theo ordered.

She obeyed quickly, lifting her hand, palm up and trembling, to Theo.

He touched her skin, and the feeling shocked her. He rolled the hand over, side to side, front to back. He placed a rock in her hand and rubbed her skin with it. At least a minute passed without words, and Ruby worried that Marquis might take notice of her. But, in spite of her fears, she found no strength to pull her hand from Theo.

"Let me see your eyes," Theo commanded.

Unable to resist, she lifted her chin. Her eyes moistened.

Theo's brow furrowed as he stared at her. She searched his good eye, noted a dullness in its center, and wondered if he knew her. He seemed so strange, functioning but somehow distant, like he kept his mind here but his heart somewhere else. She tried desperately to communicate with him through her stare, to tell him who she was, to say to him that she had finally come. After all these years she and her boy were reunited! But did he know it?

"You are a woman on a quest," Theo intoned loudly.

Ruby quickly nodded.

"You have come near to the end of it," he continued, his hands warm against her skin.

Ruby's knees quivered. She felt like she might collapse.

"Danger still awaits you though," Theo warned, his volume lower, almost as if he wanted only her to hear. "You must take care to avoid it until the time is ripe."

Ruby almost fainted. He recognized her! She felt certain of it! In spite of the clouded look in his eye, his words told her that! She wanted to shout and climb up to him and hug him long and hard but knew she couldn't.

Sensing movement behind her, she knew she had to move away. But what about Theo? He still held her hand, and she didn't want to leave him. Who knew whether or not she would ever see him again? She had learned life sometimes took strange twists, unexpected turns. If she left him now, Theo might disappear again—maybe this time forever.

When Theo looked past her and dropped her hand, she knew her time was over. But she had to do one more thing to try to reach him. She grabbed his wrist and squeezed as hard as she could.

At that instant Marquis appeared at her side and took her by the elbow. She had to let Theo go and step away from him.

"We have others who wait to see their future," Marquis hissed into her ear.

"Forgive me," she whispered, wanting now only to escape the camp so she could hurry to Beaufort to find the law. "I did not know how long to take."

Marquis pushed her into the shadows between his two wagons, jerked her bonnet off, and stared into her eyes. "I feel like I seen yo' face before dis."

Ruby held her breath, hoping with all her heart he would not remember. "I reckon not."

"Where you hail from?"

"I's from over at The Oak. Got an auntie that live here in the shanty. I come to see her today 'cause she be sickly."

Marquis grabbed her chin and turned her face from one side to the other. "I got a bad feelin' about you. Why dat be?"

"I got no way to tell."

He grabbed her by the waist and pulled her hard against him. She feared he would feel the gun in her waistband, and sure enough he did.

"What you got here?" he asked, grabbing at the pistol under her shawl.

Ruby pushed his hands away and touched the pistol but left it in place. "I got me a gun. A girl got to protect her virtues, don't she?"

Marquis eyed her hard again. "You a prettier woman than most around here. I can see where a pistol might come in handy."

Ruby decided maybe she should play along with Marquis a little instead of fighting him. "You know how to flatter a girl."

"You said you was wantin' work. I can offer you some," countered Marquis.

"I done seen the girl you already got. So what you want with me?"

"Maybe I put you to work just for me."

"I reckon that ain't the kind of labor I figure to do."

"You a Christian woman?"

"Not 'specially, but I got me a husband, a girl named Leta, and a boy too. Figure to go back to them when I leaves here."

Marquis hesitated, still staring at her. "I swear on my mother's grave, I seen you before," he said suspiciously.

Ruby slid her bonnet back over her head and decided to take another step on the risky path of teasing Marquis. "You been drinkin'," she suggested. "A drinkin' man figures he knows all the womenfolk."

Marquis grinned. "I ought to go on and have my way with you."

"You don't want me to have to use my pistol, do you?"

Marquis's grin turned ugly. "You best not threaten me, no matter how much drink I've taken."

Ruby lowered her eyes, fearing she had gone too far. When she looked up again, Marquis stood real close, his mouth right next to her ear. "Yo' husband most likely a poor man," he whispered. "Sharecropper maybe? Not able to provide what a woman like you be wantin'."

"He poor, that be true," she said, figuring to play along a while longer. Buy herself some time to get the lawman here.

"You sure you won't change yo' mind about workin' for me?"

Ruby teased some more. "You figure you gone be here awhile?"

When Marquis trembled against her, she knew his lust had overcome him. "A while maybe—so long as folks got a few nickels to spend and the law ain't too particular."

Ruby smiled. "Maybe I could think some on your proposition. Give me a few days to figure on it. That possible?"

Marquis leaned back and studied her. "You tellin' it true?"

She gave him a quick kiss on the cheek. "You keep your wagons here a few more days. Who know what the wind might blow back to you?"

Marquis grinned in an evil, crooked way, and Ruby's blood chilled. When she got back, she knew exactly what she wanted the wind to blow on Marquis.

"You hurry on back then," said Marquis. "I wait a while for one pretty as you."

After offering one final, alluring smile, Ruby hustled away, her feet pushing her as fast as she dared let them go.

Chapter Twenty-Six

Ruby and Obadiah found the Beaufort deputy just before midnight as he sat alone at the jail. Quickly they told him about Marquis and Theo. When they finished, the chunky young man yawned. "What proof you got this boy is yours?" he chided Ruby.

"None but my word," she said.

"Sorry," the deputy replied. "But we're short of men right now. And there's all kinds of troubles to tend—shootin's, robbery, drunkenness—matters far more pressin' than yours. I'd be glad to talk to the sheriff for you in the mornin', but I don't expect he's gonna do much to aid you."

Ruby wanted to argue. But when the deputy yawned again, she realized it wouldn't do any good. "Come on," she told Obadiah.

Once they were out on the street again, she stopped to figure what to do next. "We wasted time," she complained to Obadiah.

"We tried to do the right thing," countered Obadiah. "Nothin' wrong with that."

"But what now?"

"We can't just march into Marquis's camp and demand he hand Theo over to us."

"And we can't sneak into the camp and haul Theo away without someone waking up and discovering us."

"We got to get help then," said Obadiah, voicing what Ruby knew but didn't want to hear.

"It's too dangerous for anybody else!" she argued. "Mr. York and Josh Cain are gone, and I can't risk injury to Johnny or Butler . . . or anybody else either."

Obadiah sighed. "Buster be still on The Oak. Maybe he would help."

Ruby thought of the man who had treated her so kindly and shook her head. "He's too old."

"You tell me, then," Obadiah countered, obviously impatient with her arguments. "I got no other ideas."

Ruby bit her lip. She knew if she went back to The Oak and told Camellia about this, she would want to help. That might put a lot of people in danger. But without somebody's aid, they couldn't rescue Theo.

"OK," she finally said. "We'll go to The Oak."

"It will take us past mornin' for the trip," Obadiah figured.

"I can go real fast."

"You figure somebody there will help us?"

"I know it for sure."

His body weary from staying up through the night, Trenton slept almost the whole next day. When he finally did awake, just an hour or so before dark, his head throbbed even more than usual. After washing up in the kitchen, he grabbed a biscuit Calvin had left behind, swallowed it almost whole, and hurried back to his room on the second floor. For some reason today felt different than most other days—like something portentous rode the air . . . something that would change his life. The notion of dispensing justice upon the man who had killed his mother made his mood light. It had caused his hands to quiver as he washed them and a flipping in his stomach as he ate his biscuit.

Looking out the open window of his bedroom, he felt the strong breeze that blew in off the ocean. The sensation woke him up, gave him energy like nothing had in a long time. The air seemed heavy, as if it carried a storm on the way, and he welcomed it. Before the night ended, something bigger than a storm might have passed through, and that thought almost made him feel giddy.

Trenton gazed across the property his family had owned so long. The branches of the massive oak tree in front of the manse swayed in the breeze. Looking past the oak, he saw the empty fields where the rice once grew. How could anything have destroyed such a bountiful system? Wreaked such havoc on a place once filled with such magnificence? Although Hampton York and Josh Cain and their families had tidied up the place and applied fresh paint to the buildings, The Oak still seemed dead. To Trenton it was lifeless—a mere shell of what it had been. Would it ever regain its grandeur? If he had any say in it, the answer was yes.

He twisted to look for a whiskey bottle. Seeing none, he turned back to the scene outside the window. When nothing moved, he wondered where everyone was. Somebody usually worked in the garden through the day. He searched for Calvin but didn't see him either. Where had he gone? His eyes landed on the houses where Camellia and Beth lived. Was Calvin there? If not, he would be before the day ended. He would show up on the front steps, get invited inside, and eat dinner with Beth, taking the spot at the table he, Trenton, should have filled.

His sense of isolation increased as he noticed there was no smoke drifting from the houses. Where was everybody? The whole place seemed eerily still, quieter than a church at night. A wave of loneliness overcame him, and his good humor disappeared. Without his mother, he had no one to turn to, no one with whom to talk, to share his dreams, his ambitions.

Just then the wind broke a small limb off a tree and blew it toward the manse. The limb banged into the wall to Trenton's right. He watched it as if in a dream. *Everything was falling apart*, he realized. Everything he had ever wanted, ever treasured.

Angered by the thought, Trenton backed away from the window, remembering what he would do tonight. *That would fix things*, he decided. Once he had settled matters with the man who had murdered his mother, he would feel a whole lot better.

Calmed by this realization, Trenton finished dressing, left his bedroom, and headed to the barn to prepare his horse. After a few hours of drinking at Crossville General Store, he and his buddies would head to the shantytown. By morning he would have his vengeance, the Negroes would know their place again, and things would once more be right with the world.

Josh arrived on horseback at The Oak about an hour after dark, his bones weary from the long train trip home. Quickly putting away the cheap horse he had bought in Beaufort with his last dollars, he rushed to his house and through the front door. Seeing nobody in the front room, he hurried to Beth's bedroom door and knocked. When nobody answered, he knocked again. Once more he received no response. Pushing open the door, he peered inside. The bed lay empty, the covers in place.

Confused, Josh hurried to Butler's room and pushed through the door without knocking. Nobody was there either. Josh paused, not knowing what to think. He walked back to the porch and scanned his surroundings. The only light he saw came from the house where Ruby's mama and baby girl lived.

Confused by the deserted houses, he hurried to the one with the light, knocked on the door, and waited. Seconds later the door was opened by a black man Josh had never seen before.

"I'm looking for my family," Josh began. "A girl named Beth, a boy called Butler."

The man stepped back and let Josh in. Leta and Nettie were sitting by the fire.

"My name be Buster," said the old man. "You must be Mr. Josh Cain."

"How do you know?"

"Beth and Butler told me."

"You know them?"

Buster nodded.

"Beth and Butler gone into hidin' in the woods for the night," said Nettie, confusing Josh even more.

"I don't understand."

"Johnny gone. Miss Camellia and Mr. Calvin too," said Buster. "Gone to help Miss Ruby fetch her boy, Theo. A rough man named Marquis holdin' him against his will. We figure it best to hide Beth and Butler so Mr. Trenton don't see that everybody is gone and come lookin' for them."

Josh's mind reeled.

Nettie hurriedly told him how Ruby and Obadiah had come looking for help, how Camellia and the rest had decided to go aid them.

Relieved to know Beth and Butler were safe, Josh asked quickly, "You know where this Marquis man is?"

"The shantytown over near Beaufort."

"I know the place; it's over twenty miles from here."

"Yep."

Josh paced the room, wishing they had waited until he returned. What if something happened? What if Camellia got hurt?

"You know what they plan to do if they find Theo?" he asked.

"I heard Obadiah and Calvin talkin'. They figure to go after Theo at the darkest time, just before mornin', when everybody is hard asleep. If you hurry, maybe you can catch up with everybody before they do."

Josh's hopes rose as he did some quick calculations. "I'm going."

"Your horse must be tuckered out," Buster said.

"Maybe there's another one in the barn."

"You gone take one of Master Trenton's horses?" Buster asked.

"If there is one, I will."

Buster nodded and Josh thanked him for looking after his kids. Then he rushed out. If he wanted to reach Camellia before anything happened, he had to pray hard and ride as fast as he could for as long as the horse would carry him.

Ruby followed Obadiah through the dark woods. Camellia, Johnny, and Calvin trailed them. Everybody stayed as quiet as they could, and thankfully, a strong wind hid most of the noise they made. A heavy bank of clouds covered the moon. Although it had not rained, the air felt wet, like a deluge might hit them at any second. Obadiah held one lantern, and Calvin, bringing up the rear, toted a second. Other than that, nobody else carried a light. The wind blew in gusts and spurts, so Ruby knew a storm would hit before morning.

From what she could judge, Ruby figured they had walked at least five miles since leaving the main road. They had taken a deer-trail shortcut to the shantytown that Obadiah and Calvin had agreed would save them several hours and keep them from running into anybody else out on such a night. Although the trail pushed through thick woods and across a couple of streams, they had made it without incident—just a few scratches and cuts to show for their effort.

Since they couldn't move horses down the narrow trail, the two horses waited for them on the road. Calvin, Johnny, and Obadiah carried weapons—Calvin and Johnny a rifle, and Obadiah a pistol. Ruby wondered if Calvin and Johnny also had pistols but didn't ask. Hopefully, nobody would need firearms tonight. If they did . . .

When they reached a clearing in the trees, Obadiah held up a hand and halted the group. "Everybody take water," he said, his voice barely audible in the wind.

Ruby sagged down against a tree, and Camellia joined her. Camellia handed her a canteen, and Ruby took a long drink of water. They had been traveling since a couple of hours after noon.

"We will get Theo tonight," Camellia promised.

Ruby smiled and squeezed Camellia's hand. "I am obliged to you all for coming with me," she said, remembering how readily everyone had offered their aid when she and Obadiah had returned to The Oak and asked them.

"You are welcome," said Camellia. "I'm just glad you didn't try to rescue him by yourself."

"Obadiah wouldn't let me." Ruby gave Camellia the canteen, and she drank from it. Ruby raised an eyebrow at the sight—a white woman drinking after a darky. Things really had changed.

"You figure Buster and Butler can take care of things at The Oak?" Ruby asked Camellia.

"They will do fine."

"Butler sure put up a holler when you didn't let him come with us."

Camellia grinned. "He feels like he's grown. Said he knows this area like the back of his hand. But I didn't want to put him in any danger. And somebody needed to stay in case Trenton—"

"You figure he might come after Miss Beth again?" asked Ruby.

"I'm not taking any chances."

Ruby sighed and her heart raced again. "I got some fears," she admitted for the first time.

"Me too," said Camellia. "But not as many as I figured on. Seems the war took a lot of the fear out of me."

Ruby felt the same way. Given all she had already faced, what was the worst that could happen? Marquis might kill her. But she had to rescue her son, no matter how dangerous it was.

She pushed away the scary thoughts and focused on some good ones. If all unfolded as she hoped tonight, she would have her boy in her arms by daylight. Part of her couldn't believe it; another part knew it made sense. Theo's vision—the confident words he had spoken to her all those years ago when they'd been parted—was finally coming true. Perhaps not exactly as he had seen it but close enough for her.

"What will you do when this is over?" Camellia asked her.

Ruby smiled. "Obadiah and I will go back to his old place, rebuild it."

Camellia nodded. "We will all be leaving The Oak soon."

"Mr. Josh coming home?"

"Yes, he sent a telegram. I received it a few days ago."

"He find Captain York?"

Camellia nodded.

"About time," said Ruby. "The captain coming home with Mr. Josh?"

"Josh didn't say—just that he was rushing here as fast as he could."

"I expect it will please your soul to see him again."

Camellia smiled. "That's a large understatement."

Ruby's heart ached with love for Camellia—the white woman who had become her best friend. "You have been so good to me. No matter what happens tonight or after, you know I am your friend for life."

"We go back a long way," agreed Camellia. "I count you as part of my family."

Obadiah and Calvin stepped to the center of the circle and interrupted their talk. "Me and Mr. Calvin got a plan," Obadiah informed them. "When we get to Marquis's camp, we wait to make sure everybody be asleep. Then me and Johnny will take places at Marquis's wagon—one in front, one in back, so if he wakes and tries anythin' we be there waitin' for him. Mr. Calvin will watch for Rufe and the woman. Ruby and Miss Camellia will go after Theo, wake him, and lead him into the woods. If nobody wakes, we will follow real fast, and everybody will head back down the path, fast as we can go. If things go right, we can make it back to the main road, load up, and be gone before Marquis knows a thing."

He looked from person to person, as if making sure everybody had heard him. All nodded.

Ruby wondered what would happen if somebody saw them and set off the alarm. Then, with surety, she knew the answer to her own question. They would fight for their lives.

"OK then," Obadiah said. "I figure we close to five miles away yet. We keep on this deer track, move quick as we can, push hard, and cover that in two hours or so. Then we wait till everybody be settled to do what we come to do."

Ruby and Camellia stood and hugged each other. The time for talk had ended. A long trail lay ahead of them before they would reach Theo. Ruby's eyes lifted to the sky.

"You mind if I say a prayer for us?" asked Camellia.

Ruby smiled and bowed her head.

As always, Marquis waited until the last of his customers had left before he closed down his wagons and made ready for bed. Tonight, it being a Saturday, things kept going a little longer than usual. He sold eleven bottles of elixir, Theo told seven fortunes, and Mabel took four men into the back of her wagon for a little sporting time. All told, a real good night's profit.

Marquis told Rufe to drop a couple more logs on the fire, counted his coins in the dim glow of the heat, and took a swig of his own elixir. Rufe placed the logs on the fire and stood by for more orders. Marquis handed him a couple of the coins.

"Mabel restin'?" he asked Rufe.

"Yeah, drunk by now for sure."

"Theo?"

"He probably asleep too."

"I reckon we move on tomorrow mornin'," Marquis said. "Figure we done about as good here as we can for a while."

Rufe pocketed the coins and hunkered down beside him. "Where we goin' next?"

Marquis considered the sky and made some calculations. The law wanted him in Charleston and Columbia, and they recently had made stops in Orangeburg and Camden. Folks there had most likely figured out by now his elixir didn't cure every ailment they had and all of Theo's fortunes didn't always come true. "Maybe down to Savannah," he said. "Over to Atlanta from dere. People says Atlanta be a big town. A man can sell a lot of elixir in a town so large."

"You figure me to go with you?"

Marquis faced his associate. "You a free man. You go if that be yo' pleasure."

Rufus studied the stars. "Maybe it be time I took me a woman."

"A woman is a fine thing," agreed Marquis.

"I might have found one a few miles from here," said Rufe.

Marquis eyed him and chuckled. "You go on to her then. I can find me another man easy enough. Maybe for less money than I pay you."

Rufe held out a hand, and Marquis shook it.

"I stay the rest of the night," Rufe said. "Then I be gone with sunup."

Marquis tossed back another swallow of elixir, then stood and brushed off his pants. "It windy tonight," he noted. "Rain hard for sure by mornin'. Gone be a muddy day to travel."

"I got no hurry," said Rufe.

Marquis nodded, then gathered his bottle and headed to his wagon.

With fourteen men behind him, Trenton galloped his horse toward the shantytown. For once he didn't drink as he rode. He wanted to be sober when he killed his mother's murderer. A wet wind whipped about his face and blew back his hair. He wore a light brown coat and a pair of old riding pants he had found in the attic, pants his father had once worn. His stump pounded against his horse's side as he urged the animal to run faster.

Trenton thought of the mask in his saddlebags—a piece of cloth he had painted to look as horrible as possible—a crooked slit in the cloth for the mouth, red paint in the corners to imitate blood, a pair of eyes with dark circles under them, and a gaping, twisted nose. Also in the saddlebags was a robe made of an old sheet, its edges in tatters, its color spotted from other night rides similar to this one. The other men in Trenton's party carried their own versions of the mask and sheet—some more hideous in appearance than his, others less so. Either way, though, the men knew they were part of something big, something vital, something eternal. God had called them to this task: the glorious work of making sure the Negroes never claimed superiority over the whites; that the blacks kept their rightful place and learned to accept it.

Trenton held no doubts about the rightness of his cause. Anybody with any brain at all recognized the obvious inferiority of the blacks, their inability to learn, their shiftlessness, their unwillingness to care for themselves. Men like him had always given leadership to the poor and ignorant, and no defeat in war, no matter how decisive the victory of the enemy, could alter that fact. Now the cause depended on men like him—men with steel in their spines and a sense of justice in their bones—to make sure truth and justice once more ascended to their rightful places in Southern society.

Trenton and his men came to a fork in the road and slowed their horses to a walk. From now until they reached the shantytown, they would lessen their pace: first, to accommodate the narrow trail leading to the Negroes, and second, to muffle the sounds of their horses so they could take the sleeping blacks by surprise.

When they reached a stream, Trenton held up a hand and his men stopped. He quickly dismounted, and the others followed suit.

"Water the horses," he ordered. "Not far to go now."

The men quietly obeyed, each one seeing to his animal. The black man Stub eased up beside Trenton. "I reckon I best drop out about here. I done told you the house where to find the man you be lookin' for."

"You did good work," Trenton said as he handed Stub a dollar. "You come see me again in a week or so. Check what I got for you to do then."

Stub took the money and faded back into the darkness.

Trenton evaluated his men. Although he had not led men in battle, this might be better. No rules to govern his behavior here, no gentlemen's agreements, no confines of decency or morality. At night, with nobody and nothing but the moon watching, a man who knew what needed to be done lived as his own law, his own morality. What a man could impose as right *was* right, and nobody could do anything about it.

Trenton stepped to his saddle and touched the rope he found looped on the saddle horn. In just a short while, he would do the only moral thing to avenge his mother's death.

And nothing—no law, no rule, not even God—could stop him.

Ruby and her gang crouched behind a thicket as the moon briefly peeked out from the clouds, then disappeared again. Marquis's two wagons sat dead ahead of her. Nobody moved in the camp. Ruby's heart pounded. She figured it to be a few hours past midnight. They had been waiting a good while, just outside Marquis's camp. She turned to Obadiah. "Time to go," she whispered.

He nodded and she faced Johnny and Calvin. "You all set?" she asked quietly.

"Yes," they whispered.

Ruby took a big breath, then stood and made her way across the last thirty yards that separated her from her son. Camellia followed and they reached the back of Theo's wagon without incident. Once there, Ruby motioned Camellia to wait while she climbed up and in. The wagon creaked slightly as she placed her weight on it, and she froze to let it settle. Then she moved again, tiptoeing her way under the canvas and into the bed.

There lay Theo, a worn blanket tucked just under his chin. A couple of cats slept near his head, one on each side, but she saw no one else.

Ruby stared at him as tears ran down her face. He looked so peaceful, so much like the little boy she had been forced to leave behind. She marveled that he had survived and she had found him. What a wondrous moment! One of the cats shifted and lifted a paw, then settled again.

Realizing she needed to hurry, Ruby knelt, edged over to Theo, and kissed him on the forehead. His one eye opened gently, and he looked at her as if he expected her appearance. She lifted a finger and signaled for silence. He nodded and raised up and she hugged him. The cat to his left stretched and stood. Ruby released Theo and pointed to the back of the wagon. He quietly gathered a pair of old boots. Ruby moved toward the back of the wagon, and Theo followed her. She noticed the limp again and wondered what had happened to his foot. When the first cat meowed, the second one woke up. Ruby saw Camellia in the shadows as she stepped off the wagon to the ground. The second cat meowed. Theo climbed down behind Ruby and slipped his feet into his boots. The right one didn't seem to fit too well.

Ruby pointed toward the woods, and Theo nodded his understanding. Ruby slinked toward the trees, Theo behind her, slow but steady, and Camellia behind him. One of the cats meowed again, louder this time. Ruby hurried as fast as Theo allowed. She saw Obadiah, Calvin, and Johnny moving too, and her spirit soared. They were going to make it!

Then suddenly, sounds pounded to her left, in the direction of the Negro village. She heard thundering hooves, then a rifle shot. She turned, grabbed Theo's hand, and ran, Camellia following.

The hoofbeats drew closer. Others now came from the woods in front of her.

More rifle shots were fired.

A woman screamed.

Ruby reached the woods and crouched behind a thicket. A second later everyone else gathered in a circle around her and hid as best they could in the brush. A horse pounded by them, headed to the shantytown. The horseman wore a mask that looked like a ghoul and carried a burning torch.

Obadiah drew everybody closer. "It's the raiders!" he whispered, his eyes big, even in the dark. "We got to stay down!"

Another horse and rider rushed through the dark to their right. More screams pierced the night.

Ruby peered back toward Marquis's wagons and saw his head pop out, his woman beside him. A second later Rufe ran toward Marquis. Rufe and Marquis shouted at each other, but Ruby couldn't hear what they said.

More shots rang out.

A horse thundered toward Marquis. He turned and ran in terror, but the raider galloped after him and rode him down, the horse plowing over him as if trampling a snake.

Rufe rushed to the woods in the opposite direction from where Ruby watched. Although the raiders shot at him, too, they missed, and he disappeared into the dark.

Marquis staggered up and stumbled toward his wagons but then fell. Ruby couldn't tell if he was still alive or not.

The shantytown was suddenly on fire. As Ruby watched the blaze in horror, she forgot about Marquis. Why had the raiders come *tonight*—of all nights?

"We gone sneak away from here," advised Obadiah. "The raiders will do they business, then go on."

Ruby hugged Theo close, and he smiled at her.

"It's not exactly the vision you saw, is it?" whispered Ruby. "Markus isn't here."

Theo didn't speak, just shook his head. Ruby wondered again if Marquis had drugged him but didn't have time to ask.

"You'll be fine," she whispered. "Mama's got you now."

With one last look behind her, Ruby followed Obadiah as he and Calvin led them away from the burning houses and into the dark woods.

Trenton rode into the shantytown at the front of his men, his eyes squinting through his grotesque mask. Sweat ran down his face and into his neck, but he barely noticed. His men, most of them drunk, shot at anything that moved. Their aim was poor, but their desire for blood was stoked to the highest levels. Trenton kept his rifle level but didn't shoot it, at least not yet. He had another manner of death planned for tonight—one that would carry a message far and wide.

His eyes set on his vision, he steered his horse to the cabin where Stub had told him he would find the tall man with the pear-shaped scar on his face. The man had taken up with a woman and two children and now lived here, near the outer circle of the smelly village.

When he reached the cabin, Trenton reined in his horse. All around him fires were burning. As more and more shots rang out, he grimaced. Had his men actually shot anybody? Or were they just wasting ammunition? Usually they didn't shoot anyone unless somebody stepped forward to challenge them. On most nights they just fired their weapons, made a lot of threats, burned down a few houses, had their way with a couple of women, and then moved on, their thirst for violence slaked, at least for the night.

One of Trenton's men, a fiery torch in hand, pounded his horse to a stop beside him. When Trenton pointed at the house, the man tossed the torch onto the front porch. A second later another raider joined them. Trenton pointed again, and the man jumped off his horse, ran to the front door, kicked it open, and threw his torch inside.

More patient than he expected he could be, Trenton sat calmly and waited. In less than a minute, the front of the house blazed up, the door on fire. Smoke billowed toward him.

"Check the back!" Trenton commanded. The dismounted man rushed around the house, his rifle ready in case anyone tried to escape the back way.

A toddling boy appeared out of the smoke and then a screaming girl, her hands brushing fire from her long skirt. A woman pushed them forward, her hair wild and unkempt. The woman grabbed the two children as she reached the porch and threw them off it to the ground. They fell and rolled, the girl putting out the fire that had almost burned her skirt away, the boy crying at the top of his lungs. The woman rushed off the porch as it ignited behind her in a whoosh of flames and heat.

Trenton kicked his horse toward her. "Where's the man?" he shouted as she grabbed her boy.

She looked up, her eyes running tears, the boy under one arm, the girl in another, while her house burned behind her. "What man?" she screamed.

"The man who lives with you!"

"Ain't no such man!"

Trenton glared at her, then faced the man to his left. "Go!" he ordered.

"What you mean?" the man asked, looking confused.

"Into the house, from the back," Trenton ordered. "See if he's inside."

"You're loco!" the man exclaimed.

Trenton raised his rifle and aimed at the man's head. "Time is wasting!"

The man cursed, then jerked his horse and rushed to the back of the house. Trenton turned his weapon on the woman.

A minute later the man ran back to Trenton. He held a cloth over his mouth and was coughing from the smoke. "Nobody there!" he shouted.

"You sure?" Trenton asked.

"It's just one room," the man explained. "Front is burned up. Nobody in the back!"

His teeth clenched, Trenton faced the woman. "Where is he?" he screamed.

She dropped her eyes and shook her head. Trenton motioned toward the man on the ground, who moved to the woman, grabbed the little boy, and handed him up to Trenton.

"You want to see this boy ever again?" he yelled.

She let go of her daughter, rushed to Trenton's horse, and sank to her knees. "You won't hurt my boy!" she moaned. "He ain't done nothin' to you!"

Trenton set the wailing boy on the front of his saddle, his face away from him.

For an instant he wondered if he could truly hurt the child. Had he dropped that low? Become that heartless?

But the moment passed, and his anger returned fourfold. He pulled a knife from his waistband and held it in his right hand. "I am looking for your man!" he shouted. "And I will do what I have to do to find him!"

"No!" screamed the woman.

Trenton placed the knife at the back of the boy's neck. "Your man killed my mother!" he yelled. "It is him or this boy!"

The woman grabbed Trenton by the legs and pleaded with him, but he shook his head. "One more chance!" he warned. "Where is your man?"

The woman shrieked as Trenton touched the knife to the boy's skin. All around him chaos reigned. Houses burned. Women screamed. Men cursed. Gunshots sounded.

Was this what hell was like? Trenton wondered.

He pressed the knife farther into the boy's skin.

"He gone!" shouted the woman.

Trenton eased the pressure off the knife.

The woman pointed toward the woods to Trenton's back. "He gone last night!" she wailed. "Him and two buddies."

"They on foot?"

"Yeah."

"You telling me the truth?"

"Yeah! He left for Savannah. Say it not safe here no more!"

Trenton ground his teeth, his frustrations making him furious. After all this time he'd nearly had the man in his grasp, and now his mother's murderer had escaped? He raised the knife again. "You sure you're not lying?" he threatened the woman.

"I no fool!" she cried. "I know if you find him here, you gone hurt me, my babies! It's the truth, for sure!"

"If you're lying, I'll come back and finish this!"

"I not lyin'!"

Trenton shuddered with fury but dropped the boy into his mother's arms. She grabbed him and her daughter and ran. He turned toward his men and pointed his rifle to the woods. "Leave a few men to burn everything," he ordered. "The rest will go with me."

"Where?"

"After the man who killed my mother."

"You figure to catch him tonight?"

Trenton's eyes narrowed in determination. "Don't know, but I'm going to try."

The man jerked his horse around and rushed away while Trenton turned and faced the woods. Several seconds later ten men rode up.

"We got three men to find!" he commanded.

They shouted and fired excited shots into the air. Then Trenton led them away from the village and into the woods, his anger banked against the moment when he could set it loose once more.

Chapter Twenty-Seven

Back in Richmond, Lynette applied a wet compress to Hampton York's head and tried to soothe him as he tossed on his sweaty sheets. Jackson sat beside her, his eyes fearful. York had taken a bad turn, almost from the moment Josh headed out to catch the train back to the South. Sores covered his face, and his eyes burned red. Although a doctor had removed the bullet from his chest, the wound had festered and fever followed. Ever since then he had drifted in and out of consciousness—his eyes clear one minute, then bleary and lost the next. He spent a lot of time squirming on the sheets, his body fighting, his fists clenching and unclenching his covers. Sometimes he shouted and shrieked; at other times he whispered and seemed next to tears.

Lynette tried to make sense of his ravings, but for the most part, nothing fit together. About the only good news was the fact that the nosebleeds, which Josh had told her about, seemed to have stopped, at least for the time being.

York moaned and rolled over.

"You want me to go for the doctor again?" asked Jackson.

Lynette shook her head. "Nothing a doctor can do now. He'll make it or he won't. That's the way it is."

"It will be a shame if he dies . . . especially now," said Jackson.

Lynette sighed sadly. "I should have told you both earlier," she lamented. "It wasn't right for me to keep secret from the two of you the fact he's your father."

Lynette stood and rewet the rag in a bowl of water on a dresser by the bed. As she did, a knock sounded on the front door.

"Who could that be so late?" she asked.

"Hope it's not the banker," joked Jackson, obviously trying to ease the tension.

"He said he wouldn't be here until the end of the week," she said, suddenly fearful.

"Glad we got a couple more days here," Jackson noted.

The knock sounded again.

"See to it," said Lynette.

As Jackson left the room, Lynette sat by York again.

For a moment he opened his eyes, and she bent closer. "Can you hear me?" she asked.

She thought he nodded slightly but couldn't be sure. Then his eyes flickered shut again.

Jackson stepped back into the room, his face even paler than usual. "It's Tolliver from Chambersburg. He wants his money."

Lynette shrugged. "I've been wondering when he would show up. Tell him to come in here."

Jackson left the room again.

Lynette walked to the small closet by her dresser. Pulling the money out of its box, she rolled it up in the apron she wore. When Jackson and Tolliver entered the room, she pointed Tolliver to a chair.

He refused. "I won't bother you long. Just here to get what's mine and go on."

"That Jukes fellow live?" asked Jackson.

"Not sure, but I think so," Tolliver reported. "He was alive when I got him to Mercersburg, but I headed out the next day. Went to Chambersburg and packed up, then headed here."

Lynette dropped the money on the dresser and gestured toward it. "Take it," she told Tolliver.

"I claim just half," he said, starting to count out his portion.

"Take it all," she insisted. "It's not mine, and I want no part of it."

Tolliver tilted his head. "You bein' mighty generous. You figure the captain there will like that when he comes to?"

Lynette looked at York. "Not sure it matters to him."

"I just don't want him chasin' me for takin' somethin' that ain't mine," Tolliver said nervously.

"Do what you want then."

Tolliver shrugged, took a leather pouch off his shoulder, and started putting the money into it.

York stirred on the bed and Lynette moved to him. His eyes opened again, blinked a couple of times, then stayed clear.

"York?"

York raised a hand and pointed a finger at Tolliver, who paused and stared at him. "Half . . . mine," croaked York.

Lynette pursed her lips. "You rest," she ordered York. "Leave this to me."

York tried to raise up, but she pushed him back down.

"Mine," York said, more forcefully this time.

Lynette wanted to strangle him. "You're half dead because of that filthy money!" she fumed, angry as the worst of his traits showed up again. "Quit worrying about it!" She faced Tolliver again. "Take it!" she commanded. "Get it out of here!"

Tolliver's fingers got busy again, but before he could finish putting the money in his pouch, York groaned loudly and pushed up. "No!" York thundered with strength greater than Lynette knew he possessed. "I need it!"

Tolliver stopped and studied York, obviously trying to figure what to do. York pointed at him. "Leave my half," he whispered. "Keep the . . . deal."

Tolliver nodded, put some money back, and closed up his pouch. York relaxed back into the bed again and closed his eyes. With one last glance at York, Tolliver excused himself and left the room and the carriage house.

Lynette turned to Jackson. "Leave us!" she ordered him. He obeyed without argument.

She took a seat by York again. "Open your eyes!" she commanded.

York took a deep breath and did as she said. She shook her head as he watched her. "You constantly surprise me," she groused.

"Is it ever . . . a good surprise?"

She wanted to stay mad at him but realized she had no basis for it. Given what she had kept from him for so long, how could she dare throw the first stone? As she took his hand, she knew the time had come. If he died without her ever telling him, she could never forgive herself. Whether he lived or died, he had to know.

"I need to tell you something," she started.

"Tell me you . . . love me," he said.

"It's not the time for that," she countered.

He gestured weakly to the water bowl, and she filled a dipper and handed it to him. He was only able to take a sip. She put the dipper back and felt his forehead—still hot. How long would he stay conscious this time? She needed to hurry.

She grasped his hand again. "I might as well say it right out," she started.

He coughed and his chest rattled.

Tears welled up in Lynette's eyes. "It's about Jackson. He is—"

York lifted a finger to her lips and interrupted her. "I know . . . who he is."

"You do?"

"I . . . ain't a fool." He sighed. "He is my son."

"But why didn't you say something?"

He shrugged. "I . . . knew . . . you would . . . eventually . . ."

When he closed his eyes again, she thought he had fallen into a coma once more. She squeezed his hand as her tears flowed. "I didn't know I was expecting when I left you on The Oak. But I was . . . just a few weeks along."

He surprised her by nodding slightly, so she kept going. "I've wanted to tell you, to ask your forgiveness. You deserved to know. He's such a fine man."

"Does . . . he know?" York asked.

"Yes," she said gently, "and he's so proud of you."

York shook his head. "No cause for that," he whispered. "I am a rough man."

"No," she argued, "you're good in your soul. I know that, even though you cover it well most of the time. You got hard edges, sure, but we all have our sins."

He opened his eyes and stared straight at her, his look clearer than she had seen in days. "What about the money? You think poorly of me because I want it."

She wanted to argue with him, to tell him she didn't care what he did with the money, that it had no influence on the way she felt about him, but she knew she couldn't. "Money has always been your weakness. The status it can buy—the power."

"I admit that."

"Let it go this time," she suggested. "Let me take it to the authorities."

"Can't."

Frustration rose in her heart. Whether it hurt him or not, she had to talk plainly. "You tell me you love me," she began.

"Yes."

She wanted to go on but couldn't. If he didn't see it, why should she bother to point it out? For them to have any chance of a future together, any at all, he had to let these dollars go. It was the only way she would know he had changed, that he had learned from the past. But how could she say that without sounding judgmental? Self-righteous? After all, she had gone to Chambersburg to find him in hopes of getting money from him. Now she realized she was wrong in that.

He stayed quiet.

"You've said you wanted me to love you," she finally said. "But I can't do that, at least not now."

York's eyes grew misty. "There any hope you could in the future?"

She dropped his hand, stepped to the dresser, and stood over the dollars lying there. "Not as long as you keep this money."

"Come here," he pleaded.

His repentant tone surprised her. She pivoted and walked to the bed. He patted the mattress gently, and she sat by him.

Reaching up, he stroked her chin. "I got to have that money," he said quietly.

Her anger boiled over one final time. "Why?" she demanded through clenched teeth. "You choose it over me?"

His hand fell, limp against the covers, and he took a long, deep breath. She waited. His voice sounded weaker when he spoke again. "I have to have it," he whispered.

"I don't understand." She cried again, knowing then she had lost York forever—not only as the man she had come to love before she ran from The Oak but also as a friend. If he insisted on keeping this stolen money, then she couldn't care for him like she wanted. A man who clutched so hard to what didn't belong to him, who still let greed guide his heart and head so strongly, could not come to the place where he could love a woman as generously as she believed a man should.

"It's for you," he said.

For an instant she stopped breathing.

York continued so softly she almost couldn't hear him. "I got it for you," he whispered. "So you can pay your taxes, keep your house, fix it up again."

She wiped her eyes, still not sure she understood, not sure she believed. But when he smiled lightly, it dawned on her he was telling the truth.

"You got it for me?" she asked in wonder, although already knowing the answer to the question.

"For you . . . and Jackson. I don't care about it . . . anymore."

Lynette cried again, but this time not from grief. Although she didn't know what the future held—whether York would even survive or not—she did know at least one thing. Hampton York had truly changed.

She bent down to him and kissed his forehead. "Rest."

"You will use the money, won't you?" he begged. "To keep your home?"

Lynette chuckled at the twist in her dilemma. The Yankees had burned down her hotel, taken the belongings from her home. So would the Lord see it as wrong if she used the dollars to preserve her house? If she kept at least enough to pay her taxes? That's what she had traveled to Chambersburg for. Would it be stealing to keep it now, at least part of it?

"Rest," she repeated to York. "We'll figure out later what to do with the money."

York nodded lightly and closed his eyes one final time.

Lynette sat beside him through the night, hoping and praying that, come morning, Hampton York would open those big, gray eyes again.

Gasping for breath as she held Theo's hand in hers, Ruby trailed Calvin and Obadiah through the woods. Camellia and Johnny followed them, each person as quiet as possible. Ruby's face burned from the cuts and scratches she endured from the bushes and trees, and she felt blood every now and again as a branch or a thorn cut into her skin. They ran as fast as Theo's foot allowed much of the time, slowing only when the brush got so thick they couldn't rush through it, and Ruby's throat ached with thirst.

She checked the sky every chance she got, hoping for sunrise, but so far there were no signs of it. Rain fell every now and again and the wind continued to gust about, first in this direction and then in another. At times Ruby thought she heard horses behind her and she would run a little faster. But then the sounds would fade, and she would feel hopeful again that they would make it through this awful night.

After what seemed like hours, Calvin slowed to a stop as they reached a creek and crouched down by the water's edge. "Take water," he whispered.

Ruby and the rest of the group hurriedly obeyed, each one dipping their faces in the fresh liquid. When they had finished, they gathered by Calvin. Ruby pulled Theo close. It felt so good to have her boy in her arms again.

"Anybody hear anybody behind us?" Calvin asked. Ruby tried to slow her heavy breathing so she could listen but found it difficult.

"I think . . . we in the . . . clear," panted Obadiah.

Calvin licked his lips, stood, and peered back through the woods, in the direction from which they'd come. "I wonder if we should take the road now?"

"You think it's safe?" asked Camellia.

"Hard to tell," he reasoned, "but if we stay in the woods, it will take hours longer to get home."

Ruby wiped sweat off her face. The thought of taking the road scared her, but Calvin was right. It would take longer to travel through the forest.

"I think the road should be OK," offered Johnny. "We stay on the edge. If we hear anything, we dive for the trees again."

Everyone nodded their agreement.

"OK," Calvin said. "Get another drink, then we head for the road."

A minute later they struck south and east again. The wind whipped through Ruby's hair and a crack of lightning lit up the sky. She squeezed Theo's hand, praying nothing tracked them from behind.

Trenton and his men thundered their tiring mounts down the road that cut through the woods beyond the shantytown. Their torches still burned—but not as brightly as earlier. They had pulled their masks off but had not taken the time to remove the robes that covered their torsos. A lather of sweat covered the horses' flanks and the men's faces. Trenton knew they had to find his mother's murderer soon or his men would call it quits and go home. None of them liked to be seen out in the daylight. The Yankees didn't do much about what the raiders did at night, but if they got caught with their costumes after the sun rose, they could end up in real trouble. One of the men had already suggested that the Negro had escaped, but Trenton, furious at the notion, snapped at the man and told him no such thing had happened.

Pulling a whiskey bottle from his saddle bag, Trenton took a long swig. Although he had planned to refrain from drink tonight, a lot of things had changed. He put away the bottle and kept riding. The wind blew in gusts, and rain squalls moved in and out—never lasting long but never completely leaving either.

Just after he and his men splashed into a creek, Trenton reined in and signaled a halt. His men gathered around him.

"Water the horses," he ordered.

The men dropped their reins, and the horses drank deeply. A couple of men drank from canteens. Several others dismounted and slaked their thirst in the stream.

"There's a fork just ahead," Trenton said. "When we get there, I want half of us to go to the right, the other half left. We'll meet back up at the store at Crossville just after sunup."

"You sure we ought to go on?" asked the same man who had earlier proposed that maybe the black man had slid through their fingers. "This weather ain't gettin' no better."

Trenton faced the man, his anger rising from insecurity. "I *will* catch this murderer tonight," he growled. "Anybody who wants to tuck tail and go home can do it now."

The man dropped his head, and Trenton faced the rest of his posse.

"You figure the darky is on the road?" asked another of the men.

"He's got no cause not to be," said Trenton, trying to stay calm. "He doesn't know we're after him. He'd have no reason to keep to the thick woods."

The men nodded at his logic.

"OK," Trenton concluded, "Put on your masks and let's ride."

The horses climbed a slight incline on the opposite side of the creek and surged forward once more, Trenton in the lead. His energy was fueled by his need to show his men he could finish what he started—that when they rode with him, they rode with the one man who could guide them to their true white destiny.

Ruby's group pressed on through the night. The rain had stopped for a while, but the wind blew fiercely. Her feet ached, and her throat felt like someone had scrubbed it out with sharp rocks. Although the road made their going a lot easier, she still worried about Theo. More and more he dragged his bad foot behind him. In spite of his lack of complaint, he was surely exhausted. She held to his hand and swore to herself nothing would ever again cause her to let go of it. Obadiah stayed right ahead of her, turning to help every now and again, offering to carry Theo if necessary. Every time he suggested that, though, Theo shook his head and kept going.

Ruby figured it was now maybe an hour before sunup.

The group rushed down a slight incline and started up on the other side. The road twisted to the left and through a thick canopy of trees. For an instant the wind dropped, and Ruby's ears pricked. All at once the hair on the back of her neck stood up. "I hear something!" she called.

Calvin signaled a halt

There. Ruby heard it again. "What is it?"

"I don't hear anything," said Calvin.

Ruby glanced to Theo. "You hear it?"

He shook his head. Calvin motioned them forward. They rounded the bend in the road . . . and walked straight into the clutches of masked, mounted raiders, armed with torches and rifles!

Chapter Twenty-Eight

His eyes searching for the Negro who killed his mother, Trenton whipped his horse toward the clutch of strangers on the road to The Oak. At first he thought they would run, but instead, they froze and waited for him to approach.

"Where is he?" he shouted as he drew closer, his voice slightly muffled by the mask over his face.

The group was silent.

Rain started to fall again and blurred Trenton's vision some. He rode nearer but still didn't see the tall man he sought. His disappointment made his anger a deadly thing. About ten yards away he reined in his horse and stopped.

"Who are you?" he called. "We picked up your track a couple of miles back, circled around you to get in front."

A Negro and a white man stepped to the front of the group. Trenton's eyes widened under his mask as he saw Calvin and Obadiah.

"My name is Obadiah," said the black man. "This be Calvin Tessier." He pointed to Calvin. "We headin' home, not lookin' for no upset."

Trenton's men eased their horses closer, obviously wanting to see what he would do to his own brother.

Trenton tried to disguise his voice to keep his identity hidden from Calvin and hoped he would not recognize his horse in the dark. "What are whites and blacks doing together out so late at night?" asked Trenton.

"That's not your business," Calvin insisted, stepping in front of Obadiah.

"I make it my business," Trenton retorted. He spurred his horse until he stood only a few feet from his brother. Now he recognized the rest of the group, and his surprise rose. Why were they all here?

He surveyed the faces he knew so well—Camellia, Johnny, Obadiah, Calvin, Ruby. What would they say if they recognized him? What would they do? What could they do?

He almost laughed. They couldn't do anything. He owned them, he ran this county . . . at least after the sun went down. And, soon enough, the Yankees would all go home again, and he would own it in the daytime too. All he had to do was survive until that day, keep his power in place. Demonstrate that he could and would lead others in their quest for Southern freedom.

Trenton's eyes moved past Ruby and landed on the small boy standing behind her. Again his eyes widened in surprise. Theo, Ruby's son. The boy who had tried to steal a chicken from The Oak over a year ago. Trenton kicked his horse slightly and moved closer to the boy.

Holding to his mother's hand, Theo watched the masked man on the horse approach him. As the man drew within a couple of feet, a strange thing happened. Theo's head started throbbing—pain pierced from the back of the neck to the top of the skull. The man stopped his horse and stared down at him. All of a sudden Theo's vision returned: the one he had seen the night he had tried to steal a chicken from The Oak, where he had expected to find his mama. The vision that showed him how he would die.

The rain stopped once more, and the wind died. Theo let go of Ruby's hand and took a pace away from her. When he spoke, his words came out calm and steady, like he feared nothing in the world.

"I know who you be," he called into the night, a finger lifted and directed at Trenton. "You Trenton Tessier."

A gasp sounded from Trenton's men, but Trenton said nothing.

"You lied to me when you said my mama be dead," accused Theo. "Now you come to finish what we started that night."

"I'm looking for a tall Negro," said Trenton, giving up his voice disguise. "Got a mark the shape of a pear on his face."

"No such man among us," Calvin replied. "So let us go."

Ruby moved toward Theo, but he held up a hand and stopped her with an authority she immediately obeyed, in spite of his slight stature and tender years.

"No," Theo said. "This be the time."

"Take them all away!" Trenton ordered his men. "All but this one!" He pointed at Theo.

His men aimed their rifles at the group.

Theo felt movement behind him, then saw Calvin throw himself toward Trenton. But before Calvin could reach Trenton, one of Trenton's men cracked Calvin on the head with a rifle butt. Calvin sagged to the ground, knocked out cold.

"Is it really you, Trenton?" asked Camellia, her voice trembling.

Trenton glanced at Camellia but didn't speak to her.

"Take her!" he snapped at one of his raiders.

Theo watched as the man dismounted, grabbed Camellia by the waist, and dragged her, kicking and screaming, onto his horse.

"Have you become this evil?" Camellia screamed.

"Who are you to say what's evil?" Trenton asked, his voice filled with fury.

"This is wrong!" she shouted to the raiders. "All of you—you know this is wrong!"

"Get her out of here!" Trenton commanded. "Take them all!"

Ruby jumped toward Theo, but another raider cut her off and knocked her down. She jerked back up and rushed the man, but he stepped to the side and whacked her with a pistol butt. She fell to the muddy road. Picking her up, he hauled her to his horse and draped her over it.

"If anybody else does anything stupid, they'll get shot!" shouted Trenton.

Obadiah and Johnny looked frantic, but with two rifles trained on them, Theo knew they couldn't do anything.

"Two of you stay with me!" Trenton ordered his men. "The others of you take them and go!"

"You want us to kill them?" asked one of the men.

"No! They don't really know who we are, could never prove it. So take them to the store at Crossville, then let them go."

Their guns ready, the four riders forced Ruby, Obadiah, Camellia, Johnny, and Calvin down the slippery road and out of sight.

Theo waited, his eyes fixed on Trenton. "You bring yo' rope?"

"You got a sharp mouth for one in the danger you're facing."

"I knows what's gone happen," said Theo, still calm.

Trenton studied the boy, obviously curious. "How do you know anything?"

"I see visions," said Theo. "One come on me the night on your place. I see then how I'm gone die."

"What if I don't do it?" Trenton countered. "Then your vision will turn out wrong."

"Oh, my visions do come out wrong sometime," Theo stated. "But not this one. You got to do this to keep your grip on such as these." He pointed to the riders waiting on their horses beside them. "You all come out to-night for a hangin'. Figured it to be this tall man you searchin' for. But you ain't found him. You tired, you mad, you want to hurt somebody."

"I don't have to do anything," argued Trenton, almost as if he wanted to keep control of the events unfolding.

"You wrong there. You never rode in no battle in the war, so you got to show you got power. Got to prove you a man in their sight."

Appearing unnerved, Trenton glanced to his men, then back at Theo.

"You don't like me sayin' it so straight out," said Theo. "But I got it true, don't I?"

Trenton stayed still.

"You got rope," said Theo. "So be on with it."

Trenton didn't move. Theo could almost feel him wrestling with his soul. One part of him wanted to pivot his horse and ride away. Another half wanted to draw blood, to do something to make himself feel powerful against a world that had taken all his power away from him.

Suddenly one of Trenton's men moved, pulled a rope off his saddle, and threw it over Theo's shoulders.

"What are you doing?" Trenton shouted at the man.

"I'm doin' what I rode all night to do. Stringin' me up a darky."

Theo stared at Trenton but knew he wouldn't stop it, even if he wanted. It was one thing to ride away from something that hadn't started yet but quite another to stop something already underway. The rope tightened and pinned his arms to his side. The man kicked his horse and led Theo off the road and into a clearing.

Trenton followed, silent now but still moving. In the clearing he led his horse to the center and lifted his torch. "There!" he shouted, regaining his voice and pointing to a live oak tree with a stout branch about six feet off the ground. "That ought to do just fine for one short as this."

The rope around Theo pulled him toward the tree. One of Trenton's raiders threw a rope around the tree branch and looped it tight. It danced toward the ground like a snake about to strike.

For the first time Theo felt fear. No doubt lingered now about what Trenton would do. Since a lynching was going to happen with or without his leadership, he might as well get credit for it.

Theo's stomach roiled, and he almost regurgitated. Seeing a vision of his death and actually living it out felt completely different than he had imagined. His knees weakened, and he almost collapsed, but the rope around his shoulders held him up. He started to pray silently. The wind picked up again but the rain didn't fall.

"Bring him!" shouted Trenton.

The rope jerked, and Theo followed as it hauled him to the tree. He fell about halfway there, and the horse dragged him the rest of the way. At the tree the man with the rope dismounted, pulled the rope off, and pushed Theo under the noose. He studied it as if watching a dream—the rope swung and swayed in the wind.

A log stump appeared from somewhere, and a raider rolled it over until it sat about two feet high under the swinging noose.

"Put him on it!" shouted Trenton.

But Theo stepped up without anyone touching him. Part of him wanted to run, but another seemed set on seeing this through—almost as if curious to go on to death and find out what lay on the other side.

From somewhere in his head, a song came to Theo, and he started humming it under his breath. *Swing low, sweet chariot, comin' for to carry me home. Swing low, sweet char-i-o-t, coming for to carry me home . . .*

He closed his eyes and felt the noose as it was dropped over his head.

The rope scratched his neck and made it itch as somebody tightened it.

"You want a hood over his eyes?" somebody asked Trenton.

Theo waved them off. He felt drugged and wondered why. He hadn't taken any of Marquis's elixir since just after dark. He thought about Marquis and Rufe and the woman Mabel, but he didn't feel any ill will toward them. Although Marquis had cut off half his foot, he had said he did it to keep the gangrene from killing Theo. Whether that was the real reason or not, Marquis's action truly might have saved his life. And how could he blame Marquis for trying to make a living, even if he did lie and steal and cheat some to do it? That's exactly what he had done too—lied to folks about their fortunes so he could stay alive. What made him any better than Marquis? He hoped Marquis and Rufe and Mabel escaped all this.

Swing low . . . , he hummed. *Sweet chariot . . .*

"Snug it tight!" said Trenton.

The rope pinched Theo's flesh.

Theo thought he heard a sound. What was it? The Lord calling? Or something he imagined?

He felt the raiders backing up a few steps and opened his eyes. Now only Trenton stood close by, close enough to kick the stump away and leave him hanging from the branch, hanging and hanging until . . . *Swing low . . . sweet chariot, coming for to carry me home . . .*

"Go on," he whispered to Trenton. "Buy yo' soul its place in hell."

Trenton's eyes burned. "I've been in hell as long as I can remember!" he hissed.

Theo closed his eyes. What was that sound? The wind picked up.

He felt Trenton's foot on the stump, felt it kick the stump away, felt the noose cling to his throat, its strength snapping his breath away. *Swing low, sweet chariot . . .*

Lighting struck. The rain fell.

Comin' for to carry me . . .

Everything went black.

Thirty feet away, behind a tree, Josh aimed as best his trembling fingers would allow and fired his rifle at Trenton Tessier. The bullet caught Trenton in the neck, and he fell to the ground. Josh sprinted from the woods, his rifle firing at the other three men in the clearing. Two of them broke and ran, but the third dropped to a knee and pointed his rifle at Josh. Josh shot at the raider as he ran, and his aim found flesh again. The man crumpled and rolled over.

Josh reached Theo a moment later, his hands grabbing for the boy's ankles and lifting him up to take the weight off his throat. He pulled his knife from its sheath, cut the rope from the branch, and hauled Theo away from the tree.

A shot fired from behind him.

Josh dropped Theo to the ground and swiveled to face the shooter.

Trenton lay on his side, his rifle in hand, his body unsteady. As he fired the weapon again, the dirt by Josh's foot kicked.

Josh rolled to his right and shot at Trenton, knocking him out flat.

Josh watched Trenton for another second, to make sure he didn't move, then rushed to Theo again, stretching him out on the ground on his back.

"Theo!" he yelled as the rain pattered his head.

The boy didn't respond. He wasn't breathing.

Josh pulled the rope off the boy's neck and massaged his throat. Had the fall snapped Theo's neck? *Oh, Lord*, Josh prayed, *be merciful* . . .

From his left, Josh sensed movement. Turning swiftly, he saw Trenton rise once more, rifle in hand. Josh jumped at him, knocked the rifle away, and punched him in the face. Trenton fell, his head landing on the muddy ground. Again Josh watched him for another second. This time he had to be dead.

Josh hurried back to Theo and bent over the boy. Lightning cracked. Theo still didn't breathe.

"Let him live, Lord!" Josh wailed into the storm. "There's been enough dying!" Tears flooded his eyes as he pressed on Theo's chest as gently as he could and still maintain pressure.

Still nothing.

GARY E. PARKER

Josh sobbed out loud. He prayed again, this time angrily against the Lord. Against all the bloodshed he had seen in his life, all the suffering, all the hurt. If this boy died, he didn't know how much longer he could trust in the goodness of the Lord.

Suddenly Theo sucked in a big breath.

Josh paused in his praying to gently rub Theo's neck. The boy pulled in another draught of air.

Josh pressed the boy's chest again and watched as he breathed raggedly, but again and again. Josh knew then Theo would live.

"Theo!" he called again.

The boy opened his eyes and stared at Josh, as if seeing a ghost.

"You're OK," soothed Josh, his spirits rising. "You're OK."

"Who you?" croaked Theo.

"Josh Cain. I know your mama."

Theo closed his eyes. Rain spattered onto his face.

"Come on," said Josh, gently lifting the boy from the muddy earth. "Let me get you home. I expect your mama will be real glad to see you."

Chapter Twenty-Nine

About ten days later, as the sun went down, Camellia heard a wagon pulling up in the front driveway of the manse at The Oak. Curious, she dropped the dust rags in her hand, hurried to the front door, and opened it. A horse, mounted by a single man, followed the wagon.

Camellia cupped her hand over her brow to block the glare so she could see better. Her heart jumped as she recognized the visitors. "Beth!" she yelled back into the house. "Come here! Bring Calvin and Ruby!"

A second later Beth and Calvin appeared, holding hands, Ruby behind them.

"What is it?" Beth asked.

Camellia pointed down the oak-lined driveway.

"Where's Pa?" asked Beth, excited by what she saw.

"He's at the barn," said Calvin. "I'll get him."

"Round up everybody else too," Camellia urged.

Calvin hurried off.

"I'll bring Theo," said Ruby. "Leta, Obadiah, and Mama, Buster too."

Camellia smiled. She found it hard to stand still. As the wagon drew closer and the passengers saw her and Beth, they waved. Beth and Camellia waved back, their hands like windmills, side to side.

Josh appeared from around the corner, Johnny and Butler with him. Ruby stepped back on the porch with Leta in her arms and Obadiah and everybody else beside them.

Camellia grinned. The wagon reached them, and the rider dismounted.

Camellia opened her arms. "Pa!" she shouted.

York climbed slowly off the wagon. As soon as his feet touched the earth, Camellia threw her arms around his neck. He hugged her tightly for a long time, then stepped back. When Lynette climbed down from the wagon, Camellia hugged her too. And then she embraced Jackson while everybody else welcomed York.

When the greetings ended, York gazed around the yard. "What happened to that?" he asked, pointing to the huge oak from which the plantation drew its name.

Camellia shook her head as she stared at the downed giant, its thick, gnarled roots bared to the sky, its trunk prone to the ground, its branches broken and splintered. A hole big enough for a wagon to sit in lay beneath its roots. Although she had looked at it every day since the night they rescued Theo, she still couldn't believe the storm that horrible night had felled the grand old tree.

"It was ancient," Josh explained. "A storm blew through here. The next morning it was down."

York took off his hat as if in reverence, then put it back on again. "It looks different here."

"It is different," said Josh. "In lots of ways."

"Let's go on in!" Calvin encouraged. "You have to be tired."

Everybody piled into the parlor, where Josh and Butler produced several chairs. Ruby and Beth brought water. York, Lynette, and Jackson took spots in the center.

As York's eyes raked the group, Camellia could see him sizing things up.

"You look healthier than when I last saw you," Josh told York.

"I am some better, though I get nosebleeds still," said York.

"Just glad you pulled through."

As Camellia sipped her water, she wondered who would tell what first.

"Where's Trenton?" asked York, breaking the momentary quiet.

Calvin shook his head. "He's dead."

York looked stunned. "What happened?"

Josh quickly told the story. "We buried him out back," he said when finished.

"Beside Katherine, I reckon," guessed York.

"Yes," said Calvin.

York sighed. "Sorry it come to that, but it don't surprise me."

Everybody nodded. Trenton had created his own end.

"And that's Theo?" asked York, pointing to Ruby's boy, who stood by her.

Theo smiled and Ruby patted him on the head.

York glanced at Lynette and Jackson. "We got news too," he said, facing the group again. "Jackson is . . . well . . . he's my son."

Camellia felt like the grin on her face was becoming permanent. "Josh told us. Not that some of us hadn't already guessed."

"My brother has a big mouth." York chuckled.

Everybody laughed.

Then York took Lynette's hand. "One more thing. Me and Lynette, well, we're not sure what the future holds for either of us, but we're goin' to spend some time together."

"You're moving here?" Camellia asked Lynette, not sure she believed it.

"No," she said. "York is going to stay in Richmond with me."

"But you can't!" interrupted Calvin. "This place is yours!"

"Yes," said Josh, astonishment on his face that York would consider giving up what he had wanted all his life. "With Trenton gone, you can run it like you've always dreamed."

York shook his head. "I have something else now I've also always wanted. A chance to prove to Lynette I do love her. To see if we can—"

"But what about The Oak?" asked Josh.

York turned to Calvin. "It's yours. Like it should be. Your mama and me"—he dropped his eyes—"I respected her but didn't love her. I'm certain she felt the same about me. The Oak falling to me was wrong, plain and simple, and giving it back to you is the only right thing to do."

Lynette squeezed York's hand.

Calvin appeared more stunned than anybody else.

"But where will you live?" asked Josh, focused on Lynette. "Didn't the authorities take your house for taxes?"

Lynette smiled and patted York's hand. "We found a way to pay the taxes," she explained.

Camellia raised an eyebrow. Josh had told her of the money he and York had found. Apparently, Lynette had decided that keeping the money—at least some of it—didn't break any faith with the Lord.

"You're mighty kind," Calvin said, moving to York and shaking his hand. "Miss Beth and I will try to do well by the place."

York lifted an eyebrow. "You and Miss Beth?"

Beth blushed.

"Yes," explained Josh. "Seems she and Calvin have fallen in love with each other."

"So we're goin' to have at least two weddings here this summer?"

This time Camellia blushed. "Yes!"

"It's about time!" exclaimed York.

Josh walked to Camellia and took her hands in his. She nestled against his shoulder.

"Is that all then?" asked York, glancing over each one in the crowd.

Josh laughed. "Not quite."

Everyone but Camellia stared at him, unsure what he meant.

"Hold on," Josh said. "It will take me a minute to get something."

The room fell quiet as Josh rushed out. Camellia ran her eyes over the room—all the people she loved. Her heart warmed as her gaze lingered over them. Ruby, whom she loved like a sister. Lynette, her mother, who had seen her through a war. York, the man who had raised her and tried to always do right by her. Her brothers Johnny and Jackson. Beth and Butler, the friends she had helped raise as children. Calvin, a good man who had found virtue even as he fell in love with Beth; Nettie, Leta, Obadiah, Theo and Buster, people she loved because she loved Ruby.

Josh walked back into the room, his hands behind his back. Camellia watched York as Josh stepped to him and pulled an object from behind his waist.

"What you got there?" asked York.

"Something you lost a long time ago," said Josh.

Everyone leaned closer. Camellia wanted to laugh out loud. Josh handed York a metal box. Camellia knew that inside the box lay a burlap bag, and then a wood box.

York opened the box and took out the bag and the box inside. His mouth fell open as he unhinged the wood box and saw its contents. "I don't believe it," he sighed, almost at a loss for words.

"Believe it," said Josh.

"Where did you find this?"

"Buried beneath the oak," Josh replied. "When the storm took it down, I found it the next morning."

"Katherine buried it there," said York, still in obvious disbelief.

"Apparently so."

York held up a handful of dollars. "You count it?" he asked Josh.

Josh grinned. "Yes. About eighteen thousand."

York studied the money for a long time. Camellia wondered what he was thinking, what he would do next. With almost nobody anywhere having any cash, this amount of dollars made York a wealthy man. She and Josh had debated what the money would do to him. Now she wondered if they should even have given it to him. Would it pull him away from the attitude he seemed to have adopted since his latest injuries? Would the desire for power and prestige sink its clutches into his flesh once more?

Finally, York stood, the money still in his grasp. He turned in a slow circle. "Everybody gets an equal share," he said slowly.

A shocked silence descended.

York continued, "Ruby and Obadiah, an equal share for your family. Beth and Calvin, for yours. Josh, you and Camellia. Johnny. Jackson. Then me and Lynette."

"You don't need to do that," said Calvin.

York smiled. "I stole some of this money from your mama," he confessed. "Seems only right I give it back to you." He gazed around the circle one last time. "I won the rest gamblin'. So I'm goin' to take another gamble now and figure you all will know better than me how to spend this cash."

Everybody laughed again.

Camellia stepped to Josh's side. "You think we ought to take it?" Josh asked her.

She smiled at her pa, then back at her soon-to-be husband. "Pa is being generous," she teased, slipping an arm around Josh's waist. "Seems we would just tempt him too much if we don't accept it."

Josh put his arm around her as York moved to the center of the room, Lynette at his side.

"We have come through a lot," York said.

Everybody nodded.

"But we are all home now," he continued. "So let's take pleasure in it while we can."

As Camellia hugged Josh, she gazed at her loved ones once more. What a glorious sight to see them all in one place, even if only for a little while! True, they would soon all disperse again—each to their own corner of the South, where they would carve out their lives. That's the way the Lord seemed to have made things. People gathered for a while, sometimes for months, sometimes for years. But then the circumstances of Providence pushed and pulled them here and there, to this bend of the road and that twist in the wind.

Tears pushed to the corners of her eyes. Were they from sorrow or joy? Both, she realized. Sorrow at the parting that would inevitably happen, as it did with any life. But joy too—joy at the reunion she now experienced. A reunion that had taken so long to occur, an elusive reunion that at one point seemed destined never to happen.

But it had. Thanks be to God, they had overcome everything thrown in their paths and had finally come home, together, to the distant shores of her beloved native state.

Camellia thought of one more reunion she knew would come in the far distance. And she prayed that when it did, her circle of family would be unbroken. No, not everyone in the room believed in the Lord, at least not yet. But, with Lynette's influence on York, Camellia held real hope for him. And, yes, maybe Beth could guide Calvin too, although he already appeared to be a long way down the pathway to the truth.

And who knew? Perhaps Camellia could finally encourage Ruby to hear what Camellia believed: the truth that the Lord walks with us on every search of life, every journey we take, every mountain or desert or ocean we cross, no matter how high, how wide, or how distant.

Camellia's tears disappeared, and a smile replaced them. For now everyone was home and safe, and she felt glad.

About the Author

As a boy growing up in the red-clay country of northwest South Carolina, Gary E. Parker quickly came to enjoy the folklore and history of his native state. One of his earliest memories is going to Charleston with his dad on a business trip and standing by the ocean, watching the ships come into the harbor. From that day Gary loved the smell of the salt air, the sound of the ocean's waves, and the stories of the men and women who lived and died in the coastal area.

Carrying that interest in Southern history with him to college, Gary majored in history at Furman University. Feeling called to ministry, he prepared at Southeastern Seminary, earning a masters degree, and at Baylor University, where he completed a doctorate of Philosophy of Religion, with an emphasis in historical theology.

After finishing his formal education, Gary began pastoral ministry, serving as senior pastor at the Warrenton Baptist Church in Warrenton, North Carolina; Grace Baptist in Sumter, South Carolina; First Baptist of Jefferson City, Missouri; and the First Baptist Church of Decatur, Georgia (where he currently serves).

In addition to pastoring a church, Gary obviously loves writing. His previous titles include four nonfiction works and fourteen works of fiction. In addition to books, Gary has written extensively for Sunday-school Bible-study materials and national magazines.

When Gary isn't serving his church, writing, or spending time with his family—wife, Melody, and two teenage daughters, Ashley and Andrea (plenty to fill his plate most days)—he also enjoys a little golf or long-distance bicycling. After that, he mostly likes to eat, sleep, and read.

Read Books 1 & 2 in the
SOUTHERN TIDES TRILOGY

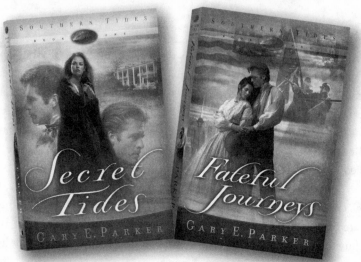

This sweeping family saga is told against the backdrop of the years before, during, and after the American Civil War. Three characters, woven together by circumstances and time yet separated by class, discover that the only things worth standing on are *family, friends,* and *faith.*

Secret Tides

Welcome to The Oak Plantation, an expansive rice plantation in the Old South. When the overseer's daughter, Camellia York, accidentally causes the death of the plantation owner, she is haunted by guilt. *Discover the startling truth about the past—and the secrets that will forever change the tides of her family.*

Fateful Journeys

Josh Cain lies at the edge of death, and Camellia, the woman he loves, must decide whether to leave The Oak to pursue the secrets of her past or stay to care for Josh and his children and risk never being able to leave. *Times are desperate, supplies are scarce, and as the war begins, brother is fighting against brother.*

Enjoyment Guarantee

If you are not totally satisfied with this book, simply return it to us along with your receipt, a statement of what you didn't like about the book, and your name and address within 60 days of purchase to Howard Publishing, 3117 North Seventh Street, West Monroe, Louisiana 71291-2227, and we will gladly reimburse you for the cost of the book.